CONTENT
MT White

To Mr. Ellis,

Thank you for your writings, your podcast and for being a reasonable voice in the wilderness of our crazy times.

MT WHITE

Twitter handle: @MatheWrite

CONTENT

"From an earth torn apart by fire and soaked in blood, spirits rise up, not driven out by the silencing of the cannons; rather, they flow in a strange way into all existing values and give them a changed meaning."

—Ernst Junger, *The Worker*

"In order that I might truly face the sun, the world itself must be destroyed..."

—Yukio Mishima, *The Temple of the Golden Pavilion*

1

I sit here looking at the page…not sure what to write…because…let's face it…

I care what you think.

And…

There's nothing more pretentious than a story about a writer, the main character, the protagonist, the "good guy", that really is a thinly veiled caricature of themselves, made worse by the level of self-loathing that determines whether said caricature is either ideal or flawed. Given the majority of writers are hypercritical, I would say most self-representations lean towards self-flagellation (I suppose it helps make the act of forming sentences that form a story more heroic).

No, no, no, it's not that type of story.

But people seem to love navel-gazing these days. Everything is so self-reflective, narcissistic…it's all about me.

It ain't all about you bitch.

But here I am…writing…scribbling away…scribble, scribble, scribble…

:sweat:

But you know that, don't you? You know everything (kind of in your job description). But you've demanded I tell you what I know, meaning you're looking for something, that something being inoffensive since you or someone can't handle the offensive…I guess. What I've given you so far hasn't been enough…or maybe you just don't like my narrative (too offensive?).

But you demand I give it anyway.

Fine.

But this won't be a memoir, literary work or even a post-factum recollection. No, no, no it's a scientific treatise. Because isn't science just the analysis and synthesis of knowledge? How is my mandate any different?

Reudelheuber_katz_Jason_report.txt

If I piss you off by omitting something or writing something that doesn't match your mutating standards—or god forbid, I'm too "offensive"—I'll just get in the next draft, right?

It's not like I'm going anywhere, right? We both know that.

And I know, the time spirit moves on regardless. And I've had time to think of my role and place in the invisible turning wheel of the age, of which I was both node and recipient in its crushing rotations but nevertheless it keeps moving…but its course isn't fixed…at least I hope it isn't…

I mean, with our social hive-mind being deteriorated, our societal corpus callosum eroded, the balance of dividing and integrating collapsed, the limbic system damaged, our precuneus, our sense of self, silenced—do you even care or notice? Maybe that's why you have me writing this?

LOL NVM.

>Thinking you're significant.

But to me it's life, my very existence…

To you, I'm sure, it's just…

Content.

*

"Kenji is coming," Yu says.

That look on her face gives me pause. I feel the fear in my gut. Whenever I think back on it all, it's the moment I start with.

"Kenji is coming."

Call it an inciting incident.

Kenji is coming…

Words that set a motion of events in to action, words that stand as a marker, doom.

Kenji is coming…

Words that are the turning point. When things change. When it all goes south. And you hate those words.

Kenji is coming…

The moment, I question everything. The moment, I feel it was all a mistake. Everything is a mistake, I think.

Kenji (Yu's husband).

Is (Third person singular present indicative of be).

Coming (What I was doing before Yu said he was coming)(yes, yes, yes, technically, different definitions but—well, a dirty joke isn't funny if you have to explain it. But you know that, don't you?).

3

Good suspenseful place to start, right? It's like a movie, right? Sucks you right in!

INT. RYOKAN-NIGHT

YU holds the keitai while standing NAKED. JASON looks up from the futon CONCERNED but also admiring her small but tight rounded ASS.

She drops phone. Turns to Jason. Looks at him.

JASON

Yu, is something wrong?

YU

Kenji is coming

It didn't exactly happen like that. We both know that. We both know the pulsing immediacy dramatic content demands which in turn has a distorting effect in execution and we both know (actually, maybe you don't know) how everyone wants to flatten a complex story with its many folds, wrinkles and tears in to one flat and simple ironed clothe but that in turn just invites its own complications, confusions, half-truths, narrative missteps and even evil.

I mean, should I start with me and my portrayal?

Am I the Jason Reudelheuber-Katz who is just here to spout Japan facts and smug musings?

OR!

The Jason Reudelheuber-Katz who had an affair with a "married" woman, who (TL;DR) might be a psychic, that led to me getting mixed up in a murder and doomsday cult?

OR!

Am I Jason Reudelheuber-Katz the hateful (half) Jewish Nazi?

You obviously don't know, since you have me here writing this?

4

Do I know? LOL
>knowing thyself
>not even once
I tell you all this because...
I care what you think.

I mean, we both know that presentation of any type, especially presentation as representation, is itself a performance, and performance is inherently false (like that one time Yamaguchi-sensei and I were at a meeting of all the other teachers on the island—Matt and Mandy both present with their respective native Japanese English teachers in tow—and we performed a lesson—*performed* being the keyword!—we acted like we were the best teachers ever, the best of friends, every lesson a gas but! It was at best moderately bullshit and at worst complete bullshit because our lessons were usually boring and I got the impression that Yamaguchi-san didn't care much for me because I didn't revere the job, nay, the profession, of teaching like he did BUT! on another performative occasion, this being the *Kenkyukai*, where teachers from the surrounding Hiroshima-ken area and student's parents observe lessons, we had the unfortunate chance of having to take the stage, where he announced we weren't just friends but "best friends", which was news to me but I didn't take it personally because I knew the tatemae game by then) and we know that memory itself is a host jester, taking events, shifting, arranging and framing them depending on the particular tint of our mental mood ring perception of the moment BUT! We also know these functions (that being presentation, narrative and memory) have been servicing humankind quite well for at least three millennia until recent.

Rewind. Shuttle back. Re-rack.

Oops. Can't do that in print.

But indulge me. We only care about the live action adaptation anyways, short-form or long form, the visualized dramatized content, right? Fuck it.

So, going back, depending on where you're reading this (my guess is somewhere off the Potomac or Seto Inland Sea—but nowhere in between), unless you're an expert working the Japan desk, you might be asking "What is *tatemae*?". And before I say "Google it", (and since I think it's important to my story) as an olive branch, I will quote my dog-eared Kodansha dictionary regarding *tatemae*: "outwardly expressed feelings, stated motivation". But that doesn't begin to explain it (kind of like the act of *tatemae* itself). For me it was the most alienating thing about living here. Yes, yes, yes—above the rabid

5

commercial consumerism that all gaijin complain about—though that might come in a close#2!

Number two certainly made its mark. Getting off the plane, going through immigration, excited to be in the land you've dreamed of since childhood, since your cousin Tyler gave you a Japanese language *Pokemon* card he found at comic book store in Seattle, on that bus from Narita to Tokyo proper, YES! It can be overwhelming to see that neon signage, the loud street noises and just noise in general telling you, persuading you, signs you can't read, where even buying shaving cream is a task, everywhere and everyone a billboard, every girl being a brand ambassador for Gucci, Pucci, Tommy, Marvel, and Louis Vuitton, and the slip 'n cultural slide continues in to your neck of the Hiroshima woods, where you're walking underground in Shareo and you see a 40-something male with perfectly coiffed hair running to catch some transportation with his Vuitton Pegase Legere and matching Keepall brown bag in tow OR! Hearing and reading the stories of girls starving themselves, saving their whole paycheck as a waitress at Jolly Pasta so they too can afford that Flower Zip tote with the monogrammed pattern *pour mademoiselle*. Even for me, from Las Vegas, NV, the US capital of casinos, neon, outlet malls and everything available on-demand, even to *moi*, it was a little off-putting. But less off-putting than say the virtue consumerism of Americans like Min saying she's buying the latest skin cream because its #ALLNATURAL, #ANIMALFRIENDLY OR! Adina liking a story about Chris Evans "fighting the racists" because that's what *Captain America* is all about, and BTW the latest installment just happens to be playing now in a theater near you. It's why it didn't bother me to see Yu, pull out her Gucci wallet to buy cigarettes at the 7-11—that and it's nice to live in a place where women care about their appearance.

BUT!

That has nothing to do with *tatemae* (or does it? I mean, we're talking appearances, right?). No, no, no *tatemae* is the student, grocery store clerk, or passerby saying "*Nihongo wa jozu,*" (*You speak good Japanese*) just because you said *Arigato* OR! Them complementing you on your chopstick skills since you didn't drop a dumpling OR! The assistant Karate teacher just looking at you throw a limp wristed jab and him saying in English "*Jay-son, good good, okay okay,*" but it only means *Jason, I don't hate you*. A system of flattery institutionalized and formalized to a degree that makes you feel our system of LIKES and "Yeah, man, I'll check your article out" with never getting proper feedback, is truly in the stone age. But you learn to appreciate the opposite of *tatemae* (that being *honne*)—actually you don't appreciate it. That's being *tatemae* and trite on my part. No, no, no, you feel a spiritual sack tap when Yamamoto-sensei tells you not to use the word *Wareware* in reference to "us" because that "us" means "us Japanese", even though your *Kocho-sensei* (*School Principal*) lauded you for knowing the word OR! When Kenji said not use the word Kimi (you) when addressing him because that's too informal and *shitsuree* (*rude*), but the real meaning being *I'm your superior in the Dojo* OR! When you asked Yamamoto-sensei at lunch about your chopstick skills and he showed you how bad your technique really was when you were just looking for the affirmation OR! When Kenji said your punches were dogshit and lacked power OR! When your English prof told you not to use second-person because you're not Jay McInerney.

Yeah, the moments of *honne* suck. But the realization of reality always does. Kinda sorta but not really like when you look at your analytics for your blog post and they don't match the number of times it was retweeted.

But I've gotten off-track.

"You Americans. Always changing, going in different directions," Yamamoto-sensei said to me, being not so bothered by my dismissive attitude of teaching but by my plans post-English teaching acquiring a chameleon like character from journalist (in Japan) to video game translator working at Capcom, Instagram influencer, translator for Instagram influencer's, or a faux Priest who only officiates dog weddings only. "I only ever wanted to be teacher," he said. But then as we walked the tourist worn paths of Miyajima, him telling me about taking his young kids ("My daughter is stupid") to watch the annual *Hanabi Taikai* (*Fireworks Show*) and how he wanted his granddaughter to learn English from the zygote stages of the womb, I told him that actually I wanted to work in the creative sphere. "Like artist?" Kind of. "Writer?" Sure. "Movie director?" Pipe dream but yeah. But I didn't know how to explain to him the current DIY culture of artistry where all skills really are necessary and how specialization of the ant variety was of a quickly passing soon-to-be bygone era. But my thoughts were too jumbled, my syntax a mess, my Japanese wanting.

I notice I'm having the same trouble in writing. I mean, I care what you think.

What if by describing I end up circumscribing; doing that circle jerk along the wrong terrain of the map? But has that ever stopped an American? Forward!

Every story in some way is about the façade of order being upturned, chaos taking its true reign, allowing the true heroes to show themselves and save the day. So, the structure of the story must be ordered. But maybe it's all a sham.

Most storytelling, most fiction, creative everything is dead. It's canned fish along with all the salty preservatives. Artificial and unhealthy flavor over the real life giving ones—did I think about this as I ate sashimi at the market overlooking Hitonose? You know, like when I made my decision? Maybe you don't know. I'll get to that later…it's MY story after all, right?

BUT!

Story is the pose and form in which we hide and disguise our insecurities, our inherent fraudulence and biases. It's how we lie to ourselves. Tell me a story. Tell me something to comfort myself, make sense of the world, to forget about my troubles. A soothing agent. A sedative. But also a stimulant. When I see people talk about the importance of story, instructing on structure, character, archetypes et cetera et cetera, I see a drug dealer, even worse a conman, pontificating on how to build a house in which to live but the edifice is made of flimsy wood. Stories are a lie and better told visually anyway, where you see, hear and feel the explosions, kisses and cum. The size of the screen doesn't matter. A book, text really, is only good for information now, data just a level above code. But even then, the information is cheap. Just one collection of text in an electric stack, upon electric shelves of text. Content upon content. All content, all art, novels, music, video games, motion pictures (long form and short form), are just in a world of their own consciousness to be accessed, referenced, re-cut and re-referenced on a whim—THINK a YouTube video about a video game featuring a quick cut of Keanu Reeves saying "whoa" while then cutting to a track by early Britney Spears as background filler, hit me *Baby One More Time*, okay I will hit you one more time but this time in gif form, hotyoungbritney.gif, the mid-riff of young Britney dancing in schoolgirl uniform (god she was hot), in a reply to a troll on Twitter, whose reply to some MSM asshole, some laid-off journalist (or rather (((journalist))) :smug:) from *NewsGrind* he told to learn to code, was a comment that made you LOLZ. Commun(al)ism of content. All content running together. Together in a void. It's just all content, content, content. And like a void, it all ultimately means nothing.

8

Nothing.jpg

A black high-res reality screen engulfing the entire horizon, consuming all it can.

But yet here I am.

How is my content any different?

Why should I even care?

Maybe a little chaos needs to reign.

Maybe

    A

Little

                                       Chaos

  Needs

                    Reign

    To

But that attitude got me in this mess.

And I can't really do anything now, here, ATM.

All I can do is…

Look at the rising mushroom cloud with one face, horror, one face laughter, one face indifferent, one face welcoming…

Call the attitude Christian, call it Zen, call it anything, call it nothing…

I tried.

I tried to be beautiful. I could try some more, supplicating before that unrequited idol.

But it's no good.

Better to be vulgar. Way fucking better (you knew that was coming, didn't you?).

BUT! While discussing the brief explosive beauty of fireworks, and how no one really watches Kurosawa's films anymore in his native land, I told Yamamoto-sensei my true fear—the fear that all my creative laboring for beauty would all be for nothing and forgotten, just like Kurosawa's films. "That is nothing," Yamamoto-sensei said. "You can be like firework: Beautiful explosion that becomes nothing. But everyone remembers explosions and memory of watching them." In other words, the memory and the associative emotions will act like a time machine of the mind where the purpose of the event wasn't necessarily important but everything surrounding and circling was. That's what would linger…like the void…which got meme planted the first month in Japan, strolling among the deer of Itsukushima with Yamamoto-sensei…

Like…

Kenji is coming.

The words linger.

>Starts there?

OR!

>Starts at the *Ryokan* in Miyajima…

OR!

>Starts when the affair begins. When did it begin?

OR!

>Starts with Jason Reudelheuber-Katz taking Yu Yamada to a love hotel. But it doesn't start there, that's just consummation.

OR!

>Starts with Jason inviting her to coffee alone day of said consummation.

OR!

>Starts with Jason telling Yu he loves her at Box Karaoke.

OR!

>Starts with Jason meeting Yu when she and her husband attend *Eikawa* the first time, happy someone in his age range is attending, and upon first meeting she asks about the Seven Deadly Sins not because she is assessing her life, her relationship to God and man, her place in the universe but because she just watched the film *Seven*, (1994. Directed by David Fincher with a script by Andrew Kevin Walker and cinematography by Darius Khondji) and is curious about the framing device. Jason explains he doesn't know much—since he wasn't raised Catholic—but he does know they consist of pride, greed, lust, envy, gluttony, wrath and sloth because he saw Seven more than once but not as much as Fincher's other work (*Fight Club* and *Alien 3* being his favorites with *The Social Network* a distant third). He then starts talking about the development of the movie itself, how Walker wrote the screenplay without an agent then pitched the agent's assistants who in turn would tell their bosses and through his hustle, he managed to land an agent, and even better, got it produced. He also mentions how *Seven* was sort of a comeback film for director Fincher because after a celebrated career in music videos and commercials, working alongside the likes of Michael Bay and Spike Jonze at Propaganda, Fincher very publicly crashed and burned with *Alien 3*, his first feature length film but really the world was against him because it followed the

iconic first two films directed by Ridley Scott (who also started in advertising) and James Cameron (who started in truck driving)—if coming after these two icons was NOT enough, he also walked in to a production shit storm since sets were built for a very different version of the film with Vincent Ward at the helm, I mean, shit, even the writing talent of Walter Hill and David Giler doing a page one rewrite of the script wasn't enough—truly a scenario of the world being against you. After the failure, Fincher was able to regroup and helm the simpler grotesque procedural and made a star out of Gwyneth Paltrow in the process and the *Alien* franchise limped on without him, I mean, one has to admit *Alien 3* is certainly more interesting than *Alien: Resurrection*, right?

>Doesn't talk the *Aliens vs Predators* movies.

>She doesn't care about Fincher canon.

>She just wants to know about the Seven Deadly Sins.

>Tries to go through each one because she is interested in the English words and really the philosophical concepts behind them because Japan is built more on shame rather than guilt, so the concept of sin, roughly translated as a criminal act in Japanese is somewhat difficult to explain.

>Gets stuck on the word and idea of lust.

                    YU

        What's wrong with it?

                    JASON

        I-I don't know. It's just
        considered in Judeo-Christian
        (a word I hate but it's
        important here) practice.

                    YU

        Ju-Christ—What? So sorry. My
        English is not good…

                    JASON

        Well, Christianity came from
        Judaism.

                    11

YU

You are Judaism? You said
earlier, ne?

JASON

Jewish. Judaism is the
religion. Jewish is the person
who practices the religion or
rather the person who is born
in to it because it's also an
ethnic group...

>Stops himself.

YU

Ah so ka. You are...Jewish?

JASON

Half-Jewish.

>Notices she's confused.

YU

You only believe half?

JASON

No, no, Jewish is also an
ethnic group. Like Japanese? My
mom is an Ashkenazi Jew—Polish.
A Jew from Poland. My dad is
German, um, of German descent.

                    YU

        I see. Jewish are very smart.
        They are good with money.

                    JASON

        Depends on which Jews you're
        talking about...

                            *

I'll stop before you say "whoa cool it with the anti-Semitism" because there's plenty enough for later (:smirk:), and I don't want this to be filled with faux movie dialogue and I haven't quite figured out the formatting.

Funny thing is, I forget where Kenji was that whole conversation (maybe the bathroom?). Nor did I ever bother to ask why Yu and Kenji didn't have any kids because procreation starts as soon as the staged vows are exchanged at the gaudy pseudo-church that is meant to look like a Hollywood wedding with a pasty whitey playing Priest and a black choir performing (if you can afford it). But you know that, don't you?

                            *

Maybe the first time we met isn't really the best starting point.

No, no, no, a better starting point would be an orgasmic *Zabriskie Point*-style explosion, right? You know a lot but do you know *Zabriskie Point* (1970. Directed by Michelangelo Antonioni with a script by Antonioni, Fred Gardner, Sam Shepard, Tonino Guerra and Clare Peploe and cinematography by Alfio Contini)? Do you know that it was a box-office disaster partially due to the 105 preceding minutes of characters staring and wandering before the conclusive fireworks?

Yes, yes, yes, let's put the fireworks up front because I need to keep your attention, right? It's about more than just my relationship with Yu, right?

Because you know this isn't some domestic drama about affairs and housewives with lots of arguments and crying about validation. It's not that type of story (Thank god).

And you should know nobody wants to read an affected domesticated story that oozes forced politeness trying to be literary. Unless it helps them feel domesticated within the right set. Like chicks. Or boomers. I'm neither (Thank god).

                            13

Literature was a mistake.

No, no, no, there are a whole other cast of characters and thrills involving sex, murder, vulgarity and the scientifically induced paranormal. But you know that, don't you? You also know the cast of characters.

Cue *Ghosts* by Japan (the band, not the country).

ROLL CREDITS

CONTENT

STARRING:

JASON REUDELHEUBER-KATZ: JACQUES DUTRONC (CIRCA LATE 70S)

YU: MIREI KIRITANI

KENJI: KIPPEI SHIINA (BUT YOUNGER)

MANDY: BLAKE LIVELY

YAMAMOTO-SENSEI: NAOTO TAKENAKA (BUT OLDER)

MATT: JACK BLACK (BUT MORE REDNECK)

YAMAGUCHI-SENSEI: HIROSHI TAMAKI

MIN: KELLY MARIE TRAN (DON'T @ ME. I KNOW MIN IS KOREAN-HAWAIIAN NOT A VIET)

MARK: ANY ASSHOLE WILL DO (FUCK YOU MARK)

You might not know the names because I changed them to protect the innocent (never know when this doc could leak), save myself, as I've been exposed guilty-as-charged, the casting choices should give you a good idea anyway of who I'm talking about.

I mean, why, waste time describing someone's appearance? Of what importance is it that Yu and Kenji both smoked, or that night we went to Karaoke she wore a gold colored loose fitting sweater, one shoulder bare, complemented by tight-fitting Evisu jeans and black high heels, a cigarette sitting between her long-nailed fingers, the lighting of tobacco accenting her

14

light brown dye job and wide smile? Is it of any more import that the same evening, in a booth behind us, came Min with new boyfriend Matt in tow, wearing a tight red turtle neck that emphasized her cleavage and muffin top, along with some jeans that weren't complementary to her hips, looking like a college professor, dressed casual for a trip to the pumpkin patch for some apple cider and gourmet pumpkin chai spice loaf cake after the hay ride? Does it even matter that some time before that Min complained of Japanese bras being "too lacy" and not plain enough, as I followed her through the city, nodding compliantly? How does that help the narrative at all save for illustrating what a lapdog cuck I was and how much my game lacked (at that moment)?

I'll try not to waste your time, I know you have a lot of content to process. Content, content, content. Content, like all your friends, relatives and frenemies on Instagram, constantly updating their feed, like Mandy did, posting a selfie atop Mt. Misen in a pink Patagonia jacket, blonde hair flowing, black Athleta yoga pants accentuating her slim curves nicely down to the black ankle boots commenting about the refugee crisis, "Beautiful view from top of #MIYAJIMA. While the view is amazing, the joy in my soul is cut short by thinking of those stranded at sea who just want to experience the same beautiful place where I now live. #REFUGEECRISIS"…I don't have time, space or memory to list rest of hashtags. And you certainly don't have the attention.

It's why most writing today is just copy writing.

You have to grab and keep attention.

Get the story started.

Keep people reading.

Short sentences and short paragraphs help.

Because our true religion and ideology is marketing.

Hence inciting incident.

But you know that, don't you?

But if you don't know who some of the actors listed above are? Google it (it's a verb now for a reason).

But you may ask, what of Adina Iscovitz? You know who she is and you know what she looks like.

*

Adina and Mandy…they saw the world in black and white terms, but so did I TBH. Our terminology was just different…

15

Speaking of terminology—trigger warning!—the word (or is it a phrase?) "N-word", will not be written here. But the word—and it is most definitely a word—"nigger" most definitely will be.

I mean, I could see some US-based minority—say a nigger—taking offense at reading the word "nigger". Will it really make them angry though? Or will they just scream about in order to create a public cry of outrage, get a little attention, and maybe a little power?

I mean, I don't get upset at seeing or hearing words like "whitey", "honky", "redneck", "white trash" or even "kike". I only got mildly upset when a nigger called me white trash in high school. "Out of the way white trash," he said walking by his pants sitting below his drawers. I didn't complain to the principal. I didn't form an outrage mob. I just moved out of the way like a cuck and remembered (and moved to Japan as soon as I could).

But I'd have been suspicious of any non-white rallying to my cause. What do they get out of it? Signaling virtue is a selfish enterprise. Maybe the signalers just want my likes or adulation. It all comes 'round to approval from others. But am I any better? After all…

I care what you think.

So, here are some words that may or may not be used: Nigger, kike, wetback, spic, raghead, muzzie, sand nigger, pajeet, street shitter, jap, chink, gook, homo, fag(got), slut, THOT, bitch, cunt and boomer (it's not comprehensive).

There may also be ideas that are unpopular like the supremacy of certain ideas, cultures, and religions over others. If the words or ideas offend you then stop reading. But you may not have a choice. You may actually have to read this as part of your government investigation work much like FBI Agents and *Washington Post* editors had to scour and dissect Ted Kazcynski's manifesto that was more right than wrong.

But for those of you reading this in the privacy of your own home or office laptop or tablet or phone, after the documents are leaked by some disgruntled government affirmative action hire, I ask why seeing words and ideas that are "taboo", things you're not supposed to say or think, I ask why do they make you uncomfortable? Is it because these words—mere words—go against long held and cherished personal beliefs that you were raised with and strongly believe in?

Or, or, or, could it be…maybe…they make you uncomfortable because after, they thought of others knowing you're reading it—this!—wrongthink!—with at least a faint curiosity and wonder, maybe even tremble, at what others might think if they knew YOU were reading THIS and may look down on you or take some form of action against you. You may be the target of discrimination—heaven forbid. And you don't want to upset your life with a veneer of stability, do you? You may talk of slaying sacred cows but really, you're just throwing rocks at an unsanctified carcass rotted to the bone. The power principle is the pleasure principle after all…

But you know that, don't you?

Do you know this probably explains my mom turning a blind eye when the real estate company she worked for was sold after the Vegas housing bust to a poo from DC by way of Bombay, or ignoring the root cause of the fits she had when she got certified as medical biller (after being laid off by same poo), dealing with non-English speakers on Medicaid—chalking it up to a "broken" healthcare system—or neglecting to recognize her new hiring manager at the hospital, a negress, only hired and promoted other dindus, or failing to see her restauranteur BF Carl getting his business profitable because of a below minimum wage greaser dominated kitchen staff, two at least with same Social Security numbers, only seeing the dollar signs and Michelin Star? Call it a boomer blind spot. But she thought she was being "edgy" by watching George Carlin, Bill Hicks and *Penn & Teller: Bullshit!* insulting Christcucks (like my dad), or renting and showing me *Dogma* (1999. Directed by Kevin Smith from a script by Smith and cinematography by Robert Yeoman) once she heard my dad became a born again (though she didn't insist on watching Woody Allen when her restauranteur BF Carl started inviting her to Temple). Selective, establishment approved, edgelordism is so 1995.

Let's bring out the fatted calf that no one dare train their sword on, see how truly offended you get then.

You may say no, no, no, you can't use those words. It otherizes and marginalizes; keep your macro and micro aggressions at bay goy. How is me pointing broad terms at you any different than what you've done with your broad, abstract, postmodern terminology of Christian, white, straight, male et cetera? I'm just playing along, widening the abstraction, the void, and opening a greater chasm for destruction. That's what we want right? It's easier to destroy something that's hollowed out and generalized, containing as much meaning as a bubblegum wrapper…right?

But does it really offend you? Does anything offend us really? Or do we just get outraged in order to show others that, hey, I think like you, I think correctly, don't come after me?

How is that any different than those who cry on command at the sight of the Dear Leader? THINK of those who arrest and narc on the non-conforming, like that Russian who turned in his "friend" Alexander (yes, Solzhenitsyn), because he wrote some letters with offhand jokes about Uncle Joe. Those who are so insecure in themselves, upset—or at least paranoid—that one doesn't conform to their beliefs, the general consensus or consensus of their peers, so they have to take action to right the wrong.

But really, it's to impress. Just like those who go against rightthink by deliberately saying wrongthink...to impress. I'm no better. I care what you think.

Whatever.

I'm sure there will be some or one who read this, maybe even write their own paper or summation of it, maybe a hyperventilating, even puritanical, yet self-important screed in *The New York Times, The New Yorker, New York* or *Vox* or *Buzzfeed* or *NewsGrind* with a headline like: "I read all of Jason Reudelheuber-Katz's Content: Here's what I found," written by some smug, probably Jewish, balding soy boy with a short-trimmed beard, or some fat blue-haired feminist who needs guys to be weak so she can get laid or some skinny fat neckbeard bugman with just as much estrogen as the feminist. But no matter, it will have good vocabulary, grammar, be heavy on moral urgency but short on any intellectual rigor. Propaganda propagating the party line.

On *NewsGrind* there will be bullet points and listicles—have to make it as click baity and easy to read as possible, right? Content, content, content, marketing, marketing, marketing:

--*It's as frightening and dark as you think.*

--*Racism, misogyny and hate is alive and well.*

And so on...

The internet was a mistake.

I'm proof of it. But I'm not a victim of it. Or am I?

Contra victimology thinking—pull yourself up by your bootstraps goy!—it's for the most part sold in terms of one should take responsibility for themselves. But, but, but it might also be an establishment ruse to shift the blame of abusive behavior from power entities to the individuals they are abusing. Look away, look away, it's all your fault. You shouldn't have taken that mortgage loan Ms. Katz, though we sell you the dream of owning a house with even a whole channel dedicated to it, and it is the ultimate status symbol, but it was your fault for taking the loan with the ballooning interest rates. Don't be a victim. In commerce, it shifts moral responsibility from the producers to consumers…if you don't like it, don't read/watch/buy it.

All your success depends on you. Make the content, work your ass off for it, put it on iTunes, iBooks, Hulu or Amazon with only a cursory posting. Just a piece of content in a vast sea of content. Promote it yourself using our platform, make yourself known, you must rise above the pack and the pack grows by the day.

I know this because I was in that pack, trying to get my content seen in the good goy way, eschewing the "Life in Japan" angle—boring!—first blogging about sci-fi anime like Riki Fukuda's crypto-Nazi *moe* magical *gyaaru* mecha space opera *First! Madchen* but after taking a break stateside the blog suffered a dry period of two weeks—an eternity—and I was on edge the whole time, unable to enjoy the coffee, burgers, outlet mall clothes runs, Cirque du Soleil shows but also pondering the loss of cultural memory as "Old Vegas" was just a ghost visible on posters and films, Sinatra and Elvis its only denizens, replaced by the latest polished jewel casinos sitting on The Strip.

More importantly my analytics had gone to shit.

And I didn't feel like writing about anime and anime products anymore.

I started looking for other product.

WAIT!

CUE *Empire State Human* by The Human League. I mean, it's not too on the nose but a lot of music cued to moving images is on the nose though most don't notice because they're too busy watching…not listening to the lyrics…rather just…feeling…feeling, feeling, falling…letting sensory waters envelop them. BUT! That's how I felt—a pure embodiment of Phil Oakey's lyrics—walking half a foot higher than the natives through the crowded streets (though speaking in a foreign tongue reduces you to a toddler level of existence and respect—but no matter!)—Japan!—that human internet for (half)Aryan's like me, who could find what they needed (if they looked hard enough) and do what they pleased with enough anonymity and lack of judgement that made it all the more exciting, the anonymous stares of the crowd having little to no effect.

WAIT!

Cue *Sound of the Crowd* (also) by The Human League. I'm walking in a crowd after all, so the track might be more fitting but it's kind of ironic because it's a lesser known single of the later (more famous) line-up of The League and I wasn't really listening to the sound of any crowd, just the flat confused ambient feedback it emits.

HOLD ON!

Cue *Big in Japan* by Alphaville because that's also how I felt walking those streets, thumbs beneath my bag straps, especially among the women, like the food court of Fukuya Mall where two school girls in plaid mini-skirts continued to stare at me and giggle until I walked over to them and they blushed, and I asked them if they thought I was handsome (they did). Don't worry, nothing further happened. It's not that type of story.

BUT!

Instead of lamenting how no one outside of a film school cared about Akira Kurosawa or no longer read Mishima, I ventured down to the used video game shops and books stores of Hiroshima City, especially around the areas of the Hondori (with excursions to shops like Alpark and SOGO), pulled out my iPhone and took photos of the shelves and piles of Super Famicom games, toys and records like the debut album of the 80s pro wrestling tag team-cum-pop star duo The Crush Gals. I posted the photos, gave a little background info, then lamented how all the work one puts in to something just ends up discarded in a pile at second hand shop.

But you know that, don't you?

Do you know with blogging, self-publishing, or what have you, you're begging, in *seiza*, head bowed low, entreating others to read your work, and (if) they read you from the perspective of superior? I mean, with establishment whatever, you're at least a little elevated on the dais and they defer the respect of same when (if) they read.

Did you know my reader response was all summed up in one user comment on either Twitter or Instagram (I forget)? That comment being, "Your site used to be good but now it's complete faggotry. I'm literally unfollowing you RIGHT NOW."???

Do you know the comment made me smile rather than frown? You do know I just kept photographing, posting and being pretentious (even though my impressions were down to single digits, sometimes just one or two).

I mean, you have to scream louder, create a ton of volume, because volume is how you get your numbers up. Quantity over quality.

Are we whores, us bloggers and social media crawlers? No, no, no, we're sluts! We put out constantly, looking for fulfillment, hoping someone will find value in our wares but the only value one assigns us is our being an easy lay.

20

They don't want to pay for it—certainly won't put a ring on it! But they might say kind things to us, maybe even throw some gifts our way in order to keep the action coming but we'll never find that ONE, the one, who will appreciate the treasure they've discovered (or at least ascribed to ourselves) and adorn us the way we desire.

BUT!

There's exceptions to every rule. We've seen them! We all have our own cyber Vivian Ward to aspire to. Hence, we keep spreading our legs, but dying inside knowing it isn't ideal, admiring and hating the select few who thrive in that ethereal center, who celebrate the chimeric prize they've found (usually "freedom") in being an e-tart.

Best tout technique in e-square is saying something controversial, like there's a globalist conspiracy, primarily ran by Jews, to control the world, subvert all races, create a serf class, where we all buy, read, and consume the same things, while keeping us in fear of the other—sand niggers today and maybe nigga niggers from Africa tomorrow, unleashing them on the unsuspecting West like a dog owner who lets their rabid German Shepherd off the leash, salivating to attack you while it's handler yells "Don't worry, he's friendly". Really, it's true. I know. I saw it on social media. From popular accounts like Ultima_Thule, OingoBoinGoy, The_ZOGfather, Andyschluss, Ernst_Jungroyper, Neu!Albion, General_TOHO and PUA's like Justin Bangs and namefags like Scott Nash. But you know that, don't you?

You also know, I could retract any statement once I get popular. Do a Soviet Style confession.

Or I could say "Hitler did nothing wrong."

But that makes me the devil.

But I certainly took the devil's bargain.

In a culture war, one can be on the side of (social) justice, hijacking all creative means of production—Poetry, literature, music, film (short form content), TV series (long form content), Capital-A art—creating humanizing compassion propaganda vehicles to spread their multifaceted diversity agenda like a mental virus to justify all sorts of violent behavior or watching and rewarding the "right" movie, the "right" book or just buying the "right" type of humane soap. Marketing with a social conscience. THINK Mandy posting Instagram an unboxing video of her newly arrived box of Tom's because she "literally had to do something to support the refugees." THINK Adina posting on Twitter Elie Wiesel quotes on August 6 in remembrance of the dropping

21

of the A-bomb. THINK her getting likes from both Hiroshima Prefectural Coordinator of International Relations Avi Feynman and Min. THINK on the same day Min posting on Facebook "Remember the Koreans who died in the A-bomb." THINK Adina replying with an article by a (((journalist))) with the headline "The case for a more multicultural Japan" with likes from Min, Matt, Mandy and Avi. THINK Min posting the next day on Facebook, "While the dropping of the Atomic bomb was tragic, we need to bring more awareness about Korean comfort women and the brutal treatment they received from the Japanese. How many LIKES can I get?". THINK Adina, Avi, Mandy and Matt (you cuck) all giving her likes with Mandy commenting, "The Japanese treatment of Korean women was just THE WORST," followed by reply from Adina saying, "It was the WORST outside of the Nazi's treatment of The Jews," followed by a reply from Mandy "I'm sorry Adina, I would never downplay the Holocaust. Just another chapter in the sins of the white race," followed by Adina saying, "I forgive YOU," with Mandy capping it off with "Thank you. I would never expect you to forgive our entire race. We don't deserve it. The more I learn, the more I think the white race is disease upon humanity," with all comments receiving likes from Min, Avi but not Matt.

But in our modern Late-Capitalist society of marketing sans deeper meaning, one needs the purest form of cynical foot soldier and villain to provide counterbalance and foil to the keep the utopian engine running. A man like me, the very embodiment of our social enantiodromia. You can be the self-righteous social justice warrior who buys fair trade coffee OR! You can embrace your inner capitalist pig, mercenary, racist or brand where all the narcissistic promises of glory find their Yes and Amen in this Devil's bargain. With raised hands we cry "Greed is Good", loving the smell of napalm in the morning as we let the hate flow through us just doing it. THINK Scott Nash on YouTube decrying globalist and BigPharma vaccinations while promoting his supplements between questions with a psychic who has connected to the ancient space race of the Lyrans who are in an eternal struggle with the Reptilians, an underground shape shifting race dwelling on earth trying to subvert all its civilized institutions. THINK e-celeb, e-Pundit and e-THOT Cary Walsh mentioning her Patreon page while being interviewed by Scott Nash about bringing a great awakening that requires we get in touch with our higher spiritual plain (and donating to her Patreon). THINK OingoBoinGoy, sub-Tweeting an article with the headline "Jewish groups linked to assisting undocumented refugees" with the comment, "Who is going to destroy who first? It's only a matter of time." THINK Ultima_Thule posting on KAI10 the merits of Fascism. THINK The_ZOGfather linking to an article on Reddit about fat female aid workers prowling refugee camps for cock with the caption "Patriarchy when? Can we get this to the top?". THINK General_TOHO tweeting "I think we nuked the wrong people. RT if you agree," with likes and RTs from OingoBoinGoy, The_ZOGfather, and even the 10th (and soon to be banned) account of Ultima_Thule's (THULEisUltimate6724899796). THINK Justin Bang's latest email featuring him sandwiched between two Euro sluts in short skirts while smoking a stogie, discussing the hustle and hard work of building his brand. THINK me spending more time on Social Media, Bangs' forums and reading posts on Kai10 (like "The True story of the Holocaust TL;DR it didn't happen") instead of reading Kawabata or preparing lessons for school.

THINK of a more balanced past where wealth was a sign of divine blessing, one fought and waged war for God, King and Country, discrimination just a form of self-protection *via negativa* and a story was just for tucking your kids in at night. :shrug:

But at night the only thing that tucks me in are those terrible words…

Kenji is coming…

Back to that inciting incident…

But consider the formatting for a "story", the bill of goods sold to writers for half-century plus: You need a beginning, hook, middle build and ending pay-off. A blueprint no different than Hoover used for vacuums or the local Japanese architect used to build the latest LEGO box that looks like all the other LEGO boxes doting the Japanese urbanscape…or even LEGO instructions themselves.

Yes, yes, yes, a story blueprint is a product blueprint. It's not art or beauty, yet we treat it as so. I mean, no one ascribes divine features or aesthetic critique to shampoo and Clorox wipes.

But…

Reducing the entire arts-entertainment complex to a cannery with superior color palette is also a touch fundamentalist, don't you think? Hard to fight the operant conditioning! No, no, no, most content is not produced with the European spirit of *art pour l'art*. It's produced in the spirt of American entrepreneurialism! The likes of Dan Brown, James Cameron, Taylor Swift and Jeff Koons are more the descendants of Henry Ford, Andrew Carnegie,

Martha Stewart and Dave Thomas rather than Tolstoy, Tarkovsky, Bach or Rembrandt.

But you know that, don't you? But if we (or just me) are going to rebel against this Progressive Consumerist Corporate Marxist super empire, then we (I) must rebel against their means of propaganda production, one being assembly line story construction that will make you forget your cares, your worries and give you your bread and circuses.

Or maybe I should just accept the bargain and be shameless with short paragraphs.

No, no, no, it's not a postmodern "the exploration of the story is better than the story" type of story. But we must proceed with meta-mutter and the Foucaultian, Brechtian, Godardian (since I've actually seen his work) and Jungerian (tell Mark thanks for recommending me to Ernst Junger)—yes, yes, yes, we must proceed, engage and utilize these tools because in this age where everyone knows everything, literary paradise is lost, so we proceed as the fallen, even if it means beating our chests outside the temple gates, confessing our sins with clauses.

I mean, postmodern lit is really, like all postmodernism, subservient to the status quo, stripping everything of meaning, a tyranny all its own, creating a void in which established corporate power can fill. After reading or watching any deconstructed nonsense one cannot wait for the latest screen adaptation of *Shang-Chi Master of Kung Fu* while really hoping Disney buys the James Bond franchise so we can finally see that long-desired hook-up with Dazzler because true power comes from providing good re: giving people what they want (confused as a need). It's why on show *Oven Talk*, the hosts OingoBoinGoy and AndySchluss, discussed how Moana is really an allegory for Ethno-Nationalism using the dialogue of "My People" and "My ancestors in an unending chain" is really just crypto language about "us" whites and how musicals like *Hamilton* are just peak fetishization of White America with AndySchluss adding "They hate us because they ain't us," rather than discussing David Foster Wallace's critiques of media culture, or how Godard and Jean-Pierre Gorin stated in *Wind from the East* the two purposes of the photographic image are to identify enemies and distort the truth (of course one could then use this as a launching pad to discuss the GUI as the next stage evolution of the image with its interactivity and endless scrolling sea of imagery taking the two purposes to next level sophistication) and if they mentioned *American Psycho* it was only in reference to Christian Bale's performance and likeness not Bret Easton Ellis' novel. But you know that, don't you? :THINKING_FACE:

Do you know why the question of "Does the profit motive corrupt the artistic process?" has rarely been asked? I mean, instead of focusing on providing revelation, catharsis or inspiration, an artist is instead turned towards providing stimulus which will persuade to purchase (or selection on subscription platform) and other practicalities that lead to stacks of cash. We may admire isolated elements (a beautifully composed sentence, a nice melody and hook, lighting, a tracking shot, et cetera) but the whole itself is usually spiritually bereft. Instead the creator or artist becomes artisan; finding pleasure in the process of construction. Kind of like me now. But I have no choice. You know that.

But do you know that at a function welcoming Hiroshima JETs, I found myself seated next to Adina and Avi and wound up in a discussion about my dislike of the *Pirates of the Caribbean* franchise, puzzling the both of them, where I could even see Avi squirm under his short beard? I had only met Adina once in Tokyo for the "Welcome to Japan" conference but now here we were the second time, at a local Viking restaurant, where the beer was flowing. "You're kidding Jason," she said. "Stop. I literally will slap you. Of all movies to criticize."

Through a slightly alcohol tinged haze I tried to explain how they're overly long, bloated in spectacle to compensate for lack of core, and completely forgettable save for how everyone liked them and how late 80s early 90s Johnny Depp is my favorite Johnny Depp but they just responded (*they* being Adina), "Jason it's just a movie…but you're still completely wrong. Completely." It's just content. But I couldn't help but think it wasn't just content because you don't spend $303 million on just anything unless you're expecting a life of return both dollar wise and brand loyalty, AKA a returning customer. To which they (this being both Adina and Avi) laughed and said (this being Avi): "The Jew is strong with this one." And both would laugh even louder in unison, to which I would reply (in my mind) that I'm more concerned with the moral implications of such a production (to which I replied to myself, "The Christian is strong with this one…still…sadly"). But that was enough of that as Adina moved on to talk to some blonde CHAD from South Africa.

And with that any goodwill and social credit I earned from my fellow JETs dissipated like the fireworks we watched at the *Hanabi Taikai* on Miyajima the next night. Call it the tyranny of first impressions. Of course, I'm referring to

25

my time in Tokyo when all the newly arrived JETs assembled, and the fresh Hiroshima pack, led by Avi went to a Karaoke joint. Min was there, as was Matt and Adina. Mandy wouldn't come until the next year. And there we were at Shidax in Shinjuku (or was it Billy Ken Kid?) a party of ten plus, sitting on their hands, in a room and not knowing what came over me, I jumped in first singing *Burning Down the House* by Talking Heads—I remember it distinctly!— footage of white families going down waterslides as the lyrics rolled slowly down the lower third providing a consumer grade Godardian level of audio-visual juxtaposition.

I sang a couple more times that night in staggered performances.

This led to the whole crew of Avi-Adina-Matt-Min surrounding me on the Shinjuku sidewalk afterwards, the neon illuminated over us a glorious halo, Matt glowingly stating in his unique Texas cadence "You were like the King in there man," followed by Min with "I know he was awesome,", Avi with "Yeah, yeah, you're definitely the king of karaoke," and Adina just smiling. Felt good, won't lie. I cared what they thought that night.

Just like I care what you think.

BTW that's the only scene in Tokyo.

MOMNDF: Shame. I wanted to shoot more there.

JRK: There's more to Japan than just Tokyo and this isn't your cue.

MOMNDF: I'm unpredictable like that.

JRK: Can you tell me the next part?

MOMNDF: No, why don't you?

My star quickly faded as we all got situated in Hiroshima Prefecture. I detected this somewhat when Matt and I met Min at Hiroshima Station in Hiroshima City to head to our Prefectural conference (the buffet being later that night), and as we discussed the best way to get there, I just kept saying "We could take the Shitty Liner" in reference to the Hiroshima City Liner but pronounced by Japanese as "*Shitty Rainaa*", but Matt and Min didn't seem in on the joke with Min finally snapping, "It wasn't funny the first time, Jason." And my feelings were confirmed as we negotiated the crowds at the train station when I nudged Matt pointing at the shop *Asse* saying, "You want to go to Ass?" with his expression not even registering a bare smile or maybe he was just uncomfortable with laughing in the presence of a so-called lady. But the day starting with jokes falling flat and ending with the derisive "The Jew is strong with this one" cemented that my star had indeed faded with the afterword of Adina teasing me the next day with a "Oh my god, Jason" followed by giggle because she noticed I had A) A *Pokemon* pencil and B) had written my name on it just like Japanese school kids, not bothering to see the irony of me reveling in commercial kitsch, trying to be my own private Warhol. And the stasis of the situation revealed itself when we all headed to the *Hanabi Taikai* on Miyajima that humid summer evening and my suggestion of taking the train to the island was ignored while they all agreed mass consensus to take the Green Line tram instead, despite it being a half hour longer ride. Of course, they all complained the trip over, with total lack of introspection that if they just listened to me they wouldn't be on the slow tram but already at Miyajima petting the roaming deer and that their democratic decision making caused this mess, which is really, in a nutshell, a reflection of late American Democracy.

Democracy was a mistake.

But I followed along like a cuck instead just taking the train by my lonesome.

Did I care what they thought? Probably. After all…

I care what you think.

But that's why, a year and a half later, that night at Shidax in Kure with Yu and Kenji, sitting in that room, sipping our drinks, my enjoyment of a coke disturbed by the obnoxious sound of all the gaijin in the hallway outside our room (a group that now included the newly announced couple of Matt and Min, along with Mandy, Adina, Avi and South African CHAD) only reinforced my decision not take up their invitation to sing in the empty air together.

Actually, re-rack that.

Let's play in real time:

As Kenji sings I notice out of the corner of my eye that Yu is wiping her eyes with a tissue. She sees me looking at her. She quickly puts the tissue in her purse and smiles.

I take a sip of my coke.

The moment is broken from the loud voices in the hallway.

Fuck, Americans are loud I think.

I look at Yu again. I roll my eyes. She smiles.

And I find that comforting. And then I notice my song, *We are X* by X-Japan is up next in the queue. Good way to drown out the western noise with a metal song. My Japanese song, my performance that impresses the Japanese for singing a song in Japanese even though I can't match Toshi's high-pitched tenor notes but every time the word "X" comes up in the chorus Yu and Kenji dutifully cross their arms in the X formation.

X!
Kanjite miro
X!
Sakende miro
X!
Subete nugisutero
X!

She then sings. A Japanese love song. I don't know the lyrical content but the harmony is pleasant, Yu's voice sincere. When she's done, I clap. She says thanks.

I continue looking through the catalogue.

Kenji sings.

Then I perform *Stronger* by Kanye West. I don't think you sing a Kanye West track, you perform them, right? Yu bobs her head, does the hand motions like she's at a rap concert, raising her arm in the air going with the beat.

Kenji plays along as well.

I'm feeling confident.

I'm feeling like I have some game. The star has returned.

But it never faded among Japanese just like a washed-up Hollywood's celebrity never fades here either. When I'm with them, I feel like I can take on the world through their smiles and encouragement becoming confident as hell. The girls laugh at my jokes, my charm taking over, as I watch them giggle, maybe they're just thrilled an American is talking to them, the ones they see in the movies, the ones they see on their TV while watching both long and short form content, like Leo DiCaprio in *Titanic* (1997, Directed by James Cameron, cinematography by Russell Carpenter with a screenplay by Mr. Cameron)— where there was even a stern warning in my welcome booklet saying, "Japanese women are expecting someone to act like Leonardo DiCaprio from *Titanic*"— it really said that, but I'm not staggered by such a task and that feeling I have here, of starting anew, my history, my background, my social status back home really being of little importance, by being here I've proven that I'm smart enough to get here, I'm a rock star in my own way and I notice more an openness from women that I never felt stateside and which I never felt being with Min, I mean shit, I can strike out with that ham beast but I at least have at least the chance of a base hit with the most casual of beauties, like Rina, an attendee of my English class, who practices experimental musical theory, whose plain-jane attire of sweat shirt, jeans and sneakers I find oddly attractive, who's in the same age range as me but who Yu told me to steer clear of, or Yuri, one of my former Junior (now) high school students, a member of Yamamoto-sensei's now defunct Ping Pong club, who (obviously) had a crush on me, who wrote in her *Jiko Shokai* (*self-introduction*) that her dream one day was to move to America and watch football every day, who I didn't have the heart to tell that it only came on Sunday's, Monday's and Thursday's, who walked home with me from school one day, gave me a piece of candy, and at that moment made me realize I needed to keep my distance but she graduated to high school and later disappeared—No, BTW, I had nothing to do with that, it's not that type of story—or even that nurse at the local pharmacy, the one who had a cute ponytail and slightly large chest that many Japanese would consider gigantic, the way she bowed, so feminine, the way she tried to speak English with me, and that attendant at Starbucks in Kure, her hair in a cute bob, her smile and chipmunk-like cheeks, almost empowering me as I met her start to the point I almost asked her out right there but held back, I had to meet Min the next day, but I've yet to return to that Starbucks, but this all makes me *harder, faster, better, stronger...*

I then see Yu.

The song is over. She claps. "You have good rap," she says (yes, she pronounced it as *lap*).

Yu's song comes up. She chose to sing an English one, *Forbidden Colours* by David Sylvian and Ryuichi Sakamoto, a vocal version of the instrumental theme from *Merry Christmas, Mr. Lawrence* (1983, Directed by Nagisa Oshima, cinematography by Toichiro Narushima with a screenplay by Mr. Oshima and Paul Mayersberg based on the book *The Seed and the Sower* by Laurens van der Post). The way she sings it—different but yet equally as haunting as the way Sylvian performs it, yet coming from her it doesn't sound like someone fighting their inner fag, a yearning for someone of the same sex, no from her its normative, but I can still hear the pain in her voice...

Before the song is over Kenji leaves the room, exits for the bathroom...

"You sing beautifully," I tell her.

"Are you sure?" she asks in her translation of the word *honto* (literally meaning, *truth*), which really should be translated as *Really?* but some asswipe decided it should be translated as *Are you sure?* and I've just ruined the moment.

But I reply, "Yes, I'm sure."

I reach across and grab her hand.

29

I don't why. Instinct.

She doesn't grip my hand, more just lets hers sit in mine. She looks at it then at me.

She smiles.

"I love you," I say. Again, I don't know why. Again, instinct, but with the heart racing at F-1 speeds.

"I love you too."

She squeezes my hand and smiles. I kiss her hand and let it go.

A kind gesture, a gentlemanly gesture for sure, Yu is blushing, her smile widening but really it was a cowardly gesture, because I knew Kenji was coming and no we haven't got to the part where Yu said "Kenji is coming" no I was just saying this in my mind, my realization that Kenji is coming and we were about the same height, and he had a temper, a temper I saw in Karate class, usually directed at the little boys, ripping their ass for such bad technique or the one time he knocked a guy out with a round house kick to the head just to teach a lesson about how he always needed to keep his hands up. I saw the guy's face. Saw his eyes almost rolling in the back of his head, him lying on the floor and wondering exactly where he was and I wonder will that be me in a few moments if I don't release Yu's hand and pretend this never happened? Because you know, Kenji the knockout artist on the unwilling is coming motherfucker.

Another song has started. *In the Air Tonight* by Phil Collins. How fitting.

I start singing.

And Kenji walks in the room as the monitor begins to flicker. Not the first or last time electronic images would flicker around Yu-chan.

*

Sorry, that was all too long.

I hope I kept your attention.

I took a break after thinking and writing those words, words that incite a range of emotions from dread to regret to submission…depending on my mood. Because I know they all lead to…

Kenji is coming.

I'll try to do better.

We're all trying to do better when it comes to writing. Got to keep attention. The playing field has been levelled—or has it been imploded? A huge sinkhole being filled to the brim with content. Content, content, content! Books, movies (short form), TV programs (long form), video games, texts, Facebook posts,

Tweets, Instagrams, Snapchat sessions, Tinder swipes, whatever else and blogs (does anyone still read those? No one read mine). And reading, true reading, is at the bottom. Visual media is that much more powerful (am I repeating myself?).

The image, the meme, is more powerful and probably more truthful than the story. It lingers with us and stays imprinted on our memories or at least mine. THINK the image of the screen flickering after I told Yu I loved her. THINK when I saw my phone flicker as I went to the bathroom afterwards at Shidax and Adina confronted me in the hallway wondering why I was "so cold" to their group and I said I just wanted to hang out with friends, and she said "fine whatever" and I said "Be that way" then she put her hand on my arm and said "I'm not mad at you, it's just some are asking questions…" and then I see Yu walking towards the bathroom as well, and I pull out my phone because I got a text from Min ("Why are you being so cold?") and a Periscope update from Scott Nash entitled "The Globalists are using the refugee crisis destroy your sovereignty", but I can't watch because this time my phone screen flickers then locks up. But you know that, don't you?

"What's wrong?" Adina asks.

"Nothing, it's just…" I look up and see Yu staring at us as she walks to the ladies room.

I can't speak for 6 billion faceless people that I don't know and will never know nor care to know but I think these images imprint themselves in my flesh hard drive more than words. Just like the physical appearance of Mandy, her image, caught Kenji's hard stare at the *izakaya* earlier that night. Just like at that very same moment Yu's glance darted between Matt and I as he stood over our table talking about Karate then inviting us to karaoke and me refusing, realizing I wasn't angry at Matt for hooking up with Min, I just wanted to be with Yu above all. Just like Adina observed same in the hallway at Shidax when I turned from my phone, to her, then to Yu and excused myself, the exoticness of the other holding sway over all life. Reminds me of when I was in 12 or 13 and my college aged Jewish cousin Abbie was staying at our place for a weekend in Vegas bringing her blonde Brazilian roommate Adriana, who looked normal enough in physique, with plain jane jeans and t-shirt, a degree of body fat but the naturally straight dirty blonde hair, and multiple ear piercings, and mischievous smile without make-up made my dick groan that much more, especially when I walked by the bathroom in the hallway, my cousin stepped out and with the door cracked I glanced Adriana putting her bra on, her nipples a quiet brown, and Abbie slapped the back of my head saying "Jason you pervert get out of here!" and before I skedaddled, I just saw Adriana's reflection in the mirror, her eyes glancing towards me with an accepting smile as she fastened her snaps.

But...

"You don't want to join?" Yu asked.

"Not really."

"No?"

"Yeah, no. I'm..." I thought about Matt nailing Min in his bed—an image that made me nauseous but then I looked at Yu, her wide smile and accepting eyes. "I just want to hang out—be with you guys. Just us. That okay?"

Yu smiled. "Of course," she said and took a long drag of her cigarette and formed an even bigger smile.

The nerves settled.

It's easy to read about game but harder to play it.

I zoned out the obnoxious bantering of my associates behind me.

I felt my phone rattle.

A text from Min: "Can we talk later?"

My reply: "Nothing to talk about."

"Don't be mad at me."

I ignored.

Before I turned the iPhone off, the display locked up, then the images started stuttering (just like later in the evening).

I hit the button on the side several times, trying to turn it off but it just looked locked up.

But it finally shut down.

I then looked up to see Yu staring at me. Same smile, cigarette close to her lips.

"Sorry," I said. "These phones..."

"It's ok," she said and took a long drag.

"You have an iPhone, right?"

"No. Sony."

"Sony? Not even an Android?"

"No. I'm too stupid to have iPhone."

"What?"

"It looks too...difficult?"

"It isn't. Really, it's easy to use."

32

"No, no, it looks too hard."

"What about Kenji?"

He held up his phone but it was the old flip kind, could be mistaken for a burner phone stateside. "Really?" I asked.

Kenji said something in Japanese. "He doesn't like technology," Yu said.

"I guess you don't either."

"No, not really."

"Huh…"

"You like phone?"

"Um, yeah."

But you know all this, don't you?

Do you know the image—especially symbols—have a power that stories and their sycophants (text) can only hope to attain? (Sorry to beat a dead horse here. I do care what you think, remember?).

No wonder the Jews—I mean, God—forbade idol worship. They have a power over man we can't comprehend. Images contain a mystical force. It's why Protestant societies, so embedded in text, get subverted so easily. They have no root images and symbols outside of a flag.

And yet…

Here I am with only words. I'll try my best to be as honest as possible. That's all I got and…

I care what you think.

But in the beginning was The Word…*Logos*…but the Word became flesh…it had to…every unseen force must make itself known through either creation or destruction.

Words, words, words—what do they mean? They have immediate value (for most), speak straight to the mind and heart. Makes the mind work, paints the picture, builds the frame, provides direct connection, a world of my own, yet a shared space. Communion. Words are authority. In the beginning, maybe really was the word, this *Logos*. The source. And here I am separated from everything with only the pen, but yet still connected to the source.

But words themselves are cumbersome. They create a muddle by trying to clarify. Never do they create the immediate sense of mysteriousness, wonder and soothing that a piece of music or an image may give. They don't immediately speak to the heart. So, I was wrong above. Words travel via the brain and then are distributed elsewhere, bringing conflict, a war between reason and the heart.

33

And writing is the most inelegant of art forms. The most entry level, the most plebian. Maybe it was more elegant in the time of the troubadour's and Shakespeare when not many could actually write. But the troubadours wrote for song and Shakespeare the stage. The Bible was more recorded than written...for posterity.

The most elegant writing is the most spare.

It's like a Japanese flower arrangement, where the spaces and exclusions matter just as much as what's present (I never asked Yu about *Ikebana* or *Kado*). Or like in Taoism where the room is defined by its openings, not the walls.

But the eastern philosophy calendar wisdom stops here. I never really studied it much. Except for the excerpts PureLight synthesized for their cultic dogma.

Writing and storytelling, with all its limited truths, creating greater perceived falsehoods and its imposition of Procrustean forms and structures, on a formless, chaotic world of moving lava, was man's original sin. It was man's way of laying claim on the vast universe, creating a limited aperture in which to frame and view it.

Yes, through other forms we can bask in the sunlight, and rays of creation, circling it, enjoying it, taking peace in knowing our insignificance. Storytelling was man becoming arrogant, a god, a tyrant saying they have it all figured out, forming then hijacking the *Logos*. Storytelling, the myths, the fairy tales, the Bible—all of it! Stories were a mistake.

See how far one can take things? But that's my thing, how I roll.

Story is all I have right now.

Writing...I have no choice.

Enough self-loathing.

Images are just as capable of lying as stories. We have images we can't trust. Not even the images of our memories but yet...they still give us meaning. The Greek (and Russian) Orthodox were on to something by treating the image as sacred. After all we see photos of a foreign land, like the *Torii* of Miyajima, the most photographed site in all Japan, or even a domestic hovel (like my mom sending photos of my Uncle Murray's birthday) and we take it all in faith we're getting the truth. Just like those instances of the screens flickering in my mind are just as truthful as the pen I hold in my hand now as I write this, forming— you may say, "creating"—my narrative, but that's normal and the *Logos* is a force of creation, not destruction.

But all we want now is to destroy. We're all deconstructing, relativizing, analyzing while really not doing anything, with nothing to build in replacement. Criticism of all stripes is just the frustrated trying to destroy the doers. Nostalgia and lament for things past are the flipside of this post-modern nihilistic coin. There is no moral duty here. There's really no moral duty at all. We're only good at analyzing then destroying, while striking a pose, thinking it means something. A privileged white disease. What doesn't come naturally to a smart (white) person becomes intellectualized, "figured out" so to speak. But putting intellectualization in to practice is a clumsy and hollow exercise because it's all thought and no feeling. It must become internalized and natural, if that's even possible.

A lot of intellectual writing comes from a place of insecurity, the need to be approved by your so-called "smart" peers but more importantly to be let others know "I'm not a plebe, my faculties are at a higher, elevated level."

I mean, we can ask questions like "If you only hear the seagull but don't see it, does it really exist?" but that won't get us anywhere. Better to just assume figments of imagination, dreams and memory are just as real as the citrus flavor on a Satsuma *mikan* upon first bite. Just relax and assume that holistic reality exists at many levels greater, with more depth, than our assumed and dismantled 2-D chessboard.

Yes, yes, yes, the post I read or meme I saw (and read) created by a chappie in Omaha just laid off at the silo manufacturing plant is just as real as the hot dog fun run on This is CNN in terms of planting its imagery, its reality, non-discriminately in my mind palace, taking, creating and triggering thoughts and emotion just as real as the Chanel Allure'd femme greeting me at the café competes with the powerful odor of the roasted beans in said café.

And yes, Yu wore Chanel Allure that day in the café, along with a scarf that kept us both warm inside.

Mandy was there that day too, but—I suppose you'd like me to discuss who these people actually are.

But you know who they are. You have their entire online history sitting in your databases on a server farm in Utah with an algorithm that can do a character breakdown, a Voight-Kampff test realized, at the speed of light after compiling all the information from their activity on Facebook, Twitter, Reddit, Instagram, Emails, LinkedIn, how many V-Bucks that had in their *Fortnite* account, if they still had *Angry Birds* on their phone and how many times they watched *Chocolate Rain* on YouTube. Do you remember *Chocolate Rain*? If you

35

don't, Google it, I understand because it was just one piece of content in a sea of content that was competing for your attention. Content, content, content!

Do you need a character breakdown from a casting call sheet?

Or do you just need to look at the metadata where the likes and engagement can give you a more satisfactory blush response than I can? We all pretty much live in cyberspace anyway. PureLight was on to something. We might not just be transcending humanity but transcending the flesh in general, becoming *Die Mensch-Maschine*.

Mandy posts a *NewsGrind* story on Facebook headlined "The Pain, Heartache and Joy of Living with a Pre-Op Transgendered Gerbil" with her only comment being the :cry: *emoji*. Min posts a link to a *Wall Street Journal* article headlined "This Tokyo Robot Brothel is Doing Big Business" with the comment "Men are literally gross". Matt hits Like. What does that say about them? I post a link to story about a famous married-with-children *First! Mädchen* cosplayer who wants to become genderless with my only comment being :man-facepalming: *emoji* with no likes or engagement from anyone. What does it say about me that it pissed me off?

You know what it says.

I care what you think.

And you'd be right. Our social media behavior mirrors something inside of us, even if it is reflecting a silent inner longing.

:shrug:

The fear of transhumanism or rather the biological changes technology has made in us have been realized too late but the malaise remains all around. Social media itself is an inherently feminine medium giving males reason to preen and enabling the worst impulses in females (but really, everyone is a woman since testosterone levels are dropping, estrogen reigning, ego's run rampant with the basic, childish and primitive need for attention constantly hitting LIKE or seeking likes, mutually assured gratification but also mutually assured falsification).

We're all just objects now, some with use, like my newest tablet, some with no use, like the obsolete Rio PMP300 MP3 player that Uncle Murray bought my mom and now sits discarded in my closet.

We've all become biological cyborgs tied to our tech whether it be through the dopamine overdoses caused by the choice to swipe left or right or the stationary lethargy created by consuming content, content, content or the adrenaline rush from same stationary position due to a first person shooter or the anabolic steroids you take so you can burn fat, build muscle and not be swiped to negative on Tinder or just having your eyes shot with an excimer laser…like I did on summer break so I wouldn't have to worry about glasses. Humans themselves have just becomes objects du jour. For a man, women are just flesh fuck puppets and since women have the choice on swiping on-screen or IRL who can blame a guy for buying Justin Bangs' latest tome so he could figure out the girl's code or hack that unzips their pants?

"Jason?" Matt, Min, Adina, Yamamoto-sensei, Yamaguchi-sensei—everyone!—asked in their respective yet compound cacophony upon seeing me sans optic lenses on a return from stateside. "You look…different," the girls said with a slight smile (one more exploit in the code discovered). FWIW Mandy was newly arrived to Japan so I was just "Jason" to her.

But who is "Mandy" to me or you? By looking at Mandy's social media history, will your idea match my casting sheet?:

MANDY (FEMALE, EARLY 20S, WHITE)

BEAUTIFUL BUT DESPERATE MILLENNIAL.

Does that description jive with her Instagram photos of her with an arm around her elementary school students, smiles plastered all over? OR! With her posting on Facebook a link with a photo of crying refugee children with the comment "When will people wake up?" OR! Her Instagram photo of a cup of coffee next to a copy of *Becoming Michelle Obama* with the comment "A cup of coffee and one inspirational woman (Not me LOL). #GOODMORNING"?

But you know all this, don't you?

But do you know that she never bothered to learn Japanese? Always depending on others to do her translating for her from Avi on down? Do you know the incident of when she was expecting a package, she left a note for the Japanese postman in English detailing when she would be in, noting the best time to deliver said package? Do you know that the only real interest she took in Japan was staying overnight at a Buddhist Temple in Nara where she could enjoy Yoga and other amenities which in turn is what probably sparked her interest in PureLight since they offered free Yoga classes to lure in potential marks?

37

I mean, it's easy to point out the evil of a cult and laugh at them but where pray tell is the individuality in wearing the same brands (THINK Mandy being a billboard for Patagonia) or being concerned about said brand or property itself rather than core values (THINK Matt talking about MCU). Where is the individuality in wearing Nikes, driving Porches, where upgrading life is really upgrading brands?

I mean, isn't being middle class, especially WHITE MIDDLE CLASS (I'll throw in our honorary Aryan's the Japanese as well), isn't it all just one huge LARP? Doing things like martial arts, going on a cruise, building a koi pond in the backyard (as seen on HGTV), dressing respectively even if it means shopping for luxury goods at Ross Dress For Less, listening to rap, or leasing a BMW. All a need to create an artificial space, to live in an empty fantasy or escape dull reality, an attempt to experience the life barbell high or low of the very rich or very poor in which they are sandwiched. Is there anything worse than the mushy middle? They don't know the thrill of a street fight or terrifying scare of a drive-by nor sailing on a yacht or flying on a private jet or being waited on hand and foot. It's aspiration for both sides!

When people experience just a food or a service of the elite, like a limo ride to a restaurant, first class plane seats or reservations at Trois Mec, it's like they've touched a higher plain of existence, giving them a smug sense of pride.

Reminds of that that time when I went to Miyajima. Where I heard *Kenji is coming...*

But when they've touched the hand of the elite, they post it on Instagram, Facebook, SnapChat or Twitter, along with their showing concern for the refugees and little brown poor children along and showing their music playlist full of exotic brown beats, even though to the regular rich or elite it may all just be banal and bourgeois and to those living in the hood just respond "y'all crazy". But it's the best advertisement the rich can get, mostly for free. A free form of brain washing, so most will spend their precious time striving to be like them, making them richer—they're the 1% for a reason! Maybe the aspirant will even sit down at their PC and start hacking away at that great idea they've always had that could be a blockbuster or make a viral video, just try, try, try to make some content go big so I can get the beach view room at the Hilton Waikiki or just some attention, striking that devil's bargain.

Kind of like when Min asked me about dropshipping and setting up a Shopify storefront because I "seemed to know a lot about the online world".

But you know that, don't you? You've seen our texts. Do they match my call sheet?:

MINSUH (FEMALE, EARLY 20S, KOREAN-HAWAIIAN)

SLIGHTLY CHUNKY, TYPE-A SECOND-GENERATION IMMIGRANT. THE MOST AMERICAN OF ALL.

You've seen her millions of questions asking me about links to this that and the other topic like writing copy, best payment processor, if generating leads on Facebook was of more use than Twitter et cetera. You probably also know of her native Korean aunt who moved from Seoul to LA to Las Vegas and made extra cash by prowling the outlet malls on The Strip, finding deals and buying 10 of everything to sell on eBay (maybe you also know why she asked me these questions instead of her aunt because I sure as hell don't).

But do you know, she asked me to accompany her around Hiroshima while she dropped cash at the international store debating between regular or Cool Ranch flavor for her monthly ration of Doritos?

"Hey Min?"

"Yeah," she asked while debating whether to buy Cool Ranch flavor or try the Spicy Nacho.

"I was um, wondering, you know, you like books?"

"Sure—but I don't really have time for reading…"

"There's um, a book store down the way…"

"I get all I need on the Kindle."

"So, you don't like…you know, physical books?"

"I just said I don't really read, and if I did no, I have the Kindle."

"So, you don't want to go?"

"No I don't."

Do you know that exchange?

Do you know that I asked her if she wanted to get dinner she said no because she needed to finish all her shopping before her bus left for Shobara? Do you know that she then asked that I take her to the *Hyaku-en* store, so she could get some utensils? Do you know her expressing her love for *Hyaku-en* stores being better than dollar stores back home? She wouldn't verbalize it but she probably preferred the Japanese version because they aren't ghetto like their US counterparts that have only one register open, slowed down to a crawl due to the Filipino who is buying 10 boxes of brown sugar, made worse by the fat redneck, one shoulder unglamorously bare, next in line who can't stop her mulatto kid in cart from crying followed by a 40-something blonde roastie in business pantsuit who just wants to buy some ribbon but with a look on her face that says "How'd I get in here?" while also asking "Why can't I get in there?", *there* being the nightclub on the strip where she used to party in her 20s, getting all fucked out but is now single, miserable and 40, in a line at the Dollar Tree waiting for the lone cashier, a fat over-powdered cheeked white boomer, unable to speak Tagalog coping with the language barrier and about to snap. I could see how Min could love its Japanese counterpart. She even said so on Facebook later that day "Can't go to the city without going to the #HYAKUENSHOP :heart_eyes:" with a photo of her holding chop sticks and a *chawan*. But you know that, don't you? Did you know I took the photo?

Do you know later that evening when I walked her to the Sogo bus station she hugged me and said "Thanks for hanging out with me today, Jason,"?

"No problem."

"I had fun. I'll let you know the next time I'm coming in to town, okay?"

But you do know of the text exchange that followed:

"I'm so bored. I don't want to go back."

"Sorry."

"It's so cold."

"Sounds like you need a good man to keep you warm."

"I do."

"Unfortunately, you took the last bus but if there was another I'd be there in a heartbeat."

"Oh! Sweet!"

"That's what they all say."

"No I mean it."

"So I'll get on the early bus tomorrow, wearing a thick sweater."

"No you don't have to."

"I can."

"No please."

"Fine. Don't say I didn't make the offer."

"Jason, you're a sweet guy and all but I just don't think that it will work with the distance."

"Yeah, haven't heard that one before."

"Don't be mad at me."

"Okay, I'm not mad at you."

But I was mad when she showed with Matt at the *izakaya* the next week and you know that by now. Just as you know that our words by now, in both text and person mean nothing which should tell us everything.

But do you know why I even pursued her? Call it a poor attempt at spinning plates. Call it desperation. Call it practicing game. Your guess is as good as mine.

*

I'm getting off course here. Maybe spending too much time talking about how everything means nothing. How much more do you need?

I mean, I could just spend the entirety of this document dwelling on a few lines of Shakesperean verse like Godard with *King Lear* (1987. Directed by Jean-Luc Godard from a script by Peter Sellars and Tom Luddy and cinematography by Sophie Maintigneux), his film shot in the back, a rumination on Shakespeare's play but also on words, images, and their meaning in general centered around Cordelia's replying "Nothing" to her father. BUT! I'd like to dwell on nothing itself (the concept, not the word) because I realized the entirety of my current malaise was hovering around, lurking…glancing…at that big beautiful nothing, that…void. The void that confirmed everything for me because if you asked me what I was about then, I'd reply "Nothing."

BTW, I might be of the rare distinction of being one who has never read *King Lear* (or watched a presentation) but have seen Godard's hard to find (well, not hard—I mean, I watched a lifted copy of the Kino Lorber VHS on YouTube) as well as Kurosawa's color-coded Japanese staging. But none of this matters. Nothing matters—except power. But you know that, don't you? You told me yourself.

You told me to sit here and write "my story" and I'm trying my best.

I mean, I could do it in the form of Platonic dialogue.

You could.

But I think that would bore you.

It would.

And confuse you.

Probably.

If I haven't confused you enough.

You're reaching your limits.

Sorry, sorry, I'll try to do better. I care what you think after all.

I know.

OR!

Maybe in the form of a commentary on the live-action version of my content with the director himself (Maybe or Maybe Not David Fincher—**MOMNDF**) and me, Jason Reudelheuber-Katz (**JRK**).

MOMNDF: Might be a good idea.

JRK: Aaaand that's your cue. Good.

MOMNDF: But no one really listens to commentaries anymore due to the demise of home video market.

JRK: Did anyone ever listen to them then?

MOMNDF: Doubtful. Save for some enthusiasts...like yourself.

JRK: So not many then.

MOMNDF: Given your existential struggle of isolation, I would guess yes. At least people are still watching movies. Are they watching?

JRK: Well, they're watching content. Or consuming it. It's a passive exercise. Kind of like how fiction reading or reading itself has declined because it's hard in this multinational state of affairs to digest fiction because processing a level of abstraction requires a good handle of language. No, no, no, pure information is easier to process.

MOMNDF: Or maybe we've all just become lazier?

JRK: Maybe. Or maybe we've just become obsessed with learning how to get ahead in this world whether it be with gold or girls, enjoying the moment rather than trying to process it scared of the present, not even daring to make art for it. After all the present does seem so fleeting. So many flee to nostalgia, a world they understand or future fantasies with a sense of hope or warning.

MOMNDF: And that's why you wrote this content?

Actually, I have no choice.

I must look in to the mirror of now connecting culture, philosophy, current events, politics, history—zeitgeist—common currency of the story or literature, ecumenical and comprehensive, all been supplanted by the ant-like specialized world of cyberspace, a global hive brain with all the info you need compartmentalized, the techno march leading us back to the primitive. No more reading except one-sentence micro blogging rudimentaries, simple meme hieroglyphs, memes that are birthed, live and die at the speed of sight painted on electronic cave walls, rainbow pooh *emoji* our common sign of the cross, audio books and YouTube sages telling us our narratives while old stories, movies, shows, ideas that once seemed fresh now seem stale. But where is our spear? Where is our tribe? All information, no soul. What's data without metadata? What's information without a story?

The present is frightening because it's different and new. But it's also frightening because if you create for it, it will all be obsolete once you click save—not when a work is complete, but when you're just done with that day's work.

But even for a completed work, you look up _____ on *insert respective APP Store name here*, select it, only to find the words "Content Deleted".

Here one day, gone the next.

An expedited form of historical corrosion that used to take centuries. THINK Papias' five volume work circa 100 AD *Expositions of the Oracles of the Lord*, which only a few paragraphs dismissively survive in Eusebius' church history (the Greek title proves elusive as well, due to lacking the body of the text in which it's used to frame the work—frame missing body and vice versa). THINK the Gnostic theologian Basilides of Alexandria's 25 volume *Exegetica* also lost and even lesser known, the surviving fragments only being those used by its detractors (fitting since most Gnostic's looked at the material world as only being worthy of flame). THINK Jason Reudelheuber-Katz's movie script *Distortion* that wasn't backed up when his laptop crashed, the only surviving copy a PDF attachment lost in the internet ether (no big loss, it sucked).

All that work, all that supposed sweat equity, wasted brain power…deleted. And you think this cheapening with electric brushes, digital palettes, pixelated canvasses, here today, gone tomorrow, content deleted, would not have an effect?

I laugh.

I tried to tell Matt this. I tried, you'll see.

MATT (MALE, EARLY 20S, WHITE)

STOCKY TEXAN CONSERVATIVE WHO CONSERVED NOTHING.

You know about his social media activity or lack of it. You've seen him like Conservative videos on Facebook that state facts don't care about our feelings and you know the links to Scott Nash clips and occasional Justin Bangs article I sent him. You know the one meme I found on Kai10 I sent joking about Jew privilege as you know his response: "I don't care that the Jews are privileged." And you know that's about as edge lord I got with him (at least) on social media.

But do you know, when we walked around Hiroshima our first weekend in country, strolling through the Peace Park and Hondori, he pointed at the street signs in English and other signs (in places that mattered) in *Romaji* and I just replied "Empire"?

"What do you mean?"

"Signs of empire."

"Whose empire?"

"Ours."

"I don't know about that man."

Do you know how I tried to broach the subject as we watched the jets take off from Marine Corps Air Station Iwakuni from his apartment in Okimi-cho and when I mentioned that I found the hardware of military fighter jets fascinating, even awe-inspiring he said, "You mean a lib like you isn't horrified of these jets of empire?"??

"I'm more bothered by the signs of empire in the US."

"Like what?"

"Like the signs in Spanish and English at the Urgent Care, the um, the driver's license applications being available in Spanish, Vietnamese, Tagalog, all that you know? That empire bothers me."

"What the hell you talking about man?"

"Never mind."

And you know from Min's texts that we did discuss this more in-depth later. And what is else there to say?

JASON (MALE, EARLY 20S, WHITE)

STRAIGHT CISGENDERED TOXIC WHITE (OR JEW DEPENDING ON WHEN OR WHO YOU ASK) (ASHKE)NAZI MALE.

You've seen the shrink's report. You know all about my internet history. Your metadata tells you that I watched a lot of videos of Cary Walsh who cared about "God, guns and the US of A" but I mainly cared that she was hot, and RT'd that I agreed with her frequently hoping to be noticed. You know that after her appearance on "journalist and activist" (but really YouTuber) Scott Nash's show, I started watching him and his sidekick the big tittied e-THOT Jimena who called out Cary Walsh for appearing on the *Oven Talk* with OingoBoinGoy and AndySchluss and confronted her with "homophobic tweets that are offensive and can't be defended" but that I found kind of funny. You know that after the interview with the psychic discussing his channeling the Lyran's and the revelation of the Reptilians and Nash's subsequent rant about their attempts to stamp out individuality, while also being sexist and having a rape culture with their demonic spirit flowing in to Japanese Emperor worship and ISIS and how their spirit of Rome was also the spirit of Nazism and how the Japanese were just "pawns" but Hitler was a full on "monster"—in short, the Reptilians are really the enemy of Liberal American values aside from their championing Central Banking and it's Scott Nash's duty (and ours) to help usher in the great awakening—but more importantly after this rant came the interview with Justin Bangs to discuss the "culture wars" and "fighting the feminists".

And you know that I started reading and watching Bangs more than Nash from that point on. Did you know I found Nash's narrative and ranting short of actual radicalism and not to mention trite and tiresome? You know that I started navigating Kai10 on a daily basis, but did you know I was particularly interested by the post by Ultima_Thule that stated "Is Scott Nash a Fed?" while some in the thread questioned if Ultima himself was an agent provocateur? Did you know that for all the posts I read about esoteric Hiterlism and Nazi UFO bases in Antartica the one post that piqued my interest the most was on that sat with no replies, quickly disappeared but posed the important question of "Whatever happened to Ultra Wide Band technology?"???

Do you know I found OingoBoinGoy's Tweet about Jewish subversion of whites via the "death cult" of Christianity—I can't remember the exact wording—but did you know I found it thought provoking? I found it more thought provoking than his recitation of the Scandinavian *Song of the Elder Edda* on *Oven Talk*. You know I watched *Oven Talk* quite a bit. But did you know that I found AndySchluss' tearful diatribe about the supposed barbarity of Allied Soldiers and the benign, heroic, character of the SS a little too much? Maybe you don't know that because you know that I watched *The Greatest Story Never Told* more than once.

Adina certainly didn't know.

45

And you think you know this is when I started my journey down the rabbit hole. This is when I embraced my inner Nazi and said yes and Amen to "Hitler did nothing wrong" but you don't know shit. You don't know the shame I felt after moving somewhat down to poverty level with my divorced Jewish mom to Las Vegas and visiting my Uncle Murray in the furniture store as he did his stand-up routine to the customers in an attempt to convince them to buy that Laz-E-Boy so they could easily consume content in total relaxation and hearing him say "I'm so Jewish I've had nose surgery three times." But Uncle Murray wasn't a bad guy, failed actor and perverted sure, but bad guy? No. And my mom revered more the works of Nathaniel Branden and Wayne Dyer more than anything about the Talmud or Kabbalah (if she read at all). No, no, no, maybe the planted seed bloomed when the cousin I was closest to from my dad's side, Tyler Reudelheuber from Lynnwood, WA—no, no, no, he wasn't an anti-Semite just a tough working class All-American who was more in to Ron Paul and sound money like everyone else in the military (TBH maybe it was him who pointed me towards Scott Nash)—he even visited me when I was studying at UCLA and he was at Camp Pendleton. We chatted about my film classes, ignored talking about the Godard class and talked instead about attending a lecture by alumnus Francis Ford Coppola and he told me his favorite part of *Apocalypse Now* were the scenes with Robert Duvall—well, the helicopter raid—and he constantly emailed me when I arrived in Japan, even putting me in touch with some of his friends from basic stationed in Okinawa. You know that but do you know when he was killed in Iraq, the story about his death on *NewsGrind*, featuring a comment by one (((Alex Lewinstein))) stating "Another dead white boy. We should be rejoicing,"? Do you know reading that and the radio silence from my mom, the lack of care or concern of anyone in my close personal vicinity, built up an instant reaction in my mind to that comment? Can you blame me for thinking "Fuck you kike"? Can you understand the first seeds being planted of thinking maybe Hitler did nothing wrong?

Didn't know any of that, did you?

Did you know I thought of Tyler as Matt and I watched the jets taking off across the sea in Okimi-cho?

*

Do you need local color anecdotes about my life in the island of Etajima in Hiroshima Prefecture? What's the purpose besides proving that yes, I really did live in Japan, in Hiroshima Prefecture, on the island of Etajima, a boat ride away from the city centers of Hiroshima-city and Kure, specifically in the Ogaki-cho district? Just like Gospel writer Mark's liberal usage of Jesus speaking Aramaic lets you feel the heavy air of Jewish Palestine and the weight of authentic testimony, I need to do same even though my story is far less extraordinary?

boringAF.txt

Do you need to know about my interview for the town newspaper and when they asked what I liked to eat, I was dumbfounded for an answer and just said "meat and potatoes" which lead to upon first meeting of Yuri and her friend Yuka they muttered something in incoherent *Etajima-ben* about my interview but said "*meeto potayto*" and giggled for the next two months saying "*Jayson-sensei meeto potayto*" *giggle giggle* upon sight of me—is this important to anything? It may be important that Yuka was the first person interviewed after Yuri's disappearance but nothing came of it save losing her giggle. What about this anecdote from a year before said disappearance: When the newly appointed *Kyoto-sensei*, with matching arrogant pomade, yelled at all students who upset him including Yuri-chan, who according to Yamamoto-sensei, he called her ugly. Does that matter? Does it help that I tell you *Kyoto-sensei* means *Assistant Principal*? It might help that upon recall of said anecdote that I thought it might be a contributing factor to Yuri's disappearance. Not everything adds up. But you know that, don't you? Do you need to know about the autistic kid Yuji who bothered me, drool always oozing from the side of his mouth, hands always together like a retard Dr. Evil, every day, always comes by my desk saying "*Jayson-sensei hana ga takai ne?*" (*You have a tall nose, don't you?*) like I needed reminding of my Jew honker? Do you need to know about Yamamoto-sensei getting in to a shoving match with kids who were all attitude, no brains and could care less about the English pronunciation of "kumquat"? Or how they mocked my Japanese pronunciation at every turn or just came up to me in the hallway trying to ape English pronunciation by slurring consonants together (a variation being "Shfrushhehfreh")? Does any of this help aside from setting the "atmosphere"?

Do you know this all might have led me to burying my head in my phone looking for escape from this backwards island life?

You may think, or even claim to know, my reading Justin Bangs work formed my attitude about women and dating but once again, you don't know shit. Do you know the formative stages started earlier, like when I was at the restaurant with Uncle Murray and the hostess asked for his phone number to page him and he replied with "Not every day a woman wants my phone number after just hello," and how he flirted with her incessantly the rest of the lunch even getting her phone number? Do you know that I told him afterwards I found the hostess a little plain and dumpy and he replied: "Jason, you can either be the guy looking for action or the guy who just likes to give off the image of getting action. An unlucky Jew like me, I like action, and I take it where I can get it"? OR! That other time when I was a little older how Murray told me about the privileged Rabbi's son he knew growing up in Oceanside who fucked every woman he could, keeping an actual notch count but whose ultimate goal was fucking a black girl. "Jungle Fever is a fever I don't ever need to catch. Maybe he was just gay and overcompensating, you know?" OR! That time when I saw my dad leave our house, head between his legs, not saying much to me, never to return while my mom looked on arms crossed and indignant? Do you know that maybe maybe maybe I partially internalized these offhand sketches and reading Justin Bangs was just confirmation finding its bias? Can you blame a guy for seeking out his work? One must consciously seek out masculinity or the dying flames of it by going to the gym or gun range or being a pick-up artist but it must be willful even though in a way it becomes an academic practice because it's unmoored from the natural cycle of modern life, only the military or law enforcement or the dwindling trades being the remaining natural vestiges. But something is better than nothing. And do you know it was a rather innocuous exchange standing outside of a 7-11, after Karate practice, that kind of got my game with Yu rolling? You know Kenji and Yu picked me up and drove me to Karate practice in neighboring Kurahashi-cho, right? Anyways, at the *konbini*, Yu looked especially good that night, wearing high heels with cargo pant jump suit, trying to do her working-class best to look as high fashion as possible and I appreciated it. It seems Kenji didn't that night. When I told her about meeting Min in the city for that upcoming Saturday she asked "Is she girlfriend?"

"No."

"Do you want her as girlfriend?"

"Not sure—I don't know—maybe not."

"So, you don't have girlfriend?"

"No."

"Do you like Japanese girl?"

"Yes—I—Yeah, I do."

"Oh, you need a Japanese girlfriend."

48

"Yeah, sure—I mean, it's hard."

A long pause. Yu looks at Kenji then back at me, takes a drag on her cigarette and smiles. "If I wasn't married, I would be your girlfriend."

"Oh, really…"

She smiles again.

"But you know, you have a—you have Kenji."

Without a beat, the smile disappears, the cigarette goes in to the trash: "I don't love him."

And you know all about our Facebook DMs and texts. You have them all. No need to rehash but as Justin Bangs said, "Our game is our story," and my story was I was the handsome and caring American and I made sure to tell her about my striking out with Min. Maybe that's why she was just as angered as I was to see Min that night in the *izakaya* with Matt which might have helped build the swell that exploded in to me telling her I loved her that night.

And you know the texts from the next week:

"Had too much fun last week."

"Me 2!!!" she replied immediately. "Are you at home sleeping? :sleeping_face:"

"No, going to the city."

"Oh, I am there!"

"Shopping?"

"Yes."

"Fun time with friends?"

"I am alone today."

"Meet for coffee?"

But do you know as I'm on the bus after hitting send, noticing out the window a bald-headed representative of PureLight passing out pamphlets, that I'm on edge waiting for her reply?

Do you know, as the speed boat crashes on the waves, going up and down, I look at my phone, hoping for a reply (but I know the signal is weak out here on the open sea)?

Do you know I hate myself as I step off the boat?

Do you know, before I get on the tram heading to the city, I look to find a message on my phone and read it with dread…

"Coffee sounds nice!!!!"

Well…fuck…do you know the complete 180 degree shift in emotion where you almost want to raise a fist in the air?!??!

Cue *Super* by Neu!

Haven't heard it?

Google it!

…

…But in retrospect, I can with full confidence say:

Meeting Yu for coffee was a mistake.

But you know that, don't you?

OR! do you?

You have me in here writing this thing…

So, there's something you obviously don't know.

OR! You just like fucking with me. Psyop by another name…

:shrug:

Yoi! Sutaato!

MOMNDF: That means "Action!" in Japanese, right?

JRK: Right…but, um, I don't really want to spoon feed every Japanese phrase to the reader…

MOMNDF: Speaking of spoon feeding, where are we again?

For your index stack on the electronic version of the content entitled **Subject: Reudelheuber-Katz, Jason,** you can label this section **The Prologue to the Prologue of the Prologue** OR **A Weekend in December.**

OR!

In a more nostalgic callback to the 90s-era terse Hollywood titling convention: **A Weekend.**

Yes, yes, yes and that makes its sequel ready-made to be titled: **A Weekend Part 2: Sunday.**

And once the prologue series is established, you can re-brand this part as **A Weekend Part 1: Saturday** because like all primary installments, it'll be the one that carries the most fondness due to its lighter tone, and healthy of explicit sex contrary to its dense Secondary, Tertiary, and Quaternary installments.

Kenji is coming.

Yes, yes, yes, he is but not yet.

You know that I told Yu to meet me at Blue Flat on the non-Peace Park side of Hondori (not sure if north or south). Do you know that café? The one that screams style over substance, the one that makes one feel hip as they walk in, where everyone else is trying look hip as well, some with their Macs, most

50

with their phones, a couple with books to look studious, thinking they're making a way in the world by learning profound things, like it gives them some advantage, but all it gives is a sense of moral superiority they think is earned by reading things their hip cultural overlords demanded they read if they wanted to be hip?

But you know it's all a game.

And I chose this café for my game.

You know on the tram ride over from the Port that I was on Kai10.org. Did you know I actually went to the Dating board first? Do the timestamps reveal that? Do they reveal I only scanned in catalog view deciding to give up after seeing the first subject line (*KAI10 HELP! MY GF WANTS TO ANALLY PENETRATE ME WITH A STRAP ON WHILE OUR DOG WATCHES*) before switching to the Politics board? Do you know my thoughts on the top post, a meme showing the Hollywood studio heads with yarmulke's painted on and their standing over the Hollywood sign with a caption "Gassing When?"? (My thought was *good question*). You know the top reply from ANON:

>*presuming gassing works*
>*presuming Holocaust actually happened*
>*presuming gas was used to kill the kikes*
>*holohoax.jpg*

OR!

The next reply from another ANON:

>*be truly WOKE*
>*know Hitler did nothing wrong*
>*know Germans and Japs really are master race*
>*wrongsidewon.txt*

Did you know upon reading that, standing on the tram, I immediately looked at the members of one of said master races surrounding me? That I saw an old man, thin, frail, bald with glasses, staring at the ground, probably wondering what had come of his life, his only saving grace being the girl standing in front of him with the pleated black short skirt and matching black stockings and that I too looked at her legs, nicely accentuated by the black flats (but mine was a glance, his was a stare)? She didn't seem to notice (too busy on her phone).

OR!

The pudgy woman sitting in front of me, clutching her purse, wearing her best dress that she bought in 1985, continually looking up at me, the other, between bouts of just staring ahead?

Did you know, I didn't feel threatened by this master race but admired the trains ran on time (the buses, not as punctual but there were external circumstances—namely traffic)?

You know I understood why many on the boards and social media, the disaffected whites seeing their neighborhoods and schools being turned in to barrios populated by hoodrats, longing for the reality championed in ads of post-war America: White picket fences, mom wearing the nice dress, dad in suit and tie and well-groomed kids named Johnny and Sally—names you rarely hear today and how Japan seemed like a haven, a high IQ ethnostate in a sea of globalization, a what-could-have-been. But did you know I noticed the dirt under the nails? The denizens of Kai10 didn't see a Japan that was a post-war petri dish using a homogenous populous to build a consumerist society from the ground up. Where girls and boys would sacrifice all to earn a spot, dedicating their existence to their chosen career, whether it be housewife, horticulturalist or hygienist, religion abandoned, the only remnant being the preservation of the historical culture that used to permeate homeland but now all surfaces...however a girl in a kimono or a tea ceremony were beautiful surfaces. Everyone looked nice and dressed nice but shallowness reigned. BUT! In a society devoid of serious crime and broken homes, did it really matter? Kai10 didn't ask such questions.

Tony Judt stated he felt the most European in American and I state I felt the most American in Japan.

Do you know I considered the middle-aged men attending idol concerts, dedicated to performing a series of cheers for their chosen pixie, performing for her as she performs for them, or when I watched an X-Japan concert on YouTube, with the crowds jumping and crossing their arms at the coaxing of the lead singer Toshi...

X!
Kanjite miro
X!
Sakende miro
X!
Subete nugisutero
X!

Do you know I asked is that better than saying *Banzai* or *Heil Hitler*? Is it better to be dedicated to something that in the end is just a commercial enterprise? Some may say that trade and commercialism gives us a more peaceful world. I say it gives us a pacified one.

>What are you saying Jason, you faggot?

I don't know.

I do know sitting in Blue Flat Café I felt like Link from *Legend of Zelda* surrounded by NPCs with faulty programming (THINK the mother and daughter who sat across from me sipping their café ole's while lightly attending their salads, not talking, just staring over each other, the daughter casually glancing at her *keitai*, the latest iPhone while her mother glanced at her older Sony flipper).

LOL was I any better or just an upgraded non-playable character?

Me waiting for Yu, betacuck earnest and early, phone out, flipping through some of the photos I took, deciding which to post on Instagram and the blog so I could get some likes—I need the traffic!—because I cared what THEY thought, I care what you think, so the pics needed editing, especially the one with that stack of early-90s FamiCom games for bygone franchises: *Yu Yu Hakusho, Pac-Man, Ranma 1/2, Aladdin, Tom & Jerry, Ultraman, Super Air Diver 2* and *Patlabor*.

How many all-nighters did the programmers pull to finish these games? How many relationships were broken because Takeshi spent all night programming instead of bothering to give his girl a call? Did he even have time for a girl? How many children missed time with their parents because they had a deadline to meet? How about that baby who almost died because both parents were busy type, type, typing away at their Silicon Graphics workstation to get *Toy Story 2* in the can? Here today, forgot tomorrow.

When David Fincher switched from film to digital I wondered if his work, his dailies and lighting tests, would be preserved for posterity or does digital just make disposable art even more conveniently disposable?

But can you blame him and not the consumer? How many consumers spent days, maybe even months, maybe even years, of anticipation for the next installment of *Star Wars, Final Fantasy, Naruto, Dragon Quest, Avengers, Super Mario Brothers, Madden NFL, Resident Evil* or *Harry Potter*? How many saved their pennies and yen, begged their parents to buy, centering their life and Christmas lists around the hot game, movie or music of the season, stood in line, took time off of school and work, got in to fights, and arguments in said line,

53

sacrificed time with those "close" to them so they could play, watch or listen only to quickly forgot discard when the new hot thing arrived? How many how many how many how many? Do you know that? Do you know?

Everyone, really.

Consumerism was a mistake.

Banal, I know. I know you know it too but that's what I thought as I looked for Yu, who was nowhere to be seen.

Kenji is coming.

Not yet. But Yu was coming and I had time to burn and content to make. Summarized the paragraph above on IG with the caption: "How many cartridges tucked you in at night?"

But you know that, don't you?

Did you know I wondered what the other patrons with their earbuds plugged in, laptops and phones out, were listening to? Was it the latest hip-hop that most likely was about a big ass booty or gettin' booty or hangin' in da club, the video probably featuring at least one helicopter and some Benjamins. The days of slappin' a bitch and doing shooting muthafuckas because they be frontin' appear to be over…at least on the popular level. People only want music from the hood if it helps them party. Reminded me of that single mom (I don't know her name), left having to raise two half-nog kids on her own, one of whom attended the elementary school I taught at. I saw her with both at the local Mos Burger, fat, no make-up, track suit, rings under her eyes, barely keeping it together, days of partying with Marines of Iwakuni over. Completely fucked out. No, she plays no further role in this story. She just reminded me of a thread on Kai10: "How ZOG uses Hip-hop to propagate it's (sic—grammar is never an online concern) agenda worldwide," listing all the Jewish music producers and record executives who championed and profited off rap/hip-hop and how it's used to get people's guards down and embrace diversity, how niggers are the only ones allowed to be unapologetically masculine so all the women will desire them, interbreed, naturally leading to a societal collapse because most of these brainwashed bitches would be left high and dry by their men once they started popping out half-niglets with their light skin and frizzy hair (Fuck, they'd almost look Jewish) giving ZOG their chance to tighten control due to all the chaos caused by fatherless kids (I mean, look at me!) and create and even more enforced police state. Shit added up. (Do you know when this was posted? I couldn't find it upon research). As soon as I read it, I remembered Adina's second-cousin on her mother's side made a

54

fortune in the music industry producing hip-hop horny juice that was able to pay for a nice yacht and mansion in Tel Aviv (A good place to sit back and relax while the rest of the world burns). Seeing Japanese, a mostly smart, kind people, listening to that noise poison, dressing in the clothes, trying to be a homey to the point that people from Africa are hired to work and model the clothing, work the stores—because face it, they all look the same to Japanese right?—thinking about it, reading about it, made me realize it was no longer cute but nefarious.

Rap music was a mistake.

Did you know Yu walked in as I thought these things? Her hair was down, one shoulder bare, her smile wide.

Did you know Mandy walked in too with some bearded boho wannabe with his hair in a bun trying to look like a Pajeet but actually blonder, skinnier and paler than me.

Chic street shitter fashion was a mistake.

Was a little surprised Mandy didn't show up with a wetback or an actual Indian with a British accent or South African CHAD or Mark (who represents everything abhorrent to her worldview yet she ignores said worldview because her ovaries yearn for the dominance hierarchy he represents). And you could tell she yearned for it as she approached me arms open exclaiming "Jason!" with a full hug, not one of those one-armed friend ones, but one locked in tight, not wearing a bra. Once released, I noticed her man-bun soyboy friend watching us with a scowl, hands in the pocket of his three stripe AC Milan soccer jacket while Mandy said "This is my friend Justin," with one hand on my shoulder as I shook Justin's weak hand, confirming his cuckiness but only doubly confirmed by her next question: "Want to join us?"

"No, I, uh, I'm here to meet…um, a friend," I said.

"Okay," she said glancing towards Yu, who was waiting in the wings. They went off to a table in the corner, probably to talk about refugees, climate change, the evils of whiteness, toxic masculinity, Dharma or whatever other bullshit, doubtful Justin would do any talking, just listening to Mandy's bullshit, while nodding politely and then wonder later why he could never get in to her pants because he was such a nice guy and gentleman, taking her bullshit in stride but only received jack shit for his trouble and then when he got a modicum of power, would probably take those frustrations out on some hapless bitch, inadequately grope her or try to get her in bed, not understanding that girls decide the difference between flirting and harassment, not to mention rough sex and rape.

Soyboys were a mistake.

"Jason?"

I turn to see Yu. She smiles and waves. "Oh, hi Yu," I say. Do I glance back at Mandy? Probably.

*

There haven't been enough breaks, I know. So, I put one there just give you a moment to sit, hit the restroom, lay down and take a nap or to readjust your attention because you've been skimming through, not really paying attention. Happens a lot in this world of which of we all have varying degrees of Attention Deficit Disorder. Makes me wish I had Autism. At least I could focus, right?

*

Honestly, I typed the break because I feel I'm avoiding writing the next part of **The Weekend** AKA **The Weekend Part I: Saturday**.

And maybe all the ranting above was just me trying to avoid it. Not because it's not hard or complex—no, no, no, this isn't the part where she says "Kenji is coming"—with tons of explosive theatrics. But because I have to look in the mirror and ask some questions I don't want answered or I think they're answered and don't want to discover different.

But sometimes you just have to go for it…

…And use humor, self-deprecation, meaningless details and meta narrative to get around it.

Because…

I care what you think.

*

Is it important that Yu ordered a latte? Actually, I forgot what she ordered but it was a safe guess given the coffee buying habits of the commercialized western world (of which I include Japan). Is it important I paid for both of us? Or that I remember that once we received our drinks, we headed towards the opposite side of the café, about as far away from Mandy and Cuck Justin as possible? Or that I also remember just walking to our table, not asking where Yu wanted to sit? (Have to maintain frame, right?)

OR!

That I remembered she didn't really thank me for buying her drink?

56

I mean, these small details don't affect the narrative in anyway, right? All details must be important to the story, right goy?

Maybe details are important in that compound effect type of way?

I go back and forth.

But that black porcelain mug, holding my dark roasted coffee with cream, sitting ensconced between my hands wrapped around it, elbows on the table, leaning slightly forward as I asked "So, what brings you to the city?" is probably of little consequence as is her reply of "Just shopping," and that beneath the table I noticed her arms extended, her mug sitting unmoored, like a black boat in a white sea of table.

She was nervous.

Or so I thought.

And I wasn't doing anything to help sitting like a road runner eager to make my move.

Thankfully, I remembered a linked article by Justin Bangs on Kai10 about posture when talking to women—maybe my first time visiting the board (do you know?)—reminding me of the pop-star but more famous-for-being-famous celebrity Gackt who at first glance you'd think was a fag with all his make-up but that's just *Visual Kei*, that's just Japan, and on variety shows he carries himself alpha, sitting casually, one arm behind his chair, making his chest appear bigger than it is, one leg casually crossing the other, relaxed, not giving a fuck about the on-air proceedings.

I know, I know, I'm doing it again—ranting.

But this rant might be important because I did same: Leaned back, positioned one arm behind my chair, tried to cross my leg but couldn't because our table hugged a wall and there just wasn't enough space. I put the leg back down. Took a sip of my coffee. "Shopping, huh?"

I know, I know, I should be entering late and leaving early, skipping inconsequential exchanges like:

"Yes, shopping."

"What are you looking for?"

OR!

The fact that I saw her body inch a little, a little squirm in her movement as she replied "Nothing special," while taking a sip of her coffee, the boat finding its anchor.

Followed by this deep observation: "It's Saturday. Just want to hang out and look around, right?"

"Yes."

"Window shopping, right?"

"Yes, window shopping."

"I was window shopping too…"

"Where…"

"Went to the used electronics store, looking at games, DVDs and all that…"

"*Ah so ka…*"

BUT!

Talking about used DVDs got me thinking about used CDs, which got me thinking about Yoshiki, the drummer for X-Japan, who played drums so hard, he'd pass out, nearly die even due to his asthma condition and when the band broke up, lead singer Toshi leaving for a cult, their lead guitarist Hide committed suicide but they got back together again…(they all do). And I thought about the sacrifice these guys make just to sell some CDs but segued to recalling Yoshiki was Gackt's friend, constantly appearing on TV together and you'd think I'd veered off again BUT! This led to my question of "Do you like Gackt?" asked in my Gackt chair pose.

The question appeared to jolt her. She tilted her head a little to think about it. "Gackt?"

"Yeah, Gackt. The popstar and celebrity. Mostly celebrity, right?"

"'Celebrity'?"

"You know, someone famous?"

"Ah yes…" she then tilted her head, thinking. "Hmm…*Gakuto-san…*"

"*Gakuto-san*, yes…"

"I'm not fan of his music but I think he's cool, you know?"

"Okay that's…that's cool."

"Do you like?"

"Like what? My coffee?"

"No, Gackt…"

"Oh, he's…he's alright. I don't listen to much J-Pop."

"Do you listen to any Japanese music?"

"I like X-Japan."

"X?"

"Yeah, sure. Yoshiki is one of the greatest drummers ever."

"*Ah so…bikkuri.*" (*I'm surprised*—I'm done translating). She covered her mouth.

"What's so *bikkuri?*"

58

"I didn't know you like…metal?"

"I'm not the biggest fan of metal. But I like X."

Important, important shit, I know but her reply of "Wahhh…Yoshiki is great, ne?" is important because she doesn't even question my liking X-Japan and is not out to hate on Yoshiki or the band. She's not even a metal fan herself but she's proud of her fellow countryman who has earned the respect of someone outside of her homeland. She's not a hater. She's not negging on me just because I like a particular band or drummer. No, no, no she's looking for a common point of understanding, to be agreeable, which relaxed me, put my guard down, subconsciously realizing it isn't a fight, but a conversation.

And just to drive the point home:

"I'd listen X any day over Arashi."

"Arashi!" Yu giggled. "I agree!"

"Or AKB48. *Hidoi.*"

"*Hidoi, ne?*"

"*Fem100 mo hidoi.*"

"*Ne!*"

Who is Arashi? Google it.

Fem100? You know about them, right? A girl group with enough promotion and innocent looks to ignite the thirst and enlarge boners of many an aimless salaryman (while probably being a high-class prostitution ring).

"You don't like Fem100?"

"No…not—it's just not my type of music."

"But they are cute girl."

"Yeah, sure. But it's all an act."

"What? Act?"

I transition to teacher mode :facepalm: "It's a performance. They're acting cute."

I knew it in the moment, just like I know now. I mean, from here I could get self-indulgent with a long dialogue exchange because I think I have a knack for dialogue and I want you to think well of me, know I have talent because…

I care what you think.

But can we get more meta about me feeding my ego with a dialogue exchange that feeds my ego demonstrating my need to feed my ego?

YU

Performance? Like actor?

JASON

Yeah, like an actor, you know?
Like…we were playing this game
in my class. I would ask the
students questions in English
and they would have to answer.
Kind of like 'Jeopardy' but it
isn't. Oh, you guys don't have
"Jeopardy" here, right?

YU

No…

JASON

Well, as we were nearing the
end of the game, one team was
close to winning, the next one
to ask a question, this girl, I
ask her, I say, 'Who is the most
handsome teacher in the
school?' She smiles, slightly—
well, a little embarrassed, but
she says, 'Jayson-sensei'.
Their team won.

YU

Wow! You're a bad teacher!

JASON

What?

60

                    YU

          You force students say you're
          the most handsome!

                    JASON

          She knew the right answer that
          would make her team win. And I
          get a little ego boost.

                    YU

          But she knows that.

                    JASON

          I know she knows that. But she
          performed the right answer to
          help her team win. She knew
          what answer would get her
          further regard—doesn't matter
          if it's true or not. Maybe it
          is true. Maybe I am the most
          handsome teacher in the school.

                    YU

          Maybe…

She smiles.
                    JASON

          Maybe?

She tilts her head.

                         61

                    YU

Okay, okay. You are most
handsome teacher Jayson-
sensei.

                 JASON

I know, right? Is it the blue
eyes that clinches it? Or my
dirty blonde hair. I know it
certainly isn't my Jew merchant
nose.

                    YU

Your nose is tall.

                 JASON

Tall?

                    YU

Hana ga takai deshou?

MOMNDF: What does that mean again? It's not on my script notes.

JRK: Hana ga takai? It, um, it means literally Nose is tall but um, I guess, means "long nose" the way we'd say it, you know?

MOMNDF: Yeah, sure, but what's the significance?

JRK: Well, um, Japanese find our, I mean, western, or is European? White? It's hard to categorize these days.

MOMNDF: Europoid works as a term.

JRK: Well, they find the Europoid nose particularly exotic since it's different than the, um, Japanese nose which is kind of um, flatter and smaller.

MOMNDF: But is there any significance to the idiom?

JRK: Well it can mean someone is prideful or boastful...as noted in this next exchange:

                    JASON

          Are you saying I have an ego?

                    YU

          No.

She giggles.

                    JASON

          Are   you   just   saying   I'm
          handsome to satisfy my ego. Are
          you just performing?

                    YU

          Maybe.

MOMNDF: We can certainly confirm your ego...
JRK: Or it can mean it can mean you have big dick.
MOMNDF: I can't confirm nor care to.
JRK: It's not that type of commentary, right?
MOMNDF: (LAUGHING) RIGHT!

                    JASON

          You're quite the actress.

                    YU

          No, I'm bad actress...

                    JASON

        So, you're telling the truth,
        then? Because you can't tell a
        lie?

She thinks for a moment, a smile cracks in corner
of her mouth as she looks away.

                    YU

        Well...we all say things to be
        nice. I am Japanese, right?

                    JASON

        Right. *Tatemae*, right?

                    YU

        Tatemae, yes.   We all do it.

                    JASON

        Yes, we're all actors like that
        in a way.

                    YU

        Yes.

                    JASON

        We all say things to keep the
        harmony—the   wa—right?   But
        what's also important is what
        we don't say, what we withhold.
        Because   we're   scared   of
        disapproval   or   what   other
        people   say   or   what   the

                    64

consequences of saying such
things might bring about. We do
it out of a sacrificial sense
of preserving social harmony.
But sometimes we lose a little
bit-maybe a lot-of ourselves in
the process.

MOMNDF: Did you really say that? About the *Wa* and harmony?
JRK: (sighing) Yeah.
MOMNDF: That's really fucking pretentious.
JRK: Yeah, well...
MOMNDF: The ends justify the means?
JRK: In this case of a narrow short term goal? Yes.
MOMNDF: I've never heard of getting a chick in bed qualified that way.
JRK: I'm full of surprises.

                    YU

Yes.

(pause)

(thinking)

(maybe processing her own
translation)

You are smart Jason.

             JASON

What?

             YU

I never think about these
things...

65

                    JASON

        Is that *tatemae* again?

                     YU

        No. I am saying honesty.

                    JASON

        Right.

MOMNDF: So you used awkward Japanese speech patterns for authenticity, not for cheap racist humor, right?

JRK: Um, uh, yeah, um, of course. If I were going for cheap laughs like the overpraised *Lost in Translation*, I'd use a lot words that had r's and l's and how they, um, get, confused but that ain't, that ain't me. I respect the, um, the Japanese effort to try and even learn and speak English. Like, I'm sure a Japanese could have a field day with my handling of their language.

MOMNDF: Yet you use racial slurs. You are full of surprises.

JRK: Well—speaking of which, I really dug the way you shot this next part. Your astringent visual scheme mixed with the Dionysian back-lighting in the modernist café setting—accurate set btw—really gave me as sense of what it would have been like had Robert Bresson and Ridley Scott teamed up to direct an adaptation of a selection from the Desire Series of Harelquin romances.

MOMNDF: That's what I was totally going for!

Jason looks over at Mandy and Justin. Mandy is talking endlessly about something, probably about the trials of her relationships while denying they all collapsed due to THOTery. And there is Justin, a sympathetic ear, leaning forward, smiling, listening to her shit like it's super important. :facepalm:

                     66

He then looks back at YU.

JASON

Wanna get out of here?

YU

Okay.

Does it matter as we exited that Mandy said, "Bye Jason. It was good to see you," or that I replied, "Um, you too Mandy. Have a good one," while waving at both her and Justin (who was too busy taking a picture of his latte for Instagram, just giving a head bob instead, like he was some suave nigga)?

MOMNDF: Well, I included it.

JRK: Yeah, yeah, you did...

Poseur's were a mistake.

I know you think I'm a poseur too.

I know because...

I care what you think.

*

>Be Jason.

>Walk along the crowded pathways of Hondori towards the bus stop on Rijodori (that cuts the shopping bazaar in half), just past the McDonald's, quietly confident your plan is working, when you suggest a visit to an art museum and she agrees.

>trusttheplan.txt

>Thank yourself for reading that post on the Justin Bangs sub-Reddit about art museums being perfect for day game.

>Remind yourself of that hook-up in *Dressed to Kill* (1980. Directed by Brian DePalma from a script by DePalma, and cinematography by Ralf D. Bode) but note there are no murders this time (yet). It's not that type of story (yet).

>Try to calm that nagging sense of hesitation.

>Forget the anxiety-ridden, guilt-based but somewhat lenient Jewish-Christian (cultural) upbringing.

>Feel the confidence that you could have your way with her if you pulled the trigger.

>Put away the fear of Kenji.
Kenji is coming.
>TFW legit fear. :sweat:
>THINK you need an incident to incite action.
Kenji is coming.
>KNOW Kenji would not go to an art museum, a government funded enterprise that overpaid to hang pictures and whatever else some faggot who ingrained himself in to the establishment and conned everyone—including himself—in to thinking it was art.

>KNOW women didn't think about these things.

>KNOW it helps them to think they are participating in some sort of fanciful activity as you figure out a way to get them out of their fanciful clothes.

>And...

Kenji is coming.

>But ATM you're trying to overcome your moral hang-ups registered in your genetic code (Protestant Aryan + Joo = Guilt^2) expressed physically on the bus to Hiroshima Castle (next to museum), keeping some distance from her, lying to yourself saying you're just trying not to attract stares and make her uncomfortable.

>Off the bus, offer your arm as she smiles, hooks hers around yours and giggles.

>Start walking to museum.

>Destiny.jpg

Do the details of the building matter? The banality and utility of modern architecture, the virus that spreads through all "modern" countries. All. Just. So. Plain. And all the same.

Modern architecture was a mistake.

OFC, it's worth noting the current exhibition was from the Menil collection in Houston, Texas. One large but culturally insignificant city loaning an art collection to another somewhat less culturally insignificant city (aside from the bomb).

Do you know if French Catholics John and Dominque De Menil

were inspired by Max Ernst's *Ten Thousand Lucid Redskins Get Ready to Make the Rain Laugh* which amounted to black dots on a piss yellow covered canvas?

Maybe they'd be amused and think it worth the price of purchase by this exchange:

JASON

Where's the Indians?

YU

(Looking around confused)

Eh, are there supposed to be
Indians?

JASON

Yes, it says 'Redskins' which
means Indians. I guess if you
squint real tight and walk up
real close, you can see some
redskins.

He squints at frame. She squints too.
JASON

Do you see them?

YU

(Giggling)

No.

OR!

This exchange regarding *The Statement Series: Yellow Painting/The Color Men
Choose When They Attack Earth* by Walter De Maria, with its flat yellow
rectangular canvas with a smaller white rectangle in the center, striking in
contrast mounted on a white wall:

                    JASON

        If you ever have an Ikea style
        home, this picture would go
        great.

                    YU

        (Giggling)

        I don't know.

OR!
The next exchange regarding blue fluorescent light placed diagonally against
a wall (not part of collection—I think but still curious of their thoughts):
        Jason looks up towards ceiling.
        Yu does same.
                    YU

        Nani?

                    JASON

        Did one of their lights fall
        from the ceiling? Should we
        tell them?

                    YU

        I don't know.

                    JASON

        If I knew I could get paid as
        an artist by going to the
        hardware store, then I would be
        doing that...

                    YU

        You want to be artist?

                  JASON

        Sure but…I've never lived in
        New York or Paris.

                    YU

        Ii na, New York…

                  JASON

        Yeah.

HE DECIDES NOT TO RUIN THE MOMENT TO TELL HER
IT'S NOW JUST ABOVE A THIRD WORLD POZZED OUT
SHITHOLE.

MOMNDF: NYC isn't that bad. You should go before commenting upon
it.
JRK: Yeah, well…

                    YU

        I wanted to be model…live in
        New York, L.A…

                  JASON

        Really?

                    YU

        Go to fashion show…

MOMNDF: Sold the glitz and glamour, huh?
JRK: I guess…

                     71

                    JASON

     So, if I need a model for my
     art, I should call you?

                    YU

     EH?!!

     (She covers her mouth in shock)

     No, no, No, I'm too old!

                    JASON

     That's for me to decide. I'm
     the artist after all.

                    YU

     EH?!!

                    JASON

     Don't worry about that right
     now.

He holds out his hand.
She grabs but holds the grip loosely.
MOMNDF: Instinct?
JRK: For sure.

But, but, but...the main part of the exhibit, *Mark Rothko: The Chapel Commission*...

Reading the description on the brochure it made a point to note that Rothko was a Russian-Jew, how the chapel was for reflection and contemplation and how he committed suicide before completion (IMO, it doesn't speak well of the product if the producer negates its value before launch but maybe Rothko knew something I'd soon find out).

Most of the paintings were various shades of black, of darkness. A bleak void.

Yes.

The void.

Cue *Radioactivity* by Kraftwerk.

MOMNDF: I love this track. It has a nice synth subtlety to it.

JRK: I'm glad I suggested it.

MOMNDF: Actually, I love this whole scene. What was going through your mind as you looked at Rothko's blank landscapes.

JRK: I understood. I don't know why but I got it. I see he got it too.

MOMNDF: Got what?

JRK: They are landscapes. Landscapes, portraits of just the meaninglessness of it all. Why waste time, money and effort for something someone might glance at, pay minimal attention to and then go on with their lives? From Da Vinci onward, was any true value added to anyone's lives? Was a greater criminal act occurring? Were people suffering and being taxed, so the elites, whether they be in church, government or corporations, were they just being used and being told that the monies are going towards something noble, something uplifting, something higher, but was it all just a massive psychosis? Was it all just bullshit? Was it all just overpriced visual content to please the self-congratulate while the normies wasted time and braincells on YouTube?

MOMNDF: YouTube wasn't around the time of Rothko. Actually there were barely computers.

JRK: Is all just the same. Content was taking over then.

MOMNDF: Right. Content, content, content!

JRK: CONTENT! CONTENT! CONTENT! YES!

MOMNDF: And?

JRK: And it just got me to thinking, actually maybe confirming it was it all just a void. Nothingness. What was the point of expending energy on cultural endeavors, trying to impress or uplift others? What was the point of a city being bomb in to the stone age, if they were to just rebuild and "modernize", just to build art museums that looked like other art museums, displaying paintings that other people, a group of experts deemed important, if all just ended in black, in nothingness, in the void? In turn, maybe all moral effort and effort in general was pointless, too...

73

MOMNDF: Including fucking another man's wife?

JRK: Right, um, yeah, including fucking another man's wife.

Kenji is coming.

MOMNDF: Or anyone?

JRK: Well, um, within reason.

```
Slow zoom in to the Rothko darkness and the
contrasting zoom in to Jason's face as he
realizes the void, the pointlessness of it all.
```

```
He tightens his grip on Yu's hand.
```

                              JASON

```
        Let's go.
```

```
She tightens her grip.
```

                               YU

```
        Okay.
```

                               *

You know what happens next, don't you?

The Title says it all: ***The Weekend Part I: Saturday Part II: Jason and Yu Fuck at A Love Hotel***

But do you know as we walked past the Rhiga Royal Hotel, SOGO, then across the crowded Kamiya-cho Nishi intersection, strolling by KFC, in to the Peace Park side of Hondori, past the Edion Electronics where I helped Adina buy a laptop, that we passed a husband keeping clear distance from his family? Do you know this reminded of a sponsored post I saw on Facebook about sexless marriages being on the rise in Japan and how they're usually instigated by the husband? *Yes, yes, yes, Yu and Kenji might be sexless*, I thought! *Maybe I'm doing them a favor!* Did you know I realized I was walking ahead, (probably) subconsciously thinking Japanese women appreciate a man who takes the lead but at first Yu looked confused as I looked towards her but then when I jogged back to her and grabbed her hand to pull her with me she smiled and shook her head?

Do you know this was near the alley that led to the Peace Love Hotel?

Maybe you do know.

Maybe Yu (or whatever her name is) told you.

Did she tell you as we approached Peace Love Hotel with its void-like white tiled exterior, that she took a deep breath, slackening her grip, looking around as we approached, slightly nervous herself?

OR!

That I held the door open for her?

OR!

That as she entered, she bowed her head towards me, her facial expression neutral?

OR!

Through the fogged glass counter, an elderly gentleman gave us an *Irrasshai*, leaned down towards the unfogged glass where you slip the cash, asking if we want to spend the night or just have a "rest" and Yu answered "rest"?

OR!

That I dropped the money and took the key?

Is it of any consequence that another older couple, in their early 40s, entered at the same time and that the man, with buzz cut, trim mustache and leather jacket held a bag with a couple of beers and the woman, obviously a house wife, wore a long flower pattern dress and dated blouse and that I avoided eye contact?

OR!

That in the elevator to our floor, it is quiet and Yu stares straight ahead and I look at her and she looks at me and smiles but it's a quick smile?

OR!

That in the hallway, a red light illuminates above each door, noting which room is occupied, ours flashing as if to say "Ready for making sex," while I see an elderly maid entering another room with her cleaning trolley of chemicals to de-sex a room as we enter ours to do opposite?

OR!

That the room itself is in dire need of update being a relic of the 80s-bubble building mania with chrome framing the mirrors over a red-sheeted bed, a faded picture of Snow White—the 1933 Disney version—sitting framed above?

Do you know the sequence of events?

Yu puts her purse down.

I put my hand on her shoulder.

She turns to me.

Hesitantly wraps her arms around me. Smiles.

We kiss.

Kenji is coming.

Or rather she puts her tongue in my mouth. Aggressively. Pressing her face and body on to mine. I lift up her sweater and find a lacey peach colored bra with a flower print (cotton though, not silk). But the cheapness of the fabric, makes me even more excited by being more inviting, less formal even if her panties don't match her bra (a low-cut white nylon polyester).

I put my hands under the front bra cup, feel her roundness and flick her nipple. We continue kissing. I then tug her panties down and she finishes by kicking them off her legs.

She's undressed me already but that isn't as sexy as me undressing her.

But you know that, don't you?

*

I would give all the dirty details since that's me.

But it's a fruitless exercise, describing the merging of our bodies, my manhood, my essence, entering her and me thrusting gently but forcefully, her feeling all the desires, all the wants, the release of hesitations, the world of pleasure invading both of us, her cries of relief as I thrusted faster, her gripping my back then my rear, eager for me to continue, and I continue with a storm and thunder she's never felt, with her letting out a cry, clouds parting, as I released myself in the dated, gaudy Disney décor of Peace Love Hotel.

Why write that ridiculous shit?

Erotic fiction was a mistake.

We fucked like rabid dogs.

And...

I care what you think.

And yes, this leads to *Kenji is coming...*

*

It all feels great in the moment. But you know that, don't you? Actually, maybe you don't know depending on who is reading this. So, for you Incel's and Femcel's, it's like the emptiness felt after finishing a task or meeting a goal, asking yourself "Now what?"

And Yu laid next to me in that tentative posture. We just felt our way around awkwardly, peppering each other with kisses, then she puts her head on my chest, I then put my arm around her but the position was uncomfortable, her hair itchy, laying on my bare chest and then...

Her phone rings.

Kenji is coming.

I see her ass, as she jumps off the bed to pick up her *keitai*. After answering she turns around towards me as she talks and I see her groomed mound. But it's all just matter of fact. Libido is in neutral, no energy to pounce. I use the opportunity to remove the filled hotel complementary condom off my cock, tossing it in the bin next to the bed.

After she hangs up the phone, she continues standing by the bed.

YU

That was Kenji.

Kenji is coming.

JASON

Is he coming?

YU

No.

>Be Kenji.

>Notcomingyet.jpg

MOMNDF: What were you thinking in this moment? You look ponderous.

JRK: I always have that look. I, um, I kind of realized then that she was an adulterer at least according to Jewish law.

MOMNDF: How so?

JRK: Well, my Uncle Murray above my mom's cries of "this is the 21st century!", told me how a patriarch like Abraham could have several wives, even impregnating his maid, yet is considered the father of Israel,

then pointed out laws in Leviticus as well and my mom's reply was he was just justifying his fucking around.

MOMNDF: I'm not sure if that really helps your case given the anti-Semitic nature of some of your comments.

JRK: It's complicated but—well, I guess it doesn't really help my case either that I felt no guilt?

I mean, Yu was the married one. I wasn't. Did she think same? Ask her. The fuzzy morality of Japan remains a mystery to me but I preferred the sexual waters of The Floating World to the harsh desert of western Puritanism.

And staring at the mirrored ceiling, seeing myself and parts of Yu, an arm and hair, standing over the bed, I thought about my reflection, about the void...

                    JASON

          How do you feel?

                    YU

          Good.

She lays down next to him, her hair once again scratching his chest.

They kiss.

I felt good.

At that moment, that's all that mattered.

So we fuck again. This time she is on top. It lasts longer since I'd blown my load already. But Yu is like an animal unleashed. The way she squatted on my cock. The bucking of her hips. The strain on her face. Her heavy breathing (no screams)(unfortunately). Her body shivering after she came, the hotel TV flipping on porn at that very moment of her orgasm, the picture and sound crackling and distorting as the screen girl masturbating started squirting "Iku! Iku! Iku! IKU! IIIKKKUUUUU!", the vibrator placed over her clit with me (a little) disappointed Yu didn't do likewise. The image cleared and became crisp as Yu stabilized her breathing as she lay on top of me, her hair itching.

She smiled. We kissed.

JRK: I love the way you shot the set flickering with all the digital distortion intercut with her moans and the exaggerated porn moans.

MOMNDF: In the moment, those aberrations didn't phase you?

JRK: Um...no...not really. I just...um...thought it was a power disruption due to high sea wind or something.

MOMNDF: And you were focused on coming.

JRK: That too.

*

It doesn't matter that I walked her to the bus stop, told her I would talk to her later or that I didn't give any reason for this (obviously, I didn't want to go back to island with her on the same bus, the same boat, same bus ride home. In short, I didn't want to get people talking).

And it doesn't matter that as I started to walk off, she reached her hand out slightly, hers brushing mine, and that I almost longingly reached for her before hesitantly placing my hand in my coat pocket.

It doesn't matter to you at least.

*

You know from my timestamp afterwards, that I was on my phone, checking Twitter and Instagram for engagement (one like) with quick dives in to Kai10, Facebook, Reddit and the Slack but do you know I was at Futaba Tosho and that cruising, Twitter, IG, FB, Reddit, Telegram, Signal and Slack made it hard to concentrate on the shelves full of discarded installments of *Dragon Quest*, *Chrono Trigger* and even non-US releases like *Final Fantasy III*, *Digital Devil Monogatari: Megami Tensei*, and *Ninjara Hoi!* (Google it)?

OR!

That I left to get some dinner at KFC, the fries tasting delicious with the chicken breast, followed by getting on the tram towards the port with more faces just focused on their phones, books or void stares?

Do you know at the Port, on the pier, I noticed a girl I've seen a number of times when I'm returning to the island, who looks at me but doesn't say anything and I do same?

I didn't go talk to her and keep those plates spinning. It's not that type of story.

No, no, no, this night, quiet dominated the boat as it bounced on the waves toward the island.

MOMNDF: I really wanted to use *Seiun* by Kitaro for this scene but couldn't get the rights.

JRK: Isn't that a little too on the nose? And didn't Michael Mann use it in *Manhunter*?

MOMNDF: He did but no one remembers.

JRK: Well, *Ridin'* by Chamillionaire wasn't close to my mental state at the time.

MOMNDF: Yeah, well, that isn't you on the screen. It's the character of Jason Reudelheuber-Katz as played by a young maybe or maybe not Andy Samberg and it fit the tone of the scene.

JRK: Did maybe or maybe not Jesse Eisenberg really turn down the role?

MOMNDF: Well he didn't want to be typecast as the maybe or maybe not Robert DeNiro to my maybe or maybe not Martin Scorsese. And he thought you were a hateful prick.

JRK: He would've made me appear too autistic anyway.

MOMNDF: And there you go.

*

Do you know walking home from the bus stop, the quiet of the small town startled me? The city with its constant noise, sensory assault but here in Etajima…nothing. The streets were only slightly illuminated by the street lights but the landscape beyond was darkened save for the lights in the houses that dotted the elevated hills. I heard crickets.

I'll stop to spare you of any literary pretentions than one feels compelled to write when describing Asian settings. No more talk of ebullient rice paddies or crackling fireflies or the songs the willows make as the wind blows.

Western lit about Asia was a mistake.

It was quiet.

So quiet that the sound other than nature—or the buzzing emanating from the light posts—will cause one to jolt. :eyes:

An isolating feeling, more than the city in a way, as you faced the expanse, the void, with the silence providing discomfort.

Or maybe I was just lonely and didn't like the person I was alone with.

But when you heard a sound…

I hear voices in the distance.

Then the street light above starts flickering.

My body tenses up.

I check my phone but it's fine.

As I approach my apartment, I notice a faint light coming from the school yard nearby. As I get closer I see a group searching through the schoolyard with their flashlights. On the street corner near my apartment, I see an outline of a figure standing across from it: Female, long hair reaching down to waist, but the appearance—pants and big jacket—reveal someone disheveled.

She turns to look at me.

Yu?

My heart skips a beat, goosebumps tingle…but only for a moment. The same feeling I get when I think of the words…

Kenji is coming.

But it wasn't her.

No, no, no her hair was black, not light brown like Yu's. Nor was she fashionable like her. But the outline looked similar in shape but the stare more focused and intense. She walked off as soon as she saw me.

I quickly walked to my door, almost leaping in to my house.

Does it matter, does it help, that I wondered if I should text Yu? Like "Hi, great time making sex today…" I debated not saying anything. I'm sure that doesn't help. Didn't want to come off like a needy cuck. But you never know when women might go batshit crazy and accuse you of rape or some shit, tell her husband, then text you "I told Kenji. Oh and by the way. Kenji is coming. To kick your ass."

So, for insurance, I just texted, "Had fun today."

I immediately got reply: "Me too!" with a :kissing_heart:. But you know that, don't you?

But do you know after receiving her text, the quiet of my place seemed even more pronounced? I thought about writing. What couldn't be a better atmosphere in which to compose a story about a spooky Ryokan in the countryside, a rendezvous gone bad, than a quiet night in the country and a faint wind starting to howl outside?

Nah.

Writing screenplays was a mistake.

Cinema is dead.

MOMNDF: Yet here we are and you watched a movie anyways.

JRK: Well, the dopamine rush of the sex and the text gave me a sedentary desire.

I chose *Demons* (1985. Directed by Lamberto Bava from a script by Bava, Dario Argento, Franco Ferrini and Dardano Sachetti and cinematography by Gianlorenzo Battaglia) from an (online) friend's (AndySchluss) Dropbox that had quite the stash of horror flicks but you know that, don't you? Do you know that summer was the horror season for Japan but I always liked watching them in the winter?

MOMNDF: I didn't know.

JRK: It's true.

MOMNDF: But I know Demons is a great choice.

You do know I had seen the movie before, right? Most content I consumed was shit I'd seen before. The new content was all the same (TL;DR: Superheroes, canned comedy with repeated gags, White people—especially men—debasing themselves in general).

But not *Demons*.

I won't explain the plot in detail—that's what Google is for—but I liked the movie-within-a-movie concept because they really didn't get too precious about it. It was more a pretext for setting up carnage.

And who doesn't like carnage?

What else am I going to watch? Especially on a dark, cold and windy night? Should I pretend I'm cultured? Should I watch Ingmar Bergman? You know with his overdone close-ups—and really he owes his debt to cinematographer Sven Nykvist—with bitches looking miserable the whole time as they hate God and the universe?

OR!

Andrei Tarkovsky with his long takes that really go too long, and his over-important, pseudo-philosophical dialogue—I mean *Stalker* was interesting but was it worth the cast and crew getting poisoned from shooting near an abandoned power plant and dying?

OR!

Robert Bresson with his expressionless thin boys in thin rooms, awkward action and drab photography, all leading up to a moment that actually means nothing in the long run and you just hate yourself for wasting 90 minutes of your life?

OR!

Martin Scorsese, where I can get off on watching tough guys act tough, and people's head's smashed in vices, while feigning deeper substance?

It's all just content, after all. Content, content, content!

So, might as well have some fun. Enjoy the show a little without fooling yourself that you're cultured…that you're superior to everyone. That you know. That you're one of them…especially if you aren't one of ((((them)))). Prove that you've been initiated in to the mystery religion. Prove you understand. Defer to the high priests of critics and trendsetters…LOL…((((critics))))…

Being a cineaste was a mistake.

So I chose to watch *Demons*.

Upon reflection, really the movie encapsulates the dreams…maybe nightmares…that occasionally visited me…being lost in a foreign place, an unfamiliar labyrinth, cornered by the dark forces approaching…lost…helpless even.

The way Berlin is filmed, with hard and harsh lighting—very much an 80s thing—but even more, the way Berlin looks…a clean European metropolis…the cultural jewel of *Mittle Europa*…before the post-Cold War overrun of endless migrants and refugees. Lead protagonist, Urbano Barberini, whose blonde hair and blue eyes gave him a sense of stereotypical European swagger and masculinity that seems so rare on screen today, is just representative of this lost world.

Ah, the 80s, the last stand of implicit whiteness the world over, before the end of the Cold War Game, before the global economy went in to overdrive, just before the colonial ((((Hollywood)))) raped and pillaged theaters world-wide. I watched these horror movies with a sense of nostalgia and loss.

The way the Italians shot horror and thrillers—*gialli*—or is it *giallo?*—even if they were trying to meet crass consumer demand, especially in crass places like the United States and Asia, they couldn't help but film with a sense of baroque grandeur and elegance that reflected their great historical culture. We may have defeated and subjugated them after the war, made them subservient to our capitalist ways—but even forced to comply, they did it their way. It had style. It wasn't just blood and tits. The former Axis countries (including France) reflected in their post-war cinema a sense of malaise and even nihilism, understanding that only high technical style (and titillation) mattered—it was the only motivating factor to even produce art because they subconsciously knew (like Celine consciously knew) that Western Civilization died at

83

Stalingrad (whether it deserved said death is the only matter of debate separating Left from Right).

But actually, I wasn't really think about this at the time or really watching *Demons* (more background noise).

I was on my phone, flipping through my photos then in to the Slack then flipping photos, and looking at the Slack. But you know that, don't you?

You know, that self-described "White Rights Activist", OingoBoinGoy, (I know, LOL, spraying thoughts or shitposting, on Twitter, Facebook, Instagram, Kai10, Pinterest and LinkedIn is "activism"…I guess you could call him a pundit, but pundits are usually paid to give their thoughts on issues with about zero qualifications and any lack of ownership or risk that come with them, and usually pundits are chicks—especially on the Right—because they just use their blonde hair, nice rack, long legs and round ass to milk money from the confirmation biases of their intellectually dulled thirsty male base), you know, with AndySchluss' help, he invited me in to a Slack (Note: we weren't using the real-time collaboration app and platform created by the company Slack ™ but a more "encrypted" variation thereof—look, you know this, I know. But it really shows the techno corporate creep in to our language and how a company becomes so associated with a technology or product that it becomes a noun by which similar modes are referred to. THINK *Coke* for Soda and *Google* for Googling, I mean, search) of fellow shitposters and you know he was the only one hanging out there at the moment. The time difference made things difficult. You know he DM'ed me a picture of an anime *Moe* chick, wearing a yarmulke with a Star of David on her person, clutching her hands like the greedy Jew Merchant cartoons.

OingoBoinGoy: You live in Japan. What u think?
Me: Like it. Got a name?
OingoBoinGoy: Thinking 'Kikechan'.
Me: How about 'Shekel-sama'?
OingoBoinGoy: LOL. Works for me. I'm gonna post on Kai10. See if Scott Nash tries to use this graphic without crediting me.
Me: :smug:
OingoBoinGoy: I'm sick of that namefag being a merchant off our content and making it good goy friendly. Fuck that guy.
Me: >Denies JQ
>Steals memes
>completefaggot.jpg

OingoBoinGoy: LOL. :100%:

Did you know around this time, was the scene in *Demons* where Barbeni's character rides a motor cycle through the...demons...while holding a *katana*, cutting everyone to pieces?

I stopped to watch it.

So badass.

Real comic book theatrics. No CG bullshit.

The scene that made the movie, sold the movie. True sizzle.

No scenes in movies like that anymore. It all looks the same.

You do know I checked my accounts again and you know I got a like on Instagram, some older chick, "ShelleyPhotos69", a Gen-Xer with a boomer heart, commented, "You paint with your photography."

>Feels good man.

And you know on Twitter, another said, "Glad to see someone is using Instagram for more than just posting selfies." Feels really good man. Someone's got to do the THOTpatrol, right? And you know the other comment: "When are u going to post some pics of Jap sluts? This shit is gay."

Do you know that I started typing, telling him to fuck off and get a life and find his own sluts, the pulsing metal beat of *Fast As A Shark* by Accept fueling the words and rage? Do you know I stopped when I saw he only had 35 followers and hid under an avatar of Stewie from *Family Guy* realizing it was a troll with paid follower count? Not worth the time.

I just watched the katana motorcycle scene again to calm down. *Pics of Jap sluts*...only thing people fucking care about. :rage:

MOMNDF: Fans suck dude.

JRK: They really do.

MOMNDF: Such a mistake.

*

You don't know this either: That night I fell asleep quickly, the sexual tension lifted, relationship with Yu consummated, instead of daydreaming about all sorts of women, ...Adina and her Khazer milkers...just motorboating them...Mandy and her long, dancer-like figure...standing in front of an open window, naked, the light accentuating her curves and pert nipples...Min...who is gross...probably has an unshaved bush...

No, no, no I was just thinking about...nothing...

Easy to do with the winter blackness that permeated my place. Easy to imagine the void, thinking for a moment about myself, about life, other, higher, things, since I wasn't thinking about banging other chicks.

The void: Call it spirit, formless energy, or call it nothingness, if that was where I was going, if that is where it all ended, is that also where it started? Are we just the sum total parts of evolution? If I wasn't willed in to existence, if there was no spiritual foundation, outside of my dad fucking my mom, then there was probably no purpose either...except what I decided is important...like fucking the women I like regardless of their attachments, relational and material...because attachments are all elusive...to the void I came from, and the void I shall return...death—nothingness—is the endpoint of everything...I'm an end unto myself.

It really is all about me.

You know, I didn't think of all this in one night—that night—and not clearly as organized as presented above. More like a jumble. But here I am writing this, and I'm easily able to summarize it. At least I'm being honest with you, unlike others who present their ideas, after having wrestled and grappled with them, putting two and two together until they finally equal four, but then present them like it was...DIVINE INSPIRATION (I've received the WORD and it is good).

No, no, no, for me that night, it was an assault of random: Void...nothingness...me...Yu...I can fuck whoever I want...or can I?...Adina...has big milkers...Mandy's legs...does carpet match drapes?...I should read Kawabata...why haven't I watched anything by Naruse?...or I can only fuck as much as they will let me and other barriers presented...because it isn't all about me to them...because for them it's all about them...

And to rough sleep I went.

But then I hear a text alert on my phone. Or at least thought I did.

Then a pounding above me. Probably my fat neighbor (an elementary school teacher).

The wind begins to howl loudly. My skin is cold. Incredibly cold. My body shivers.

In a haze, I check my phone, thinking it was Yu or maybe someone else. It's quite the haze because I can't feel the ground under my feet, almost feel out of body.

I see a light coming from the attached living room...I thought I closed my sliding doors in order to keep the heat in my room...but I slide in.

TV is on.

Yu is on the screen.

I reach out to be with her. Is my hand touching the screen or touching her? I feel I am one with her, connection of spiritual, mental, physical—all three at once, yet separate.

She has different colored eyes, one brown, one black, but wildly exotic like a wild cat, her hair moving in all directions, almost floating, manga come to life. I feel its magnetic power. "*Jason-san, Jason-san, ai shiteru yo. Ai shiteru.*" (*I love you Jason*).

Her mouth opens on the screen, I feel a warmness around my cock, I feel a warmness around my entire body as her mouth envelopes me but then she appears in front, mouth in proportion and we kiss, but it becomes a blur, I feel her, she feels me, but I see us kissing, I see our bodies entwined but I'm also feeling her wetness, and the juices flowing inside of me, I see outside and feel inside, I see the entire picture, like a *Shojo* manga panel where the ecstasy of sex is giant splash page of emotion, being and warmth.

One could say it was all a "fake" dream, but the ejaculation was very real; my boxer briefs stained when jolted awake.

I also sense the faint smell of Yu's Chanel Allure on my hands.

*

I'll be the first to tell you, **The Weekend, Part 2: Sunday** isn't as thrilling as its predecessor. It doesn't necessarily have the sequel superiority of say *The Empire Strikes Back, Urusei Yatsura: Beautiful Dreamer, Aliens, Patlabor 2, The Dark Knight, Babe: Pig in the City* or *Troll 2*. No, no, no, it's more like a Windows upgrade: Annoyance and frustration but needed to keep the machine running.

There is no *Kenji is coming*-like inciting incident. But there are incidents that lead to incitements that eventually lead to *Kenji is coming*…maybe…

MOMNDF: You really shouldn't tell people to skip ahead or let them know a scene is worthless. Makes them feel stupid for watching or reading…or whatever we're doing here…

JRK: I just like being honest.

MOMNDF: Do you? (pause) To those of you at home, he's doing a shrug. LOL SHRUG. You can only do that in text.

JRK: One advantage of text, I guess.

In retrospect, I should have included the wet dream in **Part 2** (it technically occurred on Sunday). But maybe not? Maybe **Sunday** should operate in its own narrative universe of tone, style and pacing yet still be included in this tome so you won't think I'm purposely dividing things out in order to grift (I'm not that Jewish) and well, I have no choice but to present in a lone volume.

I could write it in that boring-by-the-numbers style but being boring maybe be my greatest fear. Because...

MOMNDF: Here we go again.

JRK: Altogether now.

I care what you think.

So, the school across the street, natural alarm clock, the footsteps of students running, the trumpets of the brass band tuning their instruments—seemed like they were always tuning, never playing (even though it was Sunday), does that add anything? What about the old ladies gossiping in the parking lot behind my bedroom?

Of course, you know I checked my phone remembering the *tiing* tone last night...but nothing. Do you know I looked at my photos, thought about what to write, debating if I should write at all, but got a poetic urge...thinking about the lack of appreciation for the hard work put in by the faceless programmers who brought us games like *Fire Emblem 5*, *Final Fantasy V*, *Tales of Phantasia* and *Seiken Densetsu 3*, how the boxes are all just now sitting on a used store shelf, gathering dust? Did you know I also thought about just titling the photos *These Aren't Japanese Sluts*...or rather, *These Are Japanese Sluts* and just leave it at that? Kind of like a modern art installation, just display whatever the fuck and then give it a title...leave people to ponder the philosophy behind it.

You do know I tapped "post" on the photo game boxes sitting in a stack, hidden in a corner, with the title, *Here Are Your Japanese Sluts*, obviously referencing how programmers, box designers, and cartridge manufacturers, put out, did their best, endless hours, like a slut spends a year sprucing herself up for NBA All-Star Weekend hoping to bang a baller, but kicked to the curb afterwards, her only insurance being the baby she might be impregnated with, thus these programmers put out similar, with maybe a few accolades to show for it...and then it's on to the next one, got to get dressed up, come up with new concepts, keep turning tricks, keep the geeks thirsty and purchasing.

Did you know I thought most will walk away and just say "I don't get it,"? Fuck 'em. They aren't paying me, I don't answer to them.

First reply came from Park_City_Stephanie (THOT—obviously): "????"

My reply: "If you need an explanation then you don't understand."

But you know that, don't you?

Maybe you know (or rather thought) that I'd do something more constructive afterwards, like picking up clothes scattered on my floor (probably needed to do laundry), dishes in the sink (stack was high), or the clean stains on the commode and spillover on the floor (but I just pissed and moved on).

No, no, no, I thought about content.

Content, content, content! Thought about increasing my productivity, developing a side hustle. Meant to write out a list of things to do the night before, a tip I got from Justin Bangs from his *Will To Powerful Male* blog. But I forgot—too busy watching Demons and then falling asleep and fucking Yu on the television—that was weird—but I didn't have time to think about that. I had things to do! Had to update my blog and put the link to the latest Instagram post—felt kind of useless considering I got more traffic from IG but you never know when they might no-platform me for being a "Nazi" or some shit—speaking of my blog traffic, I also had to check the Google Analytics and see how much penetration the site was getting, and speaking of Google, I had to check to see if any of my YouTube vids, really just montages of some of my photos, were doing, but then before all that I checked my Twitter and Park_City_Stephanie replied, "I understand your photo." She understands? :laughing_face: Just a THOT trying to act like she understands, trying to front, trying to say she was at my level of intelligence, fucking THOTs always trying to prove they have brains and can roll with the boys, never fails. But before I could give her any attention, which she needed none of, I checked YouTube and found my subscribers were up…though Twitter was down. You know I went to Reddit, saw the same old political shit about the refugee crisis and PureLight's solution trying to solve the crisis through nude meditation and sex energy fields, then to Kai10 with a post entitled "Is PureLight in Japan using psychic energy to save us all?" but did you know I ignored the post (some ANON in Akron didn't know more about Japan than I) while taking more interest in a link to Scott Nash video about a Reptilian confab soon to take place in Lake Tahoe with human sacrifice on the agenda?

You know I then immediately jumped in to the Slack:

The_ZOGfather: Wassup nigga?
Me: Nuttin'
OingoBoinGoy: Nothing much or you're nutting Japs? :P
Me: Both LOL

Andyschluss: Dayum bro. Look at you. Got a picture of some of these sluts or what?

Me: LOL

Andyschluss: It's a valid question

)))Reb_Greyback(((: You shouldn't fuck a gook

Me: Why? And they're not gooks btw

)))Reb_Greyback(((: It's miscegenation dumbass

Me: We're not having babies…that I know of

Ernst_Jungroyper: Watch out! THOTs will first grab you by the cock then grab you by the wallet

Me: Speak from experience?

Ernst_Jungroyper: Divorce raped by first waifu. Fucking cunt

Me: LOL

Neu!Albion: You're both betraying your people and God's law. Doesn't get much worse.

Me: Fucking an attractive Japanese is a violation of the holy order? It's going to bring God's wrath, huh?

Neu!Albion: It's in the 10 Commandments.

Me: So we're gonna gas the kikes but defer to them on this one matter?

)))Reb_Greyback(((: God or not, fucking Japs doesn't help our cause.

Me: So I should only fuck white girls? Living in Japan? Have you seen the white bitches here?

OingoBoinGoy: Guys, guys, he doesn't live in Tennessee, he lives in Japan.

)))Reb_Greyback(((: Why's he living there?

Me: Ideal ethnostate, right?

Neu!Albion: You're needed in your homeland.

OingoBoinGoy: @Neu!Albion you're being an overdramatic Christcuck. He can fuck whoever he pleases.

The_ZOGfather: She probably dressed provocatively to cause temptation to /ourboy/, right?

Me: Yeah, she's hot.

Ernst_Jungroyper: Japs are honorary Aryans anyway. It's not like you're fucking niggers or street shitters.

Me: LOL true.

The_ZOGfather: A man can fuck whoever he wants. It's his right.

Ernst_Jungroyper: Yes, we're the final word! Not them. Fuck them and their rape allegations. That's just regret.

Andyschluss: There's nothing wrong with rape. How else did our Viking ancestors spread the seed?

The_ZOGfather: No matter who the bitch is, you must not eat out her pussy.

Me: What's wrong with that?

The_ZOGfather: It's not your job to pleasure her. You're cucking out. Bigly.

)))Reb_Greyback((((: Anti-miscegenation laws were made for a reason.

The_ZOGfather: They didn't have abortion back then. It works wonders.

Neu!Albion: Abortion has been a disaster.

The_ZOGfather: Here come the PopeFacts…

And you know the conversation swerved in to talk of abortion, that ubiquitous issue, and I'd received a text from Yu waiting for a reply…*Ohayo*…

Did you know about the knock at my door?

A loud knock.

Half-expected to hear attempts at opening my door because Japs don't respect the sanctity of private property, a western conceit—no! They just see fit to open the door, and walk right in…but only to the *Koban* section of your residence, a kind of public/private lower level space where everyone puts their shoes.

But I lock my doors. (You can take the boy out of the egalitarian indoctrinated country but you can't take the egalitarian indoctrinated country out of the boy…or at the least the principles he's internalized, like keeping the fucking door locked and wanting a private space.)

But after a few loud knocks, silence. I thought it could be a bill collector, but I had nothing outstanding, including NHK or it could have been the mailman. A "care package" from home perhaps, the one I asked my mom to send with the coffee from Platform, the café with French aspirant but ultimately French stereotyped and caricatured (at best) interior design that nevertheless beat anything here—in terms of bean and roast quality, it's only close competition being Miyajima Roasters but when I opened the door…nothing. No person or package. I thought about calling my mom and asking what the fuck but I didn't want to talk, didn't want to hear about how Uncle Murray is looking to angle in on the Professional Poker circuit or how her restaurateur BF Carl had suddenly helped her rediscover the Talmud, how she hasn't told him (yet) about her having trouble balancing payments on her new Lexus, credit card bills (from buying that Cartier watch she couldn't resist) and the mortgage (from having bought after the bottom because she had to wait for her credit to improve from the crash and subsequent foreclosure) and how Carl's nephew got a job working with Goldman-Sachs just out of Harvard or how his big brother, a labor lawyer with NBC, just married a nice Jewish girl, probably after fucking every shiksa he could lay his hands on and throw in what a mistake it was to marry my dad, a goy, a German (or of German descent rather) and how that marriage was a mistake but even so Carl could use his connections to help get his *Mischingle* future-son-in-law a finance job working the Japan desk focusing on Jewing a *Keiretsu* in to buying shit derivatives while we're on the other end of trade, profiting from their loss but I've yet to tell him Kabbalistic financial alchemy is the one trait that eluded my genetics (see mom above).

Interracial marriage was a mistake.

But before I could even have the opportunity to call mom my phone rang. Min. I declined.

Then a text: "Why are you treating me like this? What did I do to you?"

"I'm not your back-up plan." THOT. Patrolled. Felt good.

Nice thing about being in a relationship with another woman, you don't have to be phony cordial to the other women who rejected you.

Checked Instagram again. More likes with comments: "I love these games. Those were the days. Why can't they make games like this anymore?"

But you know that, don't you?

Do you know my endorphins were kicking in?

Do you know why they can't make anything like they did anymore?

Do you know my phone then rang again but with a number I didn't recognize?

>Picks up phone.

>Silence.

>Nothing.mp3

>Say "*Moshi Moshi*?" then "Hello?"

>Line goes dead.
>Phone rings again.
>Recognizes Adina's number.
I'm sure Japanese SIGINT or Softbank gave you the transcript but I know
they can have an uncooperative bureaucracy so:
"Jason?"
"Yes?"
"Oh hey, it's Adina."
"I know."
"Well, what are you doing today?"
"Um, uh…I don't know…nothing much…"
"Okay, I see, so that means you don't have any lunch plan's right? Right?"
"I'm…I'm on the island…I'm not planning to go um, you know, go in to
the city or…"
"Oh, I know, I know. I'm on the island. I'm with Mandy."
"Okay…"
"Well, we're looking for a place to eat but you know, neither of us speak
Japanese, so all this signage is you know, perplexing, and I'm famished, I didn't
eat breakfast, and Mandy doesn't know any restaurants here, so I was
wondering, you speak Japanese and all…"
"A little…"
"You speak more than we do and we were wondering if you knew a place
to eat…"
"Um, what are you in the mood for? I know this place. *Romante*, *Yakiniku*,
you know Korean BBQ, type of thing…"
"OOOHHHH…"
"What?"
"No, no, that won't do. Mandy is a vegetarian."
"Okay…that's limiting…"
"Know any sushi places?"
"Sushi is raw fish…"
"I know what sushi is!"
"But it's…um, you know, fish is, um, a meat…"
"OOOHHHH…riiiight…I don't know if she's that type of
vegetarian…know anything else?"

"I don't—I'm not a vegetarian so it's not something I usually...let me think...Chinese? How about Chinese? There's um, I think it's called *Koraiken* in downtown Etajima."

"Hold on let me check." **INAUDIBLE (INCONSEQUETIAL) FEMALE CHATTER** "Okay, we can do Ko-rak—that Chinese place."

"Okay, enjoy."

"What do you mean? You're meeting us there..." **PAUSE** "Aren't you? You're coming, right?"

"Sure."

"Gawd, Jason..."

MOMNDF: Why did you agree to meet?

JRK: Beat's me.

MOMNDF: What were you thinking at this moment? JRK: Wishing I had access to Valium, Ambien or better yet OxyContin.

MOMNDF: You really hate American women that much?

JRK: Just when 2 or 3 are gathered in girl talk's name.

And eating lunch with kike infused shitlibbery wasn't my idea of a fun Sunday, but you know that, don't you? You also know I didn't tell the Slack my lunch plans.

But did you know on the bus towards downtown Etajima, running parallel to Hitonose Bay, two tanned, fairly plain but giggling high school girls, uniforms and all, boarded and as one went to the front to get change for her fare, she noticed me and started giggling, covering her cock holster while saying loud enough to her friend, *I just saw a gaijin*, like it was a fucking *cause celebre*?

I let the comment sit.

But do you know I considered walking to the rear and lecturing them about being loud cunts and using insensitive language? Do you know I couldn't even write that with a straight face?

I know that probably doesn't help my case but...

I care what you think.

*

>Be Jason.

>Notice through the bus window, said school girls watching him approach the gaijin girls, gawking and giggling as it drives off.

>Notice Mandy looking her limousine liberal bohemian best, wearing a print bomber jacket, white t-shirt and palazzo pants, the only distraction being the assorted Aztec, Bohemian Gypsy, Turquoise, and Gemstone rings adorning each of her fingers…and nose piercing.

>stillhot.jpg

>Notice Adina looking plain with red sweater and jeans, basic make-up with her eye-brows subdued but threatening to break out and run wild.

>stilljewish.jpg

>Notice the Chinese restaurant being a little bigger than a walk-in closet.

>Sit at the rear, on the tatami, a wide enough hole provided under the table so you don't have to sit cross legged or in *seiza* (which the girls probably couldn't handle without bitching the whole time about it).

>Receive a push alert from Scott Nash entitled, "NWO Reptilian Conference in Lake Tahoe Will Determine Course of Human History."

>Adina asks: "What was that?"

>ohnothing.jpg

>:eyes:

>"I know what it is but what is the alert?"

>Say with :smirk: "The refugees. They've been attacked."

>Mandy says: "Oh my god, I hope not. That would be terrible. All those poor people…"

>"It was a joke." :sweat_smile:

>"That isn't funny."

>Adina asks: "Seriously, though what was your alert?"

>"Um, uh, nothing important."

>"Gawd Jason, don't be so defensive."

>Ignore the comment, look at the menu.

>Mandy and Adina look at their menus, then each other, and laugh.

>Ask "What?"

>Have an NPC conversation that strives to imitate a writer's room stalwart attempting to break-out. THINK in the vein of *Celeste and Jesse Forever* (2012. Directed by Lee Toland Krieger from a script by Rashida Jones and Will McCormack and cinematography by David Lanzenberg) because Adina once said I remind her of Andy Samberg and she Rashida Jones (though I'm the half-Jew in this case):

"I can't—we can't—this whole menu is in Japanese."

"Well, this is Japan…"

"Do they have one in English?"

"Um...don't think—I'm pretty sure they don't."

"Then...what do they have?"

"You want me to read the whole menu to you?"

"Yes. Do that."

"Yes, please tell us what our options are."

"I, uh, Mandy, you're, um, vegan—vegetarian—right?"

"Vegetarian. Yes. What are my options?"

"Vegetable stir fry. With rice, is about it..."

"I guess that will be fine. Does it have MSG? Are the vegetables certified organic?"

"I...um, no clue, not sure if that's a thing here."

"I guess I'll just make due."

"What about me?"

"You probably want the same...right?"

"I'm not a vegetarian? Can't you tell?"

"But most of the meat dishes are...pork—wait there's a chicken—kind of a kung pao chicken, you want that?"

"What does pork have—oh, trying to be all thoughtful of religious dietary regulations..."

"Well, more ethnic..."

"No, religious Jason. Do you eat pork?"

"Yes."

"Then you're not being ethnically or religiously observant."

"Jason, you're Jewish, right?"

"He's half. A mischling."

"I prefer the term *Mischlinge*."

"There's a term?"

"Yeah, 'mischling'."

"I'm half-German, father's side, so...you know..."

"Is that really the term you prefer?"

"I don't care. Really. I'm, uh, I'm just an American I guess."

"Do you practice?"

"I'm about to order pork dumplings. Ha ha."

"So? I uh..."

"He means no."

"Are we...uh..."

"Vegetable stir fry. Can you ask if it's organic?"

IN JAPANESE *The veggies are normal, right? Not organic?*

"They're not organic, Mandy."

"I'll take it anyway. Not like I have much of a choice."

"Adina?"

"Kung Pao chicken."

"It's kind of like Kung Pao chicken…"

"Whatever, I'll take that."

She wants the chicken and I'll take the dumplings please.

"So…what did you order?"

"I said, pork dumplings."

"Steamed or like pot stickers?"

"Pot stickers."

"I can't bring you home to mother…"

"If you did, I'd probably just quote the Gospel of Matthew to blow my cover."

"What a troll."

"I live for trolling."

"Matthew? Is that one of the Gnostic gospels?"

"No, it's, um, probably the most Jewish of the gospels actually."

"I wouldn't know. We didn't study it at the Temple."

"I haven't really studied it either—well…"

"But you know Jason?"

"Took a New Testament class for credit. Prof didn't even believe what was written, but he, um, you know, he talked a lot about Jewish roots and references."

"That is so cool…you know having a culture and stuff? Unlike, me, you know…'I'm just a white American girl'…really have nothing brag about…except privilege…"

"And genocide…"

"I KNOW. Isn't it horrible? I feel so…I can't even explain…"

"Yeah…"

"I just wish we had something ethnic to be proud of you know? Something vibrant and deep like the Jews—I mean the Jewish people or like the Thai's…I can't wait to go in the summer. It all just seems…just alive."

"I know, right?"

"Right…"

"So I envy you two. You have a culture, a proud history…"

"I'm only half. Non-practicing…"

"You should practice…"

"Yeah, Jason we'd take you in. There's some well-known half-Jews."

"Oh yeah, like who?"

"Like who?"

"David Duchovny, Garry Kasparov, Sarah Jessica Parker…"

"OMG, I just started watching *Sex and the City* like you recommended! I love it!"

"I know, right!"

"Emil Maurice."

"Emil—who? Who's that?"

"He's uh, well—he was Hitler's driver."

"Oh my god! How do you even know that?!"

"I was a history major."

"Oh god…Hitler was so—I get nauseous even thinking about him. And the Germans I've met, at least the one's now, they're so kind. I try not to even mention the Nazis, just like I try not to mention I'm an American. Oh, my god. I met this one, what's his name? Dieter. Do you know Dieter who teaches in Okinawa?"

"Don't know."

"He's a member of an anti-fascist group. Told me…get this…he's so ashamed when he told me, his great-grandfather was in the SS."

"Oh my god! Look at this!"

"What…what is it?"

"Some Japanese politician—how do you say his name, Eye-nay-zo Ta-ki-da—god I'm so horrible with these names."

"What did Inazo Takeda he say?"

"He…I just can't…"

"He said that with the looming threat of refugees, Japanese need to watch out for foreigners—especially blacks."

"I see."

"Look at this!"

"God this world is ignorant!"

"I need to stop reading the news! Makes me want to fucking kill somebody! What does it take to make idiots wake up?"

"What?"

"I can't believe...it's just...*NewsGrind* they mentioned that _____ state television showed some pro-Hitler propaganda thing. Said their struggle was the same as Hitler's. Said those who left, you know the refugees? Were traitors."

"This world is crazy. It's going crazy. When will dumbasses wake up?"

"I know, I know. That guy—these leaders are crazy. They deserve a missile up their asses. Bigots."

"With people like that leading countries...they deserve it."

"Yeah..."

Thankfully the food arrived before Adina could make the case for all-out war with East Asia—somehow tying in to the fact it benefited Israel or Mandy's brother who worked for the Council on Foreign Relations.

I'll spare you the rest of the lunch conversation (TL;DR :vomit:). It was mainly just me eating my dumplings while they talked about some Haitian author who wrote a tragic and reflective, yet magical, novel about the slave revolt in Haiti and the white genocide that followed from the perspective of the mass murderers but didn't discuss how the publisher bought her a spot on *The New York Times* Bestseller list. Then somehow a segue in to Chinua Achebe, Ta'Nehisi Coates, how great *Black Panther* was and how Mandy had never dated a nigger but thought about it. Adina encouraged her to try but understood how hard it was in homogenous Japan ("Which needs to change"), which then led to discussion of holiday plans with Mandy's brother coming to visit so it was a "staycation" because he had a conference in Tokyo, Adina going to Tel Aviv for a heritage tour, Min urging Matt to visit_____ together to get a firsthand look at the refugee crisis, ending with a cursory "What about you Jason?" and my stating that I was just planning to stay home and relax while not revealing I planned to visit Yasukuni Shrine to get the real history of World War II.

A conversation not worth the paper or time.

Except when Mandy asked me about Yu or rather "the woman" I was with day's previous and I dodged by saying, "A friend."

"Who? What friend?" Adina asked.

"A friend."

Lunch with these two was a mistake.

*

I took Adina to the bus stop so she could get back to the port. God that sentence was clunky. I'll try to do better. *As we walked, I noticed that her hair was a little tousled, the sea wind putting an exclamation point on it* (Better? I care what you think, after all).

As the wind got stronger, she soft hugged herself, rubbing her hands over her arms.

"It's nice here. So, quiet."

"It's cold."

"I don't mind."

The bus arrived, charging in almost, betraying its hefty frame (not as clunky as my sentences). When Adina took the first step she turned to look at me. "Come on. You're coming right?"

"What...I..."

"Keep me company..."

I stepped on, rolling my eyes, looked at the passengers, (some students, some elderly) then sighed loudly on the inside. As we sat down she asked, "They take Hiroshima-city bus card's right?"

"No."

"Oh. Shit. I don't know if I have enough..."

I pulled out my wallet and handed her a *Sen* note. "Here..."

She took it. "I don't—I'll pay you back."

"I charge interest."

"Oh yeah?"

"One thing I am Jewish about."

She rolled her eyes and grinned. "How about I just not ask about that girl Mandy saw you with..."

"Works for me."

I looked out towards the greenery surrounding us then those who couldn't bother to notice. Adina adjusted her purse.

"So...do you go to that Chinese place often?"

"Every now and then."

"It was good."

"I think so..."

Tiiing! I quickly pulled out my phone to check, could be Yu, but...nothing.

"It's mine...me," Adina said holding up her phone. "Min. Her and Matt had a fight."

"*Ah so ka...*"

"Is that like a habit? Just replying in Japanese?"

"*Eeto ne…*it just came out." She rolled her eyes towards me. "*Anno…Min-san?* I mean, um, Min?"

"Yeah, poor thing. Matt just won't listen. He's so cocky in his opinion, like he just knows he's right, won't even consider someone else's view or experience…"

"According to her…"

"According to—I wouldn't doubt it. A guy like him? Practically redneck. So thick-headed and intolerant. One step away from douche bag."

"But she chose—I mean, she's dating him, right? No one forced her."

"I don't know what she sees in him. Some girls just have blind spots…*ne?*"

"Stop."

"The Japanese word would by *yamete* or *yamete kudasai* to more—"

"I know *yamete*…"

"*So ka…*" She didn't bother to know Matt majored in Petroleum Engineering at Texas A&M or that his cousins were prominent players in the Houston oil scene, Japan just being a pitstop before bigger and better things, the only reason his coming here was due to his grandfather serving here in the postwar years full of stories about the "kindness of the Japanese people" and handing out chocolate to little kids…before coming home to work in oil field supplies in Midland. Basically, Matt was set. Min either consciously or sub-consciously laser locked her vision on his potential. Only blind spot for her would be the limited vision from wearing a burka while out in public if he took her to some Middle Eastern kingdom rich in black gold (Rednecks and Arabs: Two nomadic peoples who just happened to populate the land that contained the one resource the world depended on—our Spice Melange—and then making a business alliance that dictated global political events, from wars, coups to everything in-between—for the second half of the 20th century with the same amount of sophistication and grace as the main players…meaning hardly none at all. Fitting. Oil was a mistake).

The more pertinent question would be, what did Matt see in Min? A question I didn't ask.

"Yeah, men." Adina said.

I kept quiet. The bus stopped.

In front of the port entrance, a representative for PureLight handed out tracts. I ignored him.

"My phone…" Adina said.

"What?"

"It's acting…" She played with some buttons and the image of the apple appeared on her screen. "Never mind."

On the pier, sun setting, Kure visible in the distance, the wind blowing, Adina hugged herself again then opened her arms. "Give me a hug." I gave the one arm around her shoulders friend hug. "One weekend I may need to stay here…I like it out here…get away from the city…"

"With Mandy? I didn't know you two were so um…"

"Why Mandy? Why not your place? We're friends, right?"

"But…"

"But what?"

"People would talk. It's a small town."

"And you're a grown man, right? So what if they talk?"

"You don't live here…"

"Can't live your whole life as a secret…"

I noticed everyone had walked the plank to the boat except Adina. "The boat…"

"Right," Adina said looking at it. She smiled. "Bye."

"*Ja ne*…that's Japanese for…"

"I know what it means."

After she boarded I looked towards the port building. Through the glass doors, I saw the same Yu-like figure. Before I could confirm it was her, she turned away.

I heard another push alert. Probably another Nash Periscope…but when I looked at the phone screen, the image stuttered and locked up.

I turned off the phone and waited for the apple to appear.

*

MOMNDF: The magic hour shot here is incredible.

JRK: I thought so too. Even in the moment, um, waiting for the phone to boot up, I couldn't help but um, look out the windows as the bus headed back.

MOMNDF: Right, the hills, bamboo forest looming over everything, stretching to the sky, even the tall concrete walls they built on both sides of the road, fucking eyesore if I have ever seen one, can't hide the beauty of the tall green shoots what are they called in Japanese? JRK: Take.

MOMNDF: Right, fucking incredible.

JRK: Yeah, my paragraph here describing it couldn't do it justice.

102

MOMNDF: What?

JRK: Yeah, it made me cringe with its mystical, exotic orient pretentiousness, you know?

MOMNDF: It looked good on screen. And I liked how your phone rang immediately after booting up.

"What are you doing for dinner?"

"I don't know…"

"You want to meet up?"

JRK: All the sudden I was the most popular guy on the island.

MOMNDF: Maybe you're not as hated or isolated as you think.

"Are you bringing Min?"

"No, um, yeah about that…"

"Where you thinking?"

"I don't know, how about that Chinese place near the Naval Academy? What's it called? Ko-ra-ku-en or something."

"Matt, Korakuen is a garden in Okayama…and a sports/concert hall near the Tokyo Dome."

"Whatever, you know the place."

"*Koraiken?*"

"Yeah, that one."

"Uuuummm…I went there earlier."

"How about that restaurant—is it an izakaya or something—near your place?"

"*Mizutake?*"

"I don't know the name of it…"

"Look…I'm on the bus back in to town…I'll be there…give me a few minutes."

*

Of course, of course, this leads in to the all-important sub-section of *The Weekend, Part 2: Sunday* now known as *The Weekend, Part 2: Sunday: The Conversation, AKA: An Apologia for Hitler AKA The World According to Jason, AKA: Hitler Did Nothing Wrong AKA What did you and Matt Talk About?* The latter being a question more than one has asked so I will answer here though you won't necessarily like said answer nor does it probably do me any favors at any levels (most bothersome for me is my

103

argumentation, upon retrospect, isn't as airtight or reactionary enough for some but others will find it completely appalling regardless).

BUT!

I'm not going to be some post-mod asshole, teasing my way around, walking the track around the field.

MOMNDF: You kind of have been that asshole this whole story though.

JRK: Yeah, hear me out through my poor metaphor.

No, no, no, I'm getting on the field of play, with all the possibilities of bumps and bruises it could engender. The last metaphor I'll use.

MOMNDF: You shouldn't make promises like that.

JRK: I shouldn't make promises at all. Jesus was right.

MOMNDF: Is it that type of story?

JRK: It's not that type of story.

So Mizutake, busy and small, had only five tables and a secluded *washitsu* in the far corner, owned by a husband and wife with just a high schooler as extra staff. They lived above the restaurant, grandma taking care of the daughter, another elementary kid of mine, who would pop in now and then to eat. They had no dreams of expansion or franchising (like Platform back home, with its Vegas and Henderson branches and new location opening in Summerlin soon), setting up a brand by which patrons could easily recognize them, all of which must be started with huge bank (((loans))) and boomer boardrooms discussing synergies, scaling, corporate values, best practices and action plans to take to the next level in order to justify their salaries.

Franchises were a mistake.

No, no, no, they just wanted to make ends meet by serving best food and providing best service.

When the shoji door to the *washitsu* opened, I saw a group of mothers talking and drinking as their kids of various ages, from toddlers to elementary school age running around, playing.

At another table, a group of men sat and talked loudly as the wife and *mama-san*—let's just call her Yumiko—brought them mugs of beer. When they saw Matt and I, they all smiled and said "Hello" in English. At the table with them was a young boy wearing his school uniform, a white short-sleeve t-shirt and short blue shirts, yes, in the winter. His name was Shota. He came to talk to me. I tried to listen but he spoke too quietly.

And I was distracted by the petite bald-headed representative from PureLight, who entered and talked to the husband owner—let's just call him Keiji. Looked like he was seeking donations or foodstuffs. Keiji gave him a couple of bags and cash, then he left but not before glancing at me.

Things quieted down after that, the men exiting with Shota in tow saying "bye bye" with them all following the boys lead with "bye bye" muttered in drunken unsynchronized unison. The quiet provided the perfect contrived setting to have a philosophical conversation like one finds in Dostoevsky.

And it started out innocently enough:

"Look at these portions," Matt said staring over his plate of Hayashi rice. "You weren't kidding."

"You said you were hungry.".

He then dipped his spoon in to the saucy dish—I'll spare you the food porn—Matt took a bite and said "That's good. Damn good. How's yours?"

I finished my first bite of pork cutlet and put the chopsticks down. "Good."

"You mastered those things, I see?" Matt said pointing towards the chopsticks.

"I guess."

—Pause—

TL;DR: Hitler did nothing wrong.

I mean, I'm doing you a favor, so you don't have to continue reading because...

I care what you think.

And since my thinking and writing is so dangerous, so destructive, a literary Level 7 Nuclear Event, with thoughts like discarded graphite killing whoever they touch, my brain floating in open air ejaculating lethal thought isotopes where even a meal over *hayashi rice* and *tonkatsu* takes on apocalyptic consequences, you may be best suited to skip ahead to the **Prologue of the Prologue** because, hell, the next sentence might even require a cerebral Hazmat suit:

"Damn things are so hard to use. Wish they'd get with the program—I mean they're so modern and shit and they can't bother to adopt the knife and fork? Of course, I say that to anyone, like Min, she'll say I'm being 'culturally insensitive' but I feel I can say that around you, you know."

If that is too much for you, **STOP**. I write this because I care.

MOMNDF: Maybe you care too much.

JRK: Possibly.

105

MOMNDF: But I did debate even including this scene.
JRK: See...

Continue if you dare.

:smug:

Or skip to...

Kenji is coming.

\>continues reading.

\>Theconversation.txt

"You can say whatever you want around me."

"Hmph, you're the only one, I guess, you know, I'm not a racist or anything..."

"I am."

Matt laughed. "Sure you are man. But everyone is so on edge these days. Worried about every little thing people say. Lighten up, you know?"

"So what'd you say to Min?"

"What do you mean?"

"What did you say to her? Obviously, you said something that pissed her off."

"How'd you know we had a fight—I mean, an argument?"   "She texted Adina—um, I was with her, and um, her and Mandy."

"Hey now, look at you..."

"It isn't like that."

"You and Adina?"

"No."

"Mandy?"

"Don't think I'm her type..."

"Wait—"

"Yeah?"

"So...Min is just all over there advertising what happened between us?"

"Bitches talk man."

"Yeah."

"So what did you say?" Matt put down his glass and looked around. "Don't worry," I said. "Nobody here speaks English. You can say 'fuck niggers' and no one would be wiser for it..."

"Well, I'd never say that..."

"But what did you say?"

Yumiko immediately re-filled his almost empty shot glass of Pepsi. She then looked at me with a smile. Her skin was darker, and worn, a sign of years of the working-class life as waitress and maid in her husband's izakaya, but her smile was warm. Matt smiled at her and said *arigato* which might be the only Japanese he knew. He then looked at me and said, "I told a story about my granddad and his time in Japan. He said something like, 'The Japs always told me going to war with us was big mistake after seeing our tractors and bulldozers and such', but that's the way he talked, you know?"

"Sure."

"I said that to Min and she started busting my balls about how that's inappropriate language and shit and that I'm being culturally insensitive—god bless, there's that word—phrase or is it a phrase?"

"It's a term I think."

"Right, that damn term keeps popping up…'culturally insensitive'…using racist words and all that. Shit. I tried to tell her that's just how grandpa talked and they were mad at the Japs—I mean you know the Japanese, for happened during the war, but she started talking about Korean Comfort Women and how she still respectfully refers to them as 'Japanese' even though they committed all them, I mean those, atrocities during the war."

"Yeah, that's all commie propaganda. Tell Min that."

"Wait-what?"

"That whole 'comfort women' thing? It's all bullshit. With the statue outside the Japanese embassy and everything? Please. They were all just whores, prostitutes. They got paid."

"Seriously?"

"Even the US Army said during the war that a 'comfort girl' was nothing more than a prostitute or their word—'professional camp follower'—attached to the Japanese Army for the benefit of the soldiers. The Japs kn—the Japanese—knew that their men needed sex. And made sure they had it. Shipped them to Burma and other places. We allocate the resources we think are important."

Matt smirked. "And how do you know this?"

I shrugged my shoulders. "I read."

"And where'd you read something like that?"

I put my chopsticks down to think. Noticed the bowl of miso soup next to my plate that I haven't touched (no this detail is neither consequential or

107

important for the rest of the story. I just remembered it for some reason).
"I...um...maybe it was Kai10..."

"Kai10? Where have I heard that before?"

"Maybe it was on YouTube..."

"You just go searching for 'The Truth About Korean Comfort Girls'?"

"Sure—well, actually that's not a subject I'd Google unless for whatever reason I was curious in the moment."

"Which is pretty much was Google is for, right?"

"Right..." I picked up my chopsticks again to finish off the two remaining pieces of my fried cutlet.

"So you can't remember where you saw it?"

"Nope."

"So you're just going to blindly accept something you can't remember where you heard it from at face value?"

"I guess so...at least in this case."

"Why?"

"It fits."

"Fits what?"

"It just makes more sense. More plausible."

"So that's that?"

"Yes..."

Matt shook his head. "Okay, I'll just tell Min that those comfort chicks were just whores paid by the Japanese government. I'll tell her you said so..."

"Fine. Do that."

"Here I was thinking you were a liberal..."

"I don't know what I am."

"You're not a leftie?"

"I'm not a commie. That much I know. I guess..." I thought for a moment. "I guess I'm a Japanese Nationalist."

"What?" Matt smirked, leaning over the table. "Now that's a new one. You look about as Japanese as I look black or um, African...you know African-American."

"I know what you're saying."

"Yeah, it sounds ridiculous."

"If race is a social construct then why can't I be Japanese?"

"I'll agree with you there. That's bullshit, that 'social construct' shit."

"But isn't that the end goal of liberal ideology?"

108

"What? Social contruct's?"

"No, no, no, that's a tool. A tool to achieve equality, the purpose of the liberal experiment: Equality of sex, race and even outcome. Equality of everything, I guess. But the physical reality, like genetics and IQ prevents that. So, there comes in a form of secular spiritualism and alchemy to get past that— the 'social construct'. The physical externalities of race and gender differences are just in one's mind and established through power structures and hierarchies, thanks to that ubiquitous asshole: The Cis, Straight, White, Christian Male. The liberal goal is to overcome all this—to enable anyone to be anything they want regardless of material circumstances, whether biological or economic while tearing down the impediments to that end goal—complete individual freedom—even free of biology and history. Cyberspace is a tool which assists in this. I can be whoever I want or whatever I want on an any electronic platform or environment. I can be a Japanese Nationalist even though I don't have a bit of Japanese DNA. I just want Japan to thrive and exist as it is. And I'll champion that on any platform at my disposal. On the internet, social media, whatever—everyone's opinion counts, is of equal value, there's no hierarchy, I can change form whenever I want, and we all have equal access and benefits until we're banned for being an impediment to that equality."

"Whoa, whoa, whoa," Matt said putting his hand up. "I think you're taking it a little too far. That sounds like Communism."

"Yeah, 'Horseshoe Theory' or call it what you want. But isn't one of the purposes of Neo-liberal capitalism to achieve the same ends as communism? Absolute equality, material pleasure and abundance? But equality achieved through the means of the so-called 'free market' instead of state controlled everything? Instead of a Communist International that supersedes borders, we have World Trade Organizations and International Monetary Funds and Open Society Projects, Chinese and Southeast Asian elites going through a global circuit of British boarding schools and Ivy League colleges while the Arab Princes of Oil kingdoms gamble their fortunes away in Monte Carlo with palaces in Spain, Paris, Switzerland and a mansion in London all willfully sold by the host country elites, all in hope to bring down barriers that separate us by means of trade and making a buck."

"Yeah, well...if you—shit, I guess I don't like that..."

"People growing up in New Jersey, going to college here then leaving for Israel in adulthood to serve in their military or work as a judge in occupied Palestine..."

109

"Well, I don't—that's different…"

Oh Matt, Matt, you and your immediate gut responses to that word…

"So you're an American Nationalist?" I asked.

"I don't…I'm patriotic and all. Love our troops and the Constitution. Liberty, right? It's just…the sound of the word. 'Nationalist'. Makes me think of Hitler or something."

"Have you ever asked why that is?"

"Why what is?"

"Why is Nationalism such a bad thing? Why is it associated with Hitler or Mussolini? Why do we tolerate forms of Japanese, Chinese, Mexican, Israeli— you name it, why we tolerate other nationalisms? Stalinism was basically Russian Nationalistic State Capitalism…"

"Communism sucks. I won't say anything good about Stalin. Ever."

"Yeah but Stalin doesn't receive near the derision that we seem to mutually think he deserves…"

"He was our ally in the war…And you know how there are liberals everywhere in our government. McCarthy had the right idea."

"Right but Stalin soon became an enemy. And we soon found out the truth about him, gulags and purges and all that. Yet when we read an article in The New Yorker that features both Stalin and Hitler, Uncle Joe is always subtly put on the pedestal, praised as a reader of fine literature and a brilliant cultural savant while Hitler, the actual artist who worshipped Wagner and helped turn propaganda in to an art form, is disregarded as a brute. Even in criticism, one is still looked upon higher than the other, regardless of death counts, genocides and misery being unequaled. What's wrong with Nationalism, Fascism, Nazism or Hitlerism? Why's that the evil of all evils?"

Matt nervously took a sip of his Pepsi. "I think that goes without saying."

"Maybe we do need to say it. We seemed to have forgotten."

"I haven't forgotten anything."

"What haven't you forgotten?"

"The Holocaust? The six million. You should know."

"Never forget, huh?"

"Pearl Harbor, The Bataan death march—"

"Those were Japanese atrocities…"

"Right…but they were allies of the Nazis…"

"But what did the Nazis do?"

110

"The Holocaust, man! Goddamn! The way they rounded up the Jews and shit. They took over half of Europe. Invaded Poland, France and wherever else. Marched in to Russia, killing millions!"

"Assuming that is all true…"

"Assuming it is true? What the hell man!"

"Hold on, hold on. Let me make my point."

"Fine…"

"Assuming that the Holocaust, the six gorillion or whatever Jews were killed."

"Six million."

"Right the six million at Auschwitz or is it Buchenwald? I don't know, it's a depressing subject…assuming that all happened, aren't those numbers negated by the amount of Soviet atrocities committed on Russians themselves? Upwards of 50 million died under Stalin. Their whole society wiped out."

"Like I said, I won't debate whether Stalin was evil."

"Okay, but why isn't every child taught about those atrocities? Why isn't there a diary of a little kid serving time in a gulag or whose parents were arrested for saying the wrong thing?"

"I read *One Day in the Life of Ivan Denisovich* in college," (I find this hard to believe but he said it).

"But did you have any context? Do you know why you read it? Were you bludgeoned over the head with the reason why it was required reading?"

Matt thought for a minute. "I don't know. I just thought communism was bad…maybe my parents recommended it?" He took another sip.

"But it wasn't something you learned at school or seen in media—you know movies, or TV right?"

"I remember hearing about it on talk radio. And my family talked about it."

"But, you know…well, we all know…we all know about the evils of the Nazis…that's taught everywhere."

"Yeah, so? We need to know. We can't let that shit happen again."

"Wouldn't you say the same about Communism?"

"Of course…"

"But yet…there's a massive awareness gap between the Holocaust and the evils of the Gulags, struggle sessions and the killing fields…"

"So what are you saying?"

"Have you seen the movie *Steve Jobs*?"

Matt thought for a moment…"That the one with Ashton Kutcher?"

"No, the one with Michael Fassbender." I'm of course referring to *Steve Jobs* (2013. Directed by Danny Boyle—but originally intended for David Fincher—who probably would have done a better job—from a script by Aaron Sorkin based on Walter Issacson's book and cinematography by Alwin H. Kuchler), not the best flick in the world but it will serve its purpose and I won't try to be too heavy on the Sorkin-like lecture porn.

Matt thought again for another moment. "Have I? I don't know. I might have watched it. Did I torrent that one?"

"Look, it doesn't matter, but there's one line in the movie where Jobs, or the character of Jobs, rather, says, 'The two most significant events of the 20th Century—the allies win the war and this', 'this' being the release of the original Mac."

"Okay, I might agree with that. Definitely winning the war was one. I'd say maybe winning the Cold War was the other. I don't know about the Mac being so important. I never liked Apple," he said holding up his Android.

"No doubt, but context, that scene took place in 1984, towards the end of the Cold War. I won't argue about the significance of the Mac—that isn't the point—but the personal PC market, which led to all these devices," I said holding up my phone, "Where we could access a global information brain, was certainly a world changing event rivalling whatever Gutenberg did."

"Okay fair enough…"

"But the Cold War that followed World War II, the amount of money the US government poured in to technology, setting up Japan as an industrial capitalist dream, even funding Japanese research in to technologies for espionage, and microchip companies like Intel, supercomputer companies like Cray—that all flowed from the allied victory."

"Yeah, so? That's the victory of capitalism and liberty. And prosperity."

"The end of history, huh?"

"I don't know if I'd say that but you think it'd all be better with Hitler ruling the world and Japan running Asia."

"It's not about Hitler ruling the world. Or Japan running Asia. We rule the world. We live in the *Pax Americana*. Some may call it globalism…"

"I'm not a fan of globalism…"

"Why?"

"I don't want some world government telling us what to do…"

"Isn't that what we do? Isn't that what the *Pax Americana* is? Isn't it just a form of cultural, economic and military colonialism but different from its predecessors? We have bases everywhere—800 in over 70 countries. If the IRS or any law enforcement agency sets its sights on a bank for records, you better comply, right?"

"Right…fucking taxes…"

"Our cultural wares—media of all sorts—is front and center the world over. Everyone eats at a McDonald's, drinks a latte from Starbucks, or uses and iPhone or at the very least, a PC with a Windows OS, or uses Google to search or YouTube to watch videos. If we haven't colonized with arms we've colonized with manufacturing. Nike, Levis, Ralph Lauren, you name it—the world is our manufacturing base. We've made the third world safe for production of cheap wares and high profits. And if we can't export the factories, we import the workers. Our influence may be challenged more but we still have it. We're here, you and I, at the behest of a nation, a once proud empire, we're here to teach their children English, because they feel it's necessary to survive in this American dominated global world."

"And what does this have to do with Hitler?"

"Well…the narrative we use to enforce all this is—I don't want to sound like Tyrion Lannister in *Game of Thrones* but the so-called evils of the Nazis, the Axis…they really wanted to take over the world and they were bad, look at all those helpless Jews they killed…but we're the good guys…better we run the world…"

"Do you think the world would have been better run by the fucking Nazis? Fuck you! That's nuts!" Matt almost got out of his chair.

I noticed others in the restaurant turning to stare. "Let me explain."

"Explain fucking what?"

"Matt, calm down."

"You just fucking said…"

"I didn't say anything, calm down…have a beer…"

He sat down. I asked for a beer. As Yumiko brought it, smiled with hesitation this time, I smiled back and said to Matt, "It's on me, don't worry."

"You gonna pay in deutschemarks?"

"Funny but think…"

"That's hard to do when you're making statements like…fucking Hitler was okay…"

"Think about that for a moment."

"What?"

"Why are you so angry? Why get so upset at me just trying to make an objective argument from the other side? I haven't done anything. We're just talking. *Devil's Advocate*, at worst. Would you get so angry if I was defending Satan himself or Pontius Pilate, or Julian the Apostate?"

"Who?"

"You know who Satan is…don't you? He isn't Adolph Hitler by another name you know?"

"I know who fucking Satan is…I'm talking about them other—god when I drink I become a redneck."

"You haven't even had one beer."

"Mental preparation…"

"Pontius Pilate ordered the crucifixion of Jesus."

"I know that, I mean…"

"Julian the Apostate?"

"Yeah, him."

"He tried to make Rome return to Paganism from Christianity. Naturally, he's a villain from the Christian angle."

"Okay, didn't know…"

"But you do know Hitler is a monster. And I know I can play *Devil's Advocate* about the very Father of Lies himself but a defense of a failed German dictator who we vanquished in to the ash heap of history with Soviet partnership immediately causes a gut reaction."

Matt took a sip, actually a gulp, of his beer. "I don't know. I don't get your argument. You're defending them? Might as well just defend the Soviets man. They more successful, right?"

"You hate Communism right? It's restriction of economic and all types of freedoms right?"

"YES! You've read about the camps, the arrests and the Gulags, right? Shit, _____ is a missile launch away, look what they've done to their people! All those refugees!"

"You're horrified of _____?"

"I'm not horrified…"

"Well, you think they're evil, right? You think the world would be better off without _____ ruling…right?"

"Right."

Yumiko brought us more mugs of Kirin and a wider smile.

114

"Are you going to try to be an apologist for North Korea, now?" Matt asked taking his first sip. "Because if you are I might need a couple of these beers but then I might whoop your ass."

"No. But let me ask you a question."

"Sure."

"We agree that North Korea isn't ideal. And subsequently, the Chinese weren't much better but they've improved certainly. Why did we upset the apple cart then?"

"What do you mean?"

"Think about it. Korea was a Japanese territory before and during the war. As was Manchuria and Taiwan."

"Right, they wanted to take over Asia!"

"No, no—maybe but doubtful. And how's that any different than the French, Dutch or Brits having colonial occupation in Asia?"

Matt shrugged his shoulders.

"More importantly, wouldn't you say Japan could have, would have, run Korea, Vietnam, Manchuria and their occupied regions of China better than the communist governments? Wouldn't their way of life have been better?"

"Maybe…"

"Maybe. And who divided the Korean peninsula and gave half of it to the communists? If wasn't for the Japanese military trained Park Chung-hee, South Korea would have been in major trouble. Who helped Ho Chi Minh form a shadow government in Vietnam, gave them full diplomatic status and American arms to fight the Japanese and so-called 'colonialization'?"

"What about China?"

"What about it? That's…that's a different matter but we undermined the Kuomintang government after the war—we certainly didn't give them the support they needed—we forced Chiang to negotiate with Mao and Zhou Enlai. Mao's forces attacked Japanese units to provoke an invasion in the first place. The war destabilized China and prepared it for communist takeover. Maybe we should have just let Japan decimate the Maoist forces."

"So, what's your point?"

"My point is, look at all these countries, including Germany, that we divided up and gave to Soviet control. Look at the whole eastern bloc. If the war was such a victory for freedom and liberty, why'd we give up half of these liberated areas to tyranny?"

"But Hitler…"

"Look, once again, that's the boogeyman they use to get us to accept the current order. You think Germans wished for a divided nation, one ran by Communists, with the main city having an ugly wall dividing it? You think they preferred that? You think Romania was better under Ceausescu than Nazi-aligned Antonescu and King Michael? Well, Michael switched allegiances to us, but we still let the Reds take over Romania…"

"I don't—I—they would've suffered regardless…"

"Right, so now, every war, every invasion, is now waged under the pre-text as a 'humanitarian intervention' that usually makes things worse. Was Iraq better or worse under Saddam? How about Libya? Or El Salvador? Or Iran? We put the Shah in power then engineered his removal until it's possible to remove the Mullahs. Every leader of these respective countries is portrayed as the next incarnation of Hitler. We're told and re-told the story of Chamberlain giving concessions at Munich and how it only made Hitler hungrier, like a shark who tasted some fresh blood and desired more, we're told if we deal or negotiate with any world leader who doesn't line up with our ever-evolving ideas of liberal and mercantile virtues, that we are just acting like Chamberlain, letting tyranny triumph. Hitler, Nazism, Fascism, whatever—it's the eternal enemy of liberalism, the system and philosophy by which we have been raised. Nazism or fascism is the dragon that continually needs to be slain in the name of progress. The scary 'once upon a time' story we tell our children of a previously dark period. Anytime the dragon rises, whether his name be Putin, Kim, Gaddafi, Saddam, Assad or whoever—sometimes leaders who we in fact installed—it is our duty we're told to slay this dragon so that all our esoteric and constantly changing virtues at home and abroad can championed. But if they're on our side, like Stalin or Mao, or Pinochet, Marcos or the Shah, we'll overlook their evils until they've served their purpose then we'll throw them to the human rights lions of activists and historians, turning the propaganda machine against them."

Matt took another sip of his beer. "You know Hitler was a leftist, right? It was called 'National Socialism' for a reason. He was influenced by Marx. They borrowed their classification strategies for the Jews from Jim Crow laws…created by Democrats. You know that, right?"

I took a sip of my beer. "That's a modern left/right paradigm transposed on to the past. Forget the fact that a lot of Jim Crow Democrats, like Strom Thurmond, became Republicans. Was Abraham Lincoln, a Constitutional liberty loving conservative? He used most of the same tactics to preserve the

Union that Hitler did to preserve power, like suspending Writ of Habeas Corpus, invading states that lawfully and constitutionally seceded, shutting down newspapers that disagreed with him, ordering arrests of congressmen who spoke out against him and confiscation of private property and so on."

"Lincoln...well...hell, I don't know, my ancestors fought for the Confederacy so..."

"You grew up hearing he wasn't a saint, right?"

"Yes."

"So, you don't buy the story then? You're sympathetic to the other side, right?"

"I don't know about sympathetic, I mean I don't support slavery or anything. That was awful but I understand what the Confederacy was after— I mean it wasn't just a war about slavery..."

"Right. But that's what I was told in my liberal classroom on the west coast..."

"You aren't from the south..."

"Right, I'm not. I don't have much of a frame of reference. I can only go by what I was taught or care to study independently."

"Right."

"Tell me, was Andrew Jackson a leftist just because he was a Democrat? You're from Texas. I bet your grandfather was a Democrat, right?"

Matt thought for a moment. "He was. I think."

"And I bet he probably supported the Jim Crow laws."

"He might've. I don't know."

"Did he ever use the N-word?"

"I heard him say it every now and then. But mainly in a joking manner."

"Would you say he's the worst human being on the face of planet earth for talking like that?"

"No—no way. He's just joking. My god, we've become too uptight..."

"Right. We have. It's become a form of speech Bolshevism. Back to that horseshoe theory—any time we go against some sort of established moral speech standard, we're called what?"

"Racists?"

"We're called 'racists' or we're called 'Nazis'."

"That's overdoing it. I agree. They've gone too far. They're using Nazi tactics on us by calling us Nazis."

"See, I don't buy that. That's just trying to shift the boogeyman from one side to the other. Trying to call one side Nazis that was accusing you of the same thing. Both mutually agree that Nazis are the monster, so they try to project that monster on to the other side. It's puerile. There's something deeper going on."

"Like what? You don't think these Antifa, the so-called 'Antifascists' are actually fascist in the way the beat and terrorize people who disagree with them."

"No. They're just an establishment vanguard allowed to disrupt and terrorize with establishment approval."

"Isn't that what the SS, the Stormtroopers, isn't that what they did?"

"The SA you mean? They were the Stormtroopers."

"Isn't that what they did? Caused trouble?"

"Sure, but many of those groups were outlawed as soon as the Nazis came to power. And their purpose was different. They were trying to help the Nazis preserve their culture and their order from foreign influence. The groups now want to upset the culture. They're used by the establishment to make sure dissenting voices against progress—of cultural change—are silenced pure and simple. It's a form of anarcho-tyranny. The State ignores the explicit criminal acts of one group because it serves their purpose, while prosecuting the others for mundane offenses, like not filling out the right boxes on a tax form or not having their story straight after excessive interviews and find themselves penalized for perjury. These forces work together. The vanguard is doing the work of their puppet masters."

"Who's that? Who are the puppet masters?"

MOMNDF: You wanted to say Jews didn't you?

JRK: Guilty. But I also wanted him to listen.

"After the first World War, the British, Americans all of them, thrust liberal democracy, market capitalism—all that—on a country that wasn't at all suited it for it. And of course, there were the bankers who were exploiting the country for their gain. The Nazis were just a reaction against that. And wouldn't you behave the same way, if foreign powers both state and financial, came in, and started to tell you, tell Texas what to do and how to behave?"

"Of course. They tried one time. Damn UN tried to send election 'observers' to our state to see if we weren't rigging our elections."

"Right? That upsets you. But yet we do it as well. Intervening in other countries affairs but under the guise of some moral crusade whether it be helping the starving children, women's rights or establishing democracy."

"So, you hate America. Is that what you're saying?"

"No. I suppose the founding was well-intentioned. The historic, legacy Americans, those who came here to build a life and get away from English monarchic rule…"

"My people. Who've fought every war…"

"No disrespect to that really. None whatsoever. The historic Americans are fine in my book. Really, the only real Americans. They conquered the frontier with the intent to practice and worship as they saw fit; mastering the outer elements and forces so they could satisfy their inner spiritual longing and then enshrining those values in a document their ancestors—like you—rightly revere. We're beneficiaries of their genius. But everything they've fought for and sacrificed for—freedom from tyranny and rabid individualism—has been hijacked and perverted. The egalitarian European super state, free of the prejudicial practices of the old world like state mandated religion and the wars and persecutions that flowed from them, created by an admixture of Anglos, Scots, Irish, Germans and French Protestants almost immediately came under attack from a strain of foreign influence and greed wanting in on the triumph creating a new type of state religion."

"No one—I never said the system was perfect. I don't like the way things are going myself."

"But how did it get like this? Why has our technical progress resulted in a shift to taking everything private to public? Why did we ever start caring about the private beliefs of individuals? Why does that have any effect on if they should be employed or not? Now, under this new technocracy, we all live in the public square, our every action and statement under immediate scrutiny. Ideas like free speech, liberty and individual rights? These are concepts we only give lip service to. It's all been hijacked."

"By who?"

"Special interests…who want to maintain this order, the power they derive from it."

"Evil corporations?"

MOMNDF: You want to say it.

JRK: I know, I know. But I didn't want him to turn off his ears and start defending Israel.

"I'm just saying we must admit that our government, our country is under Neo-liberal occupation that has resulted in a form of Bolshevism—or at least been grossly perverted. Not Soviet style but a very particular form of American Bolshevism that perfectly suits the powerful government, corporate and financial interests. And it started with World War II and probably before that. So, they need that story of us defeating absolute evil. It has to be evil because we don't want to consider an alternative. To the keep not just order at home but also world order. This is the order we've been born in to. Just like the Chinese still revere Mao even though they've transitioned completely away from Communism—he's the father of their current order. But our order is hidden and faceless."

"So what was the point of the war again? Why did my grandpa go to war?"

MOMNDF: It must have taken a lot of strength not to say it.

JRK: You ain't kidding.

"Hate to say it, but the war was waged in the name of Central Banking…well, central everything…finance, big business…but it starts with banking."

Matt got restless in his seat and took another sip of his beer. "Oh I knew you were going there. It's all big money and greed's fault! Typical liberal bullshit."

I reached my hand across the table. Almost to grab Matt. "Hold on! Hold on! Listen, listen!"

Matt relaxed in his chair. "I'm listening. I'm getting a little tipsy anyways, I ain't—ain't—will you listen to me. Damn. I ain't going anywhere," he held up his beer mug towards the waitress.

"Think about your ancestors, the settlers. Given you're from Texas, they're probably Scottish, Scotch-Irish I'm guessing?"

"Something like that, yeah. You can call them rednecks."

"These so-called rednecks, really, their only purpose was to live their life as they saw fit, which didn't really require much finance or financial acumen. The early Americans, paid their debts with their harvests of tobacco, wheat and whatnot. The American Revolution was financed that way. A fair barter system less complicated and corrupt than the abstract English banking system. A land established by men of adventure and tenacity, think of John Quincy Adams awaiting election results while tending his plow, a time of low living but high thinking, but then combined with slavery and those later arrivals who only saw America as a land of opportunity, those who would use events like The Civil

War to play both sides, buying damaged rifles from the US government and selling them to Confederates in Texas, manipulating markets, harming farmers and producers in the process so the leeches can make whatever profit possible. Those who then came, regardless of race or national origin only had one goal: To make a fortune. Really the thing we paid deference to, regardless of morals or character were those who were rich and successful. And with that came all the financial alchemy that had been brewed in the mother country of England, which then led to more and more esoteric financial devices, becoming less rooted in material goods and resources and more the financial instruments themselves. We surpassed investment in pure material resources and evolved in to the electronic ether produced by tech. America's values followed along with it, disentangling the elements that built it—racial and national pride, religion, a love of freedom and independence to where those strands, now separated, took on a life of their own. America no longer meant for free white persons of good character looking for their own corner of land. It is now meant for anyone, who wants to practice the alchemy of finance and striving for money that doesn't really exist, that you can't hold in your hand but appears as numbers on a screen. There's isn't just a free market of goods and services but a free market of anything. Everything is for sale. Our freedom of religion has turned in to a free market of religion where the purpose isn't to put the fear of God or jolt people to think and ponder but rather to persuade to buy in and join. So a church looking for members will flatten out their message, take away sin and judgement and just keep the feels, Jesus as life coach. Better yet, why not just mix and match? We're one world, right? No race, just the human race, right? Buddha and Jesus said the same thing after all, right? Let's have best of everything and strip a great religion of any unique characteristics it may have because it might turn some people off.

"In relation, if the money and religion is abstract other things can be abstract too, like race and sex. Everything becomes fluid. One can be a Trans Zen Christian only in America. A Muslim from Dubai who has only been in the US for five years can claim ancestry with George Washington and John Adams but yet if you or I were to live in Japan or China for the same time, we would never even think of claiming relation to Oda Nobunaga or the Emperor Qin. But that's because they're nations. We're an esoteric empire built on concepts that have long been perverted. Nothing has any meaning in physical reality. So why not invade the world and invite the world?"

"Okay…" Matt said holding up his hands. "What do you want me to say?"

"Nothing."

"Then…"

"Think about every issue championed since the conclusion of the war. Think about it."

"I don't know if I can but okay. Tipsy and all…"

"Think. Think of all the things that upset you, that most so-called conservatives hate: Liberal Hollywood, 'political correctness', eroding of traditional social values, abortion, drugs, pornography and multi-culturalism, basically cultural Marxism in a nutshell. All of these things prop up the establishment. The government, the bankers, the corporations…"

"It just goes back them huh?"

"Sure. Both the establishment left and establishment right do their bidding. The left forces confrontations on all social issues and the right on military conflict. We use the social issues to wage war. Humanitarian conflict and all. World War II gave us the formula. It was our patient zero. The first humanitarian war."

"So Hitler was just a great guy, huh?"

"I'm not saying that. I'm saying the Nazis, along with the Italians and Japanese were just trying to preserve their respective order, protect their peoples from foreign—both governmental and financial influence—they were trying to preserve a traditional societal order. But we created the narrative Hitler was a tyrant, maybe he was, but we've done business with tyrants before and after. He was the evilest tyrant ever though—like the Soviets were any better—and used that as a pretext to invade Europe, then divided the spoils with the Soviets, turning the world in to our game board, to the point we're paying the price."

"How so?"

"Just like how Weimar Democracy failed in Germany, so it fails when we force liberal democracy on a people and culture by which it's a foreign concept. And the US pays the price because each time we have thousands of our soldiers killed, like my cousin…"

"Sorry about that man. I support—I mean, God bless our troops."

"Thanks. But guys like Tyler die by the thousands and we get refugees streaming in to our country from the chaos caused."

"Like what?"

"Think of all the Koreans, Republican Chinese, Vietnamese, Iranians, Sudanese, Libyans, Iraqis, Afghanis, Salvadorans and Somalians. Our

122

interventions bring them stateside. Now refugees want in to Japan and Europe too."

"But isn't that a sign of our kindness?"

"Maybe but its kindness to our detriment. As we allow the flow of others in to our countries, the native population, the legacy Americans, are left for dead like a dog on the side of a country road. But even they don't seem to care. The UN has a plan for their—our—replacement. Big business, it's become their job to keep them distracted. As long as everyone has their video games, Facebook, YouTube, NFL, NBA, NASCAR or harder drugs, like opoids. As long as they have something to capture their attention and not make them ponder the state of their squalor of their surroundings, or question why they need to press 1 for English, or why all their signage is in three different languages, then they will continue to not care. Rather they continually ignore and externalize insecurities by social issues turned political and the overseas crusades and interventions, ignoring the problems of Detroit by focusing all attention on Damascus. America is not a nation, it's an airport terminal."

JRK: I'm proud of that line.

MOMNDF: You made it up? You really said it?

JRK: Yep.

"An airport terminal?"

"Yeah, people just come in and out, without regards to their present surroundings...or maybe it's an ant colony..."

"Ant colony? We're getting biological now? Look Jason," Matt said leaning over the table. "Lookie here, I hate to break it to you but we have the greatest explosion of material wealth, prosperity and standard of living the world has ever seen. Pretty soon everyone will have a cellphone and access to the world of information—my god, it's incredible. All of this is due to capitalism. American capitalism. Can't you be proud of that?"

"Sure. I would love to be proud of that. But if anything, we've done the exact opposite. We've colonized the world with our military and capital might but yet we're not proud of it. If anything, we're ashamed to admit it. We have the greatest sense of false humility in world history. If we have an empire, a true one, why not celebrate it? Where is our 'Rule, Brittania! Brittania, rule the waves!'? Where is it? Where are our Diamond Jubilee's? Instead we're stuck in a state of pity and contempt. Pity on the poor and oppressed but also a contempt using the pathetic state of their surroundings as a reason for any sort of charitable, military or capital adventure. Why damn ourselves if we're honest

123

and celebrate our superiority in any of these matters? Instead we hide behind concepts and ideologies as being the reasons for our success, rather than just a tool in the right hands. We claim secular constitutionalism, capitalism and liberty as the virtues that brought us prosperity and we can just then overlay it and adjust it to any and every people with the same results. Because, dare we admit that we might have a biological and civilizational advantage, perhaps many might realize their core values by which they interpret the world—equality, liberty, fraternity—might ring a little false and hollow? So, we must have a little suspicion for ourselves and others to keep those attitudes in check.

"I would love to celebrate our reach and influence considering our cultural and military influence and power is unequaled in world history. If anything, can't we just be unapologetic? Just like there's a statue of MacArthur at Atsugi, shouldn't there be statues built in honor of our heroes and conquerors in every port where our influence extends with even cities named after them? Isn't that what the great conquerors like Alexander and Caesar did? Yokohama should be called 'Perrytown', Inchon relabeled 'MacArthur Ridge', how about 'Pattonburgh' for Berlin? And shit, why not, Baghdad could be called 'Bushville'. When anyone buys an iPhone or flies in a Boeing plane, or watches a Hollywood movie or television show—or hell even YouTube—or even when they're able to gas up their car –or even charge it!—they should know they're the beneficiaries of American capital and ingenuity."

Matt let out a nervous laugh. "I see what you're saying but that's…" he took a gulp of his beer. "That's going a little far wouldn't you say? Like we're better than you?"

"What's wrong with celebrating the fact if it isn't the truth? If someone loses weight do they try to hide the fact their thinner from all the fat people? Doesn't every tenet of liberalism pre-suppose a form of moral and ideological superiority? Doesn't the word 'progressivism' mean 'progress', like improvement meaning something was lacking or backward? It demands a form of allegiance like any ruling ideology except it's not to a person, a leader, or a country—It's allegiance to a thought system…"

"But, I told you, I wasn't a liberal."

"Wouldn't most conservatives call themselves 'Classical Liberals' though? Invoking the names of Jefferson, Paine and the like?"

"Sure, I guess."

"So, whether classical or progressive it is still liberalism. But naturally the progressive is more powerful in terms of staying power because it is always willfully marching forward in the name of progress. It will tolerate capitalistic finance since it gives them funds and can be used to forward their agenda. The conservatives or 'Classical Liberals' are like a retreating army constantly ceding territory. From slavery, to women's suffrage, to transgender rights and gay marriage today. They always conform to this attitude of 'progress' as its shoved down everyone's throat then try to spin how they always championed those ideals.

"They don't put up a fight and move their line back a little for fear of an onslaught. The result is a docile public who, under the weight of material need and pleasure, either obliges or is crushed for rebelling. Liberalism is used like any doctrine of the ruling class: It is a steamroller flattening anyone who stands in its way. But in this case, the steamroller is ever changing in form, with no care for consistency as long as it maintains power and the illusion of compassion and tolerance. We have an empire that we dare not call an empire, nor take pride in...because that would be hateful. Instead there is the worst combination of self-loathing mixed with moral imperative and self-righteousness. We've removed all the key vestiges of Christianity except the two most loathsome and restricting traits: Guilt and overwhelming tolerance for the other...to the point we let them overwhelm us.

"Our favorite characters in movies are the ones who embrace and revel in the chaos of destruction and superiority. The one's who know and enjoy their place and role in history: Colonel Kilgore in *Apocalypse Now*—"

"Who's he?"

"'I love the smell of napalm in the morning.'"

"Oh yeah, he's great. Robert Duvall."

"Yeah, my cousin's favorite scene. Or the drill sergeant in *Full Metal Jacket* at the beginning. Or all the characters who say 'nigger' in the Tarantino movies..."

"Hey now..."

"No one here cares...or can understand, remember?"

"Yeah, I guess," Matt said looking around.

"We like and enjoy those parts but hedge it all with guilt and a moral lesson at the end. Whereas a war or battle story used to be about the virtue of heroism and valor, a comedy to display how we need grace, a cathartic experience for the mass as whole. But now it's all just theatrics, explosions and dirty jokes, war and laughs for no reason, and then a feeling of guilt for enjoying it all. Guilty pleasure is a purely American concept."

"So…what?" Matt leaned back in his chair, taking it all in. "What now then? If it's all meaningless?"

"Watch it burn and warm your hands on the fire."

Matt sat up. "Watch it burn? You mean 'let it burn', right?"

"There's nothing to 'let' or allow. It's a process that really when you think about it, is out of our control, unless you live and work within the halls of power, but even then, the power is really out of their hands too. They can try to control the spirit of the age but it's like muzzling a rabid dog waiting to break free. But they'll hold on as tight as they can to their worldview and imposing it on the world. But the very technology brought about by their governing and economic order—the global technocratic empire of computers, cellphones, internet and social media, immigration and affirmative action policies promoted by this economic system are the Frankenstein Monster that will kill its creator."

"How so? It's brought about so much prosperity and raised the standard of living worldwide. How's that a bad thing?"

"Because it puts everyone on equal footing. Of equality, liberty and fraternity, equality is by far the killshot in Western Civilization's gradual suicide. If everyone has the same technology, the same standard of living, if everyone from Montana to Mumbai is competing for the same resources, if everyone watches the same movies and listens to the same music while wearing Nike shoes and Hanes T-shirts, if everyone blends together, mixing and procreating regardless of race or culture—but really it doesn't matter because there is no particularly important race or culture—then this whole world becomes a blank stare, a faceless crowd, an abstraction. Look at Germany and Japan after the war. Germania: A land that gave us the greatest works of music and philosophy—not to mention making us rethink religion on more than one occasion, from Luther to Schopenhauer—has been reduced to manufacturing our BMWs and techno music. Japan, since they are an island and didn't commit the bigger so-called evils of the war, got out a slightly more unscathed. But the country is one part cultural museum and one part electronics and automobile provider. The entertainment they used to endure this ignominy—manga, anime, porn and food culture—has been transferred and appropriated by us.

"An individual roaming in this world then has nothing concrete to rely on except the abstract crowd that is ever shifting. Many don't even bother to experience life, but rather sit in their rooms consumed with various sorts of flattened and generic media all day or live in the void of cyberspace. But this

126

media creates a true reality where the real events of life don't even matter. The refugees aren't so much real as is the news event about the refugees. We see the images of destruction, maybe even a dead body or two, but we have no connection to it all because we didn't experience it, because we don't live in_____."

"Min wants us to visit there, you know? Get the true story. Probably going for holidays."

"I heard."

"Adina again?"

"Yeah but look at these wars."

"Like Iraq?"

"Yeah to us, unless we serve or have family there, they are abstract. Everything is shot and recorded. We see the images of missiles being launched, drone footage of executions, the green night time haze and illuminated gun fire. And we're all so detached. It's just a real-time documentary for us. We aren't getting hit with bullets or bleeding. There's really no difference between the film footage of the A-Bomb exploding over Hiroshima and the massive explosions in any blockbuster. Watch the reels of the bombing of Dresden, with their slates at the beginning followed by detached filming of the damage below the plane, at an objective distance. It's an analytic document of destruction, not a chronicle of carnage and pain. The same with the bureaucrats who make the decisions of who to send to war. It's all just a show for them. They view it all through the lens of a screen with maybe a cursory visit to the battlefield as a show of support. But even the soldiers themselves are affected by this helming of war. Helicopter pilots trade their battle footage like we share a video from YouTube."

"Where are you going with this? I have a cousin in Iraq, are you saying—"

"My cousin died in Iraq, remember?"

"Right man…I…"

"No disrespect towards anyone in the military. These men sign up out of duty and the masculine need for adrenaline and purpose. But they're being weaponized and used by bureaucrats who don't understand the human costs. But the numbing effect of war goes from top to bottom because of technology's depersonalized effect. Everything has become a technical process instead of personal or spiritual process. Everything has become mechanized. Especially death."

"But what does that have to do with the system collapsing?"

"Because this all just creates a numbing effect. To where the numbness itself is really the only thing we feel. So, this narcotic agent of insensitivity, this mechanized system of destruction by abstraction will eventually turn inward on itself, probably on the occasion of its total victory…which is close. Of the three competing systems of the 20th century: Communism, National Socialism and Liberal Capitalism, the third option had the strongest and most robust tendencies and resources, therefore it won. Following that was the electronic, and subsequent PC and tech revolution that put a super computer and knowledge core in everyone's hands. This leveling technology was just as important as the Allies winning the war. And eventually we have to deal with the reality it created. Some will commit suicide, some will try to bring about justice and right perceived wrongs. But every system, like a religion, must work itself out to its logical conclusion which we are seeing. Secularized sanctimony can only go so far in a world of consumerist ants. We tell everyone they're unique and yet bludgeon them to think alike and consume the same products. Eventually, those who think they're special, raised that way from the womb, will want the world to know—they will lash out at it for not recognizing their notable existence…that just happens to be like everyone else's…so they'll try to crush those who even try to be contrary…because they're not as special, right? And the first blows will come. The lashing out will start. Others will realize what they've been told is a lie. They will see the apparatus for what it is. Ironically enough, the American spirit of questioning authority will help move this along as many realize who the true authority is. True rebellion will then be directed towards it. Once people realize the only feeling they get from spilling blood is one of numbness, then the flow won't stop. It'll all just be an apocalyptic movie come to life."

Matt just sat there with a smug grin. His face slightly red from probably being drunk. "Are what are you going to do, what can we do?"

"I'll probably just stay here in Japan. An island is the ideal place for someone trying to retain their individuality, right? One must either embrace the chaos or try to do their best to detach from the surrounding reality completely. I choose the latter."

"You think there's no hope, huh?"

"If a great leader arises to turn the tide or strong and brave enough to lead the way, I will follow him."

"What if it's a woman?"

"And you call me a liberal?"

"Fuck, man you know. It's the alcohol talking."

"Regardless, I desire authority. I'm not an anarchist. I respect the rules but I respect the law of nature more. But no grand authority by who we can visibly point to exists. And I have no great expectations. Now it's just a bunch of crabs in a bucket clawing for their moment of sunshine. But until something different happens, I'll try to keep it at a distance."

"You're not that so-called great leader?"

"No. I enjoy the freedom I have now. The ruler is the biggest prisoner of all. My goal is to survive the fire and maybe help stoke it if we see it rising in our favor, right?" I said with a grin.

"Fire? You mean…are you talking about death? Mass killings? What are you talking about?"

"I'm just saying—you know how celebrities champion those cleanse diets?"

"Um…not sure…"

"Well, it's basically a purge of the bodily system. A purge has a cleansing effect. Some say even a spiritual one. Through flames, things become transcendent they say…"

Matt sat up again and leaned forward. "They? How about you? You just want fucking genocide to win a…I don't know what…"

"Matt, Matt, calm down. It was just a joke dude calm down."

"Are fucking kidding! You're talking bloodshed, people dead…"

"I'm just talking hypotheticals. I've never seen someone killed. Have you? I'm just, just—you know shit can happen—no change ever comes without some form of you know, violence."

"What if I don't want change?"

"I guess that's fine. Like I said, I don't think there's much that can be done. Just sit back and enjoy your life as best as possible."

"You bet your ass I will. Fuck this is a heavy talk dude."

"I'm just—look its food for thought…"

"That's some heavy food. Almost as heavy as this damn rice."

"Would you rather we talk about Min?"

He let out a grunt of laughter. "I don't fucking know. I'm just fucking…I need another beer. I'll probably forget this whole day tomorrow…"

"How about I send you some links to just get you thinking?"

"Fine. Whatever…"

I ordered him another beer. Then called him a taxi that we shared. By the time he got to his house he was just mumbling, "Fucking bitch Min. Fuck her. Telling me how to talk…"

Thankfully the alcohol smell dissipated with Matt gone, me alone in the taxi. I sent him a link to *The Greatest Story Never Told*, him replying with :thumb_up:. I then texted him "google USS Liberty" then "google lawrence franklin scandal" and finally "google the clean break memo" not realizing I may be a little tipsy too.

"What's important about a memo?"

"It got my cousin killed."

But you know that, don't you?

Do you know about the lingering tobacco odor in the taxi?

Made me think of Yu. Briefly.

Just like now I think of…

Kenji is coming.

*

Moving on to the **Prologue of the Prologue**
OR!

Prologue of the Prologue: Interlude

With days spent at school, days of smart-ass "hellos" from the students, with their annoying smug grins, days of sitting at my desk, one English lesson to assist with, spending my time surfing Kai10—the other teachers don't know what I'm reading and if they did, they wouldn't say anything—checking emails from my mom and friends back home, asking why I don't post to Facebook my stories anymore of life and reflection about Japan. One wanting to know my routine but not bothering to give me a like or a repost. Days of checking other accounts, Slack, DM Rooms, days of annoying autism from the others debating the state of the world and how to bring about "The Restoration" usually involving gassing of the Jews, killing the niggers and forcing women to submit to White Sharia or be faced with prospect of going in to a convent, how the military was unreliable because it was "full of cucks", but war itself "was fun", while decrying the death of beauty, even OingoBoinGoy tweeting, "We need beauty in this world. (((they)))) have taken it from us," yet having aesthetic appreciation about as deep as late-period (for body building) Arnold Schwarzenegger or rather his early-period (movie career) which reached its nadir in *Red Sonja* (1985. Directed by Richard Fleischer from a script by Clive Exton and George MacDonald Fraser and cinematography by Giuseppe

Rotunno)—meaning, all surfaces, no depth, interest only when the subject is at its height of youthful and genetic energy, and even then you just want to look, not examine, why someone would lift two hours a day, obsessing in the mirror over the deltoids, wondering if they are in proportion with pectorals, triceps and latissimus dorsi, knowing they will never be perfect, the body itself in a limited time window before it deteriorates, taking anabolic steroids to keep the ship running while risking muscle dysphoria, male pattern baldness, liver toxicity, erectile dysfunction, acne vulgaris and bitch tits while fucking the maid in hopes it'll keep the adolescent vigor alive, never curious that Giuseppe Rotunno was cinematographer for Fellini, De Sica, Argento and Visconti, and considering *Red Sonja* was just a forgettable commission along with *Popeye* and *Rent-a-Cop*. But that was all me reading Slack history:

OingoBoinGoy: Remember Red Sonja? Villain was a fag.
Andyschluss: Haven't seen much Arnold. Before my time.
OingoBoinGoy: Ur a fag.

Due to the time difference, most were in bed. Even autists have to sleep. My two-cents weren't needed nor wanted.

But you know that, don't you?

But did you know reading all of it, all the pipedreams and ideal societies conjured in their minds and frustrations with nothing to show for it made me think maybe we deserved gassing ourselves?

Do you know I thought about this while sitting in my cushioned rolling chair at school?

Do you know after school I went to bed immediately to nap, unable to sleep save the five minutes of shut-eye just before hearing the engine humming outside, the thump of rap music pulsing? Kenji and Yu, arriving early as always, waiting for me to come at the appointed time with me debating not even going to Karate tonight.

First time I would see Yu since fucking her.

First time really talking to her.

But I couldn't flake out. The van awaited.

Kenji is coming.

Afterall…

So, I step towards the waiting black Honda N-Box pulled over next to my apartment. The blackness of the vehicle sitting in the black evening…the consistently throbbing but masked bass of the black music…it all projects an ominous presence.

I open the rear door, the wave of bass hitting me with a rhythmic similarity that had me wondering if it was it Jay-Z or G-Eazy? Or maybe Migos? Didn't matter.

Yu dims the volume, gives me a "Hi Jason," with smile, me returning both while Kenji gives curt head nod then puts the van in drive as we drive through the night, the chatter light, almost non-existent, the music filling in the blanks of our silence.

I check Instagram and see Min post a pic of her and Matt, arms around each other with, with dog ears and snouts superimposed over their grinning mugs, text reading, "Sometimes you fight but sometimes you forgive. I'm glad I have a partner who knows when to apologize instead of remaining in an obstinate toxic male stubbornness. The waves of my anger and rage dissipate upon sight of it…" and I can't go on. Matt cucked out. Pussy.

At the Kurahashi Town Gym, I notice Yu standing with her arms crossed, head down, avoiding eye contact, yet still keeping her smile. :shrug:

Same during practice; pacing the wooden gym floor. During opening drills, she looks at me, makes eye contact and her smile widens before I turn to Kenji to see if he noticed and find him looking away, pacing the front class on his own, barking orders. Doubtful he could see me in the back.

INT. GYM-NIGHT

On BREAK Jason, drinks from his water bottle and APPROACHES Yu.

                    JASON

          I won't be able to make the
          lesson on Friday.

                    YU

          (surprised)

          Is something wrong?

JASON

No, I have to attend a conference.

YU

Where?

JASON

Hiroshima. Well, Hiroshima City.

YU

Shi-nai, deshou?

JASON

Yes, shi-nai.

YU

What do you talk?

JASON

Just bullshit. About how we're displaced and uncomfortable with our existence here because even though we may be citizens of the world, Japan can actually be socially alienating because we're acutely aware of the fact that we are in fact not citizens here at all. We're just guests.

133

                    YU

        I see

                  JASON

        You know, it kind of gives me
        an idea of what America was
        like before its immigration
        explosion that led to its
        eventual cultural implosion.

                    YU

        (confused)

        I...

Students SLOWLY return to the gym floor. Jason
NOTICES.

                  JASON

        Yeah, never mind. Let's just
        say   all   these   gaijin
        complaining about Japan don't
        know   what   they're   talking
        about. Japan is great the way
        it is.

                    YU

        I'm glad you like Japan.

                  KENJI (O.S.)

        Jay-son!

Kenji is coming.
Actually, I came to him (or is it "I went to him"? Fucking grammar).

He stood in a crowd of mostly low-level Yakuza toughs—no, no, no, it isn't the usual American of the civilized yet exotic menace of Asian organized crime.

It's not that type of story.

Instead Kenji watched us as I held pads for the thugs and they for me, though the one with a bad bleach job seemed annoyed holding for my strikes.

He then broke it up and told us to put on our gloves and shin pads, doing the motion with his hands when looking at me.

Sparring time.

Does it matter he wore his sparring gloves, which were kind of like white cloth MMA gloves with padding only around the knuckles?

OR!

That his were stained yellow with sweat?

OR!

Do I need to explain the rules of Kyokushin Karate where only punches to the face are prohibited, kicks to the head fine? Actually, it might matter.

Kenji slowly paired everyone off and left himself with me. "You, me, *faito* (fight), Jason."

"Hai."

"Not *hyaku* (100) *paacento* (%), okay? *Powaa* (*power*) down, *okay* (*okay*)?"

"Okay."

"*Ossu!*"

"*Ossu!*"

>Be Jason.

>Throw a punch.

>Watch Kenji just absorb it in his chest.

>Circle.

>Throw lead leg like a jab, being tentative.

>copyaufcfighter.jpg

>Watch Kenji charge.

>Try to block his four consecutive body shots.

>Miss the hook punch to your chest.

>Cover-up.

>Stand there like cuck looking guarded.

>cuck.jpg

"Jason FIGHT!"

He waved me to him.

I took the bait, charged in punching, throwing punch after punch, hands down, punch, punch, punch.

>Feel yourself go down.

>See flash of green take over your vision, red, yellow and brown stars everywhere.

>See Kenji stand above you.

>knockout.gif

Kenji is coming.

See why the words make my heart skip a beat?

But this time Kenji stood above me, a grin at the corner of his face, giving me a thumbs-up, "Jay-son, okay?"

I shook my head. "Okay."

Was it a receipt? Did he know? Did he know I fucked his wife? Or did he think was just being too chatty with her? :thinking_face:

INT. GYM—CONT

Jason leans against the WALL, catching his BREATH. Yu walks up to him. She puts a HAND on his shoulder.

YU (SPEAKING JAPANESE)

Are you okay?

JASON   (SPEAKING ENGLISH)

Yeah, I'm fine.

MOMNDF: Were you really fine?
JRK: What do you think?

*

I sat on the wooden bench in the locker room, trying to clear my headache, catch my breath and trying not to faint. Didn't want to look like a total pussy.

Blondie slapped me on the shoulder. "*Jay-son, taffu (tough)*," with his thumb up and a grin. "Good."

I noticed the covered tattoos on his forearm. He noticed me noticing. He asked how to say tattoo in English. I told him.

He then pointed at it. "This. This *dento*. How say *dento*?"

"Tradition."

He tried to say it, but the positioning of the consonants made it difficult. "Tra—de—shiifer," he said with rolling tongue trying to ape English pronunciation. "This tra-di-shonifer."

"Yes," I said.

His buddies then started to bust his balls in a thick a *Hiroshima-ben* bantz I couldn't understand.

I started changing.

*

Conversation in the van was minimal at first. The pulsing hip-hop volume down a little lower. Kenji's eyes glanced at me in the rearview. I smiled. He grinned.

Kenji is coming.

OR!

Taking me home in this case.

Jason, are you okay? She asked in Japanese

I'm fine.

Yu then turned to look at me, her face animated and full of concern. *Are you really okay?*

"Yeah I'm fine," I said in English, not clear-headed enough to speak Japanese.

I wasn't clear-headed enough either to understand Yu. "*KENJI!*" she shouted and kept on talking. Maybe it wasn't shouting but just bitching and ranting, non-stop, on and on, voice almost cracking, like she was about to cry, *Jayson-san* this, *Jayson*-san that, about the only thing I could understand.

Jayson-san...

Jayson-san...

Jayson-san...

Until Kenji yelled at her to shut up. Pretty sure that's what he said through the haze of headache and *Hiroshima-ben*. Pretty sure.

She stopped. But her voice continued to be faint as she said "*Mooou...*" looking out the window. Kenji mumbled something under his breath. Sounded angry.

I felt tenser in this moment than when I was sparring. I mean, the moment lacked the more cathartic and composed process of physical confrontation, but had in abundance unhinged and unsettling status signaling of verbal confrontation. At least if you get knocked out in a fight, you're respected by both yourself and your opponent for stepping up whereas losing an argument is a wasteland of disrespect from all parties.

YU (ENGLISH)

Are you really okay?

JASON

I'm fine.

YU

Okay...

She tries to FORCE a SMILE but resigns herself to a BOW.

Kenji says something (inaudible) STERN to her and she looks away.

I respected Kenji's masculinity to stop a hysterical woman from shrieking endlessly. But she was shrieking hysterically in my defense. :gritting_teeth:

Notmyfight.jpg

Does it matter that I rubbed my temple and squinted in pain, trying not to act like a bitch? Or that the pain didn't bother me that much and I was sure I'd be sore tomorrow morning and wake up with a pounding headache?

OR! That I thought about taking some Ibuprofen even though Justin Bangs said he didn't use it due to its reducing sperm count instead opting for turmeric as a substitute?

But I didn't have turmeric. I wasn't dead and I wasn't crippled either. Decided against Ibuprofen. Didn't want to reduce my swimmies.

If anything, I poked the bruised area a little just intensify the throbbing. It felt good.

*

138

Outside my home, out of the Honda N-Box but still close, the passenger's-side window slid down *"Ganbatte Jayson"* Kenji said leaving over.

"Ossu!" I replied.

Yu gave me a faint smile and I shivered with the cold wind.

MOMNDF: This obviously gave you second thoughts about sleeping with her again, right?

JRK: Pretty obvious, yeah?

*

It does matter that after my shower the iPhone, iPad, TV, laptop (yes, I have one), Super FamiCom, even my CD player (I have one of those too)—all electronics didn't work.

Yet I had power.

And my head throbbed.

It also matters that I decided to get some fresh air, feel the cool breeze against my wet hair (sans shampoo because Justin Bangs said it rids your hair of the natural and essential oils in order to support the hair care market complex). Does it matter that it felt weird not having a phone that worked, or anything to look at, alone in my thoughts, just feeling the brief gust while the throbbing pain subsided?

What about the figure in the distance?

Feminine outline, same frame but different clothing as Yu. But as soon as I noticed, it disappeared.

Kenji is coming.

Sooner rather than later.

*

Which is a great opportunity for segueing in to ***Prologue of the Prologue: The Conference***

At the port, off the boat on the bus headed for Hatchobori, I catch up on emails from the likes of Justin Bangs (game/politics), Scott Nash (politics), Liam Bronson (game), Pacino, (one name like Madonna but more masculine and Pajeet and talking about game and politics and whatever else on his mind—like how Hitler did nothing wrong…if only he listened to Pacino), game, game, game, politics, politics, politics! Content, content, content! The modern world was going to hell!

Modernity was a mistake.

But while the world burned, we could fiddle. In fact, that was the subject line of Justin Bangs first email "While the world burns, we can fiddle,"

139

featuring photos of him in a white designer suit, and black Salvatore Ferragamo shoes, a private jet behind him, at the bottom of the air stair, posing with a group of well-dressed sluts lined up on the steps from top to bottom, blonde, brunette and everything in between.

I immediately check Twitter and see that I got an RT from Scott Nash and I wonder if the tweet will make it to his sub-Reddit. I see likes from namefags in all directions and fringe ANON accounts like _UltimaThuleIsUltimate, the biggest honor of all.

But not as big as the update stating "_UltimaThuleIsUltimate has followed you."

I dived in to the Slack.

OingoBoinGoy: Look at you nigger, RT'd by Nash of all fucking people.

Andyschluss: Can we trust you now? Are you controlled op?

Me: No. LOL. Just a premium shit poaster.

Pure text, can't do justice to our Slack. I can't insert the emoji's placed below certain comments or show the gifs, screenshots and memes that are posted. :frown:

Andyschluss: Why the big head all of the sudden?

Me: Did you have _UltimaThule follow you today?

OingoBoinGoy: @here more importantly. Look who used our kikechan meme. Justin Bangs! Lifting shit from Kai10 as always! We got the proof boys!

Me: I thought we were using Shekel-sama

A DM from Oingo BoinGoy: You're welcome.

Me: Sheeit negro that was you?

OingoBoinGoy: Yep. I recommended that he follow you. Now you got to up your game muthafucka.

Me: >Accepts mission

But you know that, don't you? Did you know I read those I stepped off the bus at Tatemachi?

OR! That I ignored Adina's call of "Jason," and continued to type and walk towards the YMCA? "Jason!" again. "God, you and that phone."

"*Nani?*" I slipped the phone in my pants pocket.

"You look happy…"

I immediately felt and urge to pull out the phone again. :grimace: "What's so important?"

"Fine, ignore me and the world around you."

I noticed others walking to the YMCA, the sea of white, mostly white, faces looking so out of place. "But the world around us is so boring?"

"I'm boring, huh?"

"You said it, not me...*ne*?"

"You."

"Me."

She slapped my shoulder. Lucky I didn't slap her.

"Are you always on your phone? Is it Twitter? Instagram? I've seen you on Facebook..."

"It's Instagram..."

"So, are you always on Insta or just when you're around me?"

"Just around you."

"Figures."

"Well, I'm not privileged like you. I don't live in the city."

"Privilege. At least you get a hotel room. I have to go back to my place for the night."

"Oh the burden..."

She punched my shoulder. I pulled out my phone. "Back to the Social Media..." she said.

"Social Media is dead. Digital reality is the future."

"That so?"

"You heard it here first."

"I'll write it down."

"Make sure you do it on a pad of paper with pen."

"Why?"

"You might lose it when you upgrade your phone. Hard copy is better."

MOMNDF: Maybe I should write that down.

JRK: Maybe you should.

*

Cue *Walking Away* by Information Society.

>Shake hands, cursory greetings, "How's_____-shi/cho?"

>Listen to smattering of complaints about the respective town, school and students (one girl got in to fight with a student, another said that three or four students groped her).

>Give stock reply of "Oh really?"

>Go to opening ceremony in concert hall, led by Adina and Justin from the café, with all the introductions and bullshit.

>Tune out reading of "award-winning" essay, by "our very own" Kim Cheong talking about how her time with her Japanese host-mother and the tense undercurrent she felt as a Korean in the home of a past oppressor (OFC she starts talking about Comfort Women).

>Look over at Matt who looks over at you.

>:shrug:

>Notice Min (next to Matt) wiping tear from her eye.

>Regret not submitting your own essay on how the Comfort Women issue was a joke and the Japanese Army probably did those women a favor.

>propaganda.txt

>THINK Female emancipation was a mistake.

>Listen to Justin say "Wow, uuuuuum, what a great essay about tolerance, acceptance and forgiveness…"

>Listen to Adina say "Right, Justin. As a Jew, I know all too well about the history of hate and what it means to face hatefulness. Hopefully, we can all learn from Kim's bravery in facing a dark history…" and on and on about the refugee crisis and whatever else.

>Feel tempted to start goose-stepping and yell out the 14 words…

>But don't.

>caring what people think.

I care what you think.

Everyone just listened, nodded their heads and feigned sympathy and understanding.

Compliance.jpg

MOMNDF: I really wanted them to look like drones here. What's the word, Non-Playable Character?

JRK: NPC, yeah.

MOMNDF: Right, I wanted them to look like NPCs.

JRK: That's not hard to do.

*

Discussion panels.

Mandy and Adina discussed whether to attend the one given by the white—of course he was white—Canadian boomer who studied and served in a Zen Monastery. Supposedly he had good things to say about PureLight. According to Mandy the head of the sect, Ando-san, had his photo taken with the Dalai Lama...

There were also rudimentary workshops on offer like "Planning and elementary school lesson", "The Technology Gap", "Dos and Don'ts of Social Media" (I could certainly speak to the "don'ts"), "Independent Japanese Study", "Building Good Relationships with Teachers and Students", and "Surviving Japanese Cultural Fatigue" (because talking about the problem makes it better).

"Which one you going to Jason?"

"I don't know. Maybe the Zen one? I don't know."

"Min wants to go to the one about surviving Japan whatever it's called."

"You seem to be surviving Japan pretty well..."

"She's getting sick of it she said. It's been hard."

"Did she re-up her contract?"

"Yeah..."

"Then why—never mind. Women."

"Yeah."

Min walked up to Matt, face full of seriousness. Kim Cheong stood next to her, also with a scowl. It's almost like you could tell from their faces that Korean-American's pussies were as dry and vacant as the Sahara.

I made direct eye contact with Kim, let her know I'm not intimidated by her permanent scowl. I smirked my best Harrison Ford half-grin. She looked away, then down. Technique I learned from Justin Bangs. Shit works.

"Jason, are you coming?" Min asked.

"Sure."

Adina, with Mandy close behind ran up to Min. "Which one are you guys going to?"

"Surviving Japan or whatever it's called."

"Oh, Avi is curating that one—he hates the word 'leading' or 'teaching'. He's like a lawyer in his language. Actually, he might be studying to become an attorney after he leaves here or a college prof I'm not sure." Trotskyist professor or lawyer—either way Jewing everyone out of their money. :face_with_rolling_eyes:

"Y'all coming or what?"

Adina looked at Mandy then glanced over at me. "Sure. We were going to see the Zen guy speak but we realized it was the same Zen guy from the Spring conference in Kobe. Remember him? Jason, you remember right?"

143

"Yeah, I remember." Only thing I remembered was him discussing something about PureLight…but I wanted to hear more.

*

I'm tempted not to even to give any more detail. But it might help explain my state of mind later.

Maybe.

No promises.

But maybe it is a promise I have to make to myself.

Because I care what you think…

*

We sat in a circle of folding chairs, the thin brown laminate folding tables, pushed to the rear of the narrow white-walled room, the fluorescent lights beating down on the exposed blue carpet. Avi, trying not look like the leader by sitting in the circle even though we all encircled him. A couple of Japanese sat next to him, a pudge named Hiroshi wearing glasses—actually had a wannabe intellectual vibe about him by even trying to ape the Jew fro, looking like a dumpier and nerdier Papaya Suzuki—and a younger woman about our age, who most gaijin men would think was an 8 because they're happy she could speak in English but hovered around 5 or 6 because she actually bothered to wear make-up (inelegantly) and a faded mini-skirt sans stockings that wanted to inch up her short legs. I tried not to look but failed.

I sat next to Matt, who sat next to Min, who sat next to Kim Cheong, who sat next to Marcelle (an Oreo from Ohio who taught in Fukuyama trying to look like a young Kathleen Cleaver but failing) and sat next to Adina, who sat next to Avi, who sat next to the Japanese, who sat next to Mariane (a skinny Arab who taught in Sera-cho by way of Michigan with multicolored hair and nose rings), who sat next to Mandy, who sat next to Irish Justin, I think he taught in Hiroshima City proper (like Adina) who sat next to me and had me wondering if he used deodorant.

In short, a room full of so much POZZ I was worried I might contract AIDS just by being in there.

Cue *Phaedra* by Tangerine Dream.

Actually, don't. Doesn't make any sense here.

MOMNDF: You should leave the music cues to me.

JRK: It's my story.

MOMNDF: It's my movie.

144

JRK: Whatever.

Everyone else looked at their phones until reluctantly slipping them in purse or pocket as Avi started by talking about the various frustrations with living in Japan and how we could get through them by focusing on our purpose of building awareness and fostering an environment of inclusion to help Japanese kids have breakthrough insights which can increase creativity and protect against groupthink while hopefully they too can be authentic about their identity while recognizing the intersectionality of the different aspects of identity and reap the benefits of what diversity can provide. "But that has challenges," he concluded with a huge grin. Adina laughed and everyone followed. "What are some of the concerns you guys have?"

Mandy raised her hand. "I can't help sometimes, how I feel like...I don't know...like a zoo animal here."

"I know that all too well," Marcelle jumped in. "Because of my skin color, my melanin, I've had kids come up to me and rub my skin as they smiled," she then rubbed her hair through her aspirant fro, "Of course they've wanted to touch my hair too. One even gave me a banana for breakfast..."

Everyone gasped in shock. I tried not to laugh.

"Right, right, I get that...I think we all have felt something like that, right guys?" He looked around as everyone nodded their heads in agreement.

"Well, I definitely felt it. Literally," Mandy said. "I was at this elementary school and this boy, came up to me, and just grabbed my breast!" Everyone gasped again. Adina covered her mouth. But I thought who can blame the kid? Mandy was a decent C-cup.

"What did you do?" Adina asked.

"Yeah," she said. "I screamed. I couldn't believe it. I just screamed then grabbed a teacher then we went to the principal's—how do you say—Ko-ucho-sensei?"

"*Kohcho-sensei,*" I said.

"Right, thanks Jason. We went to the Ko-ko, well—we went to the principal's office..."

"Right, right," Avi said.

She then laughed at herself "The teacher had such a hard time translating I think. I was SO PISSED. So, pissed. They all knew it."

"What happened to the boy?" Min asked.

"Oh, they brought him in. He bowed and apologized. But I was still angry so I just yelled and screamed at him as my teacher tried to struggle and translate.

I then insisted that he not be anywhere near me. 'Get him out of here!' I screamed. They protested, talked about how difficult it was since his mother worked at the oyster farm but I wouldn't tolerate it. I said he needs to leave for what he's done. I insisted. They all looked so confused. But I just kept screaming."

"Wow," Kim Cheong said.

Min shifted in her seat. "So…what happened?"

"His mom eventually came and took him home. She was screaming the whole time at him too. I was glad to see it. He deserved it. Literally the worst. He'll know not to do it again. Since then the boy avoids me like the plague and are always polite to me. But he rarely talks. I saw him getting punch by a couple of other boys in the class. I didn't do a thing to stop. Little shit deserved it," she giggled. The others laughed too. She shrugged her shoulders. "Sometimes you gotta do what you gotta do, right?"

"Yeah," Mariane said.

"We have to assert our rights and power. No one is going to give it to us," Marcelle said.

A faint "Right, right…" from Avi…

Giving women any voice or say-so was a mistake.

"Right, right, see that brings up a great point," Avi said. "When you feel your boundaries are violated, you need to let them know what the boundaries are. They may not know. They see the world one way, but we see ours much different."

"That's so true!" Mariane almost jumped out of her seat. "When I told a teacher that I am Lebanese, they immediately assumed I'm Muslim and started asking me about Al-Qaeda, though that's a Sunni group and my family is Shia. And then at an enkai they asked me more than once if it was okay that I drink alcohol or eat pork and I insisted to the point—I tried not to scream—that I am my own woman and I am not bound to religious restrictions, but they couldn't understand. It pissed me off. I just grabbed a mug of beer and chugged it. But I didn't eat the pork. I'm Vegan."

Everyone chuckled again.

"Right, right, but Mariane brings up a good point and an interesting contradiction—how can we teach the Japanese about the nuances of different cultures and let them know the nuances and triggers…"

"Well, I think they meant well…" Matt said.

"No! No! That doesn't mean anything," Marcelle said. "They need to learn how to uncouple the intent of what they're saying with the impact it has on others."

"That's hard to do."

"Yeah, yeah, well that's one of the challenges, isn't it Matt?" Avi said. "The Japanese aren't as progressive as we are in a certain sense. But that's the purpose of why we're here. We're here to expose them to the wider world. We're promoting our values just as much as they're promoting theirs."

(((our values)))

"That's right. It appears many have lived a sheltered life. Japan is still an island, right?" Adina said.

"Right, right," Avi said.

"So they don't necessarily have the freedom of travel and thought like we do. It being a homogenous society doesn't help either…"

"Right, right, so it's our, um, like our job to help change that. To wedge, maybe even force is a better term, our way in. We may lament the racial and gender struggles in the US and fight for justice there but this place and our day to lives has plenty of fertile ground that needs fixing."

Adina shook her head looking at Avi.

"I know all about activism. I knew that I wanted to be an activist since I was 14. I read about feminism and civil rights and started my own Twitter account," Marcelle said.

"Oh did your parents…"

"They were pretty liberal. My dad is a college professor."

"Really?" Mariane jumped in. "Mine are too."

"Oh really, where?"

"University of Michigan."

"Oh mine are at Ohio State."

"Cool, cool, so they were open to your journey? Mine weren't crazy about it."

"They encouraged me. They understood the multiple dimensions of liberation and how it's part of the black experience."

"Same, they told me how the Arab struggle is linked to a class struggle and they could also be linked to a gender struggle."

"Right, right…"

"Is it true that women leave the workforce once they get married?" Mandy asked.

147

"For Muslims?"

"No, no, sorry, I mean for Japanese."

Everyone looked around at each other.

"That sounds about right," Kim Cheong said.

"Right, right," Avi said then turned to his aspirant Jap doppelganger and asked him. "Let's ask our resident experts here. Hiroshi is that true?"

Hiroshi thought about it for a second then said, "Yes, it is true but it is change. Slowly."

"Slowly."

"That is awful," Mandy said. "Absolutely awful."

"Haven't these women seen *Girls*? Or at the very least *Sex in the City*? I think my mom watched that one," Kim Cheong said.

"I love both of them," Min said.

"Me. Too," Adina said.

"They're great. Just great," Avi said.

"Uuuum, smart shows," Justin said.

"I had a cousin who worked on that one," Adina said.

"Oh really?" Avi asked shocked. "My older brother was an assistant to one of the lead writers!"

"Get out!"

"Who hasn't seen them?" Mariane asked. Matt and I raised our hands. "Men..." the room laughed.

I noticed Matt glancing at me. He frowned a little.

Mandy then looked at the Japanese girl and asked her "Do you plan to stay at home when you're married?"

The girl didn't understand the question. Hiroshi the Jew then translated for her. She gave an uneasy smile then shifted in her chair, tilted her head and thought of an answer. "I stay home. With kids," she said.

Silence in the room.

Mandy covered her mouth.

"Have you seen *Girls*?" she asked.

The girl looked confused. "Girls? I see lots of Girls..."

"No, the show?" Mandy said annoyed. "They don't have HBO here?"

"No," I said. "They have WOWWOW, which is kind of like it but not really..."

"Well, you have to watch it..." Mandy said.

"O-okay," the girl said timidly bowing her head with a smile.

148

"See these are the attitudes the patriarchy have instilled here," Mariane said. "All this macho bullshit."

"Not good, not good," Avi said.

"Men are always the problem," Mandy said giggling.

"We are?" I asked.

"Well—not all men. We have allies," Adina said. She looked at me then Matt (who shook his head).

"Right, right."

"Men can be a part of the problem. They are the ones who are the aggressors in society. Especially the white men." Marcelle said.

"The Cis-straight Christian white male," Mariane said. She looked around. "Not sure if we have that combo in here…"

"Progress, progress," Avi said.

"Well, I'd like to think I'm Christian…" Matt said.

"What exactly are men good for?" Mandy said laughing. "Besides lifting things?"

The girls laughed.

"Uuuuum, you'll have robots for that soon enough for that," Justin said.

"Oh well…I suppose there's one other reason." All the girls laughed. Adina looked at me, Matt let out a laugh. Hiroshi quickly tried to translate to his female compatriot.

"Uuuum, they have robots for everything…"

The room laughed again.

Min put her hand on Matt's shoulder. "Guess I won't be needing you then…"

"Hey now!" Laughter again. "Well…" Matt shrugged his shoulders. "That's the beauty of the free market. It can smash the patriarchy through the invisible hand I guess."

"It's not just about the patriarchy," Adina said.

"Yeah, it's like about equal rights," Mandy said.

"Right, right…I'm not afraid of the future being female," Avi said.

"No, no, no—it's not about such binary options. That's just an enforcement of the white-male colonialization of discourse."

"That-that's uuuum true," Justin said sitting up. "Science has been dominated so long by masculine forces that that they've fit everything in to a dual pattern that—uuuum, a single X-chromosome means 'male' and two X's mean 'female'. But just because a person only has a single X doesn't mean,

149

uuuum, they're any less female. Someone with an XY can have binary-female genitalia and XX's with binary-male…"

"I'm having trouble keeping up with the X's and the chromosomes," Min giggled.

"There may be an App for that," Avi said.

"Are you talking about trans people?" Mandy asked.

"See that's the problem, this classification. Male, Female, gay, straight, trans/cis. It's trying to fit people in to little boxes…"

"Right, right, we don't want to do that," Avi said.

"Uuuum, we need to decolonize our minds as well, you know?"

"Right, right."

"When I was at Subway near Hondori…" Marcelle said, "I saw that the women's room was occupied, so I went in to the men's room. The men just stared at me. I was ready for a fight. Because this is a battle that is fought and won on the streets every day."

"Right, right…everyday…"

"Uuuum, that's quite bold…"

"You go girl," Mariane said.

"Right, my ability—I've chosen that I am a woman but it's my choice and what bathroom I use is my choice. That is my empowerment as a black woman."

"Right, right…"

"That's so courageous," Mandy said. "I almost want to clap."

"Thank you but I don't need your applause."

"I just I just wish I could be black."

"Well, that's…"

"That's cultural appropriation," Mariane said.

"Uuuuum but we just talked about chromosomes for gender discrimination…"

"There are some things we just can't choose," Marcelle said. "I didn't choose the black experience. It chose me. Just like Mariane didn't choose to be born in to Arab culture."

"More like Lebanese, which is kind of different than Arab."

"I apologize."

"I see, quite right."

"Right, right…good dialogue here guys. See how we are learning?"

"Well that is the beauty of a place like Japan. For too long, the West has not just been dominated by the Cis-straight White Christian Male culture, it too has dominated. That is the one thing I like about Japan. Even as a secular Muslim it does not feel as threatening," Mariane said.

"I have no problem with Islam," Marcelle said. "It has helped with black liberation."

"Yes, it is a rallying cry for many of the oppressed," Mariane said looking at Matt.

Adina rocked back in her seat almost sitting on her hands.

"I don't have a problem with Islam. You know Muhammed was a merchant...that makes him like the only religious prophet to come from a business background," Matt said.

"Uuuum, never quite looked at it that way before."

"Look at you with the insights," Min said patting him on the lap.

I rolled my eyes.

Kim Cheong then jumped in. "See—we say we like Japan and how open it appears to religion and other things but it does have a dark side in terms its own colonial past and racial oppression..."

"Japan had colonies?" Marcelle asked.

"Korea, Taiwan, Manchuria and some concessions in China," I said. "At least before the war. You know, um, World War II?"

"That's because uuuum, they were trying to copy the British Imperial model that was de rigeur for a superpower back then."

"Wow. Cultural appropriation at the colonial level," Mariane said.

"I uuuum, I suppose you could say that, yes."

"Lebanon was under French control, you know?" Mariane let the comment hang, then said, "So as an Englishman, you would know this first hand?"

"Well, uuuum, I grew up in Belfast. I'm from a Catholic family. But that's one reason I got away from there, to come here, I suppose. I've seen what the forces of religious hatred can do. Things have calmed down now, maybe because of diversity and immigration..."

"I know, I know," Mandy said. "I remember when I went to Dubrovnik in Croatia. Ugh, I just felt uncomfortable by all the white people there. It was like a sea of white."

"Uuuum, right, yes, and both sides of Ireland can't become diverse quickly enough. The Troubles can always spark again. I see that in the Middle East."

"Wait-wait! The Arab struggle is one of fighting oppressors. It isn't necessarily religious based or even in so-called hatred."

151

"Uuuum, neither necessarily were The Troubles. We felt a kinship with the Palestinians…"

"Guys, guys," Avi said hands up. "I think, um, I think Kim was trying to make a point."

"Sorry," Justin said.

"No, no, it's okay. I was just trying to say that Japan has its own uncomfortable history. One that it really hasn't come to grips with. Especially with its treatment of Korean women during the war and Koreans in the factories."

"Or their treatment of the refugee's now," Mandy interjected.

"Their handling of the refugee's is certainly worrisome."

"Me and Matt, were thinking of visiting _____ to see if we could help the refugee's at the source. Matt, you said something about some groups that we could go with to help—we were going to go around Christmas…" Min looked at Matt for confirmation.

He just bobbed his head up and down, "Yep, uh huh, that's right…"

"I heard PureLight is trying to help but no one…"

"Yes, PureLight has had a more progressive attitude I heard," Justin said.

"I wish we could have a religious leader like that—I think his name is Ann-do? Wish he would come to the states."

"Uuuuum, probably will sometime."

Adina then jumped in: "Japan really needs to modernize their immigration and just become more comfortable…"

"Right, right and that's what we're here to do Adina…"

"I know."

He looked at Kim. "I'm sorry Kim did you have something else to say?"

"No, no, it's just sometimes, even as a Korean now, I wonder if they still look at us as sub-human…"

"I know right! It's like I can't stand it that everyone thinks I'm Japanese and immediately they start speaking to me in Japanese."

"Ugh, literally the worst!" Kim said. "We're not Japanese but they expect us to speak it."

I couldn't help myself: "So…there's not really a way around that. They're going to assume your Japanese, right?"

"Why?" Min asked.

"Because we all look the same?"

"No—well, they can't tell the difference between, um, you know, an American or German or a Swede. So, um, they might assume…"

"It's different with Asians, Jason," Min said.

"I mean, I'm half-Jewish yet I get classified as white on every paper I sign and it's just assumed…"

"You're a P.A.W. *You Pass As White*," Marcelle said.

"Look I'm, uh, I'm just stating Japanese behavior as is. Um, like what do you want? Maybe a marker of some sort signifying you aren't Japanese?" I glanced at Adina.

Min jumped in to say, "I don't know—"

"Jason is right," Adina said. "We could descend in to hate and Nazism real fast taking that road."

"Right, right," Avi said. "We have to be constructive but at the same time we don't want to lower ourselves in to fascist practices. My Bubbie—sorry, Jewish habit—my GRANDMOTHER…" Adina laughed. Self-deprecation, another Jewish habit. "My great grandmother survived the Holocaust. She wore the Star. I don't think that's a solution…"

His Queens rat voice made me lament the failure of the Final Solution…

"Uuuum, yes, I had cousins who lived in Apartheid South Africa, it was terrible…"

Mariane then partially stood up: "You're quick to point out the practices of the Nazis and Apartheid. Let's talk about the current Apartheid that is going on in Israel. They've become Nazis in their own right in the treatment of the Palestinians and neighboring Arab count—"

Avi raised his hand, "Look, this isn't really the place—"

"Mariane brings up a point: Israel is now the white oppressor in the Middle East."

"Wait, wait—we're not white. We're Jewish. We were targeted for extermination in Europe. Israel is our ancestral homeland," Adina said.

"And to obtain that homeland, Israel has become the colonizer, even saying it must be quote-unquote 'Jewish state' meaning the minorities are second class citizens…" Marcelle said.

Adina leaned out with her hands pleading: "That's not…"

"I've been to the refugee camps in Lebanon. They're horrible, the suffering, oh my god…"

"There's refugee camps for Palestinian's?" Mandy asked.

"Oh yeah. My parents have been to the ones in Jordan. But some are refugees in their own homes in Gaza and the West Bank…"

"Oh…I-I didn't…"

"Right, right, but that's not—American Jews don't necessarily agree with Israeli policies."

"Well, are you Jewish or are you not?"

"I am Jewish, but I don't necessarily—look, I've never lived in Israel," Avi said. "And me—I don't like their behavior in the Occupied Territories."

"See look at the language you just used. 'Occupied Territories'. You've admitted it's a land under occupation."

"That's right!" Mariane said.

"And you say you're an American but American Jews have tried to undermine Black Lives Matter on campuses due to their support of the Palestinians…"

Adina almost stood up: "Wait—I've been to Israel. I have family there. It's an inclusive place. Arabs have equal rights there—rights they don't have in other Middle Eastern countries…"

"If they have the privilege of being born in majority Jewish territory. Gaza or the West Bank is no different than Auschwitz…"

"We're not Nazis—how can you—"

"The evidence is in the behavior," Mariane said.

I noticed Adina look to Avi for help but he just looked around dejected.

"Bringing up Nazis is rich," I said.

Mariane abruptly turned to me. "What? You can't deny that Israel is acting like the Nazis…"

"Who supported the Nazis? Who served in their armies?"

"What—what is this?"

"The Palestinians did."

"Uuuuum, that was a different time."

"A different time? Because the British occupied Palestine? Because the Prince of Wales was a Nazi sympathizer?"

"Well, uuuum we changed…you know Churchill…"

"That doesn't account for Israel's behavior towards the Arab world. We have terrorism and organizations like the Muslim Brotherhood because of Israel…"

"You have the Muslim Brotherhood because of the Nazis."

"What?"

"The Muslim Brotherhood was started by the Nazis to subvert British rule in Egypt."

"I'm not from Egypt!"

"I know, I know, but, but, I know my history and sometimes we need to be reminded of..."

"You can't just use history to justify injustice towards Arabs..."

"The Israeli policies are racist, that's what they are?"

I put my hand up. "Wait..."

"Let him speak guys," Adina said.

"If you don't like history and you don't like racism, should we talk about Arab racism...you know that exists right now?"

"What you..." Mariane looked confused.

"Yeah, what..." Marcelle leaned forward.

"I don't know, the, um, the slave markets in Libya? The treatment of blacks in the Sudan...or just the history of the Arab slave trade in general..."

"I don't know..." Marcelle pulled out her phone and started typing.

Mariane looked at Marcelle typing on her phone then at me, while Adina smiled, "This is a distraction..."

"I'm just, I'm just saying..."

"Right, right, guys..."

"Uuuuum, can I say something?" Justin asked hand raised. The room went quiet. "Uuuum, this may all seem important and immediate but look at the world. We could all be dead in a nuclear holocaust tomorrow. And if that doesn't get us, look at all the horrors of climate change. That could—no I'm sure it will do us in as well. I came here because I realized there was no point in raising children in a world like that. So I'm just traveling the world, trying to enjoy it before it all passes. I'm afraid it will. I wonder if these types of arguments may just push us along and make it more eminent."

"Or maybe the racists and hateful people need to be put in prison or maybe even executed—like they do to blacks—because they're refusing to be loving and inclusive..."

"Right, right, thanks Justin, and um, and Marcelle. And on that optimistic note," Avi paused. The room stayed silent. "We, um, we should probably take a break."

As we walked out the room, Marcelle shrugged her shoulders as she said, "Article on *The Huffington Post* about Arab racism..."

Mariane ran up to her, "Look, that has nothing to do with Lebanon or Palestine…we don't—I'm not a racist…"

"Oh, oh, I know you're not, I know you're not…" they then looked at me.

Matt then leaned in to me and whispered in my ear. "Maybe you were right the other night."

I half-smirked as Min gave us both the evil-eye. He turned towards her to exit with her and Kim Cheong, who glanced my way and I matched her stare.

Mandy approached both Mariane and Marcelle, the words "Palestine" and "refugees" being thrown around a lot. Justin went to go join in, probably because he was attracted to Mandy but had no way of sealing the deal.

"Since when were you a defender of Israel?"

I looked at Adina, who kept looking back at the room—actually I was probably looking around too. "Since it became a social justice rallying cry for the shrill," (translation: I could give two-shits about the plight of shitskin's) she smiled when she turned back to me. "And I like to put my nerd knowledge of the Nazis to use whenever I can."

"At least your nerd knowledge is good for something, even when it's the Nazis…"

"Implying they never did any good…"

She punched my arm. "Thanks for…" she bobbed her head back towards the room.

"Maxwell, wasn't here to help you so…" I shrugged my shoulders.

Her grin lingered as she walked back to talk to Avi.

I texted Yu. Waited for a reply. Didn't get one.

But you know that, don't you?

*

I returned to my room, the generic white wall-papered walls, the white sheeted bed, tucked so tight one needed almost Herculean strength in which to free them. Made me long for a *washitsu* even though the traditional interior was just as plain as the modern albeit with sliding doors and tatami mats but at least there was a connection to something past, instead of an empty present where the mounted idol of the plain silver Hitachi flatscreen becomes centerpiece.

I channel surfed. Old habit that felt more curiosity than servile. I mean, TV was no longer our master and we are no longer prisoner to the programming director's decisions. Stopping on NHK's news hour, listening to a moment of their stilted English translators about the American NBA (National Basketball

Association) suing the NBA (Nihon Bus Association)…they no longer had a monopoly. They couldn't control how I saw Japan or the world.

But you know that, don't you?

And I can't speak for the Japanese.

I found *Tenebrae* (1982. Directed by Dario Argento from a script by Argento and cinematography by Luciano Tovoli) on WOWWOW. Google the word "Tenebrae" and find it's Italian for "darkness". I'm glad they kept the original Romanic title (according to Google, it was released as *Unsane* in the Anglosphere).

The Japanese like Italian shit, more than they like German shit. Italy was the number one export market for anime, pro-wrestling and other pop culture before the US market really opened up. Axis alliances die hard.

But you know that, don't you?

But do you know that *Tenebrae* may be Dario Argento's masterpiece, so it should be appreciated everywhere? But of course, it's only appreciated in countries that have a sense of cultural heritage, therefore aesthetics, like Japan.

The story of life imitating art, a horror writer who discovers someone is copying the murders from his novels, who then proceeds to become and embrace the identity of the murderer himself—really what is there to say? The thriller isn't told through meta-bullshit, but through a roaming Steadicam of death and murder, with the pulsating prog rock score by Goblin giving a sense of life and verve that Stanley Kubrick could never attain with *The Shining* released the same year. Kubrick's camera was always detached and observing, with a lifeless score by tranny synth pioneer Wendy Carlos. Just like a secular Jew alienated from society and running away to another (in Kubrick's case, New York to England or in Jack Torrance's case, a hotel in the Colorado mountains). Argento's was close-up, in the shit, the blood a form of cleansing catharsis. Just like a Catholic.

The scene when the dykes are murdered, the camera slowly traveling up the walls of the building, stalking its victims like the killer himself, gave me wood. Or maybe it was just the curvy naked Latin actress with her huge tits. Hard to tell.

MOMNDF: Why do they have to be mutually exclusive?
JRK: They don't have to be I suppose.

I thought of Yu.

I dial her number.

"*Moshi mosh.*"

"Yu-chan?"

A *"Konbanwa,"* of delight.

We talk briefly. About what, I forget. Just small talk. You might have the chat logs. I glance at the silver idol but mainly just stare at the white sheets as I talk. She laughs anytime I say something. I smile inside and feel it rising. "I love you," I say. Something that comes up in a moment of emotional ecstasy, that one regrets probably later in retrospect. But I said it.

"Arigato," she says.

"Arigato dake?"

A pause.

I hear the phone muffle.

In English: "Kenji is coming."

No. It isn't that time, yet. It isn't inciting incident "Kenji is coming".

It's just her saying I can't talk right now. It needs to end there. We say our goodbyes. The line goes dead. People die onscreen.

But you know that, don't you?

Did you know you about the knock on my door immediately after or the screen flickering as I put the phone down?

MOMNDF: Did you intend the next part to be kind of surprising? Wait, wait—I know the answer.

JRK: I'm sure you know.

*

Adina casually walked in and asked, "What are you watching?"

"A horror flick."

"Which one?"

"Tenebrae. It's Italian."

She looked at the head of the bed; lightly ran her fingers across it. "Never heard of it."

"No surprise."

"You like horror movies?"

"I just like movies."

"But you seem to like horror."

"So?"

"Just saying. I've always been curious as to why people like seeing other people murdered on screen, in the sickest way possible. Especially women…"

"Horror confirms our sense of dread."

"Dread of what?"

"That fact that nothing lies beyond."

"I didn't know you're an atheist."

"I didn't say I am."

"Then what are you?"

"I'm…I don't know. I just know that we've been, you know…put in to the world, maybe willed, maybe by chance, and we try to make the best of it while we're here. Mostly we just endure it. Then we die and return back to…who knows? Death is the climaxing act, what we strive and are destined for."

"That's uplifting."

"Never been accused of being uplifting."

"Is something else up?" She put her hand on my crotch. "No one ever accused you of having a small cock either." She wrapped her hand around the erectness.

I pushed down on her shoulders. "What are you doing?"

"Suck it," I said. I began unzipping my pants.

"Eww…no."

"You don't want a Nazi cock in your mouth?"

"No it's just…"

"Not with the mouth you kiss Maxwell with?"

Then *TIIIING*. And another *TIIIING*.

Adina backed up and pulled her phone out of her back pocket.

I continued to unzip my pants. Yes, Adina and I were fucking. No foreshadowing required. Because, you know all this, don't you?

She put her phone on the counter. "Mandy. What am I going to do with her?" "How about nothing?"

She started taking off her tight pants. "No I can't just…she was talking about walking over to the Viking place for our dinner…she…" she struggled with pants leg, remaining on her right…

I grabbed her shoulders. "Here," I said. "Sit."

She sat and I pulled off her pants.

"She was talking about walking over there with Mariane and Marcelle but she didn't know directions because she doesn't read Japanese…" I pulled off her plain white panties, her slightly wild bonsai-like bush appeared.

"What's wrong with going there with them? We're all going to be there eventually…"

"Because…Mariane and Marcelle? Hello?" She spread her legs. Waited. Then sat on her elbows.

159

"What?"

"What are you asking what about?"

"Mariane and Marcelle?"

"Aren't you going to put it in?"

"Your shirt…"

"Oh god, you just have to see them…"

:shrug: Her Khazar milkers were her best feature. Why hide the positives? "I think both Marian and Marcelle were in Students for Justice in Palestine. I asked…" She struggled to pull her tight cotton shirt off. I yanked it off. "Thanks."

She began unhooking her bra. "I emailed a friend about them, because of the time zone I'm waiting to hear back but I suspect…" She slipped off her bra and the big milkies appeared in all their glory. "I think I'm right."

"Who are these contacts?"

"The Israel—"

Tiiing! Tiiing! Tiiing!

"Wait…" she hopped off the bed and pulled up her phone. She leaned to one side, her pudgy nakedness of slightly unkempt bush and big tits made me more erect. I laid down on the bed.

MOMNDF: Wait—why were you guys doing all this again?

JRK: Doing what? Talking about her possible Mossad contacts?

MOMNDF: No, you know…fucking?

JRL: Well…I thought I explained it…

MOMNDF: "Milkers" as you call them—

JRK: Khazar Milkers.

MOMNDF: Big tits aren't just the reason to have a casual sexual relationship with a girl whose race—well, fuck you pretty much hate.

JRK: Well…

MOMNDF: And Yu…

JRK: We were doing it before Yu and I ever—

MOMNDF: And you couldn't commit?

JRK: She had a fiancé or boyfriend and like you said I'm—was or you know I wasn't philo-Semitic by any stretch…but I didn't hate HER as an individual…though she could be annoying at times…

MOMNDF: So…

JRK: I can't explain.

MOMNDF: Still?

JRK: Save for...ahem...that we can't explain ourselves. We're fickle. Certain only in uncertainty. It's like that Bible verse about how the spirit—like we don't know where it goes?

MOMNDF: Or you just thought with your dick.

JRK: I'd hate to reduce it to that.

"Mandy...now...she's just sending me selfies asking which is best for Instagram."

"Put your phone on vibrate—wait anything good?"

She looked at my standing cock. "I don't think you need any more visual stimulation."

"I was thinking more about you."

"Awwww...you're such a sweetie for a Nazi." She put her phone down. "But you made me wet already."

"Oh really?"

"Yes, when you jumped to my defense against those two bitches." She hopped on the bed, mounted my cock very wet. I grabbed her tits and started playing with her erect nipples.

Tenebrae, I couldn't pause. A little annoying. But it added to the ambience as Goblin's main anthem for the film played, *"Paura! Paura! Paura! Paura!"* (Fear! Fear! Fear! Fear!) through a distorted vocoder and synth beats. I matched my thrusting to the rhythm.

Adina liked it.

That, I'm sure, you don't know.

MOMNDF: It did provide for a could visual moment synching action with sound.

JRK: "Cue *Tenebrae* theme". It's why I wrote in the script.

MOMNDF: Glad I told the script doctor to keep it.

*

TIIIING! TIIIING! TIIIING! TIIIING!

Upon hearing SMS tones, Adina was immediately off the bed. I looked at the dimples on her ass as she turned her back to me, but more from curiosity due to dissipated desire.

"More Instagram?"

"Yeah...she...by the way, I found your Instagram with no help from you."

161

"Which—oh yeah?"

"Yeah, the one will all the posts about the old anime stuff."

She turned to me as she buttoned her pants and started to put her bra on. "It's...interesting..." She struggled with the flesh footballs in her cloth cups and snapping the back hooks. I went to help her. "Thanks. You're, um, you're actually a good writer..."

"Interesting? You didn't think I had in me?"

"No, it's just..." she wrestled with her shirt. "Most blog and Instagram posting is just so...banal."

"That's a word for it. You thought me banal?"

She was done with her shirt and hopped back on the bed, laying on her elbows. "No. I don't think you banal."

I went next to her. We kissed.

MOMNDF: See why...

JRK: I just felt it in the moment.

MOMNDF: Surprising...

JRK: Look, I'm not a philosopher. I'm not here to tell you or explain all my actions and behavior. Eros is a spirit that attaches itself to other spirits like affection. I mean, there's a pool of emotions and desire getting all mixed up that I can't even begin to understand, so maybe I should be careful...

MOMNDF: Are you saying—wait, do we have another mistake? Is Jason Reudelheuber-Katz saying booty calls are a mistake?

JRK: No—not necessarily. I mean, we hardly have connection with people, so, um, sex can help us connect to connection. But at the same time, you know, we're not um, we're not pure flesh computers of code just taking in pleasure inputs, though, um, some I think would like to think us that way.

MOMNDF: Well, haven't you said something similar earlier about genetics? What are you saying exactly?

JRK: I don't know.

"You don't think I need more pictures of Japanese chicks?"

"Huh?"

"Never mind."

She snuggled next to my body. I put my arm around her. She rested her head on my chest. Part of her frizzy hair, a loose strand here and there, started to irritate my face.

"I was thinking of writing a novel," she said. "I have an aunt that works in publishing. She's the head of acquisitions."

"Convenient."

"It's about who you know right?"

"Right…"

"I'll send you a signed copy when its published."

"What's it about?"

"It's not horror."

"No surprise there." *Tenebrae* was over. I missed the great reveal of Anthony Franciosa as the killer (Spoiler alert). I turned off the TV.

"It's about a girl who moves to the big city and you know, she has this gay roommate who teaches her all she needs to know about love, life and maybe even fashion—not sure if that needs to be in there—and then she meets that charming, self-effacing kind of geeky guy, who likes reading comic books and wears thick glasses and they fall in love but then he gets a job offer that would separate them and she has to make that hard decision…"

"I got Lasik remember?"

"Who said it was you?"

"Well, I read comics…kind of…I'm more interested in the aesthetics of comics…"

"Jason…" She got off the bed and started looking at herself in the mirror straightening her hair and clothes. "It isn't about you."

"Maybe it is."

She turned around. "What? No, the story is about the girl, I haven't thought of a name yet. What do you think of Abigail? Too Northeastern WASP? I don't want her to be too Jewish either."

"Is her boyfriend black? A black nerd who reads comics? Maybe he's Republican."

"Hell no. I wouldn't—I mean I'm not saying it is bad, but I'm just when I picture him, I'm not…"

"You're a racist Adina. I can't believe it."

"The guy can't be you. I want him to be less of an asshole."

"Well, your story is about you. My story is about me."

She sat and lay down on the bed again. She started rubbing her hand on my chest before pulling away quickly. "You…getting intellectual again…you're definitely not banal…"

"No, no I was just being—look—wouldn't you say that your story is about the girl. But Adina's story about Adina?"

She sighed.

"You're saying it isn't about me. But really it is. We exist—I exist—for the sake of ourselves—for myself. We're being unto ourselves…"

"For the purpose of what?" she scooted towards me.

"For, for…I dunno…I guess to get back to our true essence. To part the clouds or sea…and get to the bottom of our true selves…"

"And then?"

"Then…death…"

"So that's it? Live, breath, have sex, then die?"

"Sure…but…I, um, you know, you also search to um, complete, to explore and discover true nature that's been clouded by all of modernity and structures, you know? You just keep looking to get closer to it."

"Then you die?"

"Yes. Death is the completion."

"Did you—were you at the Zen class today? Is that where you heard this? Did Mandy give you that PureLight brochure?"

"No. Just been thinking."

She kissed me. "You need to lighten up. I would say get laid but we've taken care of that part…but maybe that's why we just do this huh? We have things to tend to ourselves I guess. Instead of going further…"

"You have a good Jewish boy waiting for you."

"I never said half isn't good enough."

"Tell that to the Samaritans."

"Huh?"

"Never mind."

"Right. Never mind. Forget I said anything."

I thought about reaching out to her, putting my arm on her shoulder but decided against. "Forget about what?"

"Exactly." *TIIIING! TIIIING! TIIIING! TIIIING!* She pulled phone out of her pocket.

"Mandy again?"

She looked at her phone again. "No..." her stare went from casual to intense as she fingered across the screen. "It's my—a friend from college who works with—well, anyway, he—I knew it!"

"What?"

"Both Mariane and Marcelle worked with SJP I should have known...speaking of Samaritans and racism..."

"What is SJP again?"

"Students for Justice in Palestine."

"But we're not in college and..."

"And Mandy is talking about walking to the restaurant with them!"

"I'm lost..."

She sat up. Got off the bed. Started pacing the room.

"Don't you get it?"

"Somehow talking to Mandy will affect the Israeli-Arab conflict?"

"It might."

I sat up.

"Huh?"

"Mandy's brother...he works for the Council on Foreign Relations. If those two get to her, subvert her, she could influence her brother, who advises on American foreign policy and it could result in BDS gaining some traction or at least change the relationship between America and Israel..."

"So, you, we need to subvert them from subverting America giving aid and support to Israel?"

"Yes! Exactly!"

I walked up behind her. Embraced her from behind. I tightened my hold. "Now, who needs to lighten up?"

MOMNDF: There you go again...

JRK: I...I got...maybe I am a cuck.

She turned to look at me and wrapped her arms around my neck. We kissed.

"I get it. You don't care about Israel."

"Why should I?"

"Because they're your people and homeland."

"My homeland is America. My dad is of German descent from Seattle, you know, um, like Washington? My mom is..."

"Your mom is a Jew."

"A Jew from Oceanside. Not Tel Aviv. She met my dad when he was in the Navy."

165

"I don't need your family history."

"Obviously you do since you think my loyalty lies with a country in the near east, whose founding rests on…"

"On what?"

"Never mind."

TIIIING! TIIIING! TIIIING! TIIIING!

Adina pulled her phone out again. "She's in the lobby. We need to get to her before…"

"We need…"

"Please, Jason. Please!"

"Fine. Let me put my pants on."

"Hurry! Hurry!"

I put my pants on and ran out the door with Adina as she looked at her phone. "God, she's giving me selfies of herself in the lobby, now."

But you know that, don't you?

MOMNDF: I'm certainly not surprised by your actions here.

JRK: Yeah, but what about happens next?

MOMNDF: Partly surprising.

Do you know that we were holding hands but I pulled away when the elevator door opened?

Do you know I was thinking in the elevator about Justin Bangs' email and blog post from yesterday entitled, "10 Things You're Doing That Are Killing Your Frame"? Did you know, as we met Mandy in the lobby and rushed out towards the all-you-can-eat/all-you-can-drink US-style buffet that I was stewing about completely letting Adina control my frame?

You do know that I took a photo of a storefront with a Nazi Swastika and a photo of Hitler in the back alleys behind Hondori near Round One Bowling on the way there. Did you know about Mandy and Adina gasping at what they saw, while joking I'm a Nazi enthusiast? I translated the Hitler adjacent text (*Heil our prices!*). You do know that Adina took her own photo as well, don't you?

And you know I immediately posted it to the Slack as Adina prattled on with Mandy meeting up with Avi in front of the restaurant. But do you know, that I kept the phone shielded from them?

OingoBoinGoy: Causing problems I see.

Andyschluss: Probably a Kike psyop to make Japs look bad.

Me: Everything is a Kike psyop with you @Andyschluss.

The_ZOGfather: When haven't events been a Kike psyop? ZOG specialty.
Me: Doubt it. Kikes here are pissed. Especially the girl but she has Palestinians to worry about.
The_ZOGfather: Be careful. Know how the boys can cuck out from Jewess charm.
Me: But @The_ZOGfather ?
The_ZOGfather: But I knew you liked your girls yellow and short. Not Khazar with big noses.
>Posts photo of the conniving Jew but this time with long hair and tits sticking out.
Me: Haha that ain't me.
OingoBoinGoy: We know you're a good boi.

*

Does it matter me describing a sea of twentysomething's gaijin filled Yamakawa Viking liberally partaking of the buffet and beer, laughing and giggling, some checking their phone, Justin across from me discussing his being a philosophy major with the talking points being along the lines of "Uuuuum, I'd venture to say that the human race itself is just an aberration in the evolutionary cycle of the planet, a period that will pass sooner than later probably," all the while I'm checking my phone and find the tweet from Andyschluss that reads "I just want to be with my people," and think *my sentiments exactly* while listening to Adina talk about the Hannah Arendt's influence on political discourse and wondering out loud what would've happened if she met Martin Heidegger at Disney's Country Bear Jamboree?

Philosophy was a mistake.

But the girls really were just comparing Disneyland and Disneyworld to EuroDisney and how Mandy considered becoming a dancer at Tokyo Disney after her teaching stint—as conversationally as far away from Palestine as possible, with Mariane and Marcelle on the opposite side of the room, almost arm in arm, soon to be eating each other out, near South African CHAD who is holding court with three girls, Mandy looking his way, Adina attempting to block the view, while drunk Avi leaned on Adina, "Right, right..." while I looked at the Slack.

Andyschluss: You should tell those kikes to go fuck themselves. Go to the store front and give a Roman salute. Then gas them.
Me: Gas the store?

167

Andyschluss: No faggot, gas the kikes of course. Who else would deserve it?

The_ZOGfather: >Implying gassing happened.

Andyschluss: I prefer gas. It smells like…victory.

Me: I might actually tell them it's a shame the Holocaust didn't happen.

OingoBoinGoy: :smug:

Andyschluss: Why talking maybe? If you don't do it, then you're just a cuck.

The_ZOGfather: Cucks talk. CHAD's DO.

"Wait—wait! Jason, you don't like *Pirates of the Caribbean*, do you?" Adina asked.

"Right, right! The Jew is strong with him." Avi almost keeled over laughing. I chugged my beer.

"Right!" Adina laughed. She put her head on Mandy's shoulder laughing. "Jason always surprises me. First he doesn't like *Pirates* then he defends Israel…"

"Well…he's Jewish right?"

"Right, right!"

"Don't tell him. He'll say he's from California."

"I am from—"

"WHAT!?" I hear Min in a loud screeching voice.

"Jason! Jason!" Matt says waving me over.

I see Matt hovering near Randy's group (understandable) with Min hovering around him to make sure he stays in her orbit. She pushes him towards my seat, holding a plate of assorted meats and a jug of beer.

"There's no way!"

"Let him—let him!"

He walks over, almost spills some beer on me. Before I can talk, Matt says, "Jason has some real interesting—no—real different ideas about the world, don't you Jason?"

Adina looks at me.

"He does?" Min asks.

"Yeah, tell 'em Jason," Matt said.

"Tell us Jason," Adina says with a smirk.

Kim and Min look at me almost with scorn.

"Tell them what?"

"Tell 'em what you told me." Matt says pointing at them with his beer bottle.

"I've, um, told you many, um, things Matt."

"Didn't you—shit I'm drunk."

"You are."

"Didn't you say them—the Japs did nothing wrong in the war?"

A smile disappeared from Min's face. "Did you say that Jason?"

"The Japanese did nothing wrong in the war? Is that what you're asking?"

"Yes, did you say that?"

"Well, some Japanese scholars say the numbers have been overinflated, that's what I was talking to Matt about…"

"Naw, naw, you didn't say it like that…"

"How do you know? You're drunk!"

"Yeah, I am drunk," Matt laughed.

The scorn hardens on Kim as she looks at Min then me. "Jason, what did you say?"

My nervous smile turns in to a smirk.

"What does it matter?"

"What did you say?"

"Wouldn't you like to know."

Adina then stepped in between us. "Guys, all this talk of the war…"

"My favorite subject," I said.

"That's true," Matt said sitting down. Min rolled her eyes.

Adina then started talking to Mandy and Min about the Nazi storefront, and protesting or talking to the manager or staging a sit-in or inquiring if they can do latte patterns in the shape of a Swastika or is a Star of David variation possible? But Mandy had to go to the ladies room. Mariane walked past us on her phone and Adina gave her a fake grin. I took another chug of beer.

"Shit!" Adina screamed and ran after her.

"Damn. All them girls have to go to the bathroom at same time," Matt said.

"Maybe I should go too," Min said and Kim Cheong with scowl followed her.

"Will the bathroom have room for all of them?"

"Probably a line."

"Adina looked a little worried there."

"Yeah, well, Mandy…"

"What about her?"

"She's probably worried Mariane will tell her about the USS Liberty."

"What's that?"

"I told you to Google it remember?"

He took out his phone. Started trying to read. Then started laughing. "Shit man, I can't read right now."

"Ask me later then."

The girls came piling back in, Adina next to Mandy, but it was Mariane who had some friends she wanted to meet up with at the "American bar" Joey's and invited all of us.

As we walked down the other side of Hondori, past the *Neko Café*, Yellow Submarine Model shop and the Peace Love Hotel, laughter and loudness, typical and embarrassing gaijin, Adina leaned in, and whispered in my ear, "I think there might be some Palestinians there. At Joey's..."

I just shrugged my shoulders and she quickly squeezed my hand.

*

Cue *Nemesis* by Shriekback.

If you're reading this somewhere in Yamaguchi-ken, why even describe the interior of Joey's? You've been there at least once. Why describe anything? A sense of mood or atmosphere? Fuck it.

It was loud.

MOMNDF: Yeah, but I needed to capture it visually.

JRK: I always assumed it was easier to capture visually.

MOMNDF: Not so easy considering we had to build a set for Joey's on the Culver City lot.

JRK: It does look more spacious, and the extras more Asian American than native.

MOMNDF: You can tell?

JRK: Usually, yeah.

MOMNDF: How?

JRK: Asians, well, Japanese, take on the looks and attitudes of their host country. And they're louder.

MOMNDF: Example?

JRK: Well, think of Tao Okamoto in *Batman v Superman: Dawn of Justice*. Have you seen it?

MOMNDF: No.

JRK: Well, she's um, native Japanese but, she dresses like an American blonde would dress in her role, not like a Japanese.

MOMNDF: None of that matters. Most of the audience doesn't care. They care about the story. Only someone who has been to Japan, like you would notice that.

JRK: Right.

MOMNDF: And speaking of which, we're getting distracted from the story.

JRK: We are.

"OMG there are Palestinians here!" Adina tried to whisper in my ear but ended up screaming. "And Marcelle and Mariane are introducing them to Mandy!" but I was more curious about Mariane running her hand up Marcelle's back.

Before I could respond, Matt pulled me away and said he'd buy me a drink then waved Justin over to me saying we'd get along because we both think the world is going to burn. "Uuum, what's he going on about?"

"He's, you know, drunk."

"But you're worried about climate change?"

"No." I took a long sip of beer. Saw Adina get approached by a nigger in a dress shirt and jeans. Probably a military contractor. Jamal. You know him, don't you? Adina straightened up, moved her hands and kept looking towards the Palestinian table. She then brought Jamal with her and introduced him to Mandy. Marcelle tilted her head, relaxed her shoulders and played with her hair. Appears she could still go for some good black that didn't crack. Mariane froze in place, only thing moving on her was disgusted elevator eyes. Felt myself getting tipsy.

"Then why did he say something about the world burning?"

"Well, I do—I guess think the world burning will be man-made."

"Then what—nuclear war?"

I shrugged my shoulders.

"Are you a nihilist?"

MOMNDF: You shrug your shoulders a lot.

JRK: Kind of my thing.

Shrugged again.

:shrug:

"Might as well enjoy the world before it burns, eh mate? Cheers." Mugs clinked. He patted my shoulder. I watched him pat it. But some blonde soyboy with Canadian accent—I assume Canadian because he said *How you doing, eh?*—put his arm around him and they started talking.

I looked over at Min who noticed me looking, then pulled out her phone as I started talking to Matt who was talking too much with Kim Cheong while Adina went to talk to Avi laughing and saying "Right, right..." as he looked over at Justin and Canadian soyboy while Mariane went to talk to Marcelle who was talking to Jamal and Mandy but the Lebanese shrunk back as Marcelle put her one-moment hand up, eyes staying on Jamal. Mariane then ran out of the bar. Mandy ran after her but stopped when the Palestinian's by the door grabbed her for a moment to inquire while looking in the direction of the door.

TIING! I checked my phone. An @channel notification from OingoBoinGoy about some shooting in Lake Tahoe at a Globohomo conference.

But you know that, don't you?

"Jason?" Mandy put her hand on my shoulder.

"Yeah?"

"You look lonely. Come talk with me and these two guys." Her loose high waist jeans, rolled up at the ankles only seemed to accentuate her curves. Was hard to tell under her crochet elbow sleeve t-shirt if she was wearing a bra or not. My guess was no. The sitting Arabs appeared to think same. They were all smiles. I shrugged my shoulders (again) and followed her over as she patted the stool next to hers. "Sit," she said.

"I guess I have a moment," I said. Frame.

"Please," she said rubbing the seat. I sat down. After introducing them she said, "Jason is Jewish," while glancing at me and back at them.

Their smiles disappeared.

"Half-Jewish," I said. "I consider myself American. I'm not—I don't have any ties to Israel. I'm American first and last—guess you could say I'm just white."

"Why would you want to admit that?" Mandy said leaning back. "If I were like you, I'd keep the white part hidden. Unfortunately, I'm white trash myself."

"I, uh, just like to be honest about who I am."

The Palestinians nodded in agreement.

Mandy sighed. "So do I. Sometimes as a cis-gender straight white American, I just feel so guilty about what we've done to minorities—like the Arabs—around the world. You guys must hate us."

The first one, Mahmoud, with a gentle face and European smirk, rotated his glass of whiskey on the table. "We don't dislike America or Americans. Our only problem is their support of Israel." Ishmael, next to him, slightly pudgy and balding agreed with a head nod.

"That is the case with most Arab countries. They don't hate America," Ishmael said.

Mandy looked at me confused. "If it's only our support of Israel then why..."

"They're our greatest ally..." I said taking a sip. I looked at Mahmoud and Ishmael then said, "Um, that's what they say, at least right? Like the reason given?"

"Well, I wouldn't have known this without talking to—wow. I mean dialogue and understanding is best. Build bridges not walls, right?"

The Arabs nodded.

I took another long sip.

"Israel has built a wall. A fence to be exact." I said. Another sip.

"That's right," Mahmoud said. "It has been very bad."

"It's like the Israelis are acting white..." I said.

"Totally, totally."

I took a long sip.

"But some would say they just want to maintain the balance so they have an ethnic homeland for themselves..."

"We were there first," Ishmael said. "The Jews came and kicked us out."

I held my hand up not wanting to argue. Didn't really disagree with them. Felt like giving them a *Sig Heil* just so they knew we were more on the same side. The room started to moving slightly, not a hard 90 degree turn, no blurred vision, just a shallow floating.

MOMNDF: You could just say you were tipsy.

JRK: Yeah but I've already used that word.

Adina put her hand on my shoulder. "You keeping Mandy company?"

"Sure, um, just, just having a beer."

"Your face says you don't do that often."

"There's a time for everything, ne?"

"We were just talking about Israel," Mandy said.

173

Adina then sat on my lap. :sweat: The Arabs stared at us. I looked around. Saw Mandy, then Min with Kim Cheong staring as Matt smirked. "What were you saying?" she asked. I tried to lean back.

"Is she wife?" Mahmoud asked.

Mandy laughed.

"She thinks that." I turned to her "But you're engaged, aren't you, ne?"

"Stop. Not really," Adina said. "Do you speak Japanese more when you're drunk?"

"*Eeto ne…*"

"Oh god…"

"What's his name again? Your future Oto? Max? Does he know?"

"He doesn't mind…I…"

"Because he doesn't know…*daro?*"

"Not exactly…will you stop?"

"Wait—what?" Mandy asked.

"Right," I said. I looked at my mug. Empty. Fuck. "Does Avi know? Or is he like—"

"Avi is gay."

"Right, right…"

"Not that it matters."

"*So ka*—I mean, right, right…"

She lightly punched my shoulder.

I pointed my mug towards the Arabs. "Ask those guys if there's something wrong with it."

She leaned and whispered. "I don't think now is the time to be judgmental?"

"Why? You worried?"

"Why are you saying that?"

"I don't think you want to be alone in a dark room…"

"Jason…what did I say?"

"Mandy what were we talking about?"

"Israel and Palestine…but are you guys…"

"Mandy, have you ever Googled the USS Liberty?" I looked at the Arabs. "You guys know right?"

They looked confused.

"What's the USS Lib—"

Adina hopped off my lap then put her hand on Mandy's shoulder. "Don't listen to him. He's probably drunk and getting conspiratorial."

"Like you would know."

"I do know. I know you like conspiracies."

"I'd like to know more about you two…"

"I, uh, I…"

"What Jason?" Adina asked.

Mahmoud and Ishmael talked while looking at their phones.

"It's not a conspiracy. It happened."

Mandy pulled out her phone. "Here let me look it up."

"There's no need," Adina said reaching for it.

"Ahhh, I see," Mahmoud said. "This happened in 1967 during The Setback."

"Is that what you guys call it?" I asked.

"Call what?" Adina asked looking at me.

"The Six-Day War. You know where the Israelis escalated a war with Syria and Egypt that resulted in them retaliating and basically created all the Middle East trouble we have now…ne?"

"What?" Mandy said.

Both Mahmoud and Ishmael nodded in agreement.

"Oh and they also sank a US ship. The USS Liberty. *Arigato gozaimasu* Israel."

"Wait what? What does this have to do with you two or…"

"Maybe everything or…maybe nothing." I tried to take a sip but fumbled with the mug realizing it was empty.

"I'm sure you'd prefer nothing…" Adina said.

I shrugged my shoulders.

"Next, Google the Clean Break Memo and the Franklin Espionage scandal." Adina's face reddened. Saw the tears building up, the Drama Queen performance about to start, the Arabs looking on like their watching an IED explode.

"Fuck you!" Adina screamed.

"We've already done that…ne?"

"I—" tears started gushing down her cheeks. "You fucking Nazi!"

"You say that now wanting to get outraged. Which it seems that's what you're always looking for…"

"You asshole!!"

She pushed me and started slapping, again and again.

I grabbed both hands. She tried to fight. I tightened my grip. Felt the rush of adrenaline surging. "You fucking hit me again, I'll fucking hit you, got it?

175

I'm not some fucking guy you can cuck and slap and happily take it! DO YOU FUCKING HEAR ME!"

She shrunk back. "Jason…" Tears streamed down her face, fear overtaking outrage. She quickly, almost frantically, put her face in her hands and started to walk off. Mandy gave me a nasty glare then put her arm around Adina and started to walk with her towards Min, Matt and Kim Cheong. Avi walked over to comfort her as she told her biased version of events.

My freaking nerves…:angry-face: I felt a hand on my shoulder. I looked to see Ishmael passing me another mug of beer. My trembling hand took it with a thanks.

"Women," I said. "They're, uh, they're crazy."

"Yes," Mahmoud said. Ishmael nodded his head in agreement, a smile on his face.

"Fucking Jews," I said. I then looked around, surprised at myself for saying it.

Coming to Joey's was a mistake.

"Yes," Mahmoud said. Ishmael nodded his head in agreement, still with a smile on his face.

"Oh…so…I was just joking but…"

"No, they are problem."

"Right," I said.

"Did she say you were Nazi?"

"Well, um, I uh, I studied them a lot…my ancestors are German…"

"My grandfather served in Wehrmacht," Ishmael said.

"Yeah…he, um, he did?"

You can research elsewhere in the Palestinian's testimonies what we discussed but after briefly talking I realized we had a lot in common. Maybe I was being too judgmental to certain people.

Many were certainly being judgmental of me. And with all the stares and tension in the air, I felt a need to quickly leave.

I walked back to my hotel alone.

*

Min: "Didn't know u and Adina were a thing."

Me: "We're not a thing."

Min: "That's not what she says."

Me: "Didn't know u and Matt were a thing."

Min: "U just won't let stuff go."

Me: "I'll let this 1 go. We're even now."

She replied with a GIF of a black lady flicking her hand saying "Whatever" as subtitle.

But the GIF started to glitch and I received a text from Yu that said "Miss U."

But you know that, don't you?

*

It does matter that when I returned to my room, the TV was on. I thought I'd turned it off. There must have been an Argento marathon on WOWWOW because I saw a young Jennifer Connelly on my screen from the intriguing yet flawed psychic horror thriller *Phenomena* (1984. Directed by Dario Argento from a script by Argento and Franco Ferrini with cinematography by Romano Albani), released in the US abbreviated as *Creepers* (because Jewish Hollywood executives always feel they can improve a perfectly good movie just like Jewish intellectuals think they can improve a perfectly good society).

But no amount of Semitic tinkering was going to save the film. It's plot, about an innocent virginal girl who goes to a boarding school and has psychic connection with insects just couldn't really balance out the whimsical element along with the gore kinetics that Argento is really known for. The heavy metal score, influenced from Bava's Demons, featuring Motorhead, Iron Maiden, Andi Sex Gang, Bill Wyman, Simon Boswell and of course Goblin, is more of a curious footnote. But the main theme by Goblin sticks with you.

Cue *Theme* from *Phenomena*.

I looked at my phone, hoping to see a message from Yu. But the screen glitched. Then the set glitched. Digital break-up. Not like the old analog snow. No, no, no the more abrupt and sharp high pitched electronic screeches with jagged black and white lines on the screen, like it's struggling to retrieve a signal.

I turned the TV off.

I then looked at my phone. Still glitching.

TING! TING! TING!

Text from Adina.

"r u still at Joey's?"

"No."

"I can't sleep rn."

"That's ur problem."

"I just passed that Nazi store. Thought of you."

"OFC"

177

"I don't mean it that way."

"Whatever."

"Can we talk?"

"Not in the mood. Oyasumi:sleeping-face:"

No more replies.

But you know that, don't you?

Do you know I went bed thinking about Adina, but wanting to think about *Phenomena* and Jennifer Connelly? Thought about our argument. All the stares. Uneasy about what would be facing me tomorrow. The anger, the hatred, the self-righteousness, the dirty stares from Kim Cheong and my impending hangover headache.

In the middle of the night, I checked my phone again. It worked.

No engagements on Twitter or Instagram save Adina liking one of my posts from earlier in the day.

But you know that, don't you?

Do you know I dozed off with a million thoughts racing for my attention?

Did you also know I woke up barely able to gauge my senses, feeling half-conscious yet able to touch and see things in my room—like the tightly fitted sheets and hard mattress under me—but I also felt lightly afloat?

The TV comes on. I see Adina walk down the quiet Hiroshima side streets through a security camera cutting to a beautiful tracking shot. She goes outside, wipes tears from her face as she looks back towards somewhere.

She's illuminated beautifully, in a hard-lit blue—think Michael Mann circa mid-80s, when Italian Dante Spinotti was his DP—the neon reflecting off her skin, the ground wet. But there is no score by Tangerine Dream or Michael Rubini.

Cue silence.

Cue the sound of neon flickering and feet on wet ground.

Feel my body tremble.

She walks, arms crossed in a moment of contemplation. The streets are empty but she looks around, furiously.

I know what is coming. I try to scream but my voice is paralyzed. I open my mouth but only a faint moan exits. I can't even say her name. I can only watch on in fear and inevitability.

She looks around like she hears a rustling but it's just wind blowing trash around. The area seems familiar but also foreign. Signs are in Japanese, but also English, Hebrew, Arabic and Sumerian cuneiform.

She begins to walk briskly but appears lost.

I scream again, try to say "This way! Over here!" But I can't. I want to rush to her side but my body is glued to the bed.

A strong winter wind blows. She grasps herself, holds herself tightly. A knife slashes her chest. Then her face. Then another. And another. She grabs her face shocked and confused. She doesn't see the black figure behind her with red eyepatches covering the eyeholes on the ski mask...

"ADINA!"

She doesn't hear because I said nothing. Just a moan.

The figure approaches.

"ADINA!" another moan.

I feel myself kicking in the bed.

She's stabbed in the neck. Then the eye. She stumbles. Dazed. Then falls. The figure, all black save read eyes, picks her limp body up, cradling the head.

The eyes look at the camera, at me, while Adina's eyes are rolling to the back of her head. The blade is slowly placed on her throat. The red eyes move from me to her.

"ADINA!"

Still frozen. The blade digs in.

A quick slice. Blood squirts from throat. The body falls.

She lays helpless. The killer approaches, picks the head up by the blood-matted hair to expose the neck more and continues cutting, while turning to look at me. I focus on the red eyes and then the eerie unemotional display. Eyes striking fear because they're completely neutral; a cold instrument of death.

MOMNDF: Dude even that freaked me out.

*

I woke up in a sweat and the immediate reality of my surroundings, the sunlight through the window, my ability to move, my headache, my sore shoulder. I took a deep breath and looked at my phone on the bed drawer. It vibrated. A message from Yu: "*Ohayo*:hug:".

But you know that, don't you?

Kenji is coming.

*

In the shower, I felt the pain of my headache. But it was just pain. I rubbed my temples a few times and thought about...nothing really. Nothing about politics, Palestinians, Jews, immigration, white genocide—no. Nothing. I

179

recalled some of the scenes from Phenomena, then wondered what it was like for Jennifer Connelly to work with Dario Argento, then remembered there was a Japanese actress Nakahara Shoko—I mean Shoko Nakahara (got to write the name correctly for you gaijin) got her start in acting because of Connelly and then I tried to figure out which movies Nakahara was in outside of Visitor Q…but came up blank…

>Walks down hallway towards elevator.

>completequiet.mp3

>Sees no cleaning crews (no they don't have wetbacks or Filipinos to clean their rooms)

>Only sees and hears the hum of the overhead fluorescents.

*

In the lobby, I saw a crowd gathered. I looked for someone familiar or something familiar. A dark cloud permeated the room.

I felt something in my gut, that sinking feeling that you know things are off kilter, the outer mood connecting with the inner mood. You wish it was just a chemical imbalance but it's actually something deeper and darker which makes it all the more ominous.

Min cries on Matt's shoulders. Kim Cheong looks on, her scowl replaced by a frown and a hand on her friend's shoulder, tears streaming down her eyes too.

South African CHAD, the AMOG, looks up at the ceiling like he's in a state of coerced mourning, an arm around two girls, a redhead and blonde with a bad bleach job. I know both of them. One is from Atlanta, the other Cambridge, England. Mandy, head buried in palms crying, joins them. Avi gives her a pat on the shoulder and asks if everything is okay. A PureLight representative hovers towards her holding literature. He smiles constantly, bows and hands her a pamphlet. She accepts without hesitation, her mind distracted. Mariane and Marcelle both stand with their arms crossed, angry, staring at the floor. Justin is on his phone looking at Mandy.

Japanese men in suits hover, talking to different people. They don't look like effeminate teachers or hotel clerks but official.

Mandy walks over to Min. Matt lets her go so they can hug. He looks at me with cold reserve. I slowly walk over, try to ignore Min whose waterfall of tears and moaning are almost a distraction but I manage to get out the inevitable question: "What's wrong?"

180

"You haven't—" he asks sticking his head forward with an incredulous squint in his eyes. "Adina…"

My hand starts to tremble.

"What about her?"

Matt looks at Min, unsure of what to say next. Total beta. He bobs his head as if to say "follow me" but continued to look at Min almost out fear. Pussy.

"Adina…" he took a deep breath.

"Yeah?"

"Adina was found dead. This morning."

"What?"

"Yeah…they think it's murder…"

Matt's words drift off as he talks about the details of the case and how it might be related to the Nazi storefront. He starts asking questions about the Palestinians, the argument we had, but all I can do is try to look at my surroundings because I feel—everything seems so immediate. My heart races. The color of the room takes on a new vibrancy, like instantly switching from analog to high-def TV display but in an entire three-dimensional space where I feel more present and immediate than I want.

My body freezes. Like someone attacked me.

The ground underneath my feet begins to move.

The room starts to turn.

Kenji is coming.

I faint.

Pussy.

*

I awoke a few minutes later on a lobby couch. The pain in my head pulsing even more. Matt and Min stood over me. Min looked distant, like she was observing meerkats through plexiglass sponsored by Tide. Kim Cheong, scowl returned, stood behind her.

Mandy talked to the PureLight representative. He was diminutive, bald with a smile plastered on his face, he (obviously) spoke a little English because he was in conversation with Mandy who spoke no Japanese except maybe "Where's the nearest hip hop clothing store?" But this time she said, "Yeah Jason and Adina were a couple. They're both Jewish. They had a fight."

"Half-Jewish," were my first words.

"Well, half-Jew—" she then noticed I was awake. "He's awake," she said. She then walked off with the PureLight guy.

"The fight," Kim Cheong said. Her eyes stayed on me. "It was bad. Violent."

"No it wasn't you fuc—" I tried to get up but my head shot out it pain. Kim Cheong and Min jumped back thinking I was going to attack them.

Matt then leaned forward, grabbing both of my shoulders. "Calm down there Jason," he said. Mandy looked over from talking to the PureLight rep but then kept talking.

I took a deep breath.

The contempt painted on Min's face now matched that of Kim Cheong. "Let him go Matt. Leave him alone."

"What do you mean? The guy just…he fainted…"

"We need to go Matt. You see the way…"

She stopped talking and looked to her right. Matt looked in the same direction. He then looked at Min, me, the ground, back at me briefly, and said, "We'll cha—look be careful Jason. I Googled USS Liberty by the way. Interesting…" and then walked off with Min and Kim Cheong in tow.

I looked in the direction they looked and saw three Japanese uniformed men, cops obviously—no women, no female detectives like you see on the J-dramas which they probably do to ape Hollywood shows and seem "cool" or some bullshit. It's not that type of story. No, no, no approaching me were just three men in suits, impressed with their authority and happy to have something to investigate. The one in the lead bowed and handed me his business card. He was tall, lanky but confident with tightly trimmed hair. He should be played by Masaharu Fukuyama.

He introduced himself, struggled with my name, but then I said that Japanese was fine and I introduced myself.

"We need to talk to you," he said.

:squirm:

*

No I wasn't worried because they'd finger me as the killer.

No I didn't kill her.

It's not that type of story.

Though that type of story would be perfect for the likes of David Fincher…

MOMNDF: It is my type of story.

No, no, no, I was worried they would frame me. When it comes to murder cases in Japan, they are pretty open/shut—especially for the ones involving gaijin. I would have to pull my privilege card and get the embassy involved, maybe even cry anti-Semitism, to make sure they wouldn't put me in the clink. Fuck that.

"Aidee kaado?" Officer Fukuyama asks. He makes the form of a card with his fingers.

I pull out my gaijin card—literally a card that every long-term resident foreigner possesses (THINK Green Card but without the abuse). As I pull it out my wallet, hand it to them with both hands and bow, I noticed the press arrive.

I see live-trucks, reporters, women and men, dolled up, not there to investigate or ask questions—no, no, no—they are there to ask only cursory questions...who, what, when, where, why, how...but they'll dig no deeper...they'll just repeat the who, what, when, where, why and how of what they are told with the caveat of "authorities say..." but to the viewing public at large they'll be accepted as facts—especially in high trust Japan...

And I see the reporters looking at me. I see the cameras pointing in my direction, through the hotel sliding doors, with only uniform officers blocking the way, keeping their hands out, forming an imaginary line, and the reporters don't cross it...they respect the authority...they understand the relationship...they play their roles...obey the rules and you'll get your story...

I see one lady enter. She's by far the best looking of the crew, though she does look a little bit like a feminist with her bobbed hair and pantsuit. Doesn't mean she's a dyke, but probably meant she was a career striver (only dick she got was from a dildo).

But she talks to the officer. Very forward. She starts pointing towards...me.

I see Min then looking my way and trying to clear the room. She says something quietly, almost like she's trying to whisper in Matt's ear, something she doesn't want me to hear. He bobs his head, his eyes drift towards me, then back towards her—he doesn't want to stare too long—he then returns her stare to her and he walks off. I see Min talking to others: the crying Mandy, the ever-scowling Kim Cheong, Mariane, Marcelle, the darker skinned girl also from Vegas, Lynn Torres I think her name is but forget because I rarely talk to her but I'd rather talk to her than the police.

"Please," Officer Fukuyama says.

I come out of my trance and look around. "What?" I ask—in English.

"Please," he says again in English. I then see he's pointing his open hand in the direction of the door. Just past the doors sits a police car.

"Kuruma ni..." I can't even get it out.

183

"Yes," he says. His face isn't grim but he isn't smiling either.

"Hai," I say.

I then slowly stand up and walk with them towards the outside. Once again, I feel myself in the moment. The fact that everything else doesn't really matter, everything is zoomed in, the iris narrowed, the intense scrutiny invades.

I still feel the stares of the onlookers. I wouldn't call them friends but we were cordial enough not to be enemies and I wonder who told them that I knew Adina? Who said that we slept together?

The sliding doors open and I feel the flashes of bulbs, I hear the clicks. I wonder does anyone really read newspapers or watch TV news anymore? Don't they just get their news from Twitter, Facebook, Yahoo! Japan or Reddit? But the press is still present. Someone, mostly boomers, will watch the news and word will travel. Even worse, the non-Japanese news bureaus, who pretty much just translate the news reported from Japanese establishment sources will translate whatever *Yomiuri Shimbun* or Kyodo News Wire report. They won't do much digging of their own. They'll accept the wires *who, what, when, where, why and how.* And all the users on Twitter, Facebook, Kai10 and Reddit will just link to those stories. They don't have the money or time to do their own investigation. They'll just give their opinion, their understanding or perspective of events with varying degrees of authority, but mostly in the most confident or smug way possible, depending on their frame of reference… "Another white man playing ugly American," with a link to *The New York Times* version of the story on Facebook. On Twitter, someone like Ultima_Thule will tweet out, "Headline translation: Jew killed overseas, media overreacts" with a link to the *The Times* story. On Reddit it will be, "Japan is becoming more violent due to immigration. Can we get this story to the top?" with a link to *The Washington Post* article. And then on the *The New York Times* own Twitter account there will be a sub-story saying "Here's what we know about Jason Reudelheuber, the alleged killer of Adina Iscovitz." And there's my photo of me being led in to the car which they got from Kyodo.

It'll just be news content for a couple of days at best followed by maybe periodic updates. But it's just content. Content, content, content. Something to fit someone's narrative or the brand they promote. At this current rate, I might at best get a Lifetime Movie out of it. It's not deranged or bizarre enough to get the content produced that makes the the smug nerds, with their blogs and YouTube channels, to jizz their pants about…like a docuseries on HBO or Netflix or an adaptation feature or series helmed by David Fincher…yet.

184

MOMNDF: Not there yet, no.
JRK: Yeah.
MOMNDF: Too bad you can't do :shrug: irl, you know?
JRK: Yeah.

I don't wear handcuffs as I enter the car but EVERYONE stares at me like I am. Everyone snaps pictures like I am.

They might as well have just said that I'm guilty.

Worse yet, word travels. I can hear it. It will be the talk of the conference. Adina and I were having sex. How could I explain that? The secret is out. An even greater pile of embarrassment. "Jason was hitting that?"

I thanked god that I was (mostly) ANON on Social Media (with exception to my main blog linked to my Instagram)(Not that I ever really revealed my identity on that site either)(But that was the only account Adina knew about)(And her being a woman, I'm sure she blabbed it to others)(Meaning someone told the police. Who probably told reporters)(So that will all be part of the story)(Not that there was any damning evidence on the site…no I didn't murder her)(It's not that type of story). But I knew someone in the media probably told by police or told by some JET, some attention seeking THOT like Mandy or Kim Cheong who want to let everyone know how sad they are about the events that happened, or some self-important asshole, like Avi Feynman, who wants to sound concerned and thoughtful—one of these people would talk to the cameras and reveal that I had a blog and IG account. And everyone would visit it. I'd get the most traffic ever. But most would just find photos of old video game cartridges, and merchandise from a bygone era with words of lament at the ethereal nature of consumerist society. It's not Ted Kazcynski but they'll try to read through the lines and try to make the connection.

No, no, no, I'm actually not worried about that. I'm more worried they're going to read my writing. My need to sound thoughtful and important. My trying to sound poetic though I haven't read much poetry, save that one time I read *The Waste Land* in a sitting along with a few bits and pieces of *The Pisan Cantos*—but they'll see my aspirant musings, my striving for relevance.

And they'll probably laugh.

I feel naked just at the thought of them reading my work, looking at my photos.

Blogging was a mistake.

185

*

My notes read: "Inside the police station there needs to be a comedic back and forth between me and the Japanese detectives asking questions. There needs to be a comedic back and forth about if he's white, Jewish or American and the pronunciation of Adina's last name.

I mean it's kind of funny in retrospect:

"How do you her name?" he asked in Japanese.

"Adina Iscovitz?" I asked.

"Ah-day-na?"

"*Chigaimasu.*"

"*Nan to iimasu ka?*" *How do you say?* Fukuyama said.

"Ah-dee-na."

"Ah-dee-na...*deshou?*"

"*Hai.*"

"*Lasto nemu wa?*" *How about her last name?*

"Iscovitz. Isu-ko-bitcch." (Yeah, I know it reads like I called Adina a bitch but that's the phonetic pronunciation of her name.)

"Ah-dee-na Isu-ko-bitcch?"

"*Hai.*"

"Okay *desu*," he said.

"Okay?" I said. I asked with the hope that was all they needed from me. They just needed someone of Jewish extraction to help them with name pronunciation for their press release. But alas there was more

And why waste the effort? You can read their translated report.

MOMNDF: I'm sad we didn't have this scene.

JRK: We can put in the special features.

I could see this easily becoming like a bad Detective Galileo mystery, played by the namesake of the Detective Fukuyama. Murders so perfectly structured you can almost hear the tools clinking and clanking in the tool box as the writer constructs the story. An artist, looking to commit a murder, to make it the perfect work of art. He plans out it out perfectly. He selects the weapon and of course he selects the target. And of course, he's influenced by an Italian thriller that has a plot similar. It all fits perfectly. So perfectly that's it's a bunch of bullshit.

But people like that type of bullshit. It's like they want their stories to be perfectly crafted and contrived. It's like they want to think there is some order and thought even in the most grisly of affairs like murder...but they don't

186

really want to see the grisly details or the autopsy report. They want a degree of detachment. Never understood the polite murder mystery like *Miss Marple* or *Murder She Wrote*.

Actually, I do understand. It's painfully and blandly middle class, bourgeois storytelling at its worst (similar to its cousin, romance). The dirt and grit of daily life has its edges worn down and neatly rounded so as not to offend but to just move product, turning death in to a tea and biscuits affair without any degree of emotion.

Murder mysteries were a mistake.

*

>Be Jason.

>See the open office plan of the police station.

>See tall decidedly non-Japanese figures walking through the room with some degree of swagger.

>See Officer's Fukuyama and Satoh excuse themselves when they stop outside my interrogation room.

>Watch them have typical exchange of business cards and identification followed by sloppy bowing.

>rituals.jpg

>Notice the olive-skinned one took the lead, the whiter one, stocky with a closely-cropped buzzcut, standing shoulders back with confidence.

>THINK FBI.

>KNOW FBI when the Detectives excuse themselves and the two Americans entered confidently.

>yourfucked.jpg

But you know that, don't you?

You've read the FD-302 and I know you consider it more authoritative than me:

JASON REUDELHEUBER-KATZ an Assistant English Teacher (A.E.T.) in Etajima-Shi, an island adjacent to Hiroshima City and Kure City, was interviewed at the Hiroshima Prefectural Police Headquarters in Hiroshima City by properly identified Special Agents of the Federal Bureau of Investigation. REUDELHEUBER-KATZ voluntarily provided the following information in regard to the murder of

ADINA ISCOVITZ, an American national, also an A.E.T. and resident of Hiroshima City, Japan:

Mr.Reudelheuber-Katz stated his relationship with Ms.Iscovitz was "purely sexual" but also consensual and noted she was in a long distance relationship with a man named "MAXWELL" who lived in New York City, New York, though she is from Los Angeles, California.

Mr.Reudelheuber-Katz expressed his concern that Japanese murder investigations, especially those concerning foreign residents, were not given thorough inquiry and was therefore worried he might be falsely charged. Reudelheuber-Katz noted the tensions between Ms.Iscovitz and two female A.E.T.'s working within Hiroshima Prefecture who were both former members of Students for Justice in Palestine and championed the Boycott, Divestment and Sanctions (B.D.S.) of Israel which Ms.Iscovitz opposed. Mr.Reudelheuber-Katz noted several times he is "Half-Jewish" and was not a Palestinian sympathizer and that Israel is America's greatest ally.

Mr.Reudelheubter-Katz confirmed he and Ms.Iscovitz did have an argument the evening of her murder at the Hiroshima City bar frequented by American expatriates called "Joey's" but it was a personal disagreement concerning politics and national identity. He confirmed he was under the influence of alcohol when the argument occurred. He confirmed the presence of two Palestinian Arab males who were anti-Israel and admirers of Hitler whom he talked to but had trouble remembering the conversation due to inebriation. He also noted another female Hiroshima Prefecture A.E.T., MINSUH CHO from Honolulu, HI, was jealous about his relationship with Ms.Iscovitz and provided text messages from that evening to corroborate, as well

188

of texts with the deceased later that evening, shortly before her murder.

Mr.Reudelheuber-Katz reviewed and confirmed he was author of anonymous posts on the website KAI10 that linked back to his phone IP. Regarding gender relations, he wrote, "LA is full of THOTs. It's a THOTocaust," (he defined the meaning of "THOT" as "That Ho Over There"). Regarding the historical veracity of the Holocaust he wrote, "How can we even begin to verify the dead in the Holocaust? Since when have we ever trusted Soviet numbers? Where was Hitler's direct order to exterminate Jews? The more evidence I see, the Holocaust looks like a Holohoax," and a reply in the same thread to a self-identified Libertarian and another user known as ULTIMA_THULE, Reudelheuber-Katz stated, "If you ask me, Hitler did nothing wrong. If he actually perpetrated the Holocaust, that is (followed by "smirking face emoji")."

Agents asked REUDELHEUBER-KATZ about the above statements and he replied that he was just "having fun being a troll" and they did not give evidence to a malicious intent to commit murder or violence towards females, Jews or Jewish females and stated that his mother is Jewish, once again affirming that he was half-Jewish and pro-Israel.

He also confirmed that he was the administrator of the blog KATSURA'S LAIR and its related accounts on TWITTER, INSTAGRAM and FACEBOOK, where he mainly posts photographs he took of old toys and video games sitting on shelves with mini-essays full of infantile lament, aspirant artistic relevance and a heavy dose of self-importance.

Of what good is it to give any more details save the fact that the details of Adina's murder (blunt force strikes to her head, most likely hammer blows, rendering her almost unrecognizable) pretty much exonerated me because I had no hammer on my person nor could easily get access to one and that our text timestamps denote we were not near each other close to time of death? Of what good would it do to note Special Agent Murphy's annoyance at the female officer worker who bowed her head as she entered the interrogation room, set down a cup of coffee on a saucer with a thin stick sugar pack and a tiny pre-packaged cup of creamer and noting how in Japan the creamer packages are tinier because the coffee servings are tinier but it still doesn't match the American appetite for creamer and that she seemed nervous and confused when Special Agent Murphy held up said creamer packet demanding another and I had to interject and ask for an extra one in Japanese with the girl bowing upon return, taking tiny steps as she presented the creamer to Murphy, asked him if the handful of creamers she brought was enough and in English, Murphy replied, "It's fine. Thanks," to where she dropped the packets on the table and scurried out again leaving Murphy to prepare his coffee, peeling one lid after another and pouring in to his coffee to the point the black liquid had almost been consumed by white all the while asking me if I committed murder?

Would it help my case to mention upon seeing the photos of Adina's mangled body, unrecognizable, save for her too-tight t-shirt and frizzy hair now matted in blood, that I actually felt guilty for not feeling guilty or sad? Actually, actually, ackshually, that's not true. One detail in the photo, her wallet, laying on the blood-stained pavement, next to a dragonfly indifferent to the crimson liquid, with her Fluffy Fluffy Cinnamoroll charm looped through the zipper actually did elicit some sorrow because it was something I teased her about before we ever started a sexual relationship? During the summer, she asked me to go to SOGO with her because they had a Kyushu Fair on the top floor where various foods and goods from the region would be for sale and there were some scarves from Kagoshima made by a certified master craftsman. She wanted me to translate in case anything went awry. I joked I was Nazi-like in my Japanese delivery. She said she didn't mind if the Nazi could help her buy a scarf. So, I translated for her, talking to the balding, sophisticated master craftsman while she looked at the various scarves. When she finally brought out her wallet to pay, I noticed a charm looped through her wallet zipper, it's long dog ears being the main thing that jumped out at me. It was in some casual yet forced pose of cuteness that Japanese graphic designers, especially Sanrio, excel at. I teased her again when she brought out the wallet again at Tully's Coffee (to buy me a cup as thanks for my "Nazi-like translation services"). She said she thought it was cute and smiled. The thought of it, how a little trinket produced for mass consumption could make her smile, a genuine

190

smile, a smile that I would not—more importantly, COULD not—see anymore, brought about a feeling of remorse. No tears or anything. Just faint sadness. The childlike nature and joy, the purity of it, expressed in the sight of franchise charm, had been crushed by a hammer blow.

But you know that, don't you?

As you also know they released me to pursue other leads and I decided visiting Yasukuni Shrine would not be the best PR move so I decided to staycation for winter break.

:white_frowning_face:

*

"what did u and matt talk about?"

First message on my phone. From Min. Phone was blowing up. Messages from Min, Matt, Mandy and...mom. But you know that, don't you?

You know, she wrote "Oh my god, Jason is everything ok? I heard about Adina, such a tragedy..." then proceeded to spend rest of the email talking about herself and those at Temple who may or may not be related to Adina or might know one of her relations that they met on a trip to LA or layover to Tel Aviv and ending the email with "please call".

Did you know I read these on a tram, my mind zoned in on my phone, trying to cancel out my surroundings?

So, I surrounded myself with content.

Content, content, content! I opted for email content over social media content, looking at Justin Bangs daily blast with subject line: "The Only Reason I Travel and Fuck"—got my attention, won't lie—opening with: "Hey Jason, I'm going to get deep here...", proceeding to talk about how he was walking the beaches of Brittany in France, seeing all the hopeless people struggling to fit in their swimsuits, trying to squeeze some enjoyment out of life and how he realized he didn't want to be like them and didn't want me to be like them either, because that's why I'm subscribed to his badass newsletter right? I should probably upgrade, take it to the next level and join the Bangs Club, only $300 a year—very tempting considering his use of the stock photos of lingeried and very fuckable Calvin Harris *Summer* music video women—so tempting to just say fuck it and experience life and just fuck—fuck life in the pussy for all it's worth. Actually, not the deepest email. But I looked around, and saw a school girl talking on her phone while also texting and reading manga, who at least had a cheap lipstick smile. Future whore (if not presently).

Everyone else seemed to care less that a girl was murdered around their vicinity…they were too busy…living life?—no. Just…just busy moving and staying occupied.

Felt like nothing had changed.

Nothing had changed at Hiroshima Train Station: Endless ordered hordes, some foreign, most not. Heading to the Carp game at the stadium next door or standing in line around the corner at the KAB Tart shop, salivating.

I realize I got on the wrong tram and went in the wrong direction, Hiroshima Station and Mazda Stadium being in the opposite direction of where I intended.

So, I get on the bus to the Port. I never get used to the narrow passages and roads the bus travels down, how it practically rides close to the tails of the vehicles right in front.

It's night, I see the many people who might as well be faceless through the many open windowed storefronts. The grocery stores, the restaurants, the cafes. I see life going on. When I pass the different buildings, with signs of "City Home", "Wants", "K.D.S. Entertainment with sub—heading music saves the world!", "Apaman Dramatic Communication", "Texas", "Digi Fab Spot", "Tanaka Since 1919", And "Pepe le Moko Slot", a woman speed walking alone on the sidewalk, a kid in glasses, the lone student, looking down at the ground contemplating what? I wonder what's going on there. What type of lives and stories are happening? It always hits me at night rather than day. I reflect upon the city with the endless lights glistening, reflecting off one of the seven rivers giving the urban landscape a special glow. A microchip with its many circuits running and cooperating yet I stand alone, operating independently, a detached piece of the whole.

At night, the city seems alive yet lifeless. A circuit more than an organism.

Sitting next to me, an old man in tattered khakis, opens his newspaper—the only one reading a paper—with Adina's smiling face on the front page. Headline reads "American Woman Found Murdered." My face is nowhere. No photos of crowds of cars and me being escorted out. Maybe my photo appeared inside.

I dipped my head low, pulled the hood of my jacket over my head and looked at the ground level grid outside.

*

Kenji is coming.

192

Yes, yes, yes, it lingers before it happens, existing outside of the time/space continuum.

And thus begins **The Prologue** AKA **The Prologue: Countdown to Kenji is coming** AKA **The Prologue: Countdown**.

At the port, I sit in the back, meaning away from all the crowds, away from the onlookers who might recognize me, the giant windows facing the Seto Inland Sea, where Etajima lies beyond. :sweat: But no one is really paying attention to the dark expanse...no, no, no, they're paying attention to the Sony flatscreen airing whatever comedy show. But it quickly ends and goes to news.

Their news doesn't look like our news...no, no, no, their sets are brighter, with more talent that speak in hushed monotones. Top story is Adina.

>See her face again.

>See press conference with Detective Fukuyama making a statement.

>Have too clouded mind to understand him.

>canttranslate.txt

>See Avi...again?

I read the lower third with his name written as "Abi Fainman"...Avi Feynman. So that's his name? Avi thankfully gives his statement in slow Jewish Queen's English (as in Queens, New York) slow enough to make sure everyone heard him, and make me long for the Japanese overdub: "Make no mistake. Anti-Semitism is most likely the cause of this murder. Adina Iscovitz was a practicing Jew and active in both the Jewish Community and raising awareness of the type of hate that led to her murder. Others may use this as an opportunity to start a debate on the so-called 'Jewish Question', a hateful concept. They are seeking to give legitimacy to their view. A view that we must not tolerate."

Did they find a suspect? I wondered. But what came up next was a package not about Adina, her life, the reaction of her family with sympathetic still shots of photos from her childhood while her mother and father spoke about what a perfect and loving child she was—no, no, no—it was a package about racism in Japan, talking about comments made on Yahoo! Japan, B-roll of chat boards and certain rooms in Facebook, with brief mention of their American counterparts on Twitter, Reddit, and Kai10 even showing English language pro-Hitler statements from the likes of General_TOHO (with tons of followers) with a view of the TL featuring replies from Andyschluss and OingoBoinGoy.

MOMNDF: Good description. Glad they gave us rights just to use the actual package without having to recreate it.

>Sink in your chair.

But no photos of me.

And no (more) photos of Adina.

:relief:

Noticed I had still had 25 minutes until the high-speed boat left for Koyo Port. Decided to buy a ticket for the ferry leaving in five minutes.

I saw the Ferry inching its way towards the port in the black distance, the awaiting crowd starting to gather at the dock. I pulled out my phone and started checking Kai10, see if the story had broken stateside.

But you know that, don't you?

You know *The Washington Post* headline: "Murder of Jewish Girl in Japan Raises Questions of Anti-Semitism". You know I read. You know Adina's name was mentioned only briefly at the beginning followed by comments of mourning by the Japanese ambassador to the United States and the prime minister. No mention of suspects, no mention of me. But! a canned statement from Avi Feynman: "The death of Adina can be a lesson to us all about the forces of hate and intolerance and how they must be combatted." You know the story ended talking about the store with the Hitler display and mentioned Japan's "Uncomfortable history of racism and discrimination" centered around the defunct monthly magazine *Marco Polo* publishing an article entitled "There were no Nazi Gas Chambers," in 1995, while also pulling out the usual comments about Korean Comfort Women and comedian Masatoshi Hamada doing blackface on a New Year's Eve special, all ending with a quote from Adina's mom, "Adina was passionate about fighting hate. I pray that if any good can come out of this, it can stop a little more hate in the world."

You know the comments on the Kai10 post linking to the article:

"Japan doing the jobs that Americans refuse to do."

"More proof we need to follow Japan's example."

">Another dead kike.

">world mourns.

">werejoice.jpg"

"Maybe her father ordered a hit on her. She might've borrowed too many shekels from his bank."

"It's about time someone starts their own blood libel."

">One less for the gas chamber.

194

>Helping environment one dead smallhat at a time."

"A precursor to an actual Holocaust? Like for real this time?"

And finally, "The revolution is at hand!"

And you know the next post: "A Jew is murdered and everyone is distracted by the freedom fighter who attacked the NWO conference in Lake Tahoe" with a link to Scott Nash's article about there were "serious questions" about the shooting at the conference, suggesting Reptilian subversion.

As you also know when I hit refresh in catalog view, those posts, that content—content, content, content!—disappeared and the following posts took over: "How do you feel about comics erasing all signs of masculinity and femininity?", "Monarchy beats Democracy everytime Republitards", "Why we should welcome sexbots,", "Robot Apocalyspe? Yes, please!" and "MK Ultra never stopped. It just changed".

Did you know the MK Ultra story had my interest piqued? Thought it might help for a page-one rewrite of *Distortion* but I noticed the ferry had arrived, the cars leaving and driving up the ramp while the other cars waited to enter?

I started briskly walking towards the platform, feeling the cold air as I opened the door taking me outside. I started to run just a little bit.

"Don't worry, they won't leave without you."

I looked back. Saw a white guy, with black jacket and faded gray jeans, walking briskly and casually. His features were rigid and defined, his hair cropped short.

You know Mark, right?

He didn't look like Chris Pratt, younger iterations of Matthew McConaughey, Matt Damon or even Tom Cruise…one could make a case for Damon.

MOMNDF: We offered him the part actually.

JRK: I understand his refusing.

Nor the British guys who could do American accents like Henry Cavill, young Jason Statham or Tom Hardy.

MOMNDF: We didn't consider them.

JRK: Also understandable.

Maybe slightly closer to the Australians—oh those white men from down under who supply us with macho heroes these days—like a young Mel Gibson, Russell Crowe, Joel Edgarton or Jason Clarke. But even then, those comparisons don't fit.

MOMNDF: It's why we cast an unknown.

JRK: He did great job I think. Star making performance, if, uh, star making performances still existed.

He looked distinctly American. Unsophisticated, unpretentious, but also rugged, confident, practical and amicable. He smiled when I looked at him. "They won't leave without you. They never do if they see you coming."

"Uh yeah, I guess."

I slowed my walk.

"They're polite like that."

"Um, yeah, really, they are."

The Japanese men nodded to us as they waved us in the ferry. Mark followed behind me as we walked up the steel stairs. There was an open floor area for people to sit and the usual padded seating. I walked to the middle and chose a seat, nervously keeping my distance from him (should've listened to my gut instinct). Didn't feel like talking. Talked to too many Yankees as it was.

Ever engaging with Mark was a mistake.

But…

It's not that type of story.

MOMNDF: We wouldn't have a movie if it was. Well—we would've but the script would've stayed on the slush pile.

JRK: Yeah, things are out of my control. Probably for the best.

Just like it felt instinctual to go automatically to Twitter upon sitting, the first tweet being a YouTube video linked by Scott Nash showing mechanized robots leaping over logs and crushing things with their robot hands with the headlines, "The Deep State Won't Need Humans to Maintain Power". What's the point of lifting then? Or having children?

Technology was a mistake.

Below a PureLight ad was a tweet by *Japan Today* discussing how the girl band Fem100, had a "huge" scandal since the photo leak reveal of one of the member's nude, in suggestive poses with all the photos fogged and slightly blurry (I was sure I could find the uncensored ones) (Later). But there she was, Akiko Fujiwara, crying and bowing at press conference, announcing she will study at a PureLight Temple and try to clear the shame she has brought on the other 99 members. Rumor is she's used most of her earnings for a big donation. She's already been replaced by another member called Riko Takeuchi, who at least looks and plays the part of virgin well. Hopefully she learned her lesson from Akiko not to be such a whore, or at least photographically document her whoredom, so she can keep her chaste image intact for the thirsty beta orbiting male public who worship them.

Girl bands were a mistake.

The article sidebar mentioned other celebrities and their religious connections, mentioning Masami Hisamoto, soccer player Shunsuke Nakamura and Howard Jones as members of Soka Gakkai, Tom Cruise and John Travolta in Scientology, and even mentioned X-Japan's lead singer Toshi being a former member of Home of Heart and how it was all perfectly normal for celebrities to seek and explore religious experiences.

But you know that, don't you?

Do you know I considered listening to latest episode of *Oven Talk* where OingoBoinGoy and Andyschluss discussed how the United States should be divided after obvious impending Civil War where whites would finally "wake up" and become triumphant but instead was distracted by a Periscope alert from Scott Nash, with headline: "Shooting at Deep State Conference is false flag for Reptilian globalists to assert control, latest CIA document dump proves it."?

"Scott Nash, huh?"

Did you know the voice jolted me from screen? Of course, you do because Mark said it, sitting just a seat away from me. I also noticed I lost my data connection.

"Yeah, um, Scott Nash—wait, you know who he is?"

"Sure."

"Oh, it's…it's…I've never met anyone who…"

"Yeah, I know. I mean, I get it. You read and watch these guys on the net and you're all alone, you don't see or hear anyone else talking about them so you feel like you're in some sort of personal bubble."

"Right, right—shit, that's exactly true."

He extended his hand. "Mark."

"Jason."

His grip was firm.

"What do you Jason? English teacher?"

"Yeah, who isn't, right?"

"I'm not."

"You're in the military, um, uh, Navy?"

"Yep."

197

"Going to the Navy School in Etajima?"

"Yep."

"Teaching?"

"Yeah, kind of."

"Cool."

"What's Scott Nash talking about today?"

"I don't, don't know. Just got this Periscope alert, you know Periscope?"

"Sure."

"Something about a shooting in Lake Tahoe and a document dump," I said with a shrug and smile. "Seems, um, those things happen a lot these days."

"They do."

"OpSec busted."

"Right, OpSec."

"Well, it's in the vernacular now."

"For people who want to sound cool like they know intel lingo."

"Right."

"That document dump, if you scroll through it, is mostly just emails and shit. People lose their shit about all that. I think there was mention of a _____ invasion plan or something due to the refugees. Whatever. Like we're going to invade. People make plans, proposals, all the time, then they get locked away in some vault in Kabul or Washington DC and everyone forgets about it."

"Content."

"What?"

"It's all just, um, content, right?"

"Yeah, sure."

"But um, then people like Nash or Twitter go nuts…"

"For like what? A week."

"At best."

"Twitter loses their shit. Life moves on."

"You use Social Media a lot?"

"I have accounts on Twitter, haven't used it in—shit, years I think. I keep up with friends on Facebook."

"No Snapchat?"

"Only women use Snapchat."

I laughed.

"I mean, look, do women really need another platform to give themselves attention?"

I laughed again.

"Am I right?"

"Yeah, yeah."

I noticed some Japanese people looking our way, curious at the foreign language and laughter coming from us.

A schoolgirl, close to 17 or 18, her chest pushing out her collared shirt a bit, walked by our seats, tried to look away but I saw her eyes dart toward us. Mark then looked at me. "How do you survive?" he asked.

"What—I?"

"The girls. Holy shit, there aren't near as many fatties as the states. If I lived here full time, I think my dick would fall off."

Another laugh.

"I survive, I survive."

"You aren't," he then made his wrist a little limp. "Are you?"

"A gay?"

"Yeah, you aren't a fag are you?"

"No, no—no way. I, um, I kind of in a relationship."

"Right. Good. I don't understand any man getting lonely here. If you aren't getting pussy, you aren't trying."

The ferry docked.

"Want to get a taxi together?"

"Um, sure."

"Nice to find someone to talk to who isn't so…"

"Soy?"

"That's a word for it. Most of you English teacher types are…"

"Soft, soy, I know."

"Yeah."

"Going to the Naval Academy, right?"

"Right."

I told the taxi driver where to go.

"All the chicks here, the Americans or westerners—whatever you call them all a bunch of lefttards?"

"Yeah."

"I bet the men fucking cuck to them don't they?"

"Cuck?"

"Yeah, cuck. Like cuckold? Go all in with the leftie bullshit in vain hope to get in their pants?"

"No, I know what it means. It's just…I-I haven't heard someone ever say it…"

"First time for everything. But are the guys like that?"

"Yeah…some."

"Pussies," he said. "That's what's wrong with our society. Men and their weakness for poon."

"It's human nature…I guess?"

"Fuck human nature."

My head quickly moved back as to avoid a jab.

"Fuck it."

"What are you…"

"It doesn't exist. Human nature. Bullshit. We are just humans. To say there's a nature means there is some sort of preset mold in which we're formed. Do you believe in God?"

"I um, I'm…more agnostic I guess. Like there might be a spirit…I don't know."

"Well, I say our existence precedes everything else. Everything is downstream of us coming in to the world."

"It's what we make of it?"

"Exactly. It's what we make of it."

"The world…"

"The world is there be made in my image."

"What about, um, mine?"

"Yours too."

"Wouldn't you say that's a little…"

"Arrogant?"

"Yeah…"

"Sure. But the arrogant shape the world."

MOMNDF: Was it surprising hearing someone reflect the same things you said to Adina, did it make you wonder?

JRK: I was more surprised, maybe even felt a little contrarian, because I didn't want to hear my own thoughts affirmed I felt like…you know even though in retrospect he was doing poor man's summation of Sartre, I don't know, it's just—

MOMNDF: He was cucking?

JRK: No more like I needed to assert my own independent thought? I don't know.

MOMNDF: So you are contrarian?

JRK: I hate that word. Every poet is a form of anarchist right?

MOMNDF: That Nietzsche?

JRK: Yeah...I think.

MOMNDF: You calling yourself a poet?

JRK: No, not necessarily...

The taxi stopped at the gates outside the Academy. The city a stark quiet and darkness compared to the hustle bustle neon of Hiroshima, again relaxing me. "All I'm saying is it's all meaningless. Nothing before, nothing after. We shape the world. Let's have fun, doing it, right?"

"Right."

He then handed the driver some cash and then me. "Here's for the rest of your trip."

"No it's not—"

"Take it."

"Fine. Thanks." I accepted with both hands (Japanese style).

We exchanged numbers. We shook hands again. "Nice meeting you Jason."

"Same."

"See you around."

As he left and the taxi continued to my place, driving past the waters of Hitonose, and the oyster farms populating it's waters, I felt some comfort. It was nice to just have a regular conversation with someone.

And when the taxi arrived, I noticed the money Mark gave me was the exact amount it took to get from the Naval Academy to my apartment.

Kenji is coming.

Not yet.

But Mark had come.

*

I was happy to be back in my apartment, as I always was after a trip. Happy to see everything...actually everything wasn't in place. Agent Murphy told me the police had looked around. But nothing was tossed. My copies of *The War Path*, *Hitler's War*, *Culture of Critique*, and my printed out pdf of *Industrial Society and Its Future*, sat in a neat stack on my kitchen table saying *We have been here*.

Some of the resin kit figures on my modern reliquary were out of arrangement, especially Tetsuo from the movie *Akira* (1988. Directed by Katsuhiro Otomo from a script by Otomo, and Izo Hashimoto cinematography by Katsuji Misawa), with him leaning on his mutant arm. Don't have the time, space or necessity to do a full breakdown of the anime classic. It isn't related to anything. It isn't that type of story.

But still.

The mutated model of Tetsuo being out of place, was the first thing I noticed as I pulled the overhead light on in my dust filled living room. The psychic energy his body produced made it difficult to handle his powers, thus causing all sorts of deformities. This was before he became pure energy towards the end, formless, like the namesake of the film, with his psychic energy destroying a degenerate Neo-Tokyo…a second time. The film opens with the first explosion. Buddhist cycles and all that. Fitting end. Okay, I guess I did break it down a little…

I then heard the wind blow. Felt the walls shake. I put up my stuff and picked up my phone immediately after. Tried to finish the story about the Fem100 singer and her being a typical slut but I got distracted by Twitter.

Dio_LoveChild1982: "Haven't seen you around in a while."

Reply: "I'm around."

But you know that, don't you?

You know I replied because I felt an anxiety of needing to please, worried or driven by the reactions of people I will probably never, ever meet. But that's how it is. Because…

I care what you think.

But at that moment I only cared about Twitter and the up and coming actor Jeremy Silverstein tweet: "Nazis in Japan? All roads lead back to white people."

OR!

Ultima_Thule, discussing the end goal of Globalist forces with screenshot quotes from Nicholas Sarkozy, "What is the goal? It's going to be controversial. The goal is to meet the challenge of racial interbreeding. The challenge of racial interbreeding that faces us in the 21st century. It's NOT A CHOICE (not sure whose emphasis that was), it's an OBLIGATION…" then, some kike, "I think there's a resurgence of anti-Semitism because at this point in time Europe has not yet learned how to be multicultural, and I think we're (Jews) gonna be part of the throes of that transformation…", then some Euro cuck, "THERE CAN BE NO WHITE RACE. TREASON TO WHITENESS IS LOYALTY TO

HUMANITY (emphasis ??)...And the task is to bring this minority together in such a way THAT IT MAKES IT IMPOSSIBLE FOR THE LEGACY OF WHITENESS TO CONTINUE TO REPRODUCE ITSELF."

Humanity. What the fuck does that mean? About as meaningful as *human nature*. And as Mark said earlier, "Fuck human nature." Motherfuckers wanting to create the world in their image. :face_with_symbols_on_mouth:

Me: "Fuck these people."

Ultima_Thule (immediate) reply: "We know how to take care of them when the time comes."

Me: "Damn straight."

I then scrolled down to see a story on Fox News from the Berkeley City Council deciding there might need to be a "thinning of the herd". Goddamn right, there might be, but who will be doing the thinning?

Berkeley anything was a mistake.

But you know that, don't you?

Did you know I laid down in bed with my iPad?

Tried to ignore my phone. Tried to watch something on Netflix, like the easygoing dating reality show *Ainori*. On the episode I watched though, they were in Thailand and meeting a bunch of fags and Lady Boys, discussing how the predominantly Buddhist country is actually quite egalitarian in terms of gay and trans rights with Buddhist's being understanding of the lifestyle because it's not the physical world that matters but rather the world of the spirit. The flesh is of little consequence.

I tried to ignore it because I was more curious to see if the kickboxer was going to hook up with the admitted slutty half-filipino barmaid...but kept thinking about what I just read on Twitter.

:face_with_symbols_on_mouth: :face_with_symbols_on_mouth: :face_wi th_symbols_on_mouth:

>Picks up the phone again.

>Returns to Kai10.

>Sees meme with headline "Who's really in control?" with a pictures of six different Jews each designated with their own sector of power (Federal Reserve and Wall Street, Internet Spying—this Jew wears a Facebook armband, Hollywood and TV, Law Courts, Cancer Industry and, lastly, Pornography).

>Sees a post about CIA experiments with psychic energy to contact with extraterrestrial life, and how governments around the world are secretly in

touch with them as to how to use utilize them for groundbreaking technological purposes.

>interesting.txt

>Hear wind blow louder.

>Feel the cold air coming through the apartment, heater failing.

>Doze off.

>Wake up to the sun peeking through my curtains, whole body feeling cold, wind only at a slight howl.

>Fuckit.txt

Does anyone, when they're reading, really care about weather conditions? Only if it really adds to the mood of the piece, right? Like a horror story where the howling wind and creaking sounds combine to create an overwhelming sense of terror? Of course, Japanese love seasonal shit. Autumn This, Winter That. Like nature itself has something to say or something to do with our condition.

It's superfluous, lazy writing done by lazy writers. Similar to lazy filmmakers just using music as a time travel transportation vehicle.

Cue the latest hit by Ava Max.

MOMNDF: I hope you don't think that about me.

JRK: No, no, I don't.

Fetishizing seasons was a mistake.

And most weather is just transition (between scenes or chapters). It's all become habit, operant artistic conditioning. Like a musical montage of the city skyline with a rising or setting sun in a boomertier sitcom with generic music cues.

An author like Tolstoy can actually interweave the weather in to emotion and feeling. And probably Chekhov too (who I don't have time to read) because Russkies, like Japanese, have a thing for weather. Rain is just as much a character in a Kurosawa film as it is in a Tarkovsky one.

But I'm neither Russian or Japanese. I'm American, and for us, if something doesn't serve a utilitarian purpose, then it serves no purpose.

In this case, my ass was cold because of cold ass weather.

I took a shower.

You don't need to know the dirty details but the hot water on my cold skin felt good. I tried to stay in there as long as possible.

Do you need to know that out of the shower, I turned on the TV to see if they said anything else about Adina? Top story on NHK about the American

NBA (National Basketball Association) suing the Japanese NBA (Nihon Bus Association) for copyright infringement, then the Fem100 story about Akiko Fujiwara's THOTtery then local Hiroshima news but same news from night previous with rehashed soundbites of Detective Fukuyama and Avi Feynman and then quickly on to weather.

Asadora ran for 15 minutes in the background while I checked texts. You know that but do you know the most important was, "Why haven't you called me yet?" from my mom?

Close second was an email from a New York Times reporter, Jessica Rosenstein, "a friend of Adina Iscovitz's cousin" asking if I'd like to talk about my relationship with Adina and the tragedy surrounding her for a feature in the upcoming issue of *The New York Times Magazine*. You know the type of feature, right? The type that starts with an anecdote about someone or someplace obscure but who drew the lottery ticket of being the journalist's framing device? I wasn't going to be that framing device. "Jason Reudelheuber thought posting his racist comments on Reddit boards under a pseudonym was being done anonymously. He thought it was harmless. What he didn't realize was his comments would be the fuel for a hate crime the likes of which Japan as never seen," or some such bullshit. They don't understand the comments section of YouTube or Twitter itself is like the bathroom wall at the neighborhood 7-11—leave a comment and be funny.

But these stories become record in most casual minds.

Most just accept what they hear or see at face value. They have neither the time nor concern to get the particulars or ever question the account aside from what provides entertainment value.

Unless they're political junkies doing opposition research in their spare time. Like a boomer. LOL.

Boomers were a mistake.

But this uncritical information consumption can be leveraged by others than establishment media...but that isn't to be discussed at the moment...if will even get discussed at all.

I wasn't going to be a news pawn.

And none of this matters 'cept my reply: "No. I don't talk to fake news."

But you know that, don't you?

Do you know, the morning show *Asaichi* was now on with a feature on a manga about a gay marriage between a Jap (now deceased) and his whitey BF in Hawaii, and how the hubby travels to Japan to meet the brother of his deceased boytoy with a little girl character to lighten the proceedings? You always need a little girl to make it all humorous, right?

It all helps add to the light air of *Asaichi*, with its faux modern white roman arches adorned with glittering blue bathroom style tile, relaxed and casually dressed hosts, vanilla background music that every TV company around the world seems to purchase, between segments on natural home remedies and inventions by natives to make the day-to-day tasks easier—a foam roller that can also be used as a water bottle!—just glues it all together in an atmosphere of genteel acceptance away from the dirty realities of homosex.

Do you know, I switched to the NHK BS station, with its revolving 10 minutes of news from networks around the world? Top story from ABC regarded the President and his dealings with _____, the refugee crisis there and negotiations with Japan's role followed by brief mention of Adina's murder with "no leads" at the moment and a brief soundbite from Avi saying how everyone is "grieved" and they're hoping that it can be an educational moment for everyone. Then on to stories about an all-female Boy Scout troop, helping out flood victims in South Dakota.

Then on to News from a station in France—also having a refugee crisis.

You do know I returned to my phone to find Scott Nash tweeting about a globalist Nazi cabal of hitmen sent to assassinate Americans living overseas as a pretext to start an invasion or war with a link to the story about Adina's murder. Interestingly enough, Justin Bangs replied in Nash's thread asking, "Why did you hack up my interview and misquote me?" with big tittied co-host Jimena replying "You said those things didn't you? You tweeted them." With Bang's replying "Having THOTs like you on staff tells me everything I need to know about @ScottNash. Deep State Shill."

Then a Periscope alert from Justin Bangs, "Scott Nash smears Justin Bangs with hatchet job interview," with Justin explaining how he was courted by Nash to talk about the globalist conspiracy against men and how his interview was edited by a few choice quotes to make him look like a rape apologist and anti-Semite because he tweeted OingoBoinGoy's Kike-chan (also known as Shekel-sama) meme with the caption "Makes you think", pointing out that Nash RT'd General_TOHO's "Do you know who controls you?" which is obviously anti-Semitic.

And ABC news was on again but I wasn't paying attention. I turned off the set. The disadvantage of TV News is the same as teaching—you have to fill.

Fine when you're the only game in town, but Social Media has democratized the field. There is really no need to tune in anymore. Not that it matters.

TV News was a mistake.

I walked to the kitchen to turn on the radio in my kitchen. Figured I needed some culture. Some relaxation from all the noise. I found the NPR broadcast from Armed Forces Radio Network coming from the Marine Corps Air Station in Iwakuni. First the soft voice DJ talked about the Jewish composer Ari Rosenstein, and other "composers of color" doing a rendition of some German or Austrian (I forgot).

The music played. Then more music, this time with piano—maybe it was Chopin—I don't know. It all ran together. Then talk of a rendition of Bach by composer called Masayuki Uchida—with no mention of his ethnicity or his inclusion of "composers of color". They just assume we all know where he's from.

But I could barely listen to any of it. Tried closing my eyes but couldn't relax. All genteel fag stuff, outdated even, and only served the elites, polite society needing polite music.

Classical music was a mistake.

My phone rang. You know it was Agent Murphy F.B.I. but I don't trust his FD-302 or any other doc and I'm not sure if they'll give you the phone record nor will the record note my shaking hand when he identified himself:

"Did you call Jessica Rosenstein 'fake news'?"

"Um, like publicly?"

"No. In an email. Someone from the Times called our office. Said you called them 'fake news' and then asked if you're a suspect."

"Am I…a suspect…" :grits_teeth:

"No. We've interviewed the Palestinians from Joey's—"

"So it was them?"

"Didn't say that—look we're close to an official announcement. Last thing we need is you causing distractions with your attitude…"

"I didn't…look don't worry about me. I'm not saying anything. Worry more about Mandy giving an alibi…"

"Mandy? Mandy who?"

"Um, uh, Mandy, she lives on the island here with me she was at Joey's too?"

"Why would Mandy give them an alibi?"

207

"Well, um, you know, like she likes brown dud—you know brown guys? She has a thing for them."

"What?"

"I'm just saying…"

"We have a statement from her. She was on the phone with her brother at the time of the murder."

"Look, can I…never mind."

"What?"

"It's ok, I just…"

"Out with it."

"Just a question…"

"Okay…"

"How would some um, you know, social media comments affect an investigation? Doesn't evidence, you know, um, trump all?"

A quiet pause. "Everyone would love to have you arrested. Especially the media…"

"But…we all know who runs the media…"

"You're going there?"

"I'm not saying they run the entire media, you know. I'm just saying they have a high degree of influence…"

"The only thing Jews run are the fucking Synagogue's kid."

Fucking boomers. Such a mistake.

"I'm an easier target than, say, Palestinians?"

"You think the media wants to give more just cause to the Israeli military to invade Palestine?"

"How does a Jewish girl murdered in Japan give Israel a pretext to invade?"

"It doesn't. It just adds fuel to the fire."

"And I'm an easier target?"

"Frankly? Yes. A white male who made pro-Hitler anti-Semitic Holocaust denial comments online killing a beautiful Jewish girl is a media wet dream."

"She wasn't that hot."

"Doesn't matter. They'll find a flattering pic. Nobody will know any different."

"Right…" :thinking: "You know, I'm half-Jewish, really fully Jew since my mom is Jewish…"

"That could be conveniently ignored."

"Oh…"

"Once again, I recommend you clean up your online profile while you can. And keep your mouth shut unless it's mainstream media, and in that case, be fucking polite."

"I'm not a suspect?"

"No. You're not."

"Should I email Jessica Rosenstein back? Say it was a misunderstanding?"

"No. We'll handle her."

The line went dead.

Kenji is coming.

When?

Soon.

*

Does it matter I returned to the school Monday with the same hellos from the students? "Hello," one boy says with a wide smile. His two friends follow suit. "Hello." A greeting in to a world familiar but different.

OR!

That the *Kocho-sensei* took me in his office to chat, gave me his condolences and that I thanked him and bowed?

OR!

That upon return to the teacher's room I saw Yamamoto-sensei at his desk across from mine? "I read the news…" he said.

"Yeah…"

"I'm sorry for your loss."

"Thanks."

Is it important that we taught a class? Same drudgery of Yamamoto-sensei leading and me being the human pronunciation dictionary, with the students repeating the words after I say them. No one wanted to be there. Most of the kids sat looking at the floor, quiet, barely raising their voices. Others just talked while Yamamoto-sensei taught. He didn't interrupt them. But neither did I.

We both did our globalist duties and went about our way.

Back in the teacher's office, Yamamoto-sensei said he's going for a walk and asked me to join him. I agreed.

*

Doesn't matter: At school entranceway, Yamamoto easily switched from his school shoes to his outdoor ones, where I had struggle with slipping mine on. The ease at which the Japanese perform their customs and the clumsiness at which I perform them likewise give me an overwhelming sense of self consciousness. I care what they think. Just like…

I care what you think.

*

I felt the wind on my face as we walked. The sun provided little relief but I also felt the sweat under my clothes and jacket.

Walking down a few side streets, we ended up on a path leading to a bamboo forest at the foot of the small mountains doting the island but I ignored the beauty and talked to Yamamoto-sensei about the weather as Japanese are wont to do then started talking about his stress teaching and working with Yamaguchi-sensei, a backstabbing asshole who when pressed by the *Kyoto-sensei* complained that I was on my phone too much and that my predecessor was "better" and how he felt that Yamaguchi-sensei was too strict with Yuri-chan.

He then approached a green bamboo tree as it strutted out of the ground and knocked on it. He smiled while I frowned inwardly at his teacher gossip. Given his short stature and thin build, he looked almost like a wise dwarf or a lecherous sage, like Giuseppi Mayart in the anime movie *Yoju Toshi—Wicked City* in English (1987. Directed by Yoshiaki Kawajiri from a script by Kawajiri, based on the novel by Hideyuki Kikuchi cinematography by Kinichi Ishikawa).

He then looked up at the trees, like he was looking towards Heaven, paused for a moment then looked at me. "My father…he told me, as child, that the bamboo is like a miracle. Hollow on the inside yet so strong on the outside."

I didn't know how to reply. I stood there silent, looking at the green shoots.

"Do you like bamboo?" he asked with a smile.

"Sure."

He then went behind a few trees and returned with a steel folding chair, another smile on his face. "I put this here," he said. He then unfolded it, placed it on a clearing and presented his hand. "*Dozo.*"

I smiled and sat down. Closed my eyes. Don't know why. It felt cinematic so I did something cinematic. The quiet enveloped me, the only thing I heard was cars in the distance.

I opened my eyes and saw Yamamoto-sensei wondering around looking up at the trees. "Your friend, she was *Yudai-jin*…how to say?"

"Jewish. She was Jewish."

"You?"

"I'm half-Jewish, but it's more like half-Japanese, you know? I'm not religious. But...she was...kind of. It's kind of like how Japanese assumed to be Buddhist and Shinto and practice it?"

"I see...but you believe something?"

"I believe...in nothing...I guess. I guess I'm a nihilist?"

"*Ah so ka.* That helps get what you want? What do you want?"

I thought for a moment. "I don't know. I—want to be like the bamboo tree. Empty yet strong. To be blank, but not necessarily empty. Or maybe...bamboo is the wrong metaphor...maybe I just want to be like water. Formless, without shape, yet it gradually wears down the rocks as it moves past them. I just...I don't want to think."

"Hmmm..." he said looking around, while thinking.

"Thinking...reason...I feel it's all, well, um, bullshit. Our hearts, our desires have more power."

"Desire?"

"Well...no one tries to think while they're having sex, right? They just do it. Feeling, passions, matter."

"You had feelings for her?"

"Well...we...we...kind of had a secret relationship...I mean we had sex a few times." I felt myself getting sweaty though it was winter.

"Hmph. Secrets..." he looked at the ground, then looked back up. "My father studied English as a hobby. He loved Shakespeare, Sherlock Holmes and all things British," he said. "But it was the war. It was too western and he wasn't a teacher. He kept it a secret. He hid English books at home. Another secret."

"What happened to him?"

"He went to the war. He was old, but they made him fight. He died in Okinawa."

"That...was a bloody battle."

"Yes. That is why they dropped the bomb, right? Because of nasty fighting?"

"That's what they say."

Yamamoto-sensei returned to looking around. Only sounds were the wind and the bamboo trees gently swaying.

The silence felt awkward. I tried to think of something..."Did you see the movie *Kuroi Ame?*" *Black Rain* (1989. Directed by Shohei Imamura with a script by Toshiro Ishido based on the novel by Masuji Ibuse cinematography by Takashi Kawamata) (not to be confused with the other 1989 film called *Black*

Rain. Directed by Ridley Scott, with a script by Craig R. Bolotin and Warren Lewis, cinematography by Jan de Bont).

"No," he said. "I lived it."

"Oh…"

"My mom's sister lived in Hiroshima. We walked from Ondo to the city after the bomb. I saw all the death. The sickness…"

"Oh…"

"And when I came back home," he looked at me, smiled, then up at the bamboo, "I was happy to see the bamboo. The nature, yes?"

I smiled. "Yes."

"It's like everything had been destroyed. The way of life. Everything change. Now it was okay to learn English. No need for secret. Everyone wanted to learn. It was encourage. I went to college to study English. But my father could not see it…but I still remember what my father say…every day," he said looking up at the bamboo.

This was the first time, Yamamoto-sensei told me about his past. Japanese are good at keeping secrets, something I admired. What does this conversation have to do with the rest of story? I don't know.

I just felt a need to write it.

*

On the walk back, as we passed Izumi YouMe town, we ran in to an American. He wasn't in the military. He was short and stocky. Looked like Jack Black. "Don't see many non-Japanese faces around here," he said loudly. He was afraid to say "white faces." Par for the course.

His name was Matt as well (how many fucking people are named Matt in this world?).

He told us how he used to teach here 13 years ago. Yamamoto-sensei didn't know him because he was teaching in Kure—at the time. He was in town for his wife's sister's wedding and just decided to take the day to look around. He told us how the island had changed but was similar, lamenting the closing of Emi Karaoke across the street from the Pachinko parlor in Hitonose. He then pointed to the Edion store across the street from the mall.

"If I recall, that used to be called *Deo-Deo*, right?"

I shrugged my shoulders. But Yamamoto-sensei confirmed it.

"Funny how everything changes, huh?" Matt said with a shrug of his shoulders.

I found the shrug troubling.

212

*

Yamamoto-sensei noticed my unease.

Because he asked me about the exchange and unease as we returned to the school.

*

Cue *Nothing to Fear* by Depeche Mode.

The New York Times Magazine headline: "Did Hate Kill Adina Iscovitz?" Byline: "Adina Iscovitz was a Jewish advocate living in Japan. Her murder raises questions about anti-Semitic discourse in Asia."

Typical start: "It was a cold day in in Hiroshima, 480 miles away from Tokyo…" Always have to frame everything around Tokyo… "Shop owner Toshiro Yamano was sweeping the dusty front of his school uniform store when he came upon a body. 'At first I thought it was someone drunk,' the elderly man said. But as Yamano got closer, he found a body that was lifeless, lying in a pool of blood."

New paragraph: "He knew there was a problem. He knew this day would be different. Something that rarely occurs in Japan now faced him head on. A murder had been committed."

You know the rest of it.

Talk about Adina. Quotes from Avi about how she was very vocal pro-Israel activist and how that might not have sat well with others. Who were these others? Marcelle, Mariane or…me?

Matt: "I know there are some who disagreed with Adina especially her views on Israel. I've even heard some of these views in person to the point they were rationalizing the actions of a great evil like Hitler. But people like Adina helped educate me about the evils of the Holocaust. And in turn I learned about other evils, like the Korean Comfort Women. These are tragic events that must never be repeated. Unfortunately, Adina's death appears to be a repeat of these events." (What. A. Cuck.)

Min: "We're forming a new group: 'JET's Against Hate'. Our purpose will be to combat the type of ignorance that led to the murder of our precious friend Adina. Her death will not be in vein. As a Korean, I know what it feels like to be discriminated against. Looking at that monument in the Peace Park, of the Koreans who died in the blast, their only crime being slave labor, and then thinking of those women forced in to prostitution, I can't ever forget about the dehumanizing force of racism." The article noted she was in tears while saying this, while also recapping Japan's history of discrimination against

213

Koreans, mentioning the comfort women and the Rape of Nanking...even though that had nothing to do with Korea or Koreans except maybe to illustrate general attitudes and tragedies of racism.

Mandy: "As a white female, I just feel so guilty as to what my race—I get choked up even saying it because I think of all that we've done to minorities and the shame I feel. I look at all the beautiful people, especially those beautiful African children"—I couldn't continue reading. Didn't need to read about Mandy giving her own form of reparations by sleeping with a man of every race, hoping to get impregnated by a nigger so she could have a beautiful dark but light-skinned child.

The rest of the piece was the usual nonsense about the forces that inhabit the "dark side" of the internet where "anti-Semitism, racism and homophobia are common."

But you know that, don't you?

You also know my mom called me, busting my nuts for being "rude" to the reporter Jennifer Rosenstein and begging me to come "home". I hung up after bringing down her hysteric pleading.

Do you know, that she didn't realize I was home here in Japan and had to keep it that way? Looking at Adina's face for the article—they did find a flattering picture—made me ponder how be able to remain.

Do you know what my mom wanted? Have you talked to her?

I knew what she wanted.

She wanted her own little PR campaign to both the establishment and Jewry...LOL I could just say "the establishment".

But I could see her "vision": I go in front of the cameras and microphones, cry and confess, convince them that I'm a good little Hebe or the very least, not a bad goy. I'd talk about hate and what I learned. Give them a character arc of redemption.

Because everyone likes a good story.

Maybe tell them how special Adina was to me and how dangerous the menace of White Nationalism, Neo-Nazism, Masculinism and Anime Rightism really was. Maybe I could even write a guest opinion piece in a major publication about my explorations inside that "dark" world and what I learned. Maybe even start a campaign to pass some type of legislation that would make everyone feel better once it's passed.

Even though none of it would had to do with the actual murder. Especially after reading that the Palestinians were detained then released. Especially after

214

receiving a text from Min saying, "I just talked to a *NewsGrind* reporter. Pls don't come to Adina's memorial service. BTW what did u & matt talk about?"

No.

Fuck all that.

*

As logged in to the Slack a text alert covered the top half of my screen. A text from Mandy: "Just talked to NewsGrind reporter. Thought you might need to read this. Link: "Whiteness, Maleness, And Americanism Have No Intrinsic Value". But you know that, don't you?

I know you know I pasted the link in to the Slack.

Me: Sent by some THOT who finds it profound.

Ernst_Jungroyper: Delet This. NOW.

The_ZOGfather: All THOTs get the rope. Especially ones who text articles like that.

Me: 100%

OingoBoinGoy: You send a reply?

The_ZOGfather: Say you agree. Try to build common ground with her.

Me: What?

OingoBoinGoy: Delet urself @The_ZOGfather

The_ZOGfather: I'm not finished. Check your autism.

Ernst_Jungroyper: Can you be more fucking cucked @ The_ZOGfather?

The_ZOGfather: Find common ground with her. Agree with everything she says, laugh with her, build rapport, get her wet and then back off completely.

OingoBoinGoy: LOL fug.

The_ZOGfather: no better way to ruin a whore.

Ernst_Jungroyper: Fug man, I need to try that shit.

Me: LOL Thanks @The_ZOGfather But I don't hate her. She at least tries to be a good person.

Ernst_Jungroyper: Now you need the rope.

The_ZOGfather: she's not a person. she's a THOT. women aren't people.

Me: You're just jealous a girl is girl is talking to me.

Ernst_Jungroyper: projection.

215

Me: It's not projection.

The_ZOGfather: i know it's hard for you but try not to be a cuck. It hinders your relationships with both men and women.

Me: I'm not getting cucked.

OingoBoinGoy: >reminds us of gook conquests.

Me: Japs aren't gooks.

The_ZOGfather: WE KNOW. You've told us 20,000 fucking times.

Ernst_Jungroyper: You will get cucked if you act like a cuck.

Me: How do you know I'm a cuck?

The_ZOGfather: Just by the way you talk. Ur obviously blue pilled on women.

Ernst_Jungroyper: >thinks women have their own ideas on politics.

Me: Lick my balls @Ernst_Jungroyper

The_ZOGfather: like any THOT her politics have everything to do with personal expediency. she believes those things because they give her social cache.

Me: Did I ever say I disagreed with you? You should have seen the niggers she was talking to a couple days ago at a conference. The smile on her face.

Ernst_Jungroyper: this is why women need to be put in cages.

OingoBoinGoy: Wait. Isn't that the one where that Khazar got murdered?

The_ZOGfather: that bitch had some milkers on her.

Ernst_Jungroyper: i just might sell out my race for those milkers.

OingoBoinGoy: did u know her?

Me: Yes.

The_ZOGfather: that wasn't the THOT who sent you that article was it?

Me: No.

Ernst_Jungroyper: just a reminder everyone:

Posted a link to a research article with the headline: "High mammographic density in women of Ashkenazi Jewish descent".

The_ZOGfather: scientifically proven evidence of Khazar milkers. LOL

OingoBoinGoy: how much tax payer funding was required for this study of Judaic hooters?

The_ZOGfather: too much.

Ernst_Jungroyper: I should ask Justin Bangs. He's the one who linked to the article.

The_ZOGfather: @Ernst_Jungroyper you read Justin Bangs? That guy is a faggot.

Ernst_Jungroyper: I've read some of his books.

The_ZOGfather: he's a lolcow.

Me: How so?

OingoBoinGoy: Faggot used our meme. Took credit.

The_ZOGfather: Watch Scott Nash's takedown. Here lemme find link.

Then a link with title: "Justin Bangs Is a Total Fraud"

A video discussing how Justin Bangs, giving his real name (Dimitrije Kovac), is actually a failed model who then transitioned to the PUA scene. It notes that he's of "Croatian-Jewish descent" but uses the silly moniker of "Justin Bangs". Nash discussed Bangs' history of plagiarism, shaking down his one-on-one coaching clients for cash when they visited him in LA, not paying his affiliates and just being an outright liar, concluding with OingoBoinGoy's meme and ending with Nash saying "Justin Bangs with his misogynist and anti-Semitic content is not a friend to our movement and he isn't to be trusted by liberty loving patriots like you and me. I'm not here to participate in character assassination but I wouldn't be doing my duty as a broadcaster, journalist and filmmaker if I didn't warn my listeners—and really, I hate call you 'listeners' or 'fans', because I consider all of you friends—you are all my friends. And if I didn't warn my friends of the elements out there trying to bilk, subvert and distract them, then what type of friend would I be?"

Me: I enjoy Justin Bangs emails

The_ZOGfather: Holy shit! Are you that autistic? OFC you unpolluted your inbox for the very fact that's he probably a kike.

I then got a Periscope Alert from Justin Bangs at that moment: "Character Assassination! My Jewish Ancestry Explained!" I screenshotted the headline and pasted it in the Slack.

Me: LOL look at this.

Ernst_Jungroyper: Delet.

The_ZOGfather: Holy fuck. What good are you if you don't listen?

I didn't watch the Scope. I went in to my latest Justin Bangs email, just received today with headline entitled: "The Secret to Making A Comeback", quickly scrolled to the bottom without reading and hit "Unsubscribe". One less distraction.

I then got another Periscope alert from Scott Nash with the title "Should I Grow A Beard?"

I then got a text from Yu with the message: "Are you okay?"

But you know that, don't you?

*

"I'm fine."

*

I wish I replied that way.

*

But: "Hey, I know I should have reached out sooner. I don't know if you watch the news or not but you might have heard about the girl who was murdered at my conference? I knew her. I guess you could call her a friend. She was Jewish but that had nothing to do with the fact that I'm half-Jewish. It was just purely coincidence but anyways. Some in the media are doing some investigating, you might hear of some stories dropping, I don't know what really makes it in to Japanese news these days, but you might hear that we might have been more than just friends. Actually, what is the Japanese media saying? Just curious. Do Japanese even have a "fake news" problem? Or do they just have a media problem? Maybe I should search the videos by Random-Yoko on YouTube and check. Have you watched any of her videos? She talks about Japan from a Right Wing perspective. Anyways I presume that the Japanese are actually pretty guarded against things like that? Against media lies? Maybe they're protected. Maybe the media isn't out to get them? You know, because they don't have a radical fifth column inside their country trying to subvert them? Unless you count Koreans and Chinese? Masayoshi Son is Chinese so I'd keep an eye on him. I suppose you could add in the Americans there as well, especially the Jewish ones. But they're few in number. Adina was one of those of Jews. She was murdered. It might've been Palestinians or might have been this girl Min who I know. Hope you never meet her. Basically stay away from any gaijin on this island that isn't me LOL. Either way there was some Nazi store signage but it might have just been a prank with kids turning a Buddhist symbol right side up adding a photo of Hitler. You never know. I do know she was against the sign. And now she's dead. Murdered. For what?

218

I don't know. There's been a lot of talk about online. Scott Nash, do you know Scott Nash? He said it was some sort of ritualistic murder. The media, well the American media, thinks it was a hate crime. I think the Japanese media is following their lead honestly but really I don't know why she was killed. The killing was gruesome as well. Her body mangled, lying in a pool of blood, her skull cracked open from what looks like several hammer blows to the skull. Don't mean to give you the gruesome details. Sorry. But it's just, she's dead. And I knew her. A friend. And now I think someone is doing an article on me, saying a climate of hate killed her. I know that's what they're going to say, just because I shitposted online. You know the word *shitposting*? It just means that I wrote some things that were a little provocative or politically incorrect. It's nothing. Just having some fun, having a good time. They're trying to say that I'm hateful, that I'm the one who killed her. I'm the one who caused this but there's no proof that I did anything. None at all. But luckily I'm here. And it's been stressful. I'm not in handcuffs though. But it's still stressful. After we last met, I thought I'd keep my distance but I miss you. I need to see you. Everything has been a whirlwind but you're an anchor in those powerful winds. I'm sorry for not talking to you sooner. You've been so kind, so wonderful, you've been my only friends here in Japan. Really you've been one of my only friend the way we talk and the way you listen. I feel so comfortable around you. I can be myself. I hope to see you soon Yu. I love you."

Do you know I hit "send" and shook my hand from text cramp and that my heart was racing from embarrassment because I felt I let my sentimental giving nature get the best of me but I put the phone down on the table, went to look at my latest photos that were only a few weeks old but felt like a century ago, a visual time machine in to a more innocent and peaceful state of mind that just left me longing wishing for a return but I could just look not touch, only one part of my senses engaged feeling real and unreal occupying that same ethereal concrete space? Fuck.

Did you know a photo of an old cartridge of Super Mario Kart sans box struck me? Mario was all over the world, almost like an icon, just as much a part of people's lives, the console and its associated plushies sitting as a centerpiece of a room where the cross or statues and icons of Mary and Christ once stood with the Italian plumber inspiring just as many drawings, paintings and even statues maybe even more than those religious icons. But the drawings, statues and games…feathers in weight, hollow inside the shells. No doctrines and schools, dedicated to teaching and studying, no holidays and festivals

219

dedicated either nor lives ordered around prayers to this empty yet present deity. A statue of Mario will never carry the weight of Pieta yet he's ever so more present than Mary, Christ or even Buddha in Japan, and yet this isn't merchandise monotheism—no!—it's polytheistic for polythene gods. He is joined on the mantle and alters with the Nintendo canon of Link, Pikachu, Kirby, Donkey Kong and Fox McCloud. And that's just Nintendo. It also co-exists in the vacant celestial bodies with Disney, Ghibli, Square, Clamp, LEGO, Blizzard, DC and Harry Potter. Their adherents just as dedicated and radical as Christians and Muslim but their bodies, passivity and shallowness a mirror image of brittle deities they serve.

Brands were a mistake.

The text alert ring tone filled my apartment, piercing the empty quiet.

On the homescreen sat Yu's reply to my embarrassing bromide: "I see."

An immediate letdown. I cared what she thought. Just like...

I care what you think.

Why cut your wrists and let them bleed on the page if no one really gives a shit? Why open up? Why text at all? It's all just a distraction.

Texting was a mistake.

Kenji is coming.

Not quite yet goddammit.

MOMNDF: Some are just waiting in eager anticipation.

JRK: Yeah, well they can keep reading if they care.

*

Notes: "He then goes to school."

*

You know I received an email from Emily Abramson of *NewsGrind* with "Interview" on the subject line. You know it started with "Hi Jason," So friendly. "I'm doing a story on the murder of Adina Iscovitz. After talking with some of her friends, I heard that you two were in a relationship? I would like to ask you some questions if you have time."

"No," was my reply.

But you know that, don't you?

Did you know I knew what she was thinking? That she was going to blindside me with questions about whatever comments she found online, most of them innocuous?

Me: LOL some fake news journo asked me for an interview and I told her to fuck off.

220

OingoBoinGoy: LOL you tell 'em man.

Ernst_Jungroyper: Why would they want to interview you?

Me: They wanted to talk about Adina, the girl who was murdered.

Ernst_Jungroyper: >dead Jewish girl
>ofc they have to publicize it

OingoBoinGoy: Ofc they need good goy remorse for it all.

Neu!Albion: @Ernst_Jungroyper re: Hitler. He admired the British and their Empire. The Second World War was really just a ruse devised by the Americans and Soviets to bring about the impoverishment of the Britain and her empire.

Ernst_Jungroyper: Makes sense.

Neu!Albion: it's not just sense it's the truth. You must recognize that. Of course they've scotched it from the history books. Churchill sold out Britain.

Ernst_Jungroyper: :100%:

OingoBoinGoy: u see the Kai10 post about Nazi psychic research taken to US through Project Paper Clip? Ultima_Thule posted it. I think Nash is doing a video about it today. He always rips shit from Thule like the namefag but de-Judaizes it.

Neu!Albion: It's natural the US and Soviets pillaged the Nazis for their scientific research given all the great strides they made. Truly formidable.

Me: Wait—are we going after Nash now? I thought we took his side in the Justin Bangs thing.

OingoBoinGoy: Bangs was a faggot but that doesn't make Nash any lesser of a faggot. He's being a bitch refusing to talk about ZOG. I'm curious as to how he'll spin this psychic story given that it's tied to _____.

You know he was referring to recent negotiations that were ongoing with _____ who just took American Richard Kaplan hostage. Nash said Kaplan was a spook on a YouTube post while in the Washington Post he's described as a "college professor". Ultima_Thule's post noted this "professor" was indeed a ground-breaking researcher in physics and communication through mental energy transference. He was last seen in China for a conference. Meaning, he was kidnapped. But you know that, don't you?

221

Just as you know The New York Times described Kaplan's capture as "deeply alarming" and that backdoor negotiations were ongoing mainly due to human rights and how the rest of the story was vanilla with family and colleagues lamenting and grieving his capture. _____ media, described Kaplan as a CIA spy and you certainly know Ultima_Thule stated Kaplan was in fact captured because he was rendezvousing with Chinese scientists who had travelled to _____ in an attempt to assess their research in the realm of psychic technology and maybe the refugees had something to do with it. His capture was of the utmost importance and also explained why the US was rapidly pursuing negotiations. You know the President and other politicians on both side of the aisle made public statements on all the political talk shows on NBC, CBS, ABC and FOX not to mention the cable networks CNN, MSNBC and Fox News, expressing their "grave concern" at these "unwarranted actions" on behalf of _____.

Just as you know the speculation about the conference in Lake Tahoe was really about Kaplan's capture—but the shooter disrupted it, getting Nash heat.

Do you know how interesting it is watching the public figures give their performance, like the puppets they are, while seeing the true strings in places like Kai10, the curtain lifted?

Do you know why I did not mention or foreshadow this earlier? Maybe I forgot and maybe fuck you. It wasn't important to the narrative…until now.

Me: @OingoBoinGoy do you really believe that. The Washington Post says he's just an activist college professor…

OingoBoinGoy: R U really going to trust ZOG media? R U that autistic? Do I need to boot you from this slack like I just booted @The_ZOGfather?

Me: No I was just fucking with you man.

"Jason-sensei? Let's go!" I heard.

I looked up from my phone and Yamaguchi-sensei, wearing his track suit, was getting up from his desk. Fuck, I forgot we had a lesson today. Actually, maybe I didn't know and he just expected me to accompany him.

"Class?" I asked.

"Yes."

Me: Gotta hit a class guys.

OingoBoinGoy: I'm gonna hit my wife.

>Puts phone on vibrate.

Kenji is coming.

Indeed.

*

You know the *NewsGrind* article dropped Thursday night in the US but Friday morning in Japan and you know it was forwarded to me from Min with the text "The real Jason. BTW I told matt never 2 talk to u again" with a headline of "Adina Iscovitz's Boyfriend Was a Closet Nazi" and Emily Abramson's name on the byline and disclaimer: "Warning: This post contains content that is misogynist, racist and anti-Semitic"

You know the opening paragraph immediately betrayed the headline by never mentioning Nazi, "Ever heard of a Jewish man posting comments that are misogynist and racist? How about anti-Semitic comments? If that doesn't surprise you, what if this same man was the boyfriend of a recently murdered Jewish girl? We've just uncovered some vile posts from Jason Reudelheuber, the boyfriend of Adina Iscovitz, who was recently murdered in Hiroshima, Japan (480 miles away from Tokyo). The anonymous posts were done on the political board of Kai10, a haven for all things offensive."

You know the body was just screenshots of posts Agent Murphy mentioned:

"LA is full of THOTs. It's a THOTocaust."

"If she breathes, she a THOT."

"If you ask me, Hitler did nothing wrong. If he actually perpetrated the Holocaust, that is." Ofc :smirk: adding the emphasis.

"The more evidence I see, the Holocaust looks like a Holohoax."

Followed by comments from Min ("I'm shocked and appalled"), Matt ("I didn't know he was like that. I try to be a friend to all races, especially living here in Japan. I see no color. I respect the Constitution."), Marcelle ("I could always tell he was a racist"), Kim Cheong ("The way he always stared and smirked at me oozed toxic masculinity") and Mandy ("As a Cis straight white female, I just feel so guilty about what my race has to done to minorities."). Ending with a comment from my mom ("Jason is a good Jewish boy who I know regrets some things he said that can't be erased online.") (Thanks mom).

And ended with Avi Feynman talking about how he will reach out to my school board to discuss these comments but lamented how Japanese culture has a tendency to look the other way regarding incendiary comments such as the ones I made.

"Jason-sensei."

I looked through the comments.

223

"Jason-sensei."

I looked through my texts. My mom saying "Please call", one from Avi reading "We need to talk, please call", and a DM from OingoBoinGoy, with a link to the article: Is this you? Your real name is Jason and you're a Jew? Are you a Fed as well?

Me: I'm half-Jewish, half-Aryan. Not a Fed.

"Jason-sensei!"

I looked next to my desk and there sat Yamaguchi-sensei, in the same track suit. "*Hai?*"

He then started talking about some project to work on over the Winter Holiday, something he wanted to present to the class, talking about a new program in which to better teach English to kids, something about making a pivot to more internationalist style curriculum where we talk about different cultures of the world or some such bullshit. I mentioned that I've already got my lesson on Christmas for the kid's sans all the Christian trappings. And he said that he was talking after the holidays, he wanted to a bigger presentation on something. Something involving art, music and songs and all other types of something. It was all just something. Something, something, something. My eyes kept darting to the phone, thinking of what messages awaited me, what text would arrive, what type of vitriol lurked in the comments section of the *NewsGrind* article? Would I receive death threats? Would I receive unfriendings in both real life and e-life? Did I really have any friends IRL? What was the real world, and where did my real friends dwell? Where would I rather be, the confines of this fucking class or the open freedom of cyberspace? What really mattered? What really existed? I knew that it all boiled down to one thing...

I care what you think.

But Yamaguchi-sensei kept talking about something while I thought of something else with his something and my something not really aligning at all with me knowing that I'm sure he had something of concerns for his own guitar something he loved playing in front of kids, his own mini-rock god for an audience of 30, but here I was wondering about my something, a something that took up my whole mental capacity stacked upon stack with worry and anxiety towards an ethereal foggy threat of something that sits in its watchtower with cocked triggers directed at me waiting for the order, while Yamaguchi-sensei kept talking about something.

And I just nodded with the occasional *Hai* and *wakarimashita* a game I played daily, my pitiful performance all directed at maintaining the appearance of something.

I realized I needed to change something. I needed to get out of my invisible barred mind prison. I needed to do something.

I texted Yu.

But you know that, don't you?

Kenji is coming.

You know, it's soon.

MOMNDF: He can't come here soon enough.

JRK: Indeed.

*

You know this text: "Let's go to Miyajima. Stay at Ryokan!" as you know it took a while to get a reply.

But did you know, in the interim, I spent my time trying to avoid my phone, avoid all Social Media and sites like Kai10, putting it on vibrate?

Just as you know, I needed it close so I could hear it vibrate when Yu messaged me. Needed it close but I wanted it far away.

I put it on top of my lacquer black *kotatsu*, slipped my feet under the sheets, felt the warmth on my toes yet shivered up top. The afternoon sun shone through my window. Supposed to go to Karate tonight. Supposed to do many things.

I went through my photos, looking at the various ones I needed to place on Instagram but I—FUCK I COULDN'T CONCENTRATE. Heard the sounds of the kids outside walking around, jeering at each other in thick, almost indecipherable, *Hiroshima-ben*. "*Ja no!*" "*Ja no!*"

The phone vibrated!

But you know it was a Slack Push alert. My handle tagged with "Get in here!"

Did you know I was tempted, picked up the phone, held it but swiped the alert away? Begone, begone.

Still no response from Yu.

But you know that, don't you?

Do you know I decided to watch a movie but couldn't decide what to watch having torrented so much, my hard drive full of anything and everything? So much selection, so many choices, so much content—content, content, content!—It wasn't an easy mood day where the selection was easy.

MOMNDF: You should've watched *Panic Room*.

JRK: Wasn't in the mood.
MOMNDF: *The Social Network*?
JRK: Wanted something violent.
MOMNDF: *Se7en*?
JRK: Just wasn't feeling it.

After scrolling and scrolling, so many movies, so much content, content, content—content after content, I settled on the director's cut of *Death Wish 2* (1982. Directed by Michael Winner from a script by David Engelbach and cinematography by Thomas Del Ruth and Richard H. Kline) but shuttled through the first eight minutes of build-up bullshit. Just content to get the story going, a pretext for action. A movie can't just open with guns shooting and titties everywhere. There needs to be build and framing. It isn't video game. It's seduction. Like inciting incident. Like…

Kenji is coming.

Incitement is coming, really.

I jump to the scene where the wetback maid Rosario (Silvana Gallardo) is raped by a gang of diversity, vibrancy and cultural enrichment and the two whites who are just window dressing, a nod to the audience that we know it's niggers who do the raping but they can't be so explicit—have you ever heard of a multi-ethnic gang?—because the only people comforted by this cast are the kike executives signing the checks who are afraid of any sort of criticism.

But the tension Michael Winner and the editors build towards the rape of Rosario is formidable, a full two minutes of tension. The cross cuts between her in homely manner, looking simple but attractive in her white blouse and blue dress, the way the gang stalks the house and looks through the windows as she cleans with the tension of the rape itself, where Rosario is on her knees crying, a knife at her throat as she is threatened to be quiet, her skirt uplifted, her granny panties pulled to her knees, a gag put around her mouth, the nigger licking his lips—who just can't control himself as he pushes everyone else away so he can be first to enter. "Save some for me man!" The two whites don't look on with amusement but focus and even some concern, where one breaks up the proceedings and tells them to move it from the living room to the bedroom. The way she's tossed on the bed, the panties crumpled just above her knees, full bush exposed, heels still on—in fact her heels remain on the during the whole rape—while cutting to the downstairs area where whitey is worried about logistics (typical)—while Rosario's bra is ripped off in front of

226

the camera revealing her full brown nipples and the scene ending where whitey enters, slapping a crowbar in his hand, as Rosario is brought to him like a dog on all fours naked, the torn white cloth from the bra or t-shirt hanging from her neck like a leash as he unbuckles his belt and pulls down his pants while Fishburne says, "All right now, lady. Quietly. Do it nice."

Watching this, you can't help but think that Michael Winner is a man in full control. He knows the visual cues, the cutting pace that make this scene both exciting, sexually arousing yet also slightly disturbing. I only say slightly because everyone except the maid is having a fun time. It's hard to imagine Winner not having fun either, having the power to decide which woman is cast, telling her that she had to take her clothes off for the camera and be demeaned in almost every way for all of the world to see in perpetuity, while the men around her laughed and giggled about it all. I can see him auditioning the women, telling them the demands of the role, asking them if they're fine with full frontal and simulated sex, and then the day of shooting, the cameras, and sound crew all there for the purpose of filming a rape, the director in his chair, deciding the shots, deciding the placement of heels and where torn clothes, the position of the hair, in charge of the sexually violent voyeurism, yet being the ultimate voyeur himself.

MOMNDF: That is the thrill of directing.

JRK: The thrill being the power to make people act it out and perform for you?

MOMNDF: It's worth all the bullying in high school.

JRK: So, I don't think too much about this shit?

MOMNDF: No, you do.

Watching *Death Wish 2* was a mistake.

My phone vibrated.

Yu: "Ok."

Me: "Do you want to meet tonight?"

Yu: "Sorry I cannot because Karate. Are you coming?"

Kenji is coming.

Me: "Not tonight."

Me: "Go to Miyajima tomorrow?"

Yu: "Yes."

Vibrates again.

Mark: "Saw *NewsGrind*. Holy shit dude"

Jason: "Don't believe the MSM. Fake News."

Mark: "Never do. You okay?"

Jason: "Yeah, going to miyajima to get away."

Mark: "Good. Do that. Fuck them."

Jason: ":100%:"

But you know that, don't you?

MOMNDF: Yes, we know everytime you send an electronic communication, they know.

JRK: Just wanted to make sure.

But did you know when I then called the ryokan and to see if they had a room available, I expected a refusal since it was holiday season and so spur of the moment but they did have a room available, surprising me, albeit pleasantly?

Do you know I put the phone down and tried not to look at it the rest of the night, instead finishing *Death Wish 2*? Watched Bronson kill everyone with a *joie de vivre* missing from current revenge cinema and as night faded, I noticed the overhead fluorescent dominating the room yet mildly flickering. It reeked of Darius Khondji's work in early David Fincher.

MOMNDF: Darius is great.

JRK: My story should only be so lucky.

MOMNDF: He was working on a project with Wong Kar-wai.

JRK: Understandable.

MOMNDF: But maybe or maybe not Jeff Cronenweth did a great job.

JRK: He did.

But do you know I did glance at the phone screen once or twice, with its vibrations of texts received and saw its screen flickering too?

*

"Ohayo. :hug:"

"Meet me at port to go to Miyajima?"

"No. I meet you there."

"Want to have lunch there?"

"No, I have schedule. Meet in the afternoon."

I scrolled left from iMessage icon to Slack icon and saw the bright red number 20+ sitting stark, messages and tags waiting for my response.

Like a child trying to peek at the possible terror around the corner, I look at one DM from Andyschluss:

I know they're going hard on you. I don't care that you're a Jew or at least part Jew. I know you're /ourguy/. Just hunker down, weather the storm, and let this pass. We're gonna b trolling that cunty journo all weekend with sock accounts.

>Feel your shoulders drop with relief upon reading.

Me: Thx for ur support. I'm going to lay low this weekend.

Andyschluss: Go for it. Just chill.

But you know that, don't you?

MOMNDF: Didn't we talk about this?

JRK: Yes, as they and you know I got a Periscope alert from Scott Nash saying—

MOMNDF: Is Jason Reudelheuber-Katz a Deep State Plant? I know, I directed the movie. You don't need to spell it out for us. Are you that confused, you're even mixing up narrative devices?

JRK: It was a hectic time.

>Be curious

MOMNDF: Goddamn it, you are.

>Watch the first couple of minutes or Nash Periscope.

MOMNDF: This isn't the best device to describe your state of mine.

>Watch only really the first minute.

MOMNDF: Now what?

JRK: It's my fucking story.

MOMNDF: It's my fucking movie.

JRK: Well...it's not that type of—

MOMNDF: Story or movie? Which is it?

Scott Nash: Hey guys, as I've told you, there's many in the movement that have been sent by the Deep State Globalists to subvert what we're doing. The ones who are the most anti-Semitic, the ones who make the most extreme comments—let's be honest. They're fake and they're Feds. They're there to entrap you and make sure they can help build a case and to make the movement look all the worse to the mainstream media. I REPEAT: THESE PEOPLE ARE ALL FAKES!

MOMNDF: But he wasn't in your Slack with all your other Wignat pals. WTF are you doing?

>See the comments sections.

>scroll upwards and find, "Deep State Kikery yet again," and another "Imagine my shock."

Me: Can you guys troll Scott Nash too? This Periscope is full of bullshit.

Andyschluss: Sure nigga. We can take care of that faggot too.

Me: Remind him he RT'd me the "fake". Fuck you should send everything to *NewsGrind*.

Andyschluss: Fuck yeah!

MOMNDF: Wait—I'm confused.

JRK: That's your problem.

Kenji is coming.

MOMNDF: Can't come soon enough.

JRK: He is. For real this time.

MOMNDF: He better.

Kenji is coming.

MOMNDF: Stop saying that.

JRK: No.

Kenji is coming.

*

>Be at Hiroshima Station.

MOMNDF: This again?

>See the gaijin backpackers your age, treading along.

>Grasp your backpack straps and begin to question the wisdom of going to Miyajima.

MOMNDF: Um, why?

JRK: Well, um, I wasn't really geared to towards the traditional as much as I was enraptured by the overtly modern. Until, like, you, um, you see signs like "Udon for Vegetarians" written in English outside an *udonya*.

You know it wasn't written in Japanese. You know it was written for foreigners, for westerners, for Americans most likely. You know that for all their criticisms of colonialism that Americans still practice colonialism even if it's just in dietary habits. Then you see an updated story about the Nihon Bus Association (NBA) being sued by THE NBA (Nigger Basketball Association) for copyright infringement and you know who will win that fight.

230

But you also know you need to stop writing in second person and focus.

MOMNDF: It only works in the Kai10 format. True.

JRK: See?

MOMNDF: *sigh*

JRK: But, back to your...

MOMNDF: Out with it...

JRK: Um, I, um, felt, you know, a greater pull towards the urban cityscape, the stores, the cafes, the game centers where fat girls sit entranced at the consoles similar to how boomers sit entranced at the slot machines in Vegas.

MOMNDF: Boomers...

A line of them stand outside the Starbucks, the queue whiter than anything in Seattle.

American tourism in this region of the world had spiked in recent years. For what, I don't know but I certainly cared because they fucked with my piece of mind.

The way English pierces through a train in a foreign land...you become more sensitive to it.

And it was piercing all over the train. Talking. Loudly. Obnoxious with their northeastern accents; like Agent Murphy but ten times worse while scratching a chalkboard. At least Murphy had some masculine purpose to work in law enforcement, while these people, looking white, thin, gaunt, shriveled, smug and entitled in their sunglasses, tan cruiser hats, loose fitting blue jeans, khakis, parkas, and gray sweatshirts of their alma mater plastered all over. In the summer, they looked worse with their boomer uniform of short sleeve t-shirt and Khaki shirts with option between Birkenstocks or sneakers, they're wives either grossly thin and diminutive or grossly overweight, both wearing a form of waist hugging, waist high tourist pantsuit with knit top and tennis shoes. God, whatever happened to dresses? These were not men and women of military, law enforcement, construction or the manufacturing plant (they all go to Vegas). No these were boomers of the boardroom, the law office or the doctor's office. Polite society. Their wage slavery noted through their soft passive features, like drooping skin and skinny fat arms, not a dead lifter or gun owner among them.

Even worse, they actually read the news. I tried not to make eye contact with them, hoping that none of them may recognize me. But they don't read

NewsGrind. At best the closest they get to that is when Fox News or MSNBC talk about an article or have one of the "journalists" on as guests, who serve their purpose as propaganda agent (who just copy and paste Social Media posts) by providing material and talking points to whatever news org, giving aid and comfort to the championing of whatever cause or talking point that needs promotion.

And the boomers eat it up, taking everything at face value.

Just like they eagerly approach the giant Torii sitting in the sea like a kid approaches Disneyland, treating the attraction itself no less than they would a trip to see the Mouse or Universal Studios.

At Miyajima station, I walked by the restaurant that is famous for *anago*, just next to the port, but remembered what Yamamoto-sensei told me about how the restaurant raised prices due to the increased Chinese and boomer customers (the Jew boomers let their greed seep through to the Japanese like Jew osmosis, causing the Japanese to Jew on pricing).

MOMNDF: You really need to cool it with the anti-Semitism.

JRK: Seriously.

MOMNDF: As a heart attack.

JRK: You want me to cool it with anti-boomerism too?

MOMNDF: Wouldn't hurt.

JRK: Too bad.

MOMNDF: And here I thought you cared what I thought.

As I approached the ferry, thumbs under my backpack straps, I saw another boomer, this one wearing a Phillies ballcap, and fleece pullover, holding a camcorder—this guy know every smartphone has a camera?—as he approached the ferry, like he had to document every, single, moment (like boarding a ferry was important for posterity's sake). Maybe he'll show it to his grandchildren when they're looking for answers as to why they have no inheritance left.

Boomers were a mistake.

MOMNDF: There you go.

JRK: It can't be said enough.

Rather than be inside and listen to the loud sounds of Bostonian boomerisms, I stayed outside on the railing, looking at the approaching island, the *torii* sitting in the shallow water facing Itsukushima Shrine.

MOMNDF: What's a *torii* for viewers at home?

JRK: Google it.

Chinese tourists next to me, a whole family, the husband/father gaunt, his wife at varying levels of plain pudginess while his daughter just looked plain as they leaned against the railing shouting at each other in Mandarin all taking pictures with their phones.

Made me remember that Itsukushima itself was an island only meant for the Emperor and the Shogun. Closing my eyes, I could see Taira No Kiymori approaching the island in complete quiet, no trains, mechanization or loud Chinks and boomers to disturb his concentration, an island built for reverence and the elite, not tourism.

Fucking tourism.

MOMNDF: Here comes another rant.

JRK: Fuck you.

Kenji is coming.

He is.

MOMNDF: Thank god.

Tourism—when travel itself became commodified, devoid of meaning. No longer for religious pilgrimage or trade where sailing the world or taking a journey meant danger but also enlightenment, reverence or fortune. And when the fortune was made, then and only then, could one afford to see the wonders of the globe (THINK Hitler touring Paris with Albert Speer, admiring the architecture and art only after routing the historically great powers of both the U.K. and France in battle, conquering the continent), but like a late Capitalistic society the middle class must imitate the rich, and now it must duplicate itself the world over. It's not just Americans or Brits going to see the Pyramids or the Parthenon but Chinese, Indians and anyone who can pay the bill. Now travel is just an end to itself.

All for what? A momentary selfie? A shot of momentary youth or happiness? A photo in front of a monument that took years of toil to build, that had a higher purpose? Or maybe it was just to find a nice hotel, with a nice view of the eternal, so one could enjoy the momentary pleasures of life, like fucking their girlfriend or mistress (hypocrite, I know).

It only proves that we're midgets of the moment compared to the giants of the past who thought looking towards eternity.

Would they have built it if they knew this was the endgame? That it would just become a normie touristy playground?

Tourism was a mistake.

MOMNDF: I knew it.

*

I looked at my watch I was arrived at the visitor's center. Noon. Yu wouldn't be arriving in a few more hours. As diversity flowed through the welcoming area, Japanese girls in nice dresses, all made up, taking pictures of the free roaming deer while laughing, while the white women, no make-up, hair in ponytails, just accentuating their acne, in their almost matching Patagonia fleeces and cropped pants, just wading through the crowd, hands tightened around their straps, trying to wade through the waters of tourism they seemed to think they're above, I pondered what to do. I know, I know, clunky sentence.

MOMNDF: We've figured you out I think.

JRK: That's not—

MOMNDF: You're scared.

JRK: It's not.

MOMNDF: No—you're

Kenji is coming.

Well—soon.

I had time on my hands.

I stood around, rubbing my fingers together, grasping at my straps, watching the deer pick up the bag of *momiji manju* an actual Japanese tourist left on the ground, everyone giggling, except me with an energy that couldn't be settled. I walked towards Itsukushima Shrine, past all the vendors, picked up a coffee, but I as I got close, I saw elderly Chink tourists at the *chozuya*, taking the dippers, laughing as they "cleansed" themselves before entering, just standing there laughing obnoxiously, holding the dippers, taking a million photos, while also making a mockery of the Japanese who performed *chozu* correctly, reducing my patience to zero.

MOMNDF: Patience is reducing to zero. I want to see—

Kenji is coming.

JRK: I know.

Beyond that I saw people throwing their coins in to the saisenbako, then clapping their hands together twice to pray, but at Shinto Shrine, you're praying to what? It's almost like you're praying in to a nothingness. You just recognize something bigger than you. A void ultimately.

234

I also realized I couldn't take my coffee from Miyajima Roasters in to the Shrine and it tasted good.

I felt my phone vibrate. I had to go to a place where I couldn't feel it shake, where it couldn't get a connection.

*

I started my way towards Mt. Misen. Took two ropeways up just to start making the hike. In the car, there was some fatass white bitch with her skinny-fat boyfriend, attempting and failing to grow out some blonde facial hair. They both looked at me. I smiled and they stared. Maybe they read the article in *NewsGrind*. Or maybe they're just acting like every other westerner who comes in to contact with another in the wild—shock and social anxiety. Maybe we've just internalized the Japanese way of interpersonal communication, who don't talk or chat outside established social groups. Or maybe we just don't want to acknowledge the other's presence, like we want to be the exclusive gaijin to Japan. The girl took off her fleece and tried to wrap it around her yoga panted waist, to reveal a white shear top with a see-through pink bra. A little Japanese boy lifted his Hiroshima Carp hat to stare at her. I was about to ask her to put it back on but the ropeway car stopped. They got out, she shivered and she put her fleece back on while busting her boy's balls for not warning her at how cold it could be up there. Her accent was Canadian. They were headed towards a polyamorous relationship (if they weren't in one already).

I started walking up towards the peak of the mountain, on a well-paved and pebbled trail. Boomers and millennials kept to themselves as they marched the path in either their full-bodied fitness gear or loose baggy pants. Would-bangs, they were not. Many Japanese ladies trekked along with long dresses and miniskirts, some wearing jeans and flats some in heels holding their Vuitton and Kate Spade bags. Would-bangs they certainly were.

But I wasn't here to bang…yet.

I walked past the Daisho-In Temple which housed the eternal flame lit by Kobo Daishi himself, while many of the others lingered to get a coke from the vending machine, look around and play Buddhist. I continued to the peak and walked in to the viewing area that had several wooden platforms to sit and the enjoy the view in groups.

The view was beautiful—one I can't even describe.

MOMNDF: Ah the beauty of cinema not having to describe but just show.

JRK: I know.

235

MOMNDF: I know you, you know.
JRK: Fuck you.

Amid the French family joyfully talking against the railing, the random "*Sugoi*" and Japanese family chatter as they sat around the platforms relaxing, it had little effect on me.

I walked to the railing, looked at all the islands sitting on the flat Seto Inland Sea, then towards the mainland and finally the cityscape of Hatsukaichi slowly invading up the mountains like an urban bee swarm.

Kenji is coming.

Then just above that swarm sat another temple facing the sacred mountain, almost in parallel. A PureLight Temple, looking more like a formless compound, like they needed a line of sight to unify themselves with the eternal flame and Japan's sacred past.

But my sense of amazement was limited. I tried to be taken in, faked it almost, told myself that I needed to be amazed by this incredible view, *There is nothing like this in Las Vegas* I told myself but nothing took.

Save the satisfaction of my phone not vibrating.

And the view was amazing in memory.

Just like *Kenji is coming* is chilling.

At that moment though, I knew Yu awaited me once I returned to ground level. I felt a well of excitement as I briskly made my way down, not being bothered by the pathetically rotting Boomers or anti-social millennials or the well-dressed Japanese tourists who just had to look stylish no matter what they did and not being bothered by the strong breeze or by the English sign in the cafeteria that stereotypically promoted "pizza flitter" on the menu when they meant "pizza fritter", but it didn't matter what language they used because it tasted no better than a Hot Pocket. But even that didn't bother me—NO! Because Yu awaited, she would be waiting for me outside the Ryokan and things would be better, better, better and nothing could bother me. But...

He was coming.

Kenji is coming.

*

The ryokan Mizushima was an 11-minute walk from the gondola lift of Mt. Misen (don't Google. It doesn't exist). I walked briskly enough that it was probably only six minutes.

I spotted Yu from afar in the tourist traffic where she looked irritated as she typed something on her phone. I wondered if she was upset. When she got closer, I waved my hand and said "Yu!" Yeah, I shouted it.

Kenji is coming.

She looked up from her phone and a smile instantly appeared on her face. She placed her hand on my forearm.

>Be Jason.

>Want to grab her there, embrace her in the big Hollywood kiss.

>Hold back.

>Go for a kiss, aiming for her lips.

>she turns her cheek towards you right before lips are planted.

>subtlerejection.gif?

MOMNDF: You can go back to conventional narrative.

JRK: Fuck you. How about no?

Kenji is coming.

MOMNDF: Come Kenji, come.


```
EXT. RYOKAN-MAGIC HOUR

Jason and Yu stand outside the RYOKAN. Jason
looks at Yu EAGER. Yu looks HAPPY but RESERVED.
                    JASON

            It's good to see you. Feels
            like it's been too long.

                    YU

        I know.

                    JASON

        I missed you.
```

                              YU

            I missed you too, Jason-san.

He grabs her HAND to take her in to the LOBBY.
                        VOICE (O.S.)

            Kenji is coming.

   At check in, I tapped my finger on the counter, felt the goosebumps raising
on my arm, my heart beating. I ignored the robotically kind overtures of the
clerk, a politeness so natural it's been ingrained and rehearsed since birth where
it seems like a performance when they show gratitude or apologize. But I
myself performed, looking at the clerk while trying not to look at Yu, who
seemed to be staring in to her own world, or out towards the ocean, her smile
gone, until I had received my change in the tray with keycard, when she noticed
me turning towards her, the smile returned.
   Kenji is coming.

                             JASON

            What did you tell Kenji?

                              YU

            I said I was visiting friend.

                             JASON

            Friend, huh?

                (Thinks)

            Do friends usually spend the
            night together?

                              YU

            My friend is in Yamaguchi.

                              238

JASON

```
Yamaguchi-ken    or    Yamaguchi-
city?
```

YU

```
City.
```

Does it matter the room was covered in tatami?
MOMNDF: Obviously or you wouldn't be fucking telling us.
JRK: It's, um, a Japanese style room, okay?
>Be Jason.
>Upon entering room, grab her arm and pull her towards you.
>Try to stick your tongue down her throat and take her right there.
>She pulls back and puts her hand on your chest.

YU

```
I need to go to toilet.
```

>Takes her purse with her.
>Hope she's not having her period.
MOMNDF: Wait—you confused the narrative devices—
JRK: It's my story!
Kenji is coming.
I pulled out my phone and logged in to the Japan Free WiFi available on Miyajima and all major tourist locations. Messages started incoming. Five from my mom urging her to call. Min: "You can come at the Adina's memorial service only if you apologize publicly. Lemme know soon because it's 2morrow and I'll email NewsGrind. Also, what did you talk with Matt about? Don't talk to him. He's acting weirder and weirder. What did u 2 talk about?"

My reply: "Why don't you ask him. He's your boy."

Matt: "Thinking about watching *The Greatest Story Never Told*..."

Matt (again): "I watched. Holy shit. My mind is blown. I don't know what to think right now. I read that memo. I downloaded a pdf of *Culture of Critique*."

I didn't remember recommending the book to him but whatever.

239

Another text from Mandy. Hoped for it to be a nude selfie she accidentally sent to me instead of some nigger named Jayson, but instead it was a link to an article from New Republic with the headline "The Straight, White, Middle-Class Man Needs to Be Dethroned"

Ignored and went to Kai10, saw posts about the *NewsGrind* article mentioning me. Some of the comments ranged from "Jason dindu nuffin'" to an assault battle plan against those coming after me with Ultima_Thule saying "A war against Jason is a declaration of war against all of us." An ANON user asked "Why should we be supporting this Kike? He's obviously an AP." Then a debate thread about whether I was an Agent Provacateur or not sent by the federal government to undermine the movement. Ultima_Thule: "He's not a namefag Deep State kike shill like Scott Nash or merchant e-begger like Justin Bangs. He's /ourguy/ pure and simple. Trust me."

Final word.

But you know that, don't you?

MOMNDF: We know.

JRK: Fuck you.

But do you know, the phrase "He's /ourguy/", the fact he said that, that I felt a welling up inside of me, a surge of adrenaline? Someone, somewhere, defended me to a bunch of ANONs. Someone bothering to show me some loyalty. Felt good man.

I scrolled to another post that featured a statement by "JET's Against Hate" and how they condemn the violent hate of my speech and I'm hereby removed from the organization…that I was never a part of. They had already come up with five different meme parody variations featuring Hitler, General Tojo and Lee Kuan-yew, laughing while holding the statement.

The support…

:laughing:

OR!

:tear:

OR!

:laughing: :tear:

Kenji is coming.

I felt a hand on my arm.

>Yu smiles as you look at her.

                    YU

          Is everything okay?

                    JASON

          Yeah I'm fine.

He puts the PHONE away.
                    YU

          Want to take a bath?

                    JASON

          Sure.

They KISS.

                    JASON

          Take off your clothes.

                    YU

          Okay.

Kenji is coming.

He steps back against the wall.

She slips off her jacket.

She NOTICES him STARING.

                    YU

          What?

                    JASON

          Strip. I'll watch.

YU (GIGGLING)

Oh—okay.

She takes off her clothes slowly yet they slip off so easily, revealing her matching black crotchless panties and bra with hose covering to mid-waist. She slips the hose off along with her panties, her body slightly shivering.

She then unsnaps her bra to show her firm breasts with brown nipples. She's better looking than Adina…save the milkers.

She's about to grab her robe but I rush her and take her in my arms. I start kissing her until she obliges. Her skin is slightly cool with the texture of raised goosebumps. She finally obliges and relaxes her mouth in mine. I then unzip my pants, push them down quickly then push her down. She resists for a moment then looks down at my erect cock. I press again and this time she sinks to her knees, putting it in to her mouth.

The warmth of it all feels good as she covers it with her mouth. I push her head forward a little where I hear a choking sound. But then she gives it all the attention it needs between bouts of inserting and licking until finally she starts rubbing her hand to sync with the motions of her mouth. I come.

She walks casually to the bathroom holding her hand over her mouth to spit it out.

MOMNDF: That's unsuitable for general audiences.

Kenji is coming.

In our private bath, we shower first with Yu washing my back and me trying to steal a kiss from her. She seems all business but when we make eye contact, she smiles and we kiss. I take some of the suds and put them on her pert breasts, she adds some more then rubs her erect nipples against me along with soap, along with a faint smile that disappears for a moment.

MOMNDF: Must you describe?

Kenji is coming.

I put my hand between her thighs and find her only a little wet on the inside. She closes her eyes a moment and rides my hand but I stop. I wasn't feeling it at the moment, still haven't recovered from the blow job. She then kisses my cheek.

Kenji is coming.

MOMNDF: I'd be dying for the Kai10 formatting right now.

>Be in the bath.

242

MOMNDF: There you go.

I care what you think.

MOMNDF: I know.

>Sit next to each other but quiet.

>Look out towards the sea, the sun setting, and see the PureLight compound faintly in the distance.

Kenji is coming.

I then think of Adina, the murder, all the posts that made everyone upset, all the negative comments, all the articles, all the bullshit in the Slack with people calling me a faggot, but no one seemed upset there was someone murdered, her skull caved in with leaking brain fluid, curled in the fetal position helpless—no, they were more outraged someone that girl was fucking said "Hitler did nothing wrong" thinking that's what murdered her.

And no one had been officially arrested.

Kenji is coming.

I then felt a hand on my shoulder. "Jason," she says.

I turn to her, "Yeah?"

MOMNDF: Wait—this isn't scripted.

JRK: I—

MOMNDF: But when you and...well, Yu, talk...

JRK: JUST FUCKING READ—or watch!

"Doshitan?" (*What's wrong?*)—The economy of Japanese phraseology—one word, carrying a depth of meaning. English was so wordy, so bloated...

English was a mistake.

MOMNDF: You're a mistake.

JRK: We're not there yet.

MOMNDF: I'll come back for that. Until then...*rustling sound of un-micing heard*

"Yeah, I'm okay. Just thinking."

YU

Stress?

"Yeah, stress," I say.

Kenji is coming.

I look at her body with elevator eyes. Before fellatio the image of her nude figure turned me on. Longing for that before we met up today: Her tits, her skin, her bare shoulder. Now in this bath, after discharge, the reality of her naked figure, feeling her skin next to me, beads of sweat that formed on her skin from the bath, the faint smell of perfume—or was it the house shampoo? That's what sat next to me. It wasn't disappointing but maybe unfulfilling even discomforting because the discomforting thoughts remained…

Kenji is coming.

The water was hot. Onsen water is usually a degree below scorching but it didn't help with general malaise or ease the breathing.

>She starts rubbing your shoulders with her hands.

>The fingers kneading the muscle tissue feels uncomfortable and good at the same time.

>Feel a nail dig in to my shoulder.

NO!

"Ow," I quickly say.

"*Gomen!*" she says, her face alarmed, hand covering mouth.

"It's okay," I say. "It's okay."

"*Daijobu?*"

"I'm fine. It's okay."

"*Gomen, Jason-san,*" she says.

"*Ii yo, ii yo,*" I reply. But I felt the heat of the bath and it wasn't so ii. I get out. "I'm hot, let's get out."

"Okay," she says with a nod of her head.

Kenji is coming.

We find the towels. I stand there for a moment and holding a towel, she moves towards me and begins drying me off. She then dries herself off, arms raised, making the breasts hang and look bigger. Her pubic her looks ruffled yet moist.

Yet, I'm not erect.

Kenji is coming.

She slips the Yukata on me. It barely fits. Hers fits perfectly, the way it curves around her hips yet conceals her cleavage.

The meal, salmon with rice and miso soup sits prepared on a table.

Kenji is coming.

We sit down, her on her knees as I try to sit cross-legged but negotiating the robe is hard and my dick picks through a little. But the rub of the cloth against the head is stimulating.

Kenji is coming.

As Yu pours my *sake* she notices and lets out a giggle.

I smile but remind myself of the discomfort and clumsiness that comes with actually trying to act Japanese.

I as I drink the sake, Yu asks "Are you relax?"

"Sure."

"Good," she says and the smile returns.

Kenji is coming.

After the meal, I turned on the TV. The top story on NHK news is the memorial service for Adina. I go to turn it off but before I can I see Yu staring at the screen.

The signal starts to crackle with digital break-up, not snow.

"Weak antenna."

"What?"

"Nothing. My dad worked in TV. That's what he always said when there was digital break up."

"Ah...so..."

"Yeah..."

"Did you know her?"

"What?"

"The girl? On TV?"

"Yes. I texted you about it remember?"

"Ah...yes...friend?"

"Sure—yes."

"Good friend?"

"Just a friend."

"I see."

Then the TV turns itself off.

I look at Yu. Who is just staring at the ground.

"Yu?"

"Yes."

"Know much about the story? The murder?"

"Eh?" she asks pointing at herself. "Me?"

"What do you know about the murder?"

245

She starts waving her hand. "Nothing, nothing."

"Really?"

"I don't know. Only what I see on News."

"I see."

Kenji is coming.

I go to the window and push the sliding door to see the sea. The *torii*, the lights of Hatsukaichi and the light of the PureLight compound, hoping the view would relax me. It didn't. I look at the digital clock near the TV and notice it flickering.

Kenji is coming.

Yu then relaxes her head against mine. No space between our bodies. I look down at her, she's smiling, but it seems to come from a place of pain. At that moment, I thought it was just the pain of knowingly committing adultery.

Kenji is coming.

We make sex. Me on top, Yu reserved, grabbing my ass, wrapping her legs around me and, her face turned to the side to avoid kissing. Once I finish, she pats me on the back and gives me a little kiss. We lay naked on the futon for a brief moment but I feel her get up, put her underwear on and slipping back in to bed.

Kenji is coming.

I dream about being in an apple orchard again, picking up one apple but all of them have eyes and watch me while my body is slowly being immersed in water. I pick the apple anyway.

Kenji is coming.

Then both of our phones ring, almost in stereo save the different ring tongs. We both jolt awake.

Kenji is coming.

I see Min's name on the Caller ID and pick it up out of reflex.

But you know that, don't you?

Do you know Yu is on her phone too but I only see her back? "Jason? Jason?"

"Yeah, yeah? Min?"

"What did you say? What did you say to Matt? I need to know!"

"What do you mean?! Why are you asking me now?"

"He's talking about weird things like miscenganat—I can't even understand the word! Something about race mixing! What did you tell him?"

"We didn't talk about that—"

246

"He said you were right! You were on to something! You showed him the truth. WHAT DID YOU SAY?! TELL ME!"

Hitler did nothing wrong.

MOMNDF: Did you say that?

JRK: No. Wait—I thought you left.

MOMNDF: Fuck—you're right. I'll be back.

JRK: You could have at least done it in an Arnold accent.

Kenji is coming...

MOMNDF: That again...

JRK: ACKSHUALLY...

The phone goes dead.

OingoBoinGoy: What's going on fag?

Me: Why are you here?

OingoBoinGoy: Well now is the time...

>light in the room then comes on.

MOMNDF: Is it time? Why are you using—

Enough.

This was a mistake.

MOMNDF: Now you admit it.

JRK: >stops.

MOMNDF: Ur all mixed up.

MIN: "What did you and Matt talk about?"

I see Yu walking around in a panic as she puts her phone in her purse.

Before I can ask she says:

"Kenji is coming."

For real this time.

2

Kai10 Post: Why can't that faggot Jason Reudelheuber-(((Katz)))
give us a straight story?

>Be Jason.

>Be an insecure ironybro too scared to write a normal narrative
due to fear of being judged by said standards.

>Be afraid of heroes journey (what Jungian archetype is this?)

>Be afraid of beauty.

>scaredAF.txt

REPLY: Fuck you. Here's a straight story for you homosex
armchair critics that can't be bothered to work for your art.

      REPLY: Bring it bitch.

         REPLY: Here's some more content for you to consume.

        REPLY: "Content, content, content" amirite?

        REPLY: Like you need it.

          REPLY: I just want beauty in the world

           REPLY: Then why are you on
online?

MOMNDF: Maybe you should just start.

JRK: Right, the incident has been incited.

MOMNDF: And not a moment too soon.

Yu starts packing her things in the room.

"What are you doing?" I ask.

Yu doesn't answer. She paces around the room, looking for things to put in her purse while mumbling in a Japanese I can't even comprehend.

"Yu..."

"*Kenji ga...Kenji ga...*" she says not looking at me.

"*Nani?*"

"*Kenji...Kenji...Kenji...*"

I try to put my hand on her shoulder but she keeps pacing. "Yu, Yu, Yu..." She ignores me, continues to pack, continues to gather, looking under the futon, looking under other things—what the fuck was she looking for? She looks out the window, the PureLight compound in the distance and continues pacing, taking the pillows and overturning them all the while frantically mumbling, "*Kenji ga...Kenji...*"

I see her looking through my bag. I grab her arm. "Yu!"

She twists her body trying to twist away and pleads "*Hanashite!*" (*Let go!*) Looks at me, then my hand grabbing her arm and back at me: "*Jayson-san hanashite kudasai. Kenji ga...*" (*Jason please let go. Kenji is...*)

"Kenji ga what?!"

I see the straining on her face. I won't let go. Her face becomes contorted. She is no longer the sweet smile that forgives all Yu but snarling, ugly and panicking Yu. The make-up is smudged, the eye liner above her right lid to be exact—why I remember that particular detail in that particular moment? I don't know!—but it all feels like it has all changed as she tries to twist and strain and get out of my grip. "Kenji..." she cries.

"Kenji?"

"Kenji is coming!"

I look at the clock; close to midnight. It hits me: FUCKING KENJI IS COMING! I'VE BEEN SLEEPING WITH HIS WIFE!!! FUCK!

He somehow found us out. He somehow knows about us. I cucked him. The man who is my Karate sensei. The man who could probably kick my ass but given my height never felt that threatening, and I had studied some MMA videos online so I felt I had the upper hand in any real fight.

But Kenji is coming!

The real confrontation is coming.

Not an electric confrontation that could be discarded and ignored by just putting the phone down. No, no, no, a real confrontation that could leave bumps, bruises and bloody noses.

Kenji is coming.

I take a deep breath. I hear my phone ring. I let go of Yu and look at the ID wondering if it is Kenji. But it's Min. I ignore.

But the phone rings again.

Yu starts roaming the room again. She picks up her purse.

I run up to her.

"Yu let's stay. Stay here…"

"No…"

"I'll talk to Kenji…"

"No…no…no…"

She tries to fight my grip.

My phone continues to ring.

"Yu we can do this. I'll say that I forced you—"

"No Jason!"

"Yu…"

"*Hanashite!*"

She begins twisting and even tries to swing her purse but it just kind of flops in the air.

My phone rings.

"Yu!"

"Let me go…"

"Yu, you—we're going—let's stay!"

"No! Let me—"

The phone won't stop ringing. Fucking Min.

"Yu!"

"LET ME GO!!!!"

I feel the scream. Feel it reverberate throughout the room. I feel an air almost lift me off my feet. Head pulses. Feels like it's going to explode. And the ringing—I release Yu to cover my ears. A futile gesture. The noise over takes me. I begin to crouch. MAKE IT STOP!!! I see the TV flicker. The clock flickers too. A burning sensation in my leg. I look to see smoke. THE PHONE! I pull it out as it flickers, smoke coming out with Min's name and photo plastered on the screen, distorted. Fucking Min. Smoke protrudes from the rear of the television. My vision begins to blur. The odor of smoke invades me. My skin tingles. Every noise loud, every smell foul, every sight blinding, everything I touch produces goosebumps and feels slippery. But the smell of the smoke. The electrical smoke. Rubber and plastic burning. And my head pulsates. Wonder if I'm having a stroke.

The daze lifts, but the smoke still permeates the room. Feel dizzy and nauseous. I get to my knees. The smoke. The pulsing. They linger.

I stumble to my feet.

Outside I hear the sound of police sirens in the distance. If they were coming here…Itsukushima was a holy island…nothing could die on it. I couldn't die either…

I gain my balance and realize Yu isn't in the room. Gone.

I exit and hear footsteps in the hallway. People in one piece uniforms run around the corner towards our room, ignoring me. I then run towards the entrance.

I see the stares, I see people looking at me as I run through the lobby, past the giftshop that sells tchotcky things, while in my bare feet, track pants and *Attack on Titan* t-shirt.

I see Yu in the entrance way slipping on her shoes and heading towards the sliding doors that go in to the street. I see Kenji. He guides her calmly to his vehicle and leads her in to the backseat, her head down in disgrace. He walks towards the driver's seat.

I don't have time to put shoes or slippers on in the *koban*, I know, I know I didn't give this detail earlier. I apologize.

I care what you think.

"Yu!" I shout as I head toward the doors barefoot. The ground is cool.

More stares.

"Yu!"

Kenji stops to look at me. I'm ready to fight. I don't care. I'm ready. He can kick my ass. Knock me out, I don't care. I feel the adrenaline pumping. No fucks given. Knock my ass out Kenji…drop me motherfucker…I won't make it easy for you…I grab his arm, feel a firm muscle, "She's not leaving," I say.

He shakes my grip lose with his arm, and pushes me away.

I clench my fists.

Yu opens the door.

I look at her.

She reaches for me.

We make eye contact.

She puts her hand on my arm. Kenji looks at her wide eyed then at me.

I clench.

251

And that's all I remember.

MOMNDF: See was that so hard?

JRK: It was.

MOMNDF: Why?

JRK: Because I think of—

MOMNDF: Kenji is coming...yeah, yeah...

*

Actually, I do remember a dream about reptilians posing as college professors, but having human faces, the rest of their bodies serpent-like.

*

I wake up on a floor. I can't see at first. I feel a panic. Where am I?! I shout. Yu! I scream.

Slowly things come in to focus. My head pounds. The floor is my floor. My *tatami*. My living area. My apartment. The bag...the bag I brought with me to the Miyajima sits in the corner next to the TV.

I hear the trumpets of the brass band rehearsing.

Was I knocked out? Doubtful. Contrary to movie bullshit, one doesn't immediately lose consciousness after a single blow. No, it was quicker.

MOMNDF: So what would it be if it was a movie?

JRK: My guess would be sedative. I thought you left?

MOMNDF: SOON.

I wish it could be a *Wizard of Oz* there's no place like home moment. But where was my home? Why would I want to return to "reality"?

I felt heavy, could barely stand. My socks were on...but I left the *ryokan* barefoot. And my shoes...I'm sure they were sitting on the rack in the *koban*. Whoever put me here had the courtesy to abide by Japanese custom. Naturally.

I couldn't get up.

My phone was out of reach.

But the TV remote wasn't.

As my head pounded, I reached for the remote and turned on the tube hoping to see there was a wall-to-wall coverage regarding what happened. To see if I was in the News...again...or maybe for the first time.

I wasn't.

Neither was Yu.

I flipped the channels. Just the regular bullshit on most. Mostly morning newscasts, footage of Adina's memorial service and all the crying b-roll

252

followed by weather with the meteorologist using their xylophone pointing stick to tell us the obvious about how cold it was going to be as the winds howled outside my door and the hairs on my arm stood upright from the breeze.

I finally felt like I had the strength to reach for the phone sitting on the *kotatsu*. I crawled military style to the table, picked it up then positioned myself against the wall. The phone was still in the same black Otter casing I ordered from Amazon to prevent from wear and tear. I remembered the smoking from the night—or was it nights?—previous but the iPhone seemed intact. I looked at the date and it said Sunday, December 23. Two days before Christmas.

I sniffed the phone and it had no odor of smoke.

The casing was the same but the screen appeared newer and less worn. When I brought up the main screen, all my apps and icons were present. Texts from Matt and Min. One with a link to the service on YouTube and another message from her saying, "Sorry about the other night. I was a little emotional. Could you please tell me what u and Matt talked about?"

Matt: "Dude, we need to talk."

But you know that, don't you?

I hoped there was some sort of "Dear John" type message from Yu. When I looked for her iMessage history, it was gone. Nothing there. I then went to contacts to send her a new message but I couldn't find her name. Went to Facebook. Gone. Line? Gone. I looked for her profile and just got "Search Not Found" when I typed in "Yu Yamada Hiroshima". I then just typed in her name and five other girls came up who had the name Yamada Yu but looked nothing like my Yu. They also lived in places like Ishikawa and Fukuoka. And I couldn't remember her phone number.

But you know that, don't you?

Do you know, I then heard the doorbell ring? Then a series of CLACK! CLACK! CLACK! Filling the apartment? Do you know this made my head throb and the last thing I wanted to deal with was an NHK bill collector demanding payment, being belligerent and receive a punch to the neck for their troubles, especially if it was some ugly bitch?

Women bill collectors were a mistake.

But...

Could it be Yu or Kenji? I wondered. If it was Kenji, I decided I'd fight that fucker.

>Take a deep breath.

>Struggle to feet.

>Wobble a bit as you stand but manage to keep balance and slowly move in to the hallway towards the koban.

MOMNDF: You don't need to this.

JRK: You're right.

My shoes were in the *koban*.

My door didn't have a peephole, but I noticed through the fogged plastic glass and thin figure standing in front. Not Yu or Kenji.

:confused:

The figure with large glasses sitting on his nose, smiled and started asking questions in Japanese. I played dumb but he kept on asking questions. "*Wakaranai*," I said. (*I don't know, so get the fuck out of here.*)

But he wouldn't leave. He kept asking questions.

I then bowed and acted like I had to go.

He kept talking.

My head kept pounding.

He kept talking.

I closed the door.

He stopped it.

His hand reached out on the door glass. I tried to close but I felt his resistance. Fucking door wouldn't close. And my head POUNDED.

I was about to scream at him, curse him out—or rather chew him out since Japanese doesn't really have expletives. But he just smiled and pulled out a glossy pamphlet and held it with both hands.

I took it with one hand, said thanks several times then closed the door...with ease.

I took a deep breath and collapsed on my bed. The mattress felt good, even in its Japanese firmness. I repositioned my pillow and looked through the pamphlet—or was it a tract? Yellow and green spots clouded my vision while my head throbbed. It had the title in English "What is PureLight?" It discussed their religious philosophy of touching the inner core and letting the true nature of the universe rule in your soul. "PureLight is a way of looking life with a love." Obviously, they didn't love their doctrine enough to have a native English speaking copy editor. If I was in a better mood I'd refer them to Justin Bang's follower Damian Corbucci who sends out a daily email about freelancing while living abroad as a copy writer. A career path I considered when contract expired—I mean, not bad right? "Come see the PureLight.

PureLight is good. We help you find the truth and syncing with the nature. You can find the being of the universe inside your heart." Something obviously got lost in translation.

There was a picture of the founder and leader, Ando-san, with the Dalai Lama and quotes from several celebrities (like Akiko Fujiwara of Fem100) and politicians about the good work they do sprinkled in passages in both English and Japanese which had me wondering if it was a tract for actual English speakers or just for Japanese to impress them with the English passages. There was another photo of a drawn figure sitting cross legged and meditating but it wasn't Buddha. More generic. Just a faceless clear figure with blue light emitting from behind him. I assumed it was a him. Floating, emitting blue, surrounded by an array of religious symbols. They wouldn't draw a chick for religious enlightenment. But it was like something you'd see at a meditation center in Malibu. Come on in, we don't discriminate on the basis of religion. Your money is good here. Just sit, meditate, do yoga, look at chicks in their tight pants to overcome your reservations and fears that you're participating in absolute faggotry.

Malibu was a mistake. Or at least Malibu in its present form.

And my fucking head throbbed. As the words lingered…

Kenji is coming…

Where did I go wrong? I knew that if I ever saw Kenji or a man who looked like Kenji, that doom, that sense of discomfort, it would all return, gut instinct turned terrifying.

And there was this brochure.

I don't know why it captured my attention at the time. But it did. Well, I was collapsed in a bed with nothing but the brochure. Which is all that matters. Because of where it led. It's like those words, set me on a path, gave me a start, a control point on which to embark.

Kenji is coming…

There was no explanation of PureLight's beliefs…if they believed in the six ruling demons of the underworld or how their God was a ruler but not an absolute ruler or how there's nothing. Just a void and we're agents of the current chaos, trying to bring about the void, trying to actualize it through sex, through complete material obsession through—yes—an excuse to fuck ourselves crazy, killing whoever gets in our way because it's inconsequential. We just need to feed the chaos, allow it to happen. The void is coming. Just like…

255

Kenji is coming…

Why did he come? How did he find out? Why wasn't he upset to see me? Why did it all seem so calm? Why the police sirens? Was there something more urgent? Did it have something to do with Adina's death? It couldn't.

My MBTI, a test I took, paid $10 for after a lead email from Justin Bangs said I tended to jump to conclusions. Just my personality. Something programmed in with my DNA. I was programmed since birth to jump to conclusions. A mixture of German semen and Jew eggs made me this way.

I didn't want to jump to conclusions. I didn't. My head hurt too much, and I kept thinking of those words.

Kenji is coming…

And the crumpled brochure remained stuck in my hand.

I was sure that a clear looking outline of a man meditating—of course it was a man because the figure was bald, didn't have long hair and the Japanese are a fairly masculine culture, full of masculine men—at least a few—like Kenji—who haven't wholesale tolerated the that POZZed globohomo bullshit being shoved down everyone's throat but by god they were trying, and they don't advertise or champion a bunch of intermixing and fucking like crazy— well maybe they are slightly POZZed because they are consumerist, making Americans look pale by comparison and the birthrates…that unforgiving number, is going down, down, down.

I'm sure the Jews had something to do with it.

But I just couldn't prove it at the moment. And something else dominated my thoughts…those words.

Kenji is coming…

That digital explosion. The screen that flickered with digital breakup, my smoking phone…

But I remembered something else…

On my desk in the back of the kitchen, I found the membership ledger for my *Eikaiwa* class. It was all analog, written with pen on paper. The true eternal record. It had all the phone addresses and phone numbers of every member. Because Japan was high trust. They trusted me not to sell their information, not just give it away, not do something illicit. There was the contact info for Mr. Kawasaki, Mr. Honda, Ms. Toyota, Mr. Yamaha and Ms. Matsuda, the friend of Ms. Toyota, who claimed they were friends since junior high but made me wonder if they were both closeted dykes given the way they always chatted, giggled and gossiped from the back of the room.

But…

It's not that type of story.

But there was the address of one Mr. Kenji Yamada. Even though Yu did the paperwork, I remember it like it was yesterday, I remember the day they joined the class, I remembered her sitting at the corner of the classroom filling out the information while looking over at me with that smile, but there she was being the dutiful wife and put her husband's name instead of her own…just like I remember her that same day asking about the Seven Deadly Sins…

And yes, it was eerie. Her information was gone digitally, a footprint erased.

MOMNDF: Eerie shit like this is right up my alley.

JRK: I know, that's why I chose you.

MOMNDF: I really wish you didn't.

And I realized that for all our supposed friendship, I had never been to the Yamada house, never invited. But this is also Japanese custom. Only those close to a family are invited in to the house. Maybe I wasn't that close after all.

And Google Maps didn't seem to be working correctly. The address I typed in wasn't registering.

But the town was small enough, I could find their place with just the address, even if it meant asking for directions. The town was divided in to certain sections (*gun*) so I just needed to head to Saeki-gun, which was a part of the Obara section of town…near my place actually.

I just needed to walk up a hill.

I felt my body had recovered enough by this point that I could go for a short walk.

Taking some action would feel good. Like I'm doing an investigation. But…

It's not that type of story.

*

But there it was.

The Yamada house looked like most modern Japanese homes—no character. A square white box sitting on a lot. There was no garage and given the narrow spaces—even in a rural area, the economy of space is heeded—there was just a slim corner in which to fit a boxy van or *kei*-car.

No car was present in said slim space.

I walked towards the rear, hoping to find a lot or an alley where their N-Box, with its tobacco scents would be sitting, then I would I knock on their door and try to talk things out, try to figure out what happened. But…

257

It's not that type of story.

I walked up to the door, rang the doorbell. Nothing. In a way, I didn't want them to be there. I didn't want a confrontation but also felt I needed to do something. Felt I needed to confront. Fuck my fears. Or at least say I tried.

I banged on the door.

Nothing.

Is there something wrong?

The voice, elderly, came from behind me.

An *oba-san*, hunched over like all *oba-san*, pulled a steel basket and looked at me. She was barely 4'9. But amid her white curly hair, I saw someone genuinely interested in my plight.

Is Yu Yamada here?

She replied in the thickest of *Hiroshima-ben* but I heard "No", "empty house", and "long time".

I got the point.

*

That night, I knew there was Karate practice. I knew Kenji wasn't going to pick me up to take me there.

I called the taxi company and asked them to take me to the school in Kurahashi. (Amazing what you can do when you're actually passionate about something.)

The driver tried talking to me. Something about soldiers here during or after the occupation, and how kind they were to him. Once again, thick *Hiroshima-ben*, but I heard how they would pass out candy and play baseball with the kids (The common sentiment among those who grew up here).

I tried to look out the window as the taxi navigated the circular passages of the *Ondo Ohashi* (*bridge*—no need to Google), connecting one island to the other. I wanted to be silent but the driver wanted to talk.

As the taxi pulled up to Kurahashi City Gym I saw the lights on but didn't see the usual mothers and assorted others standing outside talking or smoking.

I asked the driver to stay put. Let the meter run. I knew it would be a short visit.

"*Ee…*"

As I walked around the parking lot, I didn't see Kenji's tobacco scented Honda.

I walked in to the lobby and there's no parents, no kids, and an empty gym. The fluorescents just buzz to fill the silence and reflect on a glossy floor with one kid playing badminton by his lonesome, just bouncing the shuttlecock on his racket.

I walk up to the counter and say "Karate?"—just the one word because I can't form sentence at my disbelief. The attendant says *There's no Karate tonight...* just trailing off in that Japanese way where the blank space automatically fills itself in.

Outside, I look down the street—some punks my age—were those the trashmen *yakuza*?—they walk by as they discard their cigarette butts, staring at me, eyes filled with contempt. *"Hurr, hurr, hurr"* I could hear one of them say in the distance, mocking my accent. :rage:

Karate was a mistake.

I got back in the taxi. The driver a little perplexed but yet reserved over what just happened.

I was just a fare.

*

The next night at *Eikaiwa*, the last one of the year and for the next month, we had our Christmas party in the ugly green carpeted room with Yamamoto-sensei there acting as my sometimes translator.

I asked a couple of people if they knew what happened to Yu and Kenji as we mingled. They all gave me blank stares while and shrugged shoulders.

Yamamoto-sensei leaned over to me and said, "I don't think they know what you're talking about".

They were gone and there was no reason to fight for bringing them back. I just knew, accepted, this would probably be the answer.

There was nothing I could do. Maybe there was nothing I wanted to do. The mild relief knowing that the marriage I might have fucked up had just disappeared and took care of itself. I didn't have to confront it. Only give my actions of mild investigation lip service. But the events in the ryokan lingered as did the words...

Kenji is coming.

I thought about this as Ms. Matsuda with Ms. Toyota behind her giggling asked me for help pronouncing words in Handel's Messiah which she was performing in for some choir. (I never really bothered to ask because I didn't really care.)

I thought about Yu and her disappearance as I tried patiently to pronounce every word Ms. Matsuda pointed at, followed by her writing notes in *katakana*,

259

followed by Ms. Toyota giggling at my pronunciations as she tried to repeat them.

But before I could lose my shit. I just thought of Yu. That last moment she stretched her hand towards me and then became enraptured in the lyrics of Handel. In fact...

Cue Handel in flashback.

MOMNDF: Not right now.

JRK: I never learned Handel in public school.

MOMNDF: What did you learn?

JRK: We studied Snoop Dogg and Tupac.

MOMNDF: Why?

JRK: Because American cultural education was ruined by Jew faggots.

MOMNDF: That's bit hyperbolic wouldn't you say?

Public education was a mistake.

But the laughing and giggling wore thin. We finished up and Takata and Toyota exited shoulder to shoulder. Maybe they were cold. Or maybe they were priming themselves to go down on each other, while their husbands were out drinking.

MOMNDF: You've watched too much Japanese porn.

JRK: Probably true.

*

Yamamoto-sensei walked with me on the way home. It was dark with a somewhat low wind chill.

"Yamamoto-sensei, do you remember Kenji and Yu Yamada? Do you know what happened to them?" (I thought I'd accepted it. Guess not.)

"Yamada-san?"

"It's like they disappeared."

He stopped to think. "I don't know..."

"Right..."

"Some people just disappear. You know *yonige*, right? How you say in English?"

"I don't know—something like 'run away' or 'escape under the cover of night'—there really isn't a direct translation."

"I see," he said. He then looked towards the moon. "People are disappear. Nasty times."

"Who is disappearing?"

"Remember Yuri-chan? She disappear…" he just held out his hands like they disappeared like dust.

"Do you know why? Why would someone disappear? Were her parents in debt? Was there maybe something else?"

Then Yamamoto-sensei stopped walking.

He looked off in the distance and there was the same nerdy PureLight rep leaving the entryway of a house. He then backed towards the edge of street, away from the lamp.

"PureLight," I said.

"Yes. They're nasty. Nasty group."

"Like *Aum*?"

"I don't know…I don't like them."

"And people are disappearing…"

The crickets were the only ones talking.

The PureLight rep turned a corner and disappeared. We kept walking.

"Do you think maybe they could be the reason people are disappearing?"

Yamamoto-sensei started ahead, almost in a trance, before answering. "I've known Americans for a long time…"

"Yeah. And?"

"They either talk too much giving their opinion. Or they ask too many questions."

"Which am I?"

Yamamoto-sensei laughed.

"Both, I know." :shrug: Like it was a real fucking problem. Like Japanese were perfect.

"My father always said 'A man shouldn't talk.'"

"It seems most Japanese men follow this advice."

"Yes," he said as we approached my house. "But I didn't follow his advice." He laughed. "Merry Christmas" he said waving goodbye.

That night the wind picked up as soon as I got home. I felt cold and wrapped myself tightly in my sheets. I felt the walls rattle. Tomorrow was Christmas I realized.

I could barely sleep.

*

I wish I could be distracted right now by Twitter, Line, Instagram, SnapChat, YouTube, Netflix, Reddit, and Facebook. But wishes don't come true.

I face the blank page, well, the blank lines and…nothing.

When I have no distractions, I want them. Because here I sit alone in this room with just pen and paper. Just me and the page.

It does explain why my writing suffered, my sense of aesthetics never up to par. Distractions, distractions, too many distractions.

But how did I get in this room?

I remembered Yu saying something about…Yamaguchi.

My friend in Yamaguchi…

*

You know as I got on the tram at the port, headed to Hiroshima Station, I logged in to the Slack and found some Christmas morning autism.

OingoBoinGoy linked to a tweet by BavarianBobby (whose avatar was a blonde in classy, unrevealing dress while standing in a grain field) that read: "Yule is originally European. Christ is not," with a photo of a Yule altar in her one-bedroom apartment.

OingoBoinGoy: Maybe I should invite her in here.

Neu!Albion: Watch it mate.

OingoBoinGoy: u know it @Neu!Albion. xianity converted to Germanic paganism not the other way around.

Neu!Albion: i won't debate that.

OingoBoinGoy: debate what? That nowhere in the bible is December 25 mentioned? It's the birthday of Sol Invictus, the sun god.

Neu!Albion: that's common knowledge.

OingoBoinGoy: yet we all still practice. Xianity is just a gloss over a very pagan holiday.

Neu!Albion: regardless, Europe is still a Christian continent.

OingoBoinGoy: since when? The churches in Europe are just tourist traps.

Me: I would say Merry Christmas but damn.

Neu!Albion: You can give me a proper Happy Christmas. I would not protest.

OingoBoinGoy: ur just butthurt because everyone's waking up that xianity is a cucked crypto kikery.

Neu!Albion: it was Jews who killed the Christ.

262

OingoBoinGoy: and jesus was a jew. A Jew named Yeshua. Don't hide under latin meaning.

Me: I guess no one cares about Scott Nash going on the NewsGrind show?

OingoBoinGoy: No one gives a shit about that. Nash is just trying to save his ass by bowing down to ZOG. Like he doesn't do that enough but never naming the Jew. He's cucking on the Kaplan story.

He is of course referring to the capture of Kaplan in _____. Nash, stealing a source from Kai10, claimed that Kaplan's kidnapping was intentional because he was getting too close to psychic truth of contact with extraterrestrials that was monopolized by the Globalists and Reptilians—and he got roped in with the Lake Tahoe shooting.

Nash issued denial after denial regarding his connection, deleting the videos of his accusations from YouTube and Twitter, claiming it was all a globalist plot to get him censored all the while asking his viewers for support by clicking on the link below and purchasing some of his "Celestial Power" supplements or just making a cash donation to his PayPal or a recurring Patreon subscription for exclusive sneak peeks in to his next earth shattering stories or taking it to the next level and joining his club *The Celestial Order* with IRL meet-ups in your city with the goal of combatting the evil influences of globalist society that only costs $499 to join. Televangelism gone secular and paranoid.

But the clips still existed and sat in the archives of cyberspace.

Justin Bangs reveled in the story, naturally, shitposting for a couple of days, even trolling Nash on Twitter to get blocked for his trouble.

Then Ultima_Thule posted on Kai10, "This is what happens when you fuck with Kai10 Scott Nash. Don't steal our stories. Just further proof all should stay away from grifter's like Justin Bangs and Scott Nash."

But you know that, don't you?

But do you know I was almost off the tram during this exchange?

OingoBoinGoy: Stop talking about these vanilla e-celebs. JFC.

Neu!Albion: Helped distract you from the Christian history of Europe.

OingoBoinGoy: @Neu!Albion i don't have time for your christ cucking either.

Neu!Albion: Happy Christmas to you then mate.

263

OingoBoinGoy: Yes. I'm going to spend the day celebrating the endless life cycle, the festival of fire and thanks to the god of fertility, and Wotan himself. But u xtians will just call the blandly commercial xmas tree, the yule log, the mistletoe and Santa. B O R I N G. I don't need crypto kikery in this slack aka Christcucking. Go cuck somewhere else.

DM from Andyschluss: @OingoBoinGoy is being a real faggot. WTF.

Me: Maybe he's just having a period celebrating X-mas alone.

Andyschluss: He's married. Why would he be alone?

Me: Maybe he's having marital troubles?

Andyschluss: Fuck him for acting like this.

Me: He'll get over it.

Andyschluss: He shouldn't be bringing that in here.

Me: Sometimes it's hard to keep things compartmentalized.

Andyschluss: u would know.

Me: I would.

*

I slept walked through Hiroshima Station, past it's boomer coffee queues, secular Santa's and other glossy attempts at celebrating a feigned corporate Christmas—on to Iwakuni.

Iwakuni…you know all about Iwakuni. No need for me to give a travel log of the city. I could talk about the churn of elderly tourism or the slight differences between *Hiroshima-ben* and *Yamaguchi-ben* but won't or how Iwakuni is just over in the next prefecture of Yamaguchi. But I won't. Fuck it. Why was I going there? Why? Ah yes…

YU

My friend in Yamaguchi.

I went in the vein hope, or just in vein, or just an excuse to have some fresh air away from the eerie anchor that submerged me on the island. Maybe I could somehow, just by blind luck, run in to Yu, have some closure, or not.

I walked from the train station, it's bilingual signs dominating the landscape to accommodate the US Marines and their families stationed there, walked and walked and paid my ticket to cross the Kintai bridge with its multiple curvatures and cars parked on the pebble river bed below.

I looked around casually for Yu or Kenji or some sign, some happenstance that she might be around, maybe admiring the architecture of the bridge with its combination of Chinese influence and Japanese ingenuity…and nothing.

Not around.

Across the bridge, and around the tourist shops immediately populating the other side, I continue to look, heading towards the statue of Sasaki Kojiro, the ropeway leading to Iwakuni Castle in the distance. Nothing.

I start walking aimlessly yet purposefully towards the ropeway entrance when I notice the red eyes.

The red eyes.

The night…the red eyes stalking Adina…

But that was a dream.

No. It wasn't me.

It's not that type of story.

But the dream lingered, as did the glowing blood eyes, like eyes of the white snakes of Iwakuni. There was a sign, for museum displaying the unique snakes of this region. White snakes with red eyes.

I stared at the sign.

Started thinking. Started jumping to conclusions. Started wondering about the possibility of Yu…no…no…no…just jumping to conclusions…but those eyes…and the figure who committed the murder it was about the same height as Adina…it didn't necessarily have to be a man…no…no…no…STOP.

"Whoa, you know him too? Talk about coincidence—or is it synchronicity? Have you read Jung?" the voice jolted me…it's testosterone fueled confidence followed by a slightly feminine yet western giggle.

I turn and there's Mark with—Mandy? He's winter casual in almost the same gear I met him with at the port. His smirk practically sewed in, complementing Mandy's perma-grin next to him. He's just a bit shorter than her but she's enraptured by his presence.

When he notices me noticing him, I step back in surprise and mutter "*Bikkuri shita*" then walk towards him.

"Look you're practically a native. You even surprise in Japanese!"

Mandy laughed (of course she did).

"Merry Christmas, is what I should be saying. Merry Christmas," he said walking to shake my hand.

265

"Yeah, um, Merry Christmas."

I then held my hand out to Mandy, wondering what her reaction would be considering the *NewsGrind* story and the backlash and her texts—"Merry Christmas, Jason" she said with a light hug, and tentative smile.

"Merry Christmas."

"I probably should be saying 'Happy Holidays', but it just comes out so naturally."

"Nah. You're fine. We all celebrate Christmas, right? Hell, they even celebrate it here, right? Right Jason? You're the Japan expert, right?"

"Well, it's kind of more like, um, you know, a Valentine's Day kind of thing, here, you know?"

"Do you have a hot date?"

Mandy laughed.

"No, um, actually I—" I looked around, "I just came…"—*why are you here Jason?*—"I'm just…I'm looking around, I guess. You? You have a hot date?"

"Nah. That's not my idea of spending Christmas."

"Uh huh," I said. Mandy wore a smile indicating that she was at least somewhat amicable today. "So you two, um, know each other, or something?"

"Nah. We just ran in to each other. Not every day you just see a tall blonde girl walking around."

"He was escorting me back to the train station."

"You never know who might attack. Like what happened to Adina. Mandy says you both knew her?"

"I mean, yeah, you read the *NewsGrind* article right?"

"Right," Mark said.

I tried looking at Mandy but she looked at Mark, smile faintly cracking. "I mean," Mark said. "Sorry, sorry. Too soon. I mean, blondes are a premium here so be careful…"

"Stop it."

"You know someone on the Marine Base?"

"No. My brother. He's here doing some research. Or actually he used it as an excuse to pay me a visit. He had some speaking engagement but stopped over to say hi for Christmas."

"CFR is having a conference here?"

"No. Tokyo. But he flew over."

"Why isn't your brother walking you—"

"What was the conference for again?" said cutting me off.

266

Mandy rolled her eyes with a smile, "I told you."

"Tell us again, so Jason can know."

"Something about media literacy, the challenges of disinformation and how it causes to more hate in the world."

"I think the world might need more hate, right Jason?"

"Stop."

"Next time you see your brother, ask him about The Inquiry. See if he knows what I'm talking about. Jason knows what I'm talking about, don't you Jason?"

"Jason knows. Look at the smile! Jason, I knew you'd know."

"Stop," she said giggling with her mouth shut.

I smiled. I did know. You don't? Google it.

I noticed some Japanese passerby's staring at us as we talked. Really as Mark was being loud and obnoxious and Mandy lapping up every word of his. I shouldn't have been surprised or disgusted that Mandy's moral outrage around me was immediately reduced to flirty banter around Mark. I wasn't surprised. More disgusted.

"Jason, did you read Kai10 today? Did you see that post?"

"Um, no..."

"Dude, you gotta read it. It was pretty wild shit. Trust me, you have to read it. Read it before it disappears."

"What is this?" Mandy asked.

I shifted on my feet and put both thumbs under my straps.

"Kai10? You know that board where anything goes. A lot of conspiracies and shit. Wild stuff. Conspiracy guys like Scott Nash plunder a lot of their news from there. Today...wew, it was pretty wild. Jason goes there."

"I know...a hate site..."

"Hate site? Listen to that! Is that what your brother told you. He just doesn't like competition!"

She put her hand over her mouth while placing another on his shoulder.

"You haven't read it, have you Jason?"

"No."

"Read it. Trust me. You better get there fast, because you know the rotation is on that place."

"Right, right."

Stories were there one day and gone the next. Just one long continuous stream of content. Content, content, content!

But you know that, don't you?

"Well!" Mark said. "Enough about who controls the world. Us peons need to live in it. We were going to visit Iwakuni Castle but the ropeway was shut down. You know a good place to eat?"

"Um, well, are you looking for a regional food?"

"Sure, whatever. Mandy isn't going to eat anything anyway, are you Mandy?"

"You might be eating alone."

"If it comes to that."

"There's *kawara soba*—it's, it's, this type of uh, soba noodles served on a stone."

"Is that what the *kawara* is?" Mark asked pronouncing it as *kaweara*.

"Yeah."

"Okay," he looked at Mandy. "What do you think?"

She shrugged her shoulders. "Sure."

"Let's do it," He then looked at me. "Jason, you coming?"

"No, um, I uh—I have plans."

"Alrighty then, have a good Christmas. Don't be too lonely."

"Okay."

We shook hands.

I then looked at Mandy, unsure what to do. She then walked over to me and gave me another hug. "Have a good Christmas," she said.

"You too."

They then walked off to the restaurant. Not hand in hand or arm in arm but smile to smile.

I tightened my grip on my straps and looked towards the ground walking back towards the bridge and the train station, every now and then looking up, hoping to see the figure or personage or outline or any hint of the memory that was Yu.

But found nothing.

But you know that, don't you?

*

You also know before entering the train back to Hiroshima, I went Kai10 to find the latest posts, letting it load on my screen so I wouldn't have to fight connectivity issues. You know the post: The Hidden History of Robert Kaplan.

"One piece of the story behind Kaplan's capture in _____: His partnership with Dr. Norifumi Uchida, a Japanese expert nerololgist measuring brain waves and brain energy. At first it was just theoretical

268

discussion between Kaplan and Uchida exchanging research and notes. But after the success of the dystopian SF anime *Akira*, and their potential at weaponization, both governments decided it was worth moving forward to explore this new realm of warfare. With funding from the Japanese government and CIA, Kaplan and Uchida used orphaned children (female twins because their brains mature faster) and modified their brains so they could communicate. An irl version of psychics. But the program then disappeared. I can find no more documentation. But it might provide a key clue in to the reasons for Kaplan's disappearance."

First ANON reply: "You're high ANON"

The next: "You might be on to something."

ANON after: "He is. Uchida's Sempai was Dr. Noriyuki Takada, a pioneer of neurology. What's left out of his bio is he worked as a partner with Nazi scientists on their psychic research."

The Next: "And those same Nazi scientists came to the US under Project Paperclip to work on MK Ultra and Project Monarch."

Next: "And you know who Kaplan's mentor was? Gerhard Muller. One who came over from Germany. Part of Paperclip."

Last: "We did it Kai10!"

ANON: "LOL
>give fag Scott Nash more material for his show so   he can hate bait on Nazis?
>retarded.jpg"

Next ANON: "How will they ever recover from that burn?"

And on and on.

I didn't know why it made Mark excited to mention it. I wanted to do more research on this psychic program but I didn't have data connection.

And I noticed the same digital interference.

I looked around to see if anyone else was having the same problem. I just saw a plain girl in a plain school uniform looking at a note while also looking out the window. Another in blue uniform with gray sweater, working on her bangs and makeup, talking to someone the duration of the trip while also flipping through manga on her phone.

MOMNDF: You've already mentioned that girl once.

JRK: Oops. Faulty memory.

And the words lingered upon site of my screen became distorted...

Kenji is coming.

The words sat, conjuring anxiety, fear and regret.

And they wouldn't leave.

*

Decided to go to the Hiroshima Museum of Art. They still had the special exhibit from the DeMenil collection in Houston. The same paintings that I managed to use my charms on Yu. I thought maybe in the vein hope that maybe I could see her here, prowling the paintings, contemplating, my own Christmas miracle, a moment of happenstance.

But I also knew I wouldn't find her. No serendipitous moment of reunion and romance.

It's not that type of story.

But I wanted it to be. As I walked through the first gallery ("From Romanticism to Impressionism") featuring paintings by the likes of Delacroix, Courbet, Millet, Corot, Boudin, Manet, Monet, Renoir, Sisley, Degas and Pissaro, as I walked glancing, trying to find some meaning, some feeling of inspiration, I saw a man, looked to be Arab—was it one of the Palestinians from the bar?—He stared at Degas' A Woman in the Tub (1891. Pastel, carton 71.5x71.0 cm), admiring the plump painted ass of that anonymous eternal peasant. He admired it until he noticed me noticing him admiring a painted ass. He looked at me with a stare then returned his gaze to the walls and kept on walking. He wore a white sweat shirt and gray jeans, with his olive skin and black hair providing a striking counterbalance—fuck you, I'm in an art museum, I notice these type of connections given the environment.

Was he one of them? Was he there the night Adina was killed? Was he one of the ones detained? Why was he released? Why's he going against his religion looking at naked women instead of thinking of ways to get in the arms of 72 virgins?

I glanced over at him again, without trying to notice, while also trying to contemplate Manet's *Woman with a Gray Plumed Hat* (1882. Pastel, canvas 55.0.35.3 cm).

I didn't get it.

He left the curved room, his walk congruent with the curvature of the floor and the walls.

I looked at the Degas—nice ass—and then quickly walked out of the room in to the next one ("Post-Impressionists and Neo-Impressionists") featuring paintings by Signac, Seurat, Toulouse-Lautrec, Rousseau, Bauchant, Cezanne, Gaugin, Van Gogh, Redon, Bonnard, Vuillard, Munch, Lesidaner and other artists who've earned the honor of only being referred to by their last name. God forbid the day if I'm ever referred to as Reudelheuber-Katz. A day, that forward thinking, makes me realize I need a *nom de plume* to hide my partial *nom de Jew.*

But as I entered the room, I looked for the Arab. Looked both ways. The room was open with nowhere to hide. I realized this is turning in to some bizarre play on that scene that in *Dressed to Kill* (1980. Directed by Brian De Palma from a script by De Palma and cinematography by Ralf D. Bode)—

MOMNDF: You've already mentioned Dressed to Kill and its credits.

JRK: Fug.

It's not that type of story.

I'll stop there.

Like I stopped to look at Van Gogh's *Daubigny's Garden* (1890. Oil on canvas 53.2x103.5 cm), the centerpiece of the entire museum, and more importantly for the city of Hiroshima, the main collateral the Bank of Hiroshima uses to stay solvent. A work of financial art in itself. There were all the paints, the oils reflecting the light, a shine and pop that isn't reflected in books or the internet.

But I didn't get it.

Van Gogh, the "tortured artist" and "misunderstood genius" who had psychotic episodes, even severing his ear while no one bought or cared about his paintings. The thought of toiling away, day after day, on portraits that no one cared about, painting, pleading and hoping that someone would "get it" all the while they didn't get it, driving one to the point of madness and eventual suicide. And all for what? Glory and adulation after death? He didn't receive any of the benefits, being more tortured than artist and more misunderstood than genius. Why toil away in poverty just to be confounding, then wait for the rest of humanity to catch the trend wave after the fact and use your hard work and vision for their overpriced vanity purchases? Fuck that.

Van Gogh was a mistake.

271

I thought about the Arab—*was he there that night? Why was Mandy nice to me today? Maybe I should have eaten kawara soba with her and the jarhead. Why was OingoBoinGoy being such dick?* And those words…

Kenji is coming…

This is ridiculous.

Enough shallow shit tier art criticism.

It's not that type of story.

I try not to feign sophistication but try is the operative word.

A long sigh, and I moped about the museum looking at the paintings hoping to see…something. But the divine spark wouldn't flicker (only bad metaphors).

And all the art and money dedicated to all this shit. All the remaining sands on the shore that is the commercialized art world after the oceans of church and state patronage receded. Fucking joke. All the money wasted, all the print and talk. Such a waste. For what? So people can feel sophisticated, superior, part of the in-crowd because they're talking and looking at capital-A Art? It was all just paint on a canvas. All just chosen to be important because someone or some group somewhere in power—probably Jews—deemed the art important and "priceless" to the point whole banks and fortunes are wasted on conceits. Fucking ridiculous.

Art was a mistake.

In the final room ("Ecole de Paris"), I ignored the paintings of Matisse and Picasso and decided to sit on the couch provided in front of the triptych painted by Leonard Foujita, a Japanese artist who introduced Japanese techniques (gold foil backgrounds, *mensofude* brushes etc.) to illustrate western themes and settings—in this case a narrative of the Virgin Mary and Christ (*Annunciation, Adoration of the Magi, Descent from the Cross*).

The third painting of Jesus being lowered had my attention, especially the strange way his figure appeared with the assist of Japanese ink, rather than just the paints one finds in classical renderings.

But as I looked at the figure of Christ, I decided to sit, contemplate, I closed my eyes, took a deep breath—it was Christmas afterall and there were no paintings of Wotan for me to consider—and with eyes then opened I looked at Jesus, Yeshua or Joshua depending on who you ask, and…couldn't understand. Why did he and the apostles following—why did they die for an ungrateful, uncaring and unknowing mass? They say now "love and salvation" like it's a forgone heroic conclusion, but why did they "love" them, whether it be Jew or Gentile, who mocked, spit, hated and had them arrested and executed? Why? Why love those assholes? What was so lovable to rise above the contempt of Caesar? And why did this so-called love conquer the world's greatest empire?

I won't explain. Doubt I'll even give an answer. It's not that type of story.

But those questions lingered at that moment.

Why sacrifice for anyone? Especially those you don't love yet even know? Why give your life for the wicked, if it will never bring a recompense—even generations later—in (vein?) hopes that they will come to worship the same god as you? What reward was there in sacrifice for dim possibilities of conversion? Did those thoughts ever travel through the minds of Peter, Paul, John, Matthew, Mark or even Jesus himself?

And seeing the way an agnostic yet pagan culture like Japan is harmonious you wonder what's the advantage of even bringing Christianity to a place like this, and wonder if Rome and greater Europe were better off without it.

"Pretty smart, isn't it?"

A British accent—the Arab!

He sat a cushion away from me with a quiet smile on his face. His hands were at rest, palm down on the cushion, like he was enjoying a breeze but trying to hold himself in place.

"Yeah," I said. "I guess."

"Fitting to admire on Christmas, yeah?"

"Huh...I was, uh, thinking the same thing."

"Are you American then?"

"What was the giveaway?"

He grunted with a smile.

"Where in America?"

"Me? Well, Las Vegas I guess. But I've also lived in Seattle and LA. But I lived longest in Vegas. My childhood, was, um, a tour of the west, I guess."

"They have many museums like this in Vegas?"

"No. Unless you count the Neon Graveyard."

"What's that then?"

"That's where all the unused neon signs of Vegas go. It's like a capitalist graveyard, really. I mean, I don't mean to get political or economic..."

"It's okay mate. I understand."

"And, uh, you? Haven't we met?" I asked trying to push this conversation towards some sort of line of investigation.

273

He squinted. "Don't think so."

"Oh, because, I, um spent a late night talking to some Palestinians. I mean they were good guys and all, but it was late, that whole night was a blur…"

"I'm not Palestinian."

"Oh, right, British, yeah…"

He smiled again. "My family lived in England, yeah. But we're Assyrian Christian not Muslim."

"Christian huh?"

"Yeah. Our origins are from Iraq and Iran and Turkey. I speak Aramaic which is the language that Jesus spoke."

"Oh…and your family like immigrated to, um, England?"

"Yeah. My great grandparents were removed from our ancestral homelands 100 years ago in an Islamic genocide."

"No homeland?"

"Not at the moment I'm afraid."

"I see, I'm uh sorry to hear that. You know, many, or maybe some, at least a lot on the internet I guess, they feel that we're—whites, Europeans—you know we're losing our homelands."

"Who are your ancestors?"

"Uh, um, mostly German and Jewish. My mom is Jewish. But my dad is German—well, of German ancestry in Lynnwood, Washington—well, Seattle."

"Have you ever been to Israel?"

"Me?" I laughed. "No. Like, I've never even been to Europe or England. Um, I mean, I'd like to go, well to um, Europe, Like Germany and France, those places. Especially before it all falls apart. Especially Germany."

"You consider yourself Christian or Jewish then?"

"No, no I—I don't really consider myself. I mean, my dad is a Christian, a practicing—Protestant…evangelical you know—very American. My mom is sort of practicing Jew. But me? They…I don't know. Talking with those Palestinians, I understand the appeal of Islam. It all seems more…"

"Macho, eh?"

"Macho? I guess, sure."

"Islam is different in the West than east."

"Yeah?"

"Muslims in the West are more insecure about their identity here—I guess I can say here, yeah? Japan is the West, yeah? Or rather just in the modern world in general. The groups are either highly conservative reactionary or highly liberal…"

"I can understand that."

"You can, eh?"

"I can. Surprisingly. Western politics is going in that direction."

"In the east—I mean there's no surveys or anything—but in places like Iraq the young are less religious. There's underground Christian conversions. Islam is secure but not as secure as people think. Especially in this modern world. The truth is young Muslims don't all fast, they are sexually promiscuous, they are also modernizing. They are just at an earlier stage of it than the West is."

"Modernity…"

"Non-religious Europeans, and Americans too I guess," he said looking at me, "They see Islam's hold on its adherents to be threatening."

"Right. I think…"

"Yeah?"

"I think for many younger people it's nice to see a group of people believe in something. Especially now. Here. Where everything seems just…cheap."

"I agree. The anti-religious materialist epoch is coming to a close. Who will be there to pick up the pieces? Islam? The Church?"

"Or something else? Nazis maybe?"

"Already been tried mate. Didn't work. Probably just accelerated things if anything."

"Right…"

"The Near East was once the Christian region in the world. Perhaps it's time in Europe is also ending. What can be done? I don't see a solution. I just try to have some faith."

"I, um, I have faith that Japan will survive whatever comes. They're more robust than many world cultures."

"Indeed they are mate. But we aren't Japanese."

"Right."

"I'm sorry what's your name again?"

"Jason."

"Ishaia."

We shook hands. His grip was firm. I wondered if his name was a form of "Isaiah" but didn't bother to ask.

"Nice to meet your Jason. Are you a teacher?"

"Yeah. And,um, you?"

275

"No. Just touring. My sister is a teacher in the city here for one of the private schools."

"Nova? Geos? Aeon?"

"Forgot the name. Thought I'd look at the art while she's working. We need to focus on art and reuniting the church. Not in that order necessarily. We've lost power but it's a good opportunity to renew our institutions and philosophy."

"So you have faith? That, like you know, it can be fixed?"

"Faith is all we have. Even if the West collapses. God is still God. He's in control."

"You're not upset? You don't want to invade Iraq or wherever and take back your homeland?"

He stood up. I did as well. He looked at the painting of Christ then said, "When you grow up hearing stories of genocide and forced migration, all of those stories can stir in you a heart for revenge. Nothing can keep it at bay. Not even Christianity itself."

"But that's natural, isn't it?"

"Certainly. But the way the memory of violence can darken the hearts of survivors…it can be hopelessly embittering and just lead to more violence."

"But…what's the alternative? Especially if people want me or my people dead?"

"Well, that's our job—I mean it's the Christian's job—to show a way towards self-sacrifice and empathy for our fellow man."

"But that could lead to just more death for the better people."

"Perhaps. But you're American, yeah? Your country is how old? Not even 300 years?"

"Something like that."

"The cycle of violence and revenge as gone on for thousands of years and will go on. And all nations will perish. All of them. The Sumerians, the Egyptians, Babylonians, Persians—all disappeared or altered by types like Alexander the Great, whose empire perished with his death. Then Rome, then Byzantium, which called itself Rome, and so on. I say it's better to be a sacrificial lamb than a devil."

"But what about…you know those who remember…the remnant?"

"Well, God help them all in their suffering. Something we can learn from the Jews, eh?"

"Maybe. I mean they never let us forget do they?"

"Right," he said. "Good meeting you and Happy Christmas."

"Merry Christmas."

*

Do you know waiting for the tram I felt a sense of relaxation talking to the British Assyrian, and I lingered on his words, thinking of counterarguments, mainly, why the fuck would you sit by idly and let your people be massacred?

I decided I'd rather be a devil.

Actually, I'd made that decision a while back.

But you know that, don't you?

Do you know at the stop near Hondori, I notice Mandy entering the tram, her smile from earlier gone? The tram is once again crowded and she's standing while I'm sitting. I lightly shout her name and motion for her to sit down. The men, the older one's in business suits look up to her as she passes by.

She then sits down silently and pulls out her phone to start looking at it, immediately flipping to NewsGrind.

"Hey, um, did you have a good Christmas with your, you know, brother?"

She just shrugs her shoulders.

I then get a Periscope alert on my phone. Mandy's eyes roll up towards me that say superior in every way as they quickly return to their point of origin.

The alert from Scott Nash read "The Truth About the Lies of the NewsGrind Interview".

But you know that, don't you?

Did you know I heard Scott Nash's voice coming from Mandy watching the NewsGrind piece? It's introductory package with alarming concern music, "On this NewsGrind Christmas special, a journey in to the dark web of extremist conspiracies…" followed with quick edits full of Scott Nash greatest but damning soundbites, you know, the usual: "9/11 was an inside job", "Mandalay Bay had multiple shooters—it was a globalist plot!", "The President is a 33rd level member of the Illuminati," "We're under Reptilians control!", "Psychics are being harnessed to leverage government control" et cetera et cetera ending with "There's a conference in Lake Tahoe of the world elites and they are in panic mode right now, so they are meeting to figure out how to ratchet up control for their overlords" followed by flashes of his tweets including his RTs, like the one from General_TOHO that read "Do you know who controls you?" concluding with excerpts of news reports of a shooter and ambulances cutting to the mulatto host seated with Nash like a kind but determined interrogator, "First of all, you have a lot of detractors, but

277

shouldn't you take some responsibility for your comments that caused a woman close to retirement to be shot?"

Of course, the denials come immediately with "No, no—that quote is out of context" with a juxtaposed edit showing an uncut version of his quote on YouTube, followed by the next question: "You've had known white supremacist misogynists like Justin Bangs on your show, why would you even give people like him a platform?" followed by immediate disavowal's and subsequent soundbytes that seem to support Bangs' worldview like "The globalists want to bring about a white genocide!" and "Every bitch needs a good slap on the ass sometime" like they were actually said back to back in the same episode though the shirt colors, one hipster garage workshirt with "Earl" nametag and the other a black Slayer t-shirt. "I no longer associate with the likes of Justin Bangs, and I apologize to my viewers or any out there offended by his speech. He has shown himself to be a sexist, racist and fraud."

Then another Periscope alert followed by superior eyeroll from Mandy. Justin Bangs this time with title: "Scott Nash shows his true nature as backstabbing piece of shit!"

But you know that, don't you?

As you know on the *NewsGrind* piece, the reporter then rolls video, has Nash watch the monitor of a little girl from her hospital bed who was shot at Mandalay Bay, who talks about being paralyzed for life followed by funeral B-roll of the of the black lesbian security guard shot by one his "fans" at Lake Tahoe. "What do you have to say them, Scott? Are lizard people to blame for their sorrow? Or are your fans?"

Before he can answer they show the end of the shooter's Facebook Live stream, the camera falling to the ground with him as he screams "SUBSCRIBE TO SCOTT NASH FOR THE TRUTH!"

Then live Skype streams of both families appear on a monitor for Nash to look in their eyes and answer.

His answer is inconsequential. The stage has been set. The propaganda executed at Porsche precision. A single camera drama or multi-camera soap with stilted plots, and engineered situations to take place on a finite number of sets that populate every episode, with forced, tired, and polite storylines and choreographed reveals could not have done it better. This is where the true drama and the true stakes were.

But Nash's answer, like you didn't know, was, "Of course the reptilians are not responsible for their sorrow. But I can't control who listens to me or their actions…"

Put a fork in him he's dead.

Riveting content. Excellently staged. Riefenstahl couldn't have done it better (and I would know. I've watched *Triumph des Willens*, *Olympia* and the lesser known *Der Sieg des Glaubens*).

I start watching Nash's Periscope where he's watching the *NewsGrind* piece in real time with his big tittied Latina THOT co-host Jimena. The comments as they scroll up vary from "You're doing God's work Scott!" to "This is what you get for being an agent of ZOG" from Ultima_Thule himself, "Tell them the truth about the Jews Scott!", and even AndySchluss chimed in with "Merry Christmas cuck kike faggot!" all the while Nash explained to Jimena how malicious the editing was, playing raw video of the interview that he taped himself with his iPhone. "They're coming after me because they know how powerful I've become. That's why they attack me." "The MSM is afraid of you Scott!" said the commentator Patriotic Granny 1776 almost similar to the next one, "I love you Scott! I want your babies!" to the generic "Don't let the lamestream media keep you down Scott!"

But you know that, don't you?

Do you know I look at Mandy and say "It's um, uh, kind of funny, isn't it?"?

"What's funny?"

"You—and um, you know me. You're watching the NewsGrind piece on uh YouTube and um, on Periscope I get the alert from Scott Nash and I'm watching his reaction, his trying to explain it all you know. It's like opposite sides of the coin. Kind of funny, right?"

"No."

"It's not. You don' think—"

"Oh…god…" Literal :facepalm:.

"What?"

"I can't believe—actually, after the NewsGrind article on your VILE comments, I can believe it. I can believe that you would support someone like Scott Nash. That white trash…"

"He's from Dallas. Like you."

"I know. It's nauseating. There's a reason I moved to San Francisco. Aren't you from LA?"

"I just went to school there…"

"You should know better too. You have a college education."

"Yeah, so, what does that even me—"

"It means you shouldn't be making awful comments like you did on that site—what is it 'Kay ten' or something?"

"Kai10."

"Whatever it is. Whatever. It's just a hate machine. The things…"

"What things?"

"What you said…they're just…"

"It's just shitposting—like you—"

"It's risible! You know what that means?"

"Of course—"

"I got nauseous just reading those comments to think—"

"Look, I can expla—"

"Sure you can. But I don't want to be a hateful Nazi! Matt is now repeating—"

"I—I haven't even chatt—talked, um, Matt—well he's…"

"You're trying to recruit people to your hate—"

"Like your side is perfect—"

"My side? Like there's sides? Justice and decency only has one side."

"Sure it does. If you even know what they mean—"

"I know more than you!"

"Says who? You're fucking ZOG tool brother?"

The Tram stops.

"GO FUCK YOURSELF JASON!" Mandy screams for the whole tram to hear. The remaining passengers try not to stare but rush the exit. Mandy tries to exit quickly but gets stuck in the queue of card scanners. She then tries to move ahead, saying "I can't be around. I can't. Sorry. *Gomen*. If only Adina…" almost mumbly, pushing herself ahead of the crowd, no one, even the men, fighting her as she bulls forward off the tram.

She didn't realize we would have to be on the same boat going home. I decided to keep my distance for the bitches safety and not cause an international incident. I saw her talking on the phone, in hysterics (probably to Avi) and only heard the words, because they were so loud that those sitting in their padded chairs trying to watch the variety show hosted by Downtown were looking in her direction irritated and probably wondered by what she

280

meant when she said "he said my brother was a tool of something—I don't even understand," (probably looking to call some diversity police on me).

As the boat coasted along the waves, the sun set where it was hard to admire the view. I never bothered to wonder where Mark was considering he lived in Etajima (I thought), while Mandy sat in the rear by the door to make as quick of an exit possible while I sat in the common area up front, everyone seated near me on the bench trying to focus on their paper or phone as I remembered my sense of excitement coming over here, coming to Japan. But now that I was there for two years on, I realized I had an attitude of what now? Japan seemed like an unreal place, fantasyland, until I arrived. Then it just was, it just is. It became normal and banal. Most experiences are like this, I guess. It's something you strive toward then once you have it, it loses its uniqueness and has challenges of its own.

A blonde was pissed off and looked down on me, just like one would at home. I was alone. Here. On a boat going to a remote island, when I could be alone, at "home", in one of the many casinos, working as dealer or just walking through the alienating *whirr* of the slot machines.

If I disappeared from Etajima, Japan tomorrow, no one would care. Just like no one in Vegas or LA or Seattle cared when I left it.

And those words lingered. Even more heavily than Mandy's recent tirade, but she added to the weight of the consequences…

Kenji is coming…

And coming to Japan was a mistake.

*

Yu is on the screen. I try to shout to her. "Yu!" But she just stays stationary, docile, immovable to my cries. "YU!"

Nothing.

She sits in a black chair. She looks down towards her feet. Her hair is a mess, hanging covering her chest her clothes loose.

"Yu!"

She then looks up. Slightly.

Distortion comes from the screen. The interference—lines, lines, lines thick and black, occupy the screen jagged in assorted angles.

My phone too.

Then outside—I'm outside now—I start walking around a corner, towards the parking lot behind my apartment, I know she's there, I know.

The PureLight Temple sits in the background. It looms over me, replacing the moon.

I hear a faint feminine voice—almost like a whisper. "Jason."

I turn to look.

I wake up.

I sit in bed trying to sleep. Trying to return to that dream, but can't.

I just lay looking at the wooden ceiling as the words linger only to reinforce my discomfort.

Kenji is coming.

*

TIIING! TIIING! TIIING!

I jolt up.

OingoBoinGoy: @General_TOHO GET IN HERE—NOW!

You know @General_TOHO the avatar of Godzilla's face imposed on General Hideki Tojo's body, military uniform and all, was my handle on both Twitter and Slack, and everywhere else I shitpoasted.

But do you know, my hand trembled as I depressed the Slack icon in half-sleep? You do know the direct message from OingoBoinGoy with a link to a post on Kai10, and then successive links to posts on 4Chan, 8Chan, and out in to the mainstream of Reddit, Twitter and Gab, with Scott Nash in mid-Periscope (my other alert), "The Dark Nazi Underground Is Full of Degenerate Fake Perverts"

Kai10 link from Ultima_Thule: "I've made a mistake in trusting Jason Reudelheuber-Katz, AKA General_TOHO. I've received screenshots of personal messages between him and Stephanie Kyle, AKA Park_City_Stephanie. Normally I would not post such gossip but Kyle is the wife of Wayne Kyle, AKA OingoBoinGoy. These screenshots are of Jason and Stephanie sexting. OingoBoinGoy should patrol his wife better because you never trust a THOT. And Jason Reudelhuber-Katz should not be in our movement. He's obviously an agent of subversion."

I would write "but you know that, don't you?" but you may not know that given the suspicious nature of Ultima_Thule.

Do you know the photos listed are one of Stephanie, blonde, not particularly gorgeous but full figured and curvy standing outside…Park City I guess, in full ski uniform, smiling? Her husband, Wayne is then in the next picture, balding, with goatee, wearing a Hawaiian shirt, emphasizing his paunch, post-acne cratered face, looking like a fucking loser.

You know our messages:

Stephanie: "You need to come back to US. We need you. I need you."

Me: "Japan is getting old. Maybe I will. I need some blonde in my life."

Stephanie: "LOL. I'm blonde everywhere. Not fake. All natural."

Me: "Like a good Aryan girl. Not sure if I believe you though."

Stephanie: "Do I need to prove it to you?"

Me: "You do. Show me."

Have you seen the pic of her sitting down, legs spread, showing her blonde taint?

Me: "It might be you because I like what I see."

Stephanie: "Need to see it all huh?"

Me: "I do."

Or, the next selfie of her in the mirror, fully nude, her full tits and pink nipples, blonde locks hovering just above them, standing slightly cross legged?

Stephanie: "Good enough?"

Me: "I suppose."

Stephanie: "What else can I do to convince you?"

Me: "Touch yourself."

Stephanie: "You would like that."

Me: "So what?"

Stephanie: "I might squirt on to my phone screen though."

Me: "That makes it hotter."

Stephanie: "LOL ok."

Next was just a screen shot of her touching herself. Not the full video she sent. Just my reaction, "That will get any man hard."

Stephanie: "Nothing makes my husband hard."

Me: "Ur husband has a problem."

Stephanie: "That's why I need you Mein Fuehrer"

Me: "Maybe I'll just go to Park City and not tell you. Just break in to your house and take you."

Stephanie: "OMG that makes me wet."

Me: "Put you over the dinner table and take you from behind."

Stephanie: "Yes. God, I'm touching myself."

Me: "Cum inside of you while I pull your hair."

Stephanie: "I hope you make me pregnant."

And that the was the only message posted. There were several more. But you knew all this, right?

Just as you know the comments on Kai10:

ANON#1: ">Trusting a THOT
>Trusting a KIKE
>Can't get any more shit tier"

ANON#2: "Do we need any more proof the Jews just want to take our women and use our children as blood sacrifices?"

ANON#3: "Whoever murdered his Khazar girlfriend, made a mistake and murdered the wrong merchant."

ANON#4: "Is there anyone in this movement who is not a FED, Kike or THOT (or all three)? Serious question. Not memeing."

I watched a little bit of Nash's Periscope with big tittied Jimena, "That's how the globalists subvert these movements. They send in agents like this Jason and have him build up a following, distract everyone with Nazism, then it turns out not only is he Jewish, but he's also sleeping around stealing the women of others in their so-called movement."

"So true," Jimena says.

He then looks at the camera: "Folks, this is why you need to stick with people you trust. Those who don't hide behind fake names pretending they're a playboy or those hiding behind fake accounts claiming to be Japanese when in fact they're perverted Americans wishing they were Japanese."

Justin Bangs posted on Twitter: "If only Wayne the Hawaiian shirt Nazi knew the truths of Judaism, game and hypergamy, he wouldn't have gotten cucked. And Jason Reudelheuber-Katz could also have benefitted from my advice in my latest book *Bangs, Bitches and Branch Swinging*.

But you know all this, don't you?

Stephanie.

Fucking THOT bitch cunt.

Been messaging back and forth for a while. She had my doxx. You know, dumb fuck that I was gave it to her. Those messages were from before Adina's murder—she knew about Adina, about Yu, said it turned her on. Maybe even a couple of days before. BUT YOU KNOW THAT! YOU KNOW after the murder I stopped messaging her. You know she kept asking where I was and I ignored. You know she leaked the photos to someone. You know they somehow got to Ultima_Thule.

I checked my Twitter sock account for General_TOHO. "This account is no longer active." Not the first time I was banned and while I considered buying an alt-account, I figured it wasn't worth it. My account for JasonDoesJapan, my normie account, was also no longer active as was my Instagram, and my blog for *Katsura's Lair* taken down by the server admin for "hate speech".

It was over.

>Never trust a THOT.

OingoBoinGoy: @General_TOHO thanks for revealing to all of us that you're just a degenerate kike who wants to ruin marriages!

Neu!Albion: You shouldn't be allowed in more countries mate. Go ruin Israel next.

Me: @OingoBoinGoy I didn't know she was your wife.

OingoBoinGoy: Bullshit. You're an agent of subversion. End of story.

)))Reb_Greyback(((: And who's fault is it from letting him in here?

OingoBoinGoy: @)))Reb_Greyback(((now is not the time to be a faggot.

)))Reb_Greyback(((: I always thought we were letting too many in here. The discussion has gone down hill. @General_TOHO just wanted to talk his Jew degeneracy.

Me: I'm only half-Jewish, I don't even practice. I've never been to Israel. Have you guys read my tweets?

OingoBoinGoy: How can we? You've been banned from Twitter dumbass. As have I and most of his in here because of this shit! Gab is now under pressure from ZOG to delete your accounts as well because they're saying it's already led to one death.

Me: I didn't kill anyone. Adina was murdered by someone else!

Ernst_Jungroyper: So you admit to knowing that kike?

OingoBoinGoy: @Ernst_Jungroyper you obviously missed the news: @General_TOHO was fucking her. They were probably scheming on how to undermine our movement. Someone did us a favor by murdering her.

Me: That's not what happened.

)))Reb_Greyback(((: I'd believe you if you actually murdered her.

Neu!Albion: Why are we even still talking to this bloke?

Andyschluss: Jason betrayed us all.

Me: thx @Andyschluss way to defend friend. KYS.

Andyschluss: No u. Friends don't lie to each other.

Me: I never lied to you.

OingoBoinGoy: You're done Jason. Delet or Go get some shekels.

Me: You're all faggots.

You can no longer access this Slack

But you know that, don't you?

Text from Min with a link to a NewsGrind Link: "Boyfriend of Slain Jewish Girl Linked to Nazi Social Media Accounts". "I now know what you and Matt talked about. No need 2 ask anymore. Don't ever talk 2 me again."

The article, once again was a collection of my most polarizing tweets under the General_TOHO account:

"Do you know who controls you?" ("An obvious anti-semitic reference")

"A THOT once told me to hit her. I didn't because I never give a THOT what she wants."

"Rape served a purpose. It was a way for the strong to spread their seed. That way the women really had no say in the matter."

In a reply to a white privilege article:

"America: 2% Jewish

 Harvard: 25% Jewish

Billionaires: 35% Jewish

Military? Only 0.3% Jewish

We have to talk about Jew Privilege"

A posting of two photos: One with Neo-Nazis on one side and the other a group of Ghetto blacks with my caption: "Pick the better neighbor".

A posting of a photo with two different plaques at Auschwitz: One from 1948 (4 Million died) and 1989 (1.5 Million died), with my caption: "Never forget".

My posting of the meme I found in Kai10 of Jesus saying he fed 3000 Jews fish and bread juxtaposed by Hitler saying he made 6 million Jews toast.

"We always talk of Russian influence. What about Israeli influence?"

And on and on.

They were purposely meant to get a reaction, meant to get attention, because…

I care what you think.

And even then, I was ejected. Wrong of me to even think an electronic tribe was viable.

That was a mistake.

Social Media was a mistake.

Doing any sort of political activism and thinking it would make a difference was a mistake.

Then when I attracted some women, some who were turned on by my posts, they fucking turn on me. I wasn't giving her some attention so she doxxes me. All women and their goddamn attention.

Women were a mistake.

*

I try watching a movie, something different, something by the Duplass Brothers but I forgot the title with all its navel gazing, talking, plotting, and ironic mundaneness.

I then try an action flick. Then a doc about action movies but they get so precious about the tropes—fuck! This content. I can't enjoy anything. No content in the world could make me content. All a bunch of shit. A bunch of shit content. Content, content, content! A waste of my goddamn time.

Movies were a mistake.

I then check Kai10 because it's the only site I've not been banned from. There's a post about "Japan's Hidden Psychic Program" and more about Robert Kaplan and Masayuki Uchida's research in to psychic technology. How they implanted neurotransmitters in twins, to send communications via Ultra Wide Band signals, which is explains why the government banned it from usage…but…when then these signals are used, due to their intensity they can cause forms of digital interference both when they are communicating and when they are trying to remotely hack devices.

But you fucking know that, don't you?

MOMNDF: They fucking know!

JRK: Fuck you!

MOMNDF: I'm out of here! Racist bastard!

JRK: For real this time?

MOMNDF: Count on it!

Kenji is coming.

The break-up, the snow, the jagged edges, my phone burning. Was it all just a dream or…

No…

But anything is possible.

Kai10 was closer to the truth on many things except what they wrote about me.

I called FBI Agent Murphy but he didn't pick up. Just an answering machine. You may or may not know the message: "Hi, um, agent Murphy this is Jason Reudelheuber-Katz. Um, you may have seen some news drop about me, I had no control over that, and um, I'm not an agent of subversion or spook or anything, I'm sorry that I didn't disclose all my accounts to you— honestly, I thought it was irrelevant but I wanted you to know if you are still investigating the murder of Adina, I may have a lead. Her name is Yu Yamada. She's disappeared completely from this town with her husband Kenji. I'll be honest: We were um, were fuc—having an affair. But she's gone. I can't find her. And she might have somehow found out that I was in a relationship with Adina. I have a theory—"

Answering machine cut-off.

A knock on my door.

Yamaguchi-sensei stands at my door, looking cautious and nervous.

God, had they read the *NewsGrind* article too? Was I going to be fired due to pressure from the SPLC?

"*Eeto*, Jason-sensei, you know Yamamoto-sensei? He is, um, the hospital. He had…" he looks at his phone, Google translate, then to me. "He had stroke?"

"Yamamoto-sensei had a stroke?"

"Yes. Yesterday."

"Oh."

"He is in hospital. He wants to see you."

*

Yamaguchi-sensei drove me to the small hospital across from YouMe town, near where Yamamoto-sensei and I walked. He was silent hardly asking a question or even bothering to make small talk. I wondered…did he know? Did they know about the incident with Yu, the *NewsGrind* stories and such? What did they know?

Regardless I knew my job was about to get shittier with just Yamaguchi-sensei sans my elderly friend Yamamoto-sensei…the one person I could call a friend, the one who revealed his secrets to me—but that's only in retrospect.

At the time, I just saw my friend sedate in a bed.

288

In the room, like all hospital rooms, sat Yamamoto-sensei attached to the machines, part of his face limp. His fat daughter greeted us, the one he once told me was stupid but she was the one there with him. Upon entrance, she leaned towards her father and spoke to him like a baby in a way to say "Look who is here!"

Yamamoto-sensei's eyes went wide as he tried to wave. "Jason-sensei!"

I bowed lightly and shook his hand while Yamaguchi-sensei let out a fake laugh saying "he is so happy to see you Jason," then started talking to his daughter.

I managed to crack a smile.

Looking at Yamamoto-sensei, in his gown, sitting in lifeless surroundings, some rice sticking to the corner of his mouth on the paralyzed side unaware of it all, barely aware of who I am yet said (in English): "I thought you disappear! I thought you gone. So many people disappear!"

Continuing: "I so happy to see you! So happy! I thought you disappear! I thought you were...gone! So many people disappear!"

"Well, um, I'm here Yamamoto-sensei. I came here to see you."

"I know, I know. Thank you. Thank you. You good man Jason. Good man. I know."

"I think some would disagree..."

"No. You good. I know. You came to see me. I so happy to see you! So happy! I thought you disappear! I thought you were gone! So many people disappear!"

I then went to Yamaguchi-sensei and asked, "Why does he keep saying that?"

Yamaguchi-sensei then said, "Um, *eeto ne, nan dake?*" he said to himself. Quietly, he leaned in "Um, Yuri—you know Yamauchi?"

"Oh um, yeah, yeah, we talked about it."

"But we don't know what happened to her. His daughter said he would not stop talking about it and even say you ask about disappearance?"

"Well, I had a...friend who disappeared."

"The girl who was killed?"

"No. Another. It's just like one day, she disappeared."

"Ah *so ka?*"

"*So desu.*"

"People disappear all the time. You know because they are in trouble. And Yuri-chan, she have problem."

289

"Right, in trouble…" Right, right, I'm sure the Kyoto-sensei constantly yelling at her and calling her ugly helped.

Before I could say that—like I was going to say that :rolling_eyes:—Yamamoto-sensei's daughter came to me with an envelope. And handed it me bowing with both hands. A letter of some sort.

"This is letter for you from Yamamoto-sensei," he said.

"Yes, Jason! I wrote for you."

"Thank you," I said bowing.

"I thought you disappear! I thought you gone. So many people disappear!"

"I'm not going anywhere."

Decided to read the letter later.

*

Yamaguchi-sensei then drove me to the school instead of back home.

Kocho-sensei told me that they had been contacted by the Hiroshima Board of Education about the article that dropped and "pressure" they received. I only knew one person who worked in the Hiroshima BOE—that kike Avi! Mother. Fucker.

Kocho-sensei, smoking in his office, with an apologetic smile said they now have to review what was said and even though they believe in the right to free speech that I had violated my contract by participating in public political speech that could bring harm on the school and the city.

Meaning I could embarrass the shit out of them. They were already receiving phone calls from journalists asking about me.

"Enjoy winter vacation, okay?"

I knew what this meant. My contract renewal was in January. They were going to wait for the press to slip over and then not renew. That's what they always did. No one is ever "fired". They just don't have contract renewed.

I knew I would probably get the same treatment if lucky.

But if the heat continued, with Adina's death, followed by the bad press, especially if it got in to the Japanese press, they would cave in to the new mob.

Fuck.

And I knew they would cave. They cared about what other people thought. Japanese way. Just like how…

I care what you think.

Nobody had any fucking balls.

When I returned to the teacher's room, with the half-speed winter break vibe, only half assed club activities keeping everyone occupied, everyone made sure to avoid eye contact with me, including Yamaguchi-sensei.

I opened the letter Yamamoto-sensei gave me, read its content, because at least he took time to hand write content, but the words were just words. They meant nothing given the pressure of everyone trying to divert their attention from me, the shame object occupying their shared space. So, they typed on their laptops that would be obsolete in a year or two, in their chairs that would be obsolete also in a year or two, in a building that if lucky would be standing for 20 years at max, and me? I would be gone. Off back home as my seat is warmed by some other gaijin who will laugh and play clown human dictionary for the kids and all involved.

Fuck you all.

I checked my phone. Saw the *NewsGrind* article texted to me by everyone (including Mark). But you know that, don't you? You know the top reply #Trending on Twitter was by one (((Howard Zuckerman))): "Jason Reudelheuber-Katz was a mistake of humanity. If that racist kills himself my only response is 'Thank you!'"

I'm a mistake.

Jason Reudelheuber-Katz is a mistake.

Cue *Photograph* by Gary Numan. Perfect in the following with Fincher-like photography.

MOMNDF: Don't rope maybe or maybe not me in to this.

JRK: I thought you left.

MOMNDF: I'm officially GONE. You're on your own.

JRK: Giving me over to Satan?

MOMNDF: I don't even know what that's referencing.

The teachers just saw Jason the teacher, and now Jason-sensei the attention attracting missile that might spice up their dull mundane material lives. But they didn't care. They didn't know the real Jason, the one who posted photos with thought provoking passages on Instagram, or the Jason who practiced Kyokushin Karate, or the Jason who loved the wife of the lead instructor or the Jason who shitposted only as General_TOHO—actually, they did know that hence the silent scorn. And they didn't know Jason the fuck buddy to Adina or Jason the son to a mom who was blowing up my phone ("You need to call now! This has been so stressful for me!") or the Jason who just wanted to sit at home at night watching movies and reading, while shitposting—no, no, no, I was just *Jayson-sensei the embarrassment*. And to the rest of the world I was Jason the racist mistake. But what did they know? What do you know? Did they or you know the Jason who sat and binge watched Dragon Ball Z on the weekends due to a last minute cancellation by his father who had retreat to attend or the Jason who looked at his *Pokemon* card given to him by his late cousin Tyler Reudelheuber with the *Kanji, Hiragana* and *Katakana* all forming a sea of imperceptible phrasing that required a Rosetta Stone that could only be attained by study and mental effort and that I Jason Reudelheuber-Katz was ready to dedicate myself to the task? Do they know the satisfaction of finally being able to read said card and find the *Pokemon* in question was *Clefairy* but in Japanese was called *Pippi* all the while made more poignant that I dug the card off my shelf to translate it on the day I found out Tyler Reudelheuber was killed in action by some raghead in a land that didn't value his life? Do they know the Jason who went to the library with his uncle on those weekends his mom had a conference to attend on The Strip and wandered the shelves checking out books about the Far East on a gradual scale of those with pictures to those with hardly any and studying the history of WW2 in and out because it involved Japan but also the Nazis—I'm sure they claim to know I took an interest in Nazi Germany—but do they (or you) know that the books that piqued my interest most were those with two page spreads of Kiyomizudera in Kyoto and Itsukushima-jinja here in Hiroshima and the occasional photo of *kado* with the flowers arranged with empty space in mind? Do they know the Jason who discovered Japanese films in college, the ones of Kurosawa, Mizoguchi, Kitano, Shimizu and Ozu, who stayed for the entire screening of *Seven Samurai* when many had left since it was past the required class time limit to attend a screening so he could see the last reel, one of the glories of world cinema, and that last shot of remaining ronin who realized that even though the won, they really lost? Or do they know the Jason who walked down the evening streets of Century City looking towards the Hollywood Hills in the background, or past the studio lots, thinking the gates were too tall or he was too small, lacking courage or the 13 year old Jason taken by his Uncle Murray to the Thomas & Mack Center to watch *PRIDE 32: Real Deal in Vegas*, the first US show promoted by the now defunct Japanese (and Yakuza ran) MMA company, who looked at the sea of Japanese faces watching the spectacle of Mark Coleman getting pummeled by Fedor Emelianenko, the crowd mainly on the side of the Russian not the American but the showing of respect afterwards, the bloodied Coleman consoling his crying daughters as the Russian showed him nothing but deference amid the cacophony of Japanese voices, and realizing not just these people know how to put on a show but there's another universe out there, one of violence but bookended with respect, where blood and beauty meld and you don't care that Uncle Murray is off trying to get a word in with Harrison Ford, reminding him that he was the funny guy at craft services during the shooting of *Hollywood Homicide*, you just focused on the Japanese pageantry and polite crowd realizing this was just a parody of the real deal, that being Japan itself, and you wanted to see reality but bided time by begging Uncle Murray to use his connections to obtain comps to the next show and he gave that boy his birthday wish and how excited he was to see *PRIDE 33: The Second Coming* at the same Thomas & Mack but end up disappointed to see the Japanese Takanori Gomi lose to the cocky and showboating Nick Diaz but at the same time felt happy for Diaz because many had written him off and even he was gracious in victory or The Jason who when he got his letter from the Embassy saying he was hired to be a JET realized that reality was fulfilled or the Jason who traveled to places like Kyoto and Himeji castle alone because company was just tiresome or the Jason who warmed his feet under the *kotatsu* during winter finding a kindred spirit reading Mishima, such a joy that he went to Mos Burger and turned his phone off, just so he could finish Spring Snow while sipping a coke and slowly eating french fries or the Jason who loved movies but also loved Japan but really didn't know what to do with his life, just taking the path of least resistance, whatever was easiest, so JET it was, because the path was easy as was starting a blog or a sock account on Twitter and accepting an invite from Andyschluss in to a Slack, or just being with Adina, who was easy going enough in private that he didn't mind being around her in private, though commitment meant choosing and she never forced the choice—behaviors enabled by his malaise—a malaise with the world that might have been just having no clear path in it because he knew in his heart of hearts he wanted to really work in the arts but he was fearful after seeing the struggles and failures of his uncle and yes that maybe fear is what dominated his decision making in both relationships and career choice but unfortunately he wasn't clearheaded enough to understand at the time and this Jason had only one constant—that being the Land of the Rising Sun, Japan itself, and that too was being taken from him. Yes, yes, yes, this Jason Reudelheuber-Katz was a mistake.

293

And the other teachers, even the English-speaking ones like Mandy, Min and Matt, they didn't give a fuck about the real me. I was just an object to them. First one of pity, now one of scorn.

In cyberspace, I barely exist now. A distant memory on an endless horizon.

Every part of me has been divided up. A man in divisible parts and that's how I see everything—in divisbles thinking I can keep myself and everything around me compartmentalized, not an individual but just a dividual.

And in this cheap building, on cheap chairs, pounding away at cheap keyboards, while at home watching movies that I found the cheapest way, there was really no long-term eternal goal in mind.

Things used to be built to last, now they're built to please and serve a "purpose" while sucking any life out of the place. Probably because we, the dividual population at large have no life to celebrate.

We're all sleepwalking no matter many claims of "wokeness" we make.

Fuck.

Boomers, Japanese, Chinese, Koreans, Blacks, Mexicans, Jews, Palestinians, Arabs and Whites—everyone—cogs to serve the corporate capital overlords more productively and loyally. Look at the great progress that all modern society has lived up to.

The product has not suited the hype. It's all now just censorship and persecution for all who disagree. But yet, we just try to imitate these macro patterns to micro behaviors. We need to be subservient to consume. We need to others subservient to us to consume. Consuming things like content. Content, content, content! Mini-empires unto ourselves. And no one care(s)(ed). No one at all gives a shit. Everyone just wants attention or a chance to fly first class.

Hitler did nothing wrong.

But saying that makes me a mistake?

Jason Reudelheuber-Katz is the mistake?

Maybe it's true because...

I care what you think.

But you know that, don't you?

You know I'm a mistake.

You're a mistake. They're a mistake. It was all a mistake. Fuck everyone.

Humanity was a mistake.

Pretty much my conclusion in this whole affair.

But you know it doesn't end there.

It's not that type of story.
But you know that, don't you?

*

Min texted me: "Matt has disappeared."
Of course, he has.
"Wait. Aren't you guys in _____ ?"
No reply.
Of course.

*

Text from Mandy: "I literally shouldn't be texting you. But I've been studying PureLight online and I think it can help you. Help you transcend all these problems. Please contact me if you want help. But you have to want it. Maybe you can redeem urself by helping some refugees"

I have to want it? Helping refugees?

Fuck that cunt!

Texted Mark: "Shit's falling apart. Mandy invites me to PureLight…"

Mark: "Maybe you should listen to Mandy more…"

Upon reading that I nearly through my phone across the restaurant above the fish market overlooking Hitonose. Yamamoto-sensei brought me there once for lunch so he could complain about Yamaguchi-sensei. The eyes of the patrons, when I made eye-contact with a few of them—all comforting feel good smiles and stares. Indifferent to me and what I so-called "represented".

As I ate hamachi sashimi and looked over the bay, I noticed someone get up from the table next to me. A brochure had been left sitting on the table.

Another one for PureLight.

I thought about flagging him down but he'd already exited.

The brochure was different than the one I was given before. It was all in Japanese with only a few words of English sprinkled throughout.

But I noticed, seated near the guru in lecture sitting pose, was a woman about my age at his right hand. The resemblance…no. I got to thinking…no.

Cue *Random* by Gary Numan.

I stared.

No.

I pulled it closer to my eyes to examine more closely.

No.

It was Yu.

A spitting image.

295

The woman, the right-hand lady or hand maiden of the local cult—she was too close to the guru in almost every photo. It couldn't have been. No way.

But it was.

It was a face etched on to my memory. It was her.

I texted Mandy: "I'm interested."

She immediately replied: "We'll go tonight."

Me: "Fine."

But you know that, don't you?

But you don't know what happens next.

It's why I'm here writing, isn't it?

3

I look at the faces on the bus as it slowly negotiates the narrow roads towards my stop and I wonder if it's my ultimate end—or just a transition, a line we as a society and individuals must cross to embrace and move forward in to a new reality and being. But ATM, I'm on a bus. A public bus filled with public people. The old lady fighting saying *yokoisho* with each step she takes down the bus stops, the other elderly madame looking ahead, might as well be lifeless, years of toil etched in her face, the lone high school boy and high school girl with faces buried in their phones, or in the girl's case, just looking towards the floor, her soul gone astray.

The words linger.

You know the words.

Kenji is coming.

Why did it come to this?

Kenji is coming.

Why am I doing this?

Kenji is coming.

Why do I feel unmoored?

Kenji is coming.

Why must I feel the arms tingle, hairs rise and heart beat?

Kenji is coming.

Why, oh, why? Fuck my life. I press the button for the next stop.

Kenji is coming.

The bus stops. The bus driver says, "*Hai, Yamamoto-bashi desu.*" (*Here is Yamamoto bus stop*—but enough translation)

Yamamoto-bashi. An area with the same *Kanji* as Yamamoto-sensei. I think of Yuri who he mentioned disappeared. I feel like I was disappearing. Would the bus driver say my name next?

*

Cue *Rubycon* (7" version) by Tangerine Dream.

297

The wind lightly blew as the compound stood planted like a Lego construction in the short distance, dwarfed by the mountains of Akizuki.

Mandy stood in her red Patagonia puff vest with, black v-neck ribbed sweater, gray leggings and Kate Spade purse dangling from her arm. She had no other belongings but I noticed her hair was now cut short, almost same as mine, with her hair parted at same side, ear with multiple piercings exposed, accentuating her thin neck.

As I got off the bus, she looked at me with reserved contempt trying not to make eye contact but standing like a school teacher going through the motions, trying to do her duty.

"This way," she said pointing her head towards the compound and started walking leaving a trail of tension I feel hitting me as I follow.

"Did you hear from Min?"

Without looking back at me, she said, "No."

"She texted. Said Matt disappeared?"

"He did?"

"Here let me…" I searched for the text but couldn't find it while Mandy ignores and keeps walking, the wind the only sound. "I mean, they said they were going to _____ for vacation but that place is dangerous with the refugee crisis and all and now my text disappeared…" Mandy kept on walking. And I muttered, "Everyone's disappearing."

"What?"

"Everyone just seems to be disappearing?"

"Who? Matt's just being a baby probably. I don't know what Min saw in him."

"No. No. There's Matt, sure, but there's that girl, her name is Yuri, my, my, my um, English teacher…Yamamoto-sensei I visited him in the hospital. He said she disappeared. And Yu…"

"Me? I'm here."

"No, my—her name was Yu. A friend. She disappeared. Along with her husband Kenji. I was wondering if maybe you saw anything on the news? Like *Japan Times* or *Yomiuri Daily*?"

"No. I don't watch the news here."

"Just *NewsGrind*?"

"Just about."

"Adina too…in a way."

"Adina was murdered. She was killed."

"But by who? No one has been arrested. There was those Palestinians but they were released."

"I don't know."

"But you know, that, um, I made some racist comments on Twitter."

A frustrated sigh as we approached the double doors to the front of the facility. Building non-descript as always with steel doors reminiscent of those of a school auditorium.

A bald headed male attendant in white robe opened and bowed. He asked something in Japanese.

"Where here for classes," Mandy said.

The man appeared confused.

"CLASSES!" Mandy said.

I stepped forward and said it in Japanese.

The man immediately acknowledged, bowed and said *There's no yoga classes today.*

I turned to Mandy. "He said, um, there's no yoga classes today."

"Well, that doesn't matter. I just want to learn and help the refugees. You want to learn and help too, right?"

"Have you ever been here?"

"No."

"So, you didn't have, um, a plan? Do you know what classes are on offer or if refugees are being helped here?"

"No, I, um, just thought…like meditation and stuff—they have that right? Their English portal said they did as well as statements about the refugee crisis."

I tried to explain to the attendant.

So, you are interested in our doctrine and refugees? He asked.

Yes.

But we don't speak English here.

I speak Japanese. I can translate.

But we have no classes right now and no refugees are here.

We are just curious. I looked back at Mandy. *We are seeking.*

I see. One moment please.

He then closed the door and walked off.

"What's going on?" Mandy asked.

"I don't know."

"What did he say."

"He said, 'one moment' I—have you ever bothered to study Japanese?"

"No."

"Why?"

"There's always someone around to translate."

THOT.

I know, I know, that type of thinking probably is what got me at the front door of PureLight. But I couldn't help but think it even though I tried immediately to discard it.

The door opens again and the attendant waves us in.

We oblige.

*

There was a *koban* as always and places to put our shoes. I heard laughter coming down the hallway. The building smelled of incense.

The attendant presented a pair of slippers for both of us on the elevated stone floor.

As I struggled to slip my shoes off and put them in a box, which Japanese call a *locker* even though it has no locks, I looked at Mandy untying her shoes as she tried to look around.

"How did you hear about this place? How did you know it would be good for me?"

"I just read the brochures and looked online. Seemed interesting thought some charity work could help you. Might help meeting some less fortunate people too and help them."

"What? I went to a public school with an assort—do you know anyone who practices or attends?"

"No."

"Then…"

"Well, Mark. Mark that military guy? He recommended it. He said their philosophy was interesting. Mentioned also the refugees. I was curious so I researched."

"And couldn't find anyone else to come with you?"

"Well, you're here," she said putting her slippers on.

"You needed a translator…"

She bowed to the man, poorly, sloppily, ignoring me. THOT!

As I stepped up with my back pack, he waved his hands and tried to remove it. He then placed in the koban area on the floor near the "*locker*". This last detail has nothing to do with anything.

Just a fixed memory from what happens next.

300

Like…

Kenji is coming.

Last time I write that sentence.

*

We both sat cross-legged on the tatami floor looking around the room, silent, the sound of faint group laughter and some aggressive talk in the next room over. The attendant returned with a burly man, sporting tightly trimmed hair and a rigid jaw line. He wore the same cotton white tunic and cotton white shirt, yet also had a red sash around his chest. His stare said surprise but also suspicion.

"*Tate*," he barked.

I stood up and Mandy followed my lead. She leaned in and asked, "What does he want?"

"He wants us to stand."

He put his hand up. "*Shizuka ni shite.*"

"What?" Mandy uttered.

"*Shizuka ni shite.*"

"*Anno…*" I pointed to Mandy and said she doesn't understand Japanese.

Then why are you here?

We're interested in PureLight. The philosophy…and helping refugees.

She doesn't speak Japanese?

I'm her translator.

Are you interested in PureLight too?

Yes.

He then pointed to the wall. I looked at it then back at him.

"What's going on?" Mandy asked.

I put my hand up. "He's asking us to be quiet."

"Why?"

"Just…"

The man continued in Japanese and put his hands against the wall like he was being frisked by police. He then pointed at me then the wall. Obviously, he was some sort of security officer.

I slowly moved towards the wall and placed my hands in position. The security guard—call him Kazuo (who could probably be played by a younger version of the boxer Guts Ishimatsu), began to search me when Mandy said: "Jason, what's going on? Why are they searching you?"

Kazuo stopped, turned and started talking to her more aggressively.

301

"Jason!"

"Mandy!"

"Jason!"

"*Oi!*"

"Mandy, shut the fuck up! They want us to be quiet! There's some sort of, um, security thing going on."

Mandy was quiet as my body trembled during pat down. Kazuo then talked to the attendant. He brought a clear bucket and put my wallet, phone and keys in it.

He then motioned to Mandy.

"What?"

"Let them frisk you. Security and all that."

"I'm not…"

"You need to do it."

"FINE!"

Kazuo frisked her down then took her purse and put it in the bucket. The attendant then left the room.

"Where are they taking—"

"*Shizuka ni shite!*"

I put my hand up towards Mandy.

"Just—um, Mandy, heh, just let me do the talking. That's um, why you wanted me here…after all."

If being an asshole required that Mandy shut the fuck up, I was going to be an asshole. Fuck it all.

I asked where they're taking our stuff. He said it was to check the equipment for bugs and surveillance. The attendant then brought a pair of folded garments and handed one to each of us.

I took mine and Mandy took hers hesitantly.

"*Nuide. Chenji,*" Kazuo said doing motion of changing clothes.

Kazuo and the attendant stood stationary as we held our new clothes.

"They want us to change." I looked at Kazuo. "Now."

"While they're here?"

I asked Kazuo if it had to be done here. He said yes because of security precautions and how there have been spies trying to get cameras in the building.

We're not spies.

You have to prove that.

"We have to change here with them watching."

"What?"

"Just down to underwear—something about security and people trying to sneak bugs and cameras in."

"We're not spies. We just want to help—"

"They don't know that."

"I don't know. Maybe we should go…" Mandy started for the door. "Where's my purse? Where's my stuff."

"*OI!*"

Kazuo pushed her back.

I then grabbed her arm.

"What's going on?"

"*Yamete!*" I said putting my hand out in panic. "*Yamete kudasai.*"

I tighten my grip on Mandy's arm. "Look, I think there's um, some sort of paranoia, and we're only making it worse."

"But they want us to…"

"We're only making it worse by resisting. It makes us more suspicious…have you really had problems taking off your clothes before?"

"What? Are you saying I'm some type of—you're such a prick. I don't know why I reached out to…"

I put my finger up and looked at Kazuo. He looked on with intense black eyes and suspicion. I then lowered my head. "I, um, I won't look. Change, um, change behind me."

"But what about them…"

"They won't hur—"

"You're sure."

"Sure, yeah."

"Fine."

We changed as Kazuo and the attendant watched. Quickly. They put our clothes in another bucket and took them out of the room. Mandy and I were identical in dress.

Are you two twins?

No, I said.

Brother and sister?

No. We're not related.

He ran his hands over his head. *You look like twins with the short blonde hair and same haircut…*

"What's he saying?"

303

"He thinks—he's asking if we're twins."

"Why?"

I shrugged my shoulder. "We all look the same to them."

She shook her head dismissively as the attendant then brought us both clipboards and handed them to us.

"Information forms. They want us to fill them out." I then told Kazuo that Mandy couldn't read Japanese and I would need to talk her through it.

"*Dozo*," he said motioning his hand to the ground.

"So, what's this?"

"You write your name there."

"In English or Japanese?"

"Japanese, well, English…here just give it me."

She handed me the clipboard and I started filling it out. Only sounds I heard was Mandy's breathing as she fix stared at the wall with a permanent scowl, the ticking hand of the analog clock and a slight howl of wind outside. I tried to fill the small box on the form, meant for brief *Kanji*, not long-form *Katakana*, guessing how to spell Mandy's name.

I then heard a commotion at the door.

Kazuo went to talk to another attendant, who was followed by a diminutive man also wearing a red sash. Their talk seemed somewhat abrupt and brief, Kazuo defensive.

Kazuo came back to us and said, "*Hai, stoppu.*"

He asked for the clipboards. I said we weren't finished. He said it wasn't necessary.

The same man in red sash then entered, holding a couple of laptops. Call him Koji the computer guy (he could be played by Takayuki Yamada).

Koji opened the laptops to a screen from the English portal of PureLight. He then clicked to a form that was in English. He smiled. "*Hai, dozo.*"

Fill this one out instead?

Yes.

I told Mandy.

"At least I can read this."

The form asked for the typical name, address, phone number et cetera but then asked for things like social media handles, and web site addresses. I wrote down everything. Let them know I'm General_TOHO, fuck it. I even wrote down my ANON ID for Kai10. I just didn't give a fuck anymore. No fucks given.

304

Koji took both our laptops and left the room.

Kazuo shut the door.

Just Mandy, her breathing, me, the tick of the clock and the wind.

…And the laughter down the hall.

We both stared at the floor. The wind was almost in competing gusts. I heard some foliage moving from its bursts. And the clock…not a *tick-tock* but more just, *tick, tick, tick*…

"Maybe we shouldn't have come here," Mandy said.

"Huh…"

Faint laughter down the hallway heard again.

Tree branches heard swaying by the powerful wind.

Tick, tick, tick…

The door burst open with Kazuo and few of his men. They pulled us up. "Jason! What's—"

"*Damare ya!*" Kazuo shouted at her.

"Jason!"

"*Damare!*"

"Say we just want to help—"

"Why?!"

I then blacked out.

*

Not really sure if I blacked out. Just the last thing I remembered. Everything after that was a blur or even a blank. No, no, no, there's no need for quick cuts between unfocused and blurred images with heavy breathing, off-kilter camera angles and overexposed lenses.

Just black.

*

My body felt weak again as I awoke. I saw white walls, tatami floor, a sheet over me, a pillow underneath my head. I felt something on my head, something rubber, I then heard an electric buzzing sound, like one you would hear in a hospital—what are those called?

But I didn't want to get up.

I felt tired, my body relaxed, my eyes heavy.

No sound of wind, or the tick of the clock or Mandy's disgruntled breathing.

No, no, no, just the warmth of the sheets and darkness.

305

I just wanted to sleep. I had no phone to grab or notifications to check, or a job to rush to or questions to answer. I had freedom to rest, so I closed my eyes again.

I saw the rest of facility, floating through it, as if on air, because in my dreams especially half-slept ones, I never feel like I'm walking, and there I was floating through the building, endless rooms of tatami mats, women and children both, sitting down, a multicultural mix, some Indian, others refugees from_____, Mandarin heard in the background, and I continued gliding. Saw someone on a screen—screens everywhere!—and there were my tweets and Kai10 comments posted as those in their white uniforms and white tunics looked at them and analyzed them, and then on a screen appeared YU.

I walked to the screen and tapped it, sliding my hand across as her body slid from the screen out of the TV, in to a handstand then in front of me. She smiles.

The room turns dark.

"Yu?"

I'm now strapped in a chair. The room has a red glow along all corners, I see shades of Mandy, Min and Matt casually postured as they look on, while on the other side is my friend Miguel from high school, an Argentinian who always told me he was Italian or a German depending on his mood that day and joked about having Nazi ancestry.

And on the screen, there appears my Line messages with Yu, me leading her on, trying to flirt, there's my Facebook messages with Park_City_Stephanie, me pushing her and saying "Where's the nudes?" then there's the tweets, "Every business cares about green so they need a little grease" with a picture of Mexicans crossing the border then mowing lawns. "I preferred California when everyone looked like The Beach Boys not the Barrio Boys," "Why are there no nigger's dressed as Santa Claus? Because last time a prison had a chimney was during the Holocaust," ending with the usual "LA is full of THOTs. It's a THOTacaust," and "The holocaust was a holohoax."

My whole body shakes as I feel the dread in my soul, the reds in the room brighten, and the demon headed figure appears faintly in the screen background, horns round like a goat.

And then more messages of me and Stephanie talking, then Yu, then that girl from Canada who was DMing me with political questions, who I eventually pushed to show me some nude selfies, and she did but I didn't like her bitchy attitude, so I blocked her.

306

Then all the messages from Adina.

I start crying.

Uncontrollably.

STOP! I say but I can't open my mouth.

"I'm horny, want to meet?", "Yeah sure," god it looks all so clumsy and embarrassing now, and then when you see "what are you doing this weekend?" me saying "going out", "have fun!" she then she asks "what are we?" and I don't reply then two days later her reply "forget that I asked that" and then my reply "why don't you ask Maxwell" and then...

The screen flickers. I see a few flash frames of Dr. Robert Kaplan viewing this all from a Skype camera, his face partly curved, reptilians walking behind him, some appearing—flickering—in front of me, the green scales on their skin a vivid reality.

I feel a hand on my arm. The lights come up in the room, but I only turn to see Yu's face—my god it's all so cinematic—and all that I see is her, dressed in her boots—weird because shoes are supposed to be off inside—and her leather jacket, her hair curled and her mouth opening in perfect English "We can make this go away."

Then I awoke.

The reality of the room made itself felt.

And the door opened.

Three men appeared, two men were small but timid with the silhouette of Kazuo looming over them. They lifted me as I couldn't stand on my own.

They led me down a hallway (unsure if it was night or day). They stopped outside some sliding doors. I heard a man talk in a high pitched Japanese voice followed by laughter.

I wondered where Mandy was for a brief second.

Koji the nerd then came to us and said something to Kazuo, my brain too tired to concentrate. Kazuo flicked his head towards the doors and the room, but Koji said chigau and pointed towards another room.

Kazuo told the men to take me to the other room.

*

In this room, there were monitors on the wall, some with pictures of a bald-headed guru and quotes written in elegant *Kanji* next to him, but there were also feeds from NHK World News and CNN International in Japanese, another screen switched between different social media feeds of Japanese news orgs and those with #PureLight in their posts—majority in Japanese. Men, or were some women?—I couldn't tell because they were all so thin, all bald heads and soft features—almost a unity in their appearance but they all sat in the *seiza* position in front of quad monitor screens, typing, clicking, surfing websites, blogs and feeds, analyzing some sort of information.

The attendants got a zaisu chair and positioned me for back support. Koji then put a black lacquered table in front of me as attendants, I think they were women, poured us both tea. They left for a moment then returned with tablets.

"Japanese, okay?" Koji asked.

"Okay."

You are American?

American.

Your name, it's hard to pronounce.

It's German.

We did some research. We saw the articles. You are Jewish.

Yes, my mom is Jewish. My dad is of German descent.

Do you practice Judaism?

No.

What do you believe?

I…believe…in nothing.

Are you an Athiest?

No. It's just…it's hard to explain in Japanese. But I like the ideas of Zen and Shinto.

That's fine. All is fine.

It is?

Yes, you are seeking truth.

I…I try or tried.

Our goal is to become one.

One?

A what?

A unity?

Yes, PureLight is about unity. Unifying all ideas and all humans.

I see.

You say you believe in nothing. That's because the nothing is unity. You're very smart.

I looked around at all the computers. The attendants above him typed on their tablets—but I noticed one behind me—were they recording our conversation?

You're interested in the computers? Electronics?

It's just all the screens…

308

We've looked at your online history so we can tell you are an expert on many things and…

I took a deep breath. Click, click, click of keyboards and mouses, the gentle hum of the PC fans all made the rhythm of my heart race faster.

You are a deep thinker.

I exhaled.

What?

You have a deep understanding of the world. The nature of women. The nature of who controls the world.

The Jews?

Yes. The Jews. You understand they are a problem.

I sat up.

I was just trying to help expand ideas.

Yes, you were. We can see. We need your help.

You need…me?

Yes, we need you. Our English outreach is very limited especially with people who speak English and understand things like you.

So, what are you trying to do here?

People are trying to stop understanding. They are trying to stop PureLight from helping Japan and the world attain enlightenment. The Jews are a part of this.

Really? I mean you believe this or notice this?

Yes. They use their power through the western governments. But we, like you, are trying to change this.

How?

Digital reality is the future. We have immense power to bring truth and enlightenment through the digital realm. There is no physical presence. We can be anywhere at anytime, we can be anything. You can be boy or girl, man or child, American or Japanese. We are transcending physical form and borders while also bringing truth to everyone. It is almost close to Nirvana. We want to bring the world closer to Nirvana.

I stared at him and tried to take it all in. The click, click, click of keyboard and mouses dissipated.

Do you understand?

I understand.

Ando-san has seen what you've written, he wants to meet with you, he thinks you can help us. He directed his hand towards the portrait of the bald-headed man on the wall, framed by elegant Kanji. His gentle but stern face, was enhanced by his black eyes. *Ando-san thinks you are a gift from Heaven.*

309

I would like to meet him.

*

They took me to another room, one that was small and had a monitor in it. The attendants brought me a *zaisu* and put it directly in front of the television, while also giving me another brochure to read in clunky English.

Kazuo talked to the two attendants, buzzing them with questions. He took their answers with reserve then tried to shut the door but the attendants held it open. Kazuo let them through as they placed a black lacquer tray of rice, tofu, pickled vegetables and eggplant, bowing on their way out. Kazuo then closed the door.

I learned in the video that PureLight adhered to Buddhist practice of the *shojin ryori* vegetarian diet. Honestly, I didn't care. Food was food at that point. I was hungry.

The video was mostly in Japanese though it tried to show as many shots of non-Japanese as possible to make it look as international as possible.

But my thoughts…they were in another place. Flipping through the literature…my god my spirit felt free.

I discarded it and tried to concentrate on the video with its shots of space, the planets, stars, solar systems, clouds, and beautiful Japanese mountains all dissolved with the stationary view of Ando-san talking, a short yet virile man in complete control and assuredness discussing his philosophy, and I looked at the screen thinking because it was slightly difficult to understand his beliefs as he described then surrounded by the historical religious symbols of both East and West. Something about meditating and opening a third eye and seeing Buddha, Brahma, Vishnu, Shiva, Zoroaster, Jesus, Nostradamus and Amaterasu herself telling Ando-san of a great prophecy regarding the fate of humankind and how he must bring the message to Japan then the world. He then talked about the state of modern humans and how we only focus on the material reality of getting as many material goods as possible, overloaded with unnecessary anxiety and how the realm of cyberspace is pulling us away, calling us to a higher place but dividing our loyalties between the spiritual and the material and only being used for coarse purposes.

I realized I wasn't in one place. Yes, yes, yes, back to the individual/dividual! Parts of me were many places scattered about. There was Jason the English teacher, Jason the son, Jason on Instagram, Jason on Twitter but also General_TOHO on Twitter and Kai10 but also the Jason who fucked and messed around with girls like Stephanie, the Canadian…Yu…and Adina.

There was no unity. No individual. I was a man divided, spread out through different modalities and forms, from physical space to cyberspace. I needed unity. I saw people meditating on the screen, so I pushed away the *zaisu* and sat Indian style, closing my eyes and pinching my thumb and forefinger together. I was formless and I just needed to embrace it. Embrace the void.

For once in my life, I felt relaxed.

I didn't feel the need to go anywhere. It was easier than I thought to empty myself. Maybe because nothing was there. It was all just movies, photos, books and websites. All just content. Content, content, content. That's all that filled me and it could be easily expelled with no attachments, especially without my phone around, where my true soul resided. I saw the real world around me, this small room, the faceless people—it was all really of little consequence. My true home was in the online void. And it had been cut off from me with bans and banishments. But maybe I could resurrect and help PureLight conquer that realm. Maybe there were higher truths. I meditated on creating an AI program that would learn and post on my behalf across a dozen or dozens upon dozens of accounts, where others could learn because after all, I was going to die anyway, we were all going to die, but the words and wisdom could live online forever. I needed to frame my whole physical purpose around this.

In the video, Ando-san said life was just an aberration, a contradiction between the spiritual unities of birth and death—yes! Death was really all there was. Death was the way forward. I needed to prepare for this death.

I'd found the leader I'd been looking for.

*

Another knock on the door and again, there was Kazuo of security with his bald-headed men—I was pretty sure they were men. But I stood up on my own, feeling my strength to walk.

"*Kite*," Kazuo said.

He led me down another hallway, and opened two sliding doors to a vast room, with everyone sitting in *seiza* while Ando-san was onscreen, a monitor sitting on a dais, speaking, the crowd a white clothed unity.

Except for Mandy.

She sat at the back of the wide room, uncomfortable in *seiza*, uncomfortable in just general posture.

Ando-san said something.

Laughter.

Mandy doesn't smile but looks confused.

Kazuo sits me down next to her. He then taps her on the shoulder, and she notices me. Her look says broken. Her short hair is slightly disheveled, her make up gone, earrings gone too, redness is under eyes from some form of marathon crying. She tries to crack a smile when she sees me. Tries to reach her hand towards me but returns it to her lap then looks down.

More laughs. A white cloud of generic faces laughing.

Kazuo then tells me to translate for her.

"Do you understand?" I whisper.

She turns her head towards me. "Understand? I don't."

"That's why, um, I guess that's why they brought me here."

"I don't know what's going on."

"Why? Didn't you talk with the computer—"

"I only talked to that security guard. Well we didn't talk. They brought me an iPad or something and I talked about my life and family photos on Instagram. And they asked about my family, then just about me and my desire to help refugees. And my dreams. Oh my god, those dreams...I saw...everything...it broke...it was like a miracle..."

I noticed some of the faces looking towards us.

The video onscreen continued.

"I've seen everything too. Everything."

"What is the video saying?"

I listened. Then tried to talk.

"The void brings a purifying um, a purifying light that makes us holy. Everything, holy, you know? We must get back to this path of holiness by embracing our true nature."

"How do—"

"Hold on."

I listened.

"Well, we've been held captive too long by the modern world. Everyone is controlled by the media. Fast food, and, um well, I guess instant food—unsure of translation, it's all lowering the life expectancy and destroying health. It's destroying our ability to think. We are too controlled by base desires like pornography and sex, too controlled by seeking out money, wealth and gaining possessions."

"Oh, he's right."

"We have to return to the primordial, the natural state of being. Civilization and technology has weakened our senses as we've put too much goodness and pacification on a pedestal. We must bring about a purification of karma."

"But…"

"Hold on…"

I listened as he talked about computers and electronics. "Cyberspace is now our second consciousness. Oh this is what I talked about with the tech guy. You haven't talked to him?"

"No."

"Basically, cyberspace is our new consciousness. It is the perfect place to reach Nirvana. There is full objectivity. No sensitivities or physical desires exist. Neither do feelings. Our desires taken care of regardless of the other. And we see those desires for their true useless value."

"What?"

"Wait, wait, I need to listen…"

"Something about the world being your idea. You bring everything through consciousness, through your reflective power and abstractions. If the world is your idea, then to remake it, you must become blank. That is why we go in to cyberspace. To become blank. So, you too must become the void."

"Oh…"

"You're more free by the less important things are. Don't think about money to get money. To accomplish more, don't do anything."

"So true. That's true."

"The rage within you comes from your desires. Your ego. Your 'I'. The problem is, you want too much. You want everything for yourself. You need to recognize the absurdities of these wants and problems. They're, um, they're not real. They're only in your mind. To achieve Nirvana, you must put these things to death. Even your toy collection."

The crowd laughs. I giggle. Mandy lets out a roaring laugh. "It's true, it's true." Some look back at her but immediately return to the screen.

"The 'I' does not exist. You do not exist. You are just an extension, a face, of collective spirit. You must extinguish these desires, these thoughts, these things that rage within you."

A tear run down Mandy's cheek.

"You must empty everything. The way to enlightenment is a void. You are the being by which the void comes in to the world."

313

I don't know if he is talking to me or Mandy or the others. Is it me or the collective "you"? He used the Japanese word *anata* not *anata-tachi* which is the plural.

"In the future, there will one day be a purification of all the karma. Enlightenment realized for all and that all will be one."

"I want it."

Now tears stream down both our faces.

Everyone then started to sit in circles, I was confused about what do. I started scooting to a circle but then Koji stopped me. *You and her just be a pair.*

"What do we do, Jason?"

Koji explained.

"We, um, we are to just talk to each other and," Koji talked more, "Then, we...I'm supposed to be neutral. I'm just going to listen. And then after the bell rings, you listen to me. No judgement. We just answer the question."

"What's the question?"

"Who am I?"

The bell rang.

We faced each other sitting on our knees. "Do we start now?"

"Yes."

"Do I go first?"

"Sure."

"Okay. Who am I?" She thought for a moment. "And you're just going to look at me?"

"Yes. Until the bell rings."

"No judgement?"

"No."

I stared at her. Tried my best neutral expression, focusing on her deep blue eyes, the longer blonde bangs that betrayed her short cut, her now empty earlobes where rings and studs used to sit and the white cotton tunic as she said, "I'm a woman. I'm the daughter of Charles and Laura. I'm the sister of Jack. I'm from San Francisco. No—I'm—I'm from Houston, Texas. I'm white. White from Dallas, Texas. From River Oaks. No, Highland Park. Whatever. I'm rich, I'm privileged. I'm the daughter of privilege. I'm smart? Maybe. I'm a dancer. I'm empowered. I'm a feminist. I'm woke. I'm liberal. I'm...I'm confused. I live in Japan. I'm an English teacher or assistant English teacher but I'm...I hate the kids. I hate them. I...I hate most people. I hate how no one cares. I hate racism. I hate hate. I hate you. You're—I'm sorry. I—hate

314

what happened to Adina. But I'm also hateful. Oh my god. I'm so hateful. I hate my family. I really hate my brother. I'm such a bitch. I'm a user. I use everyone. But also, I'm needful. I need others. I'm a slut. A total slut. I feel the pain of it. The pain of just using and fucking. I need medicine for it. I'm a user. A user of drugs—I hate—I hate the pain. I'm…" tears rolled down her face. "I'm confused. I think I'm smart. I think I know it all. Think I have it all but…I don't. I have nothing. I know nothing. I'm—"

The alarm went off. Mandy quickly wiped the tears from her eyes with her sleeves. She put hand on my lap, stared in to me with her baby blues, "Go. Sorry."

"Who am I? I'm Jason Reudelheuber-Katz. Reudelheuber is my dad's name. From Washington near Canada. Katz is my mom's name. It's Polish…well Jewish. I'm half-goy/half-Jewish. But…I want to be white. A gentile. But everyone wants me to be Jewish. Maybe I am Jewish. Maybe I can't deny my roots. Maybe I'm everything. Actually, maybe I'm nothing. No, no, no, I'm confused. That's what I am. I'm confused. No, no, no, I think that I want things to be simple. I just know that I'm a man, or that I want to be a man. I know that I want to be white—but what does that even mean? I am technically 'white' but I don't feel like it. Never mind. Maybe I want to be German. I'm a Nazi or I want to be since they don't really exist. I'm poor but I want to be rich. I'm unknown but I want to be famous. I'm—I love movies. I'm a cinephile. I love art. But I hate movies and art. I love women. I'm a pervert. But I hate women. I love Japan. But I hate it too. I'm…I'm a racist. I hate everything and everyone. I hate this world…" I felt the tears stream down my face. "I—"

The alarm goes off. Mandy places her hand on top of mine. We stare at each other, the noise of others standing in the middle of circles around us screaming at each other, sounds of physical altercation while everyone watches doesn't move us. We continue staring at each other. In seems we are in that room, staring, talking, screaming, for days (maybe we were) but it all ends where it started: Both of us sitting in *seiza*, hands on our laps, eyes locked, but this time just repeating over and over, "I am nothing, I am nothing, I am nothing…"

And I realize I'm not even looking for Yu in the crowd.

*

I tried to sit in my room to meditate. Focus on the void but I was too overcome with my calmness. Thoughts—thoughts of possibilities!—raced

315

through my head as I sat criss-cross apple sauce mindful at the world of potential ahead of me.

I didn't care for my belongings in my apartment or my job or that I would get fired or what people would think of me, I mean, I care what you think, but at that moment I didn't care, the liberation song singing loud in my heart.

But then my door opened.

Koji and his two attendants. He waved with his fingers pointing towards the floor—Japanese style—beckoning me to come.

I went.

Kazuo stopped Koji in the hallway. They talked for a brief moment. Something about Ando-san. Something he told Koji to do. Kazuo didn't seem to know about any of this and buzzed Koji with questions. *What does he want to talk about? Why now? Why Jason? I don't know. He just told me to bring him.*

Kazuo continued down the hallway past us.

*

The door opened in to a dark room, red trim around the corners, like my dream. The floor was rubber too. A 72-inch flatscreen sat mounted on the wall displaying only white noise.

Koji told me to stand in the middle of the room as I heard the mechanical sound of something being lowered. I looked up and saw a black sphere-like object descend towards me. I couldn't make out its shape and immediately recoiled.

Koji and his attendants held me in place.

Relax.

They strapped some sort of harness to my head.

Koji and his attendants then left the room, closing the door, blackness enveloping me.

I stood alone in the dark, my only light being the red lines in the corners giving the room shape…and the white screen. The only sound was my heavy breathing as I looked at the monitor.

Breath in.

Breath out.

In, out.

In, out.

In.

Out.

The monitor switched from white, to a live camera feed of Ando-san sitting on a dais, looking slightly wide due to the locked hard camera and its wide-angle distortion. Two women, with full heads of hair but no make-up, presented tea in front of him then bowed and walked out of frame. In the corner of the monitor I could see one was Akiko Fujiwara of Fem100 and Yuri—was it Yuri? It at least it looked like her. They were about the same age, but Yuri was only 14—

Jason-san?

Yes.

Do you know who I am?

Yes.

Who am I?

You're Ando-san.

What do you think that means?

I…you're just like us?

That is right. You are very smart. It takes a lot of people years to figure that out.

Thank you. I'm not that smart.

False humility has no place here. You are smart. I'm just a messenger and I need people like you. Because we are all messengers. And we need to spread enlightenment. It takes many acting as one.

I want to help you.

I will not turn you away then.

I laughed.

I'm glad to see you laugh. Japanese don't laugh enough but it seems Americans always laugh. I saw that a lot on television as a young boy.

We can be loud.

It's okay. We all have our differences. But we all have our similarities.

Yes…I guess so.

You have a question? I can tell.

Yes, um, where are you?

It doesn't matter.

You're not in Hiroshima?

I'm everywhere and anywhere. That is the magic of our technological age, right? The way we can connect.

I…I suppose so.

317

I was never afraid of technology. I understand it's true essence—which is to unify us, and bring us together in to one. We must embrace it and therefore let its infinite possibilities overtake us.

Yes.

I know you are an expert with technology too. People are jealous of your talent and your ability to see.

But it got me in to trouble…

People ahead of their time always get in to trouble. Those first to notice, those first to see. Many are uncomfortable with the truth.

You've seen what I wrote?

Then all my posts appeared on the screen. "Holocaust was a Holohoax," "Hitler did nothing wrong," "LA is a THOTacaust", "Time to talk about Jew privilege" and so on and so on. I felt indifferent to the words but felt my skin tremble knowing I could be judged for them.

Don't worry Jason-san. Your writings might be crude but that's what people need to understand in these times. You are telling the truth in your own way.

But everyone…

You've been freed. Being honest without fear is the greatest freedom of all. We are privileged to have you with us. If you want to help…

I want to help. I feel so at peace here.

Good. And I feel at peace just seeing you that way. See how we can help each other?

I grinned.

But it's not so you can just be at peace. We need you for the next challenge facing our world.

I translated what he said in my mind.

If you think I can help…

You can.

How? Through posting? I can start some new accounts, I can train your people how to do subscription churn, creating anonymous accounts…

Relax, Jason-san. Relax. Take deep breathes please…

I took deep breathes.

Close your eyes.

I closed my eyes.

Felt my breathing.

Relax…

Deep breathes…

In and out. In and out.

In, out. In, out.

In.

Out.

Then an electric jolt stung the back of my head.

When I popped my eyes open, I just saw white. Like that scene where Morpheus lectures Neo in *The Matrix*. But as my eyes opened, the room became engulfed in twilight, stars, the planets and the universe itself with plastic and material goods like houses—but American houses—cars—but American cars—Smart phones, pots and pans, video game cartridges, *Pokémon* cards and an Emoji Poo plush floating above me and around me.

We elevate things, material things above the spirit, and it has made us weak. We value a false goodness too much. The only cure for this is a destruction of the old attitudes. A radical change.

A resistance?

No.

All the material goods disappeared. Just the universe remained.

An awakening.

Everything in the Universe then began to brighten.

An awakening of spirt and consciousness, that makes people embrace the void.

How?

I heard you studied Zen?

A little.

Have you heard the Zen proverb of the man who attained enlightenment just before he was struck in the head with a sword?

N-no.

Cut to a Japanese man in traditional clothes being suddenly struck with a boken at the temple but just as contact is made, the universe bursts from the head overtaking me.

Well, no need repeating. You just saw it.

I understand.

In order to liberate the souls of this world, we must be the swordsman that strikes.

How?

We are the enlightened ones. We are the carriers of the sword. We must be like Shiva.

Shiva?

Do you know?

N...not really.

Several statues of the Hindu god appeared before me, as I walked through the temples alone, his likeness elevated.

Shiva is the destroyer. But also the creator. And like Shiva we must bring chaos but also bring life.

Why chaos?

Because it will have a purifying effect, bringing us in to unity.

But what type of chaos?

There is no need to concern with that now. In due time, the seals will open.

The seals?

You know the Christian scriptures don't you?

Those seals? The Seven Seals?

Correct. You're very smart.

I know about them.

And you know when they're opened, chaos will reign.

Yes...

And the Horsemen will come.

I saw scenes of destruction, scenes of my own mind of nuclear wars, death in the streets, babies crushed, tears flowing with blood and everyone distraught—

Then black.

Before that...the enemies of this world...

Gold coins started to fall before me...Men pledging allegiance the all-seeing Eye of Providence...men wearing yarmulke's rubbing their hands with them—but then a flash of lightning revealing their green scales and reptilian skin...

The enemies of this world must be revealed. They have powerful weapons.

Flashes of atomic explosions at the universal level! Spaceships, guns, missiles, lasers!

I then felt a jolt to my head.

I tried to fall down but then felt myself weightless and floating.

But we have our own.

Who?

I continued floating, feeling weightless...the stars above me and below me...

Ancient Indian scriptures tell of two angels, two women, who bring enlightenment to the world. That is why we have so many young women serving here. It only helps our goal of helping the world reach enlightenment. After all, Nirvana comes before destruction.

Yes. I see it! I understand!

320

But we also have one of the angels
You do? We do?
Yes. And you know the other.
I do?

Suddenly I felt an electric pulse go through my skull. I felt a vice gripping my head, the room itself shook with visible electric bolts forming above me, the room started shaking just like when Yu said LET ME GO but this time I grabbed the harness and wanted to shout LET ME GO but just let out a primal scream.

Until. Nothing. Just white. Like the white on the monitor when I entered the room.

The pain vanished.

I look to my right, and see a tatami floor, a black lacquer table, my TV and…my living room. But sitting across from me is a female with jet black hair. I sit down. On the monitor, Ando-san's face is in extreme close-up smiling as the girl sitting in *seiza* looks up at me.

"Yu!"

But the monitor appears in front of her.

Meditate on this Jason.

The room then returned to its dark and red.

And I collapsed to the floor, the rubber padding my fall.

*

Back in my room, still in my hypnagogic state, tired from the adrenaline dump but still feeling awake, I felt my head rise from the pillow and floating through the hallways again, navigating the different rooms consciously wondering if this was a dream or if I'd accomplished a step in PureLight meditation by going external, my flesh a discarded rag.

In one room, there are men-like women but there is Akiko Fujiwara walking around attending to the babies who seem neglected lying in cribs of fecal matter, leading in to an industrial room with a giant microwave leading to a loading dock with a female figure standing in the distance in the blades of grass at the feet of the Akizuki mountains going towards the sea.

I hear the wind then feel it. I step off the dock but then am suddenly far afield from the compound, a distant dwarf to the surrounding mountains. The winter breeze blows hard and I cradle myself as I feel my skin against the thin cotton. It's of little value.

I see a young Japanese girl, in school uniform, standing in the distance, framed by the dock garage opening, locked in hard stare at me, her face sad. She holds up a generic smart phone, then a screen appears. I see the image clearly.

Yu.

But with black hair and variant eye colors. One black, one brown. She smiles.

"Yu!"

I reach to grab her but am only cradling the phone. The breeze gets stronger, I feel colder, and cradle the phone like a child.

I'm not who you think I am. Neither is Yu.

Where is Yu? Who are you?

Yu doesn't exist.

She doesn't? Then who—

Yu as you know her, is really my sister. Her name is Hanami.

"Beautiful flower."

Yes.

And you are?

I am Hanako.

"Flower child."

We are twins. We've had a connection ever since we were born. It's what kept us close even during a traumatic childhood. We were poor and our mother died when we were young. We were sent to live with our grandmother in Saitama. We were the butt of jokes. All the kids would make fun of us.

The image on the phone flickers. Hanako is poked in the brown eye by a group of boys and they laugh.

I was the ugly one, Hanami would feel it and try to defend me.

Another child, Yu—no Hanami—runs to her defense but they slap her and push her to the ground. One kicks her. The rain starts to fall. The boys laugh and walk away. Hanami lays down crying. "Hana-chan, Hana-chan," her sister says as she nudges her.

I felt her pain. We could feel each other's pain.

Then a van arrives. Men take them and put them in a van.

We were sold to the government. For experiments.

I see myself, Jason Reudelheuber-Katz, wearing a lab coat, holding the hands of the girls, smiling at them, as I walk them down the corridor. I bring them in to a dark room top-to-bottom covered in 90s electronics: Professional-

322

grade 4x3 Sony Trinitron CRT's, Computer box monitors, CD-ROMs, pagers and a couple of Tamagotchi I give to the girls to play with.

Professors Robert Kaplan and Masayuki Uchida appear on monitors looking on.

Both girls are strapped in to a chair and a power drill starts.

They used us as guinea pigs.

All the monitors go blank, covered in analog snow, sparks everywhere, everyone runs in a panic while Hanami and Hanako, now grown, smile at each other.

We could now talk to each other through our minds but it wasn't working as the scientists wanted. The changes they made to our brain affected us differently.

Men run around shouting about "damage to her hypothalamic-pituitary axis and her right frontotemporal cortex"

Hanako lays on an examining table. "We may have a case of asomatognosia," I say.

"No, no, no, it's alexithymia," the other me says.

The twins sit at a table. Hanako appears almost paralyzed but grips a pencil as does her sister. Yu/Hanami draws a three-dimensional picture of a cube. Hanako draws a flat picture.

Yu—I mean Hanami—struts down a street, the sound of stilettos hitting the pavement.

Hanami could act normal. She could live like nothing happened. They could program her. But me…

Hanako's body is limp paralyzed in a wheelchair, her hair is disheveled, her variant eyes locked on me, as her mouth seems stuck in mid-speech, looking at me from the doorway of my room.

You are also perfect Hana-chan. Ando-san appears next her, backlit by the hallway light. You just embraced a different world than her. You were given a doorway in to a more special world, that of spirit. They discarded you but we found you. Ando-san then looked at me, then down at Hanako.

I thought I would never see Hanami again. But you found her Jason-san.

When?

When she met you Jason-san.

Me?

Yes. I could feel her love for you.

Images of us laughing and being together appear on the phone next to my pillow. Memories that never happened. Like us in the park or at the movies or at a nice restaurant or dancing in front of the Eiffel Tower but they felt real—real as rubbing my eyes. Dreams I remembered, dreams that felt as they had occurred and as real as the instant disappointment I felt upon waking.

I knew she loved you. I'm glad after so long, she was happy…but…

But? But—what?

But I woke up, to my door bursting open.

*

"Koi ya!"

I jumped up and followed Kazuo to the room.

*

I was brought to a room with only a tatami floor and some mounted monitors. Koji sat with a laptop on a table as Mandy across from him in *seiza*.

I need you to translate.

Sure.

I then sat down in *seiza* between them but out of the line of sight.

"What do they want Jason?"

"They want me to translate for you?"

"About what?"

Koji talked.

"They want to know about your brother."

"Jack?"

"He works for the Council on Foreign Relations."

"Yes."

"They want to know everything you know."

"That like, he's in Tokyo?"

"That's a start I guess."

She didn't know much. She just knew things in general in Tokyo. I filled in most of the blanks since I knew parts of the city and some of the details of the conference from reading Kai10. You can read the separate briefing and interview I gave.

Koji put his laptop down. Then Kazuo walked in to the room.

What's going on?

There's some people we want answers about.

Who?

Look at the monitor.

The wall monitors flipped on. Matt and Min appeared on respective screens. Both tied up and on their knees, bloodied.

324

Mandy screamed.

*

"You're not helping Mandy!"

"Guys please! Please calm down!"

"I want out of here! I want to leave!"

Matt and Min were on two separate screens, Min on left, Matt on right, in front of a white sheet but in close proximity as they talked to each other.

"It was your fucking idea to come here!" Matt yelled to his left.

"Shut the fuck up!" Min yelled to her right.

The video feed was Hi-8 grainy. Couldn't tell if it was from within the compound or elsewhere.

Mandy kneeled in front of the screens almost begging. Tears streamed down her face. "Guys calm down! Please! It's nice here! It's really nice!"

Kazuo held a microphone and screamed *"Shizuka shiro ya!"*

"It's your fucking fault! It's your fault we're here!"

"Shut up! Shut the fuck up!"

"Shizuka shiro ya!"

He handed me the microphone. *Tell them to shut up.*

"I should have never followed you!"

"Too late!"

"Guys…"

"It was you're idea…"

"Matt? Min?"

"Hey did you…"

"Matt? Min? Please be quiet."

Both looked up.

"Jason!" Matt yelled. He tried to reach for the ceiling.

"Jason! Jason! Jason please tell them release us."

"OI!" Kazuo screamed.

"Guys, be quiet…"

"Listen to Jason guys," Mandy sniffled.

"Jason man…they abducted me. There was a driver. One grabbed me, while one grabbled my legs…they did the same to Min…"

"They did Jason…"

"I came here to visit—looked around from the Kai10—then walked away then they fucking nabbed me on the way back to the bus station—they kept asking me about you. I think they thought I was you!"

325

"Then they took me because Matt mentioned me!"

"Bitch they asked about my girlfriend!"

"Wait, who? I'm confused."

"*SHIZUKA SHIRO YA!*" Kazuo screamed.

Two men then ran on to the screen. One kicked him in the face, the other in the ribs. Min ran in from the right she was punched and thrown to the ground.

They continued to kick Matt. Again. And Again. And Again. His face and to his ribs.

"*Yamete kudasai. Yamete!*" Kazuo then pushed me. I stumbled back and fell towards Mandy, surprised he'd be so aggressive towards me. I tripped head first in to a table in the corner. "Jason!" Mandy screamed. Kazuo pushed her head to the floor while screaming "*DAMARE YA!*"

He grabbed the mic and ordered the men to take them to another room. Matt's blood appeared on the white sheet.

Min cried, "Help! Help! Help!"

"What's going on?" Mandy said. Her tears dropped on to the tatami. "Why can't they just be peaceful. We're trying to be loving."

As the side door opened. Koji walked up to Kazuo but was pushed away. The side door then automatically shut.

"Mandy what happened?"

"I don't know…I don't know…"

The image on the monitors changed.

I could hear voices and talking from the stationary mic somewhere in the room but it faded in and out as Min or Matt or Kazuo approached the mic.

I stumbled up, shook my head and walked to Koji. *What's happening?*

They are obstacles.

What?

They are trying to ruin our mission.

But…he said you took them? Kidnapped?

No. He was a spy. He said he knew you. He then asked for her to come. She is a spy too. They are part of CIA. She might be a Korean double agent.

What? No they're English teachers. Of course they know me.

It doesn't matter. They are trying to hurt PureLight.

How?

Since they have been here they have been causing nothing but problems. Always asking questions. Arguing with us but not answering our questions. And then you and Mandy came...

But we're not...

We know. We know is an ally and who is not.

How would you know if I'm not an ally? Do you speak English?

Koji doesn't answer he just looks at the screen.

Mandy's head was still buried in the tatami, crying.

"What's going on? What's happening? Why? Why them? Why can't they be peaceful? They are always fighting. Always."

I looked at the screen. It was mostly dark, and padded—was it the room I was in earlier?

Matt could barely stand. He leaned against the wall. Kazuo spread his hands out wide pointing at them then bringing them together. "*Shiai shiro!*"

Matt stayed against the wall barely standing. Min looks at Kazuo with confusion.

"What—I can't..." her voice trails off as she tries to circle away in to the corner of the frame. She looks around helplessly knowing there's no escape.

Kazuo then walks to her trembling in the corner and pulls her towards Matt.

"*Faito,*" Kazuo says.

Min backs up crying. "No, no, n..." her voice trails off backing in to the corner.

They don't understand.

Koji hands me a microphone.

Please translate.

Translate?

Tell them...they need to fight each other.

Or what?

Or they will both die.

"What's happening? What's..." Mandy looks at the screen puts her head back on the tatami, this time burying her face in her hands.

Koji thrusts the microphone in to my shoulder almost jabbing it. *TRANSLATE!*

"Matt and Min," they both look up as if they hear the voice of God. "Guys, they...they say you must fight each other or else both of you will die."

"—son!" Min yells. She walks in towards the speaker. "What did we d—" she drifts off as Kazuo approaches her.

327

"They say you are both obstacles to the cause and have caused nothing but trouble. They say you want to hurt them. They say you are an enemy."

Min walks towards the frame "—ot enemies!!" she then walks away again from Kazuo.

TELL THEM THEY NEED TO FIGHT!

"Guys…you have to fight or else you'll both be…"

"Help Ja…" her voice cuts off. Kazuo grabs Min's head and slams her against the wall. He slams it again and again and again the only sound I hear is a distant "—op" for stop.

She falls to the floor as he knees her to the face again and again and again and again.

"STOP!!!!!!!!!"

Koji grabs the mic and hits me on the side as I fall back. I clutch my head dizzy as I see Min's mouth spitting blood from drowning in it from her collapsed lungs. I hear her voice gurgling.

I then see the men enter and a noose drop in to frame. My head pounds. They stand Matt up on a chair, he just mumbles something incomprehensible, they put his head through the noose, tighten it, then kick out the chair from under him. His legs kick and flail, but stop as his white pants turn brown from fecal release. His body turns slightly towards the camera as his tongue hangs out.

"Why, why, why?" Mandy mumbles. "Why couldn't they…"

"*Oi,*" Koji says. He pulls me up by the arm.

My head still pounds but I walk as the door is opened. I'm taken through a dark hallway, to a metal door that opens in to a dark room. There is the body of Matt hanging, the smell of shit in the air. The men tidy up the blood. Kazuo grabs me by the arm, then takes me to Min.

I can't recognize her face but the smell of brain fluid makes me nauseous.

I bend over and vomit.

"*Oi!*" Kazuo screams. He then lightly kicks me with palm of his foot. I fall over. I stand up as Matt's body is being lowered and put in a body bag.

Kazuo looks at me dead eyed.

He points to Min and Matt.

This is what happens to those who try to stop us. Understand?

I understand.

*

I sat in my room. Told to meditate.

Thoughts of Matt and Min's limp bodies haunted me. I kept replaying Kazuo kneeing her in the face over and over. She defenseless, at his mercy, and her going limp. I had wanted to do that to her for a while.

Matt not so much.

But the way they treated me in the past. The way Matt cucked as her puppet. In a way, I was relieved that I no longer had to face them, see the judgement that was always permanently planted on their faces when they read about me on *NewsGrind* or some other SJW rag. They were ground up the face of true power. The power they held over me was gone in an instant.

Did Ando-san approve of this behavior? Did he know all that was going on here? I mean, he knew this wasn't the way. I'm sure he'd be shocked and disapproving if someone told him.

Did this make me an accessory to murder? I wondered. Probably best that I stay at the compound. Stay within the confines.

Probably best to disappear.

Not that anyone cared.

By staying here, I knew that I had to do my best to navigate these waters so that I didn't end up like either Matt or Min. I had to survive. Which meant displacing my inner reality and being separate from what existed physically.

But I had plenty of practice in that regard.

*

I started floating through the rooms again. I glided past the padded room where a teenage girl was circled by dogs, dressed in white cotton, clutching herself as they attacked and tore her limb from limb, then in to a room with a giant microwave, with Matt and Min's bodies being loaded, dried to the point they looked like zombies, then placed in vats of acid in order to dissolve, forever away in existence as their ashes float out in to a backdoor loading dock with the same figure of Yu—no Hanami or was it Hanako?—she had dark hair so it was Hanako standing in the distance. I reached out and touched her screen but then woke up to sunshine in the doorway.

*

Koji and his attendants took me back the dark room, arguing again en route. Back to the black and red surrounding me, as I tried to sniff the blood and fluid of Matt and Min. The metallic odor of blood, the pungent smell of an oozing brain, lingered.

Harness on my head, the monitor went from white to Ando-san and his attendants leaving him stage right.

"Hello," he said. His use of English jolted me.

"Um, hello."

That's the only English I know, forgive me.

Of course, since you have to listen to my poor Japanese.

No, no. You speak Japanese well. Truly.

Thank you.

I thought of Koji. Did he speak English?

What's your question?

Are there are other English speakers? I was wondering about your attendant.

They speak some English. But not like you.

But there are other members who are English speakers. It's a world-wide movement. I can't be the only one...

Jason-san, you are now asking too many questions. You are important in your own way. Just like Mandy is in hers.

Why's she important?

It is of little concern for you right now. We are here to talk about your contribution and what you can do.

I see.

I can tell you're upset. I heard about your friends.

They weren't really my friends.

But you knew them.

I did.

I honestly wish I was there. It seems the Hiroshima branch needs some work. For that I apologize. I know seeing them die probably caused you much pain and confusion.

I hesitated to answer. He did know. He knew what was going on here. The image of Min being beaten, then Matt's legs kicking, trying to prevent death at the last instant—the smell—the—

Their spirits are free.

Free?

Yes. The world is your object, your clay to mold. If you look at their death as some sort of sad event, it will be sad, but if you look at it as a moment of joy, it will be joyous.

Joyous?

"Happy?" That's how you say it in English, right?

Yes, "Happy."

It's a moment of freedom. There is no difference between flesh that is animated and flesh that is inanimate. The only difference is the life force living within them. This life force is eternal as it connects and gathers in to a unified field. They are only returning to source. "Be happy, ne."

Okay. I'll be happy.

You have doubts...

Well, it's a radical change of mind for me. I've never thought of things that way...

Then you must start. Meditate on this.

I will.

We need you for the next phase.

I'll try to help.

I felt the jolt again to my head. There was Hanako sitting with Ando-san, crippled in her wheelchair. I was in the room with them, Hanako hovering above me like a judging angel and me on floating tatami floor while the guru stood inside a square television box, while reptilians started to flash around me as the fluorescent lights flickered.

Time is of the essence. The forces of the world, like the US and their Japanese government puppets are plotting all sorts of attacks against us. Ways to infiltrate us. Like your friends.

Matt and Min?

Yes.

They weren't spies. I've known them for a couple of years.

Maybe they weren't but we have to be careful. And we have to prepare.

How?

Reptile humanoids jumped in front of me! Mouth open, fangs out! I tried to leap back but they disappeared.

You know them?

I...I do...

I knew you would. They are the true rulers of this world. They have the ability to communicate with aliens and even angels. They run the world governments and banks and are doing everything in their power, using the world governments to stop the awakening from occurring.

How...how can I help?

Ando-san disappeared from the monitor.

Yu appeared. Or Hanami but I knew her as Yu. There was she was with her beautiful blonde hair, all smiles, as we walked together in the rain.

Hanako looked at me sans blinking. *We need you to find her Jason-san.*

But I can't find her...I tried...she's disappeared.

I know. I know she loved you. I'm glad after so long, she was happy...but...

What?

331

I sensed there were barriers.

On the TV screen appeared footage of Adina. Video from a Facetime session appeared "Hi, Mom this is Adina. I'm sorry I couldn't be there for your birthday but Happy Birthday." Her mom asked about me, that boy she was seeing, "Jason? There hasn't been much movement on that. Taking things slowly." "You better hurry up because I need grandkids."

Taking things slowly…

Then there she is inside her hotel bedroom, crying. The video is grainy.

No…Stop…

Cut to another shot.

Another angle of grainy video, Adina looks up. "Hello?" she asks. A knock on the door. She hears her name. "Jason?" She walks to the door excited and checks her hair quickly in the mirror, adjusts her ponytail.

The knocking gets louder.

"Hold on."

She opens the door.

Stop. Please stop.

The door opens. "Jas—"

The only thing visible is red eyes and a hammer coming down. Again and again. As Adina's body goes limp.

NO!

It was done for you Jason.

NO!

Hanami needed your love. Not her.

NO!

She is just flesh Jason-san. Her spirit is free.

She helped us Jason-san.

She helped us.

But…but Adina.

She's free.

And it brought you to us.

It did.

But I didn't come after she died…it's been…

Ando-san's face, a full headshot, appeared on the screen. *Other things brought you here too.*

Then all my posts appeared on the screen. "Holocaust was a Holohoax," "Hitler did nothing wrong," "Rape has its purposes" and then the messages between Stephanie and I.

You hacked me?

No.

We liberated you.

You're needed here.

We need you.

What do you need from me?

We need you to bring Hanami to us. We need her.

Ando-san dominated every corner of my sight.

We need our angels. With two we can bring about Nirvana.

How?

Think of their connection. What it can do.

Quick cuts of missile launches, stop lights going dead, plane crashes, the stock market tanking, a power plant explosion—a glorious menagerie of destruction.

Together they have the power to unleash these forces of chaos, and bring us all to embrace what is inevitable.

The void.

Yes.

…

We know you are one us. Fate has brought us together Jason. We need you.

Someone finally needed me.

I've already looked for Yu—I mean I looked for Hanami. She's disappeared. I can't find her.

We will find her the same way we found you. We will project your image, because our last happy memory was of a blonde gaijin…

And there I am on the screen, escorting the two little girls in my lab coat, the image of me flickering and changing with the image of the real scientist. There's a resemblance. We—no I—no him! Are doing psychological tests, showing them pictures. The two little girls clap and laugh as we—no, he—does basic psychological drills, like Rorschach tests, tapping shoulders while the other responds, drawing on the palm of another while the other's hand moves, he wears glasses just like mine, he smiles just like me, and the girls smile back at me. I become him.

333

We use this equipment and Hana-chan's power to project your image and bring her to us.

The screen flickers. A bolt of pain goes through my head. I scream, but I can't open my mouth. Nothing comes out. I feel paralyzed. I see Professor Kaplan in the corner of the screen looking on through a webcam.

I feel myself transporting, I see myself on every screen, every monitor, I see the images of Yu—or is it Hanami?—and I kissing then I'm kissing Hanako, we're in bed, making love, then I'm in a field with a two of them, then doing the psychological tests again, holding up the cards, then I whisper in Hanako's ear and tell her a secret, she laughs, the laughs then break up the screen, they break up everything, the screen has-a-ton-of-digital-interfere-nce-jag-ged-lines-eve-ry-wh-ere-wh-ere-is-An-do-sa-n?

Jason...stay strong...almost there.

More Kaplan...he shakes his head in the negative.

Jason!

Sparks fly from the roof. The smell of burning plastic. I hear in Japanese Maybe there is another way. My head pounds.

Footsteps on the floor. What's going on? The monitor is busted as smoke lightly protrudes from its rear.

Kazuo runs in to the room with his attendants as Koji arrives with his own. I'm dizzy. I can't stand.

An attendant brings a fire extinguisher on the monitor. My body is limp. I start feeling nauseous but hold it back. My head pounds again with the smell of smoke and soda acid.

But then Kazuo grabs me by the arm and picks me up. I have trouble with my balance. The room starts turning. Kazuo and his henchman prop me up as Kazuo starts arguing with Koji and pointing at me.

*

We go to the main hall. But it is empty. Mandy sits in front of a screen of Ando-san, in *seiza*. She wears a wide smile.

"Hi Jason."

I try to wave as Kazuo and Koji place me on a *zaisu* in front of the smiling electronic face of Ando-san, the man I had just talked to.

Kazuo then looks at the monitor.

He speaks English better.

I look at Koji.

334

Mandy puts her hand on my arm. Her eyes look glazed over. "They need your help. Ando-san wants me to visit him. I'm being prepared. He said so."

I looked at the screen and tried to rub my temples, trying not look at the bright light. I can barely move. The room turns. Ando-san speaks.

Mandy waits. Then taps my arm. The lights. The fucking lights. Stars. Oh, the stars. My stomach. "Jason?"

"What?"

"What did he say?"

"I—"

Koji steps in, "Your brother? He is Council—how do you say?" he pokes my shoulder.

"What?"

"'Council of Foreign' how do you say?"

"Council on Foreign Relations?"

"What about CFR Jason?"

"I don't know."

Ando-san talks again. Says something about me being disconcerted from our talk. "What's wrong Jason?"

"I don't know. I just don't feel…" I feel my breathing get shorter, my heart bumping faster.

"Please," Koji says tapping my shoulder. "The Master say."

"I…"

"*OI!*" Kazuo slaps the back of my head.

And the glare of the fluorescents, my stomach.

"THE LIGHTS! CAN WE DO SOMETHING ABOUT THE LIGHTS? I'M SICK!"

I'm sick. Can we turn them off? It's making me sick.

TURN THEM OFF!

Kazuo glares at Koji then heads towards the switches, bringing the lights down.

I close my eyes.

I'm sorry, can we start from the beginning Ando-san?

Yes. These two have done enough to make things difficult but hopefully you can help Jason. SIT DOWN BOTH OF YOU!

Kazuo and Koji obey.

"What did he say?"

"Nothing, don't…"

"Please tell me."

"He just said these two are no help. There must be some feud."

What are you talking about?

Sorry Ando-san. She just wanted to know what we discussed.

He smiled.

I understand. That's fine.

"What did he say?"

"He just said he understood."

"Okay, great."

Her brother…he works for Council on Foreign Relations?

He does.

He then looks to Mandy and speaks as I translate.

"Are you ready to serve us?"

"I'm ready. Tell him I'm ready," she bows towards the monitor.

He speaks again.

The darkness of the room brings a clarity. Just the glare of the LED reflecting off Mandy's white skin, the way a few of her blonde locks hang suspended—"Jason?"

"What?"

"What did he say?"

"He said you're very privileged that you can be used."

"How?"

Ando-san speaks again. I see her looking at the screen with a wide smile content in ignorance. The room still turns as did my stomach.

My head starts to throb but I only think about the trembling of my hand. "Jason?"

"Oh, um, they said they want you to go meet your brother."

"Meet him? Is that all? That's easy. When?"

"Before he leaves Tokyo."

"But he's busy he has a conference."

"They want you to go to the conference."

"Oh. I can do that. When are we leaving?"

Ando-san speaks. He has such a huge grin. Speaks with such a calmness.

"Jason? Jason, come on why do I need to keep asking you—"

"Mandy…" The throbbing, the lights my stomach.

I fall over. The darkness of the room envelopes me.

"OI!" Kazuo screamed. He ran to my chair, lifts me up then calls for Koji. Ando-san starts screaming at them.

ANSWER HIM! TRANSLATE!

"JASON!" Mandy crawls over to me but Kazuo kicked her shoulder to push her off.

STAY AWAY! Then he looks at me. *TRANSLATE!* I say nothing. *TRANSLATE!* He punches me again. Ando-san screams at him to stop.

I fall over to the other side. Koji pushes me back up as Mandy crawls over him, with a loud cry. Ando-san yells again. Then Koji slapped Mandy again and again then pushes her away.

"Translate," Koji said.

I look at the eyes of Ando-san in the monitor.

I look at Mandy cradled and grasping her face, realizing she had blood coming from her nose.

I'll go. Send me.

That is not your purpose. Her purpose is start the process of enlightenment early.

She's not ready.

That's not for you to decide.

I've know her longer than you.

You must obey.

"Jason?"

I feel a blow against my head. Then a kick to my ribs. And another kick.

"JASON!"

SEND ME! I'M JUST A JEW. I'M EXPENDABLE!

Mandy runs to me but Kazuo pulls her by the hair and throws her back.

What? What did you just say? STOP! STOP THIS! Ando-san almost looks helpless from the monitor trying to control events.

Kazuo looks at the monitor then points at Koji.

He never told you?

Koji then appears in front of the screen and bows, trying to explain.

Mandy starts crying, grasping her head. "Jason! What's happening? What's happening?"

The Master yells at both his minions. Then the screen goes blank.

Kazuo kicks me in the head. I don't feel the kick. I just feel myself rolling. The room. The darkness. The white light flickering from the monitor.

The room becomes a meadow. I see my dad, his figure, walking in the distance. I hear Mandy scream. Kazuo and Koji yelling at each other as they

337

pull on her hair—"AHHHHHHH!!!!" Her screams pierce the room. I've relegated myself towards death. I see a darkness on the horizon which then becomes a room, it becomes black, but there are red outlines showing the corners of the room with red faces appearing, they look like devils, my body shakes, they start laughing, the laughs, the howls overpower me, I can't move—paralyzed again—but I see the flashes of a table, a stone flask on top of it, a very simple one, with a wooden table and mud hut style walls and standing before me is Jesus himself, he opens his hands, I see the wounds— right through the robe on other side visible!—I see behind him robot sentries marching, with visor faces, like the old school Psilon's on *Battlestar Galactica*, it all seems natural, no CG, all feels in the now—now, now, now—"JASON! HELP!" Mandy screams—Jesus himself is expressionless but all too human, his face full of sorrow, so sorrowful that he really isn't Christ but Jesus—no Yeshua—but that burning quiet presence emanates from him so much so that I grasped his hand and press the wounds against my face that I can feel cartilage and the bone protruding.

"AHHH!!! STOP!!"

The screams bring me back.

She lays there, whimpering, reduced to blood and tears, as Kazuo and Koji bring their attendants to pull her out of the room, almost in slow motion as she tries to get to her feet but is slapped hard to the ground as I lay there wondering, is it time? The black haze forms over me, dizzy…I see stars but I mainly see black, but yellow forms appear in the void.

All I can see is drowning in cold grey sand…

Cue *Art of Life*.

The opening part of the first movement, which would be fitting for the soundtrack when this scene is adapted…it starts slow…a pondering on death…

The same thing I ponder at that moment. Maybe it was the moment to personally embrace the void, to make it reality. The weapons were locked, the seeds of destruction planted. I feel the black embrace me.

As the weight begins putting itself on me, my breath leaves me, it becomes harder to breath, I feel like surrendering. Why am I even fighting? What's the point?

All that I had lived for, the sum of my knowledge, all about movies, music, books, video games, relationships, society at large—nothing could help me in this moment. It all feels like a waste.

I don't know how to set me free to live
My mind cries out feeling pain…
The building shakes.

And there lay Mandy. Blood covering her face, once pretty. She was such a manipulative bitch bringing me here. So POZZed. So much the embodiment of everything I hated. Her screams are no more. Just whimpering. I see her tears clearing the blood from her face.

Can't go back
No place to go back to
Life is lost, flowers fall
If it's all dreams
Now wake me up
If it's all real…
Just kill me.
The guitars start up.

But there wasn't a void. A flicker of my dad and Jesus—don't worry it's not that type of story but—

She looks at me. The tears clear enough dry crusted blood that she looks to wear a mask. Her body is paralyzed on the ground, she's disheveled and pathetic, her mental mask of confidence destroyed. But I see the white of her eyes, they capture my stare. I see someone broken, desperate and helpless. I see a pleading in her eyes.

Kenji is coming…
Jason FIGHT! I remember Kenji saying. *FIGHT!*
Yoshiki's drums start here. The guitars flare up too.
Her stare.

My decision. Kenji's words hit me harder.

Jason FIGHT!
The heaviness of it all. I can just let it all end now. Or I can choose not to. I can risk it all for something, but I don't know what. But I realize I don't want this. I don't want it now. I want to see Yu again. I want to see the Seto Inland Sea again, like I always see it on the boat ride over. I want to revisit Hiroshima Art Museum again…maybe view the triptych with a new set of eyes, I want to see the mountains and the trees, I want to see my friends, I want to make some friends, I want to hurt, I want to feel, I want to love, I want to experience—as hard as that all is—I want to see the Sistine Chapel, I want to see Adam

reaching out to God, I want to see God in life instead of tempting fate and seeing if he really exists right at this moment—but it's not that type of story.

Time for thinking is over.

The guitars start to rev up… faster and faster…gathering strength.

And Mandy…she's paralyzed.

The drum beats get faster, more rhythmic.

No time for hesitation. Now or never. *Jason FIGHT!*

The metal explodes. Heavy drums and guitars in powerful unison.

I jump on top of Kazuo, who is on top of Mandy. I start punching. Punching him as fast as I can. Again and again and again. He's surprised. No time to let him gain his bearings. He covers his face with his hands as he gets in the fetal position. I knee him the face, again and again and again. His body goes limp.

The drums pound.

Koji tries to step in. He pulls the back of my shirt. I punch him in the balls then palm strike him to the face—one Karate move that just came for me but I palm strike again and again and again then pull on his body to stand then knee his face again and again and again. Then push him to the ground but I turn to Kazuo and stomp my heel against his head again and again and again where blood starts to squirt out and cover the tatami. The surrounding attendants are paralyzed as they are stunned at my aggression.

I see Mandy's hand and pull her from the blood pouring from Kazuo on her face but I grab both of her hands as I feel her heavy body collapsing and failing to stand, I pull her up, I hug her, I feel her breasts beneath the clothe rub against my chest, but it all seems so unsexual because we just need to get the hell out…I look at Mandy who is breathing heavy, blood running down her nose, staining her teeth.

"Mandy let's go."

I pull her along and open a door to the corridor. I feel her adrenaline set in and I feel her start walking on her own, I keep hold of arm as I start to run, "Can you run? Let's run."

We run.

The metal beats surge.

I'm making the wall inside my heart
I don't wanna let my emotions get out
It scares me to look at the world
Don't want to find myself lost in your eyes

I tried to drown my past in grey
I never wanna feel more pain
Ran away from you without saying any words
What I don't wanna lose is love

We run down the black hallway and as women, some with children clutching, stare at us, they cry as the building shakes and the lights flicker above us but I'm just trying to find a door, any door, that could lead to another room, any room. I open door after door, the building shakes, find one that opens, that goes in to some sort of kitchen where I see the women on the floor under the metal preparation table wondering if it's an earthquake or raid but I decide to grab a knife because you never know who might confront us, I see another door on the side of the kitchen, I pull Mandy toward it, "This way! This way!" I yell, while seeing some men following behind us where they try to grab Mandy but I wildly slash the knife towards them as they back off at the many slashes, cuts and thrusts, where I kick the door and fall back a little then run in to with my shoulder to only enter a labyrinth room where there is industrial equipment, like a huge microwave to remove the moisture from anything. But we keep running. I wonder if this maze has an end, my worst fears come true. But I keep running. I make sure I have Mandy but we hit a wall—THUD!— and I look along it for another entrance, some sort of, some sort of something, there had to be something, something there had to be a way out and at the corner I see a loading dock, I see a garage door shaking as the building rattles wondering if it's an earthquake but I pull Mandy, past the heat and smells as I hear the commotion of men behind us. I get towards the door and press every sort of button imaginable and one opens the gate but the other closes it so I press the green one again and the door begins to slowly open as I start to breath or realize my breathing as the building shakes more and more rapidly and I hear screams but two of the attendants see us and begin to run toward us, the door only half open as I start to push Mandy "Run! Leave! Crawl!" she starts to go under and I start to roll too but I'm still holding the knife like a dumbass and as I roll it pierces my abdomen but I roll off on to the hard pavement, I look at my side as the blood starts to pour out "You're bleeding" but I don't care. I pull Mandy as I see a field and lights in the distance, and we start to run, run as fast as we can until the lights get closer and closer but they seem so distant. I see flashing police lights, hear sirens, see almost a whole brigade towards the front of the building so I pull Mandy towards those lights. Let's run, run, run, run, run until we can get in their safe arms, but as we get

341

close I stumble and things start to fade, I wonder if this is death, I fall to my knees, I begin to breath heavy, Mandy stops running as she sees me collapse returning to me "Go!" I say "Run!" I hear her footsteps off in the brush and I begin to feel the cold wind on my face, the stars over me, and the mountains in the distance as I smell the salty sea air and I wonder if I'm going to see the void or Jesus himself, or just God in general and finally get some answers, but then I hear the clunking of equipment, the metallic sound of guns being carried, and a figure standing over me, Kenji, he had come, weird person to see in the afterlife and then I heard a familiar voice in English, "Yeah, that's him," and I close my eyes.

*

I wasn't dead. I'm not writing this from the grave. It isn't that type of story. But you know that, don't you?

*

I woke up, in a hospital bed at Marine Aircorp Base Iwakuni and a black nurse looking at my IV. She smiles. "You're up finally." I feel my head throb with pain. The television in the room has CNN on talking about a terrorist attack that occurred in Tokyo.

"He doesn't know, does he?" the nurse says.

I look to see who she's talking to and see Mandy sitting at my bedside with a copy of *The Brothers Karamazov* in her lap in a casual track suit. Her face is bruised all over. She stands up and approaches my bed with a smile. "Good morning."

I hear the sounds of jets taking off.

"Yeah, how long…"

"Just a day or so…Happy New Year…belated. I realized I never said that to you."

"Oh, it's that time huh?"

"The base is on lockdown. No one can leave."

"Why?"

"There's been a bombing at a hotel in Tokyo."

"Your brother?"

"My brother is fine. It was a different hotel. The Keio Plaza in Shinju— how do you say that?"

"Shinjuku."

"A bombing there. Some bankers were meeting."

"Jews."

342

"I don't know."

"Pretty sure it was Jews."

"Already?"

"I'm…it's just—who did the attack? Al Qaeda? North Korea? Do they know?"

Mandy looked down, at the TV then at me. She bit her lip.

"They say it was PureLight."

4

You know the mainstream media story. I know it by heart because my set was glued to CNN all day was set in stone: PureLight an apocalyptic cult in the vein of Aum Shinrikyo but tailor made for the Information Age, had—at least to speculation and preliminary investigations—participated in computer hacking, wire fraud, murder, poisoning, child trafficking of minors due to the predilections of its leader Masanori Yamauchi also known as just Ando-san, and a hotel bombing. You know the main story in the English press is the possible links to the murder of Adina Iscovitz who protested a store that had Nazi signage, that, turns out, was a store run by a PureLight shell company. You know the assailant was listed as 18 year-old Kazuo Yamada, a disaffected youth and adherent to PureLight, who heard some teachings or read some literature of Ando-san and decided it was his duty to take care of The Jew and cleanse Japan of their influence, this same Jew who was causing trouble at the same business he where he worked as a clerk. You know Avi Feynman did several press conferences and told of how next week, he is going to meet with leaders inside the Japanese government to talk about how they could help promote understanding and cultural tolerance in such a homogenous country like Japan, hoping they might be open to taking in more refugees. He ended one press conference with a quote from Elie Wiesel that's projected at the Hiroshima A-Bomb Museum:

We Shall Remember
We Must Remember
For only in memory
Is there some hope for us all

You know they reminded everyone of PureLight's anti-Semitic writings as you also know they didn't exploit that angle too much because Japanese were the ones who mostly died even though that didn't stop the anchors from speculating on motivations or bothering to dive in to the beliefs of PureLight itself instead just emphasizing some choice quotes from one tract.

But did you know the one thing I didn't see on the news was anything about the Akizuki compound, save some random shots when discussing the bombing and subsequent police raids? I had no idea what the internet or Kai10 was saying. I had no phone. But I was curious because they started reporting on the case of two imprisoned Americans on _____ television with Professor Robert Kaplan.

I saw footage of someone who looked like Matt and someone who looked like Min sitting in some sort of interrogation room discussing that they had been captured and treated well. After seeing the hostage videos multiple pundits collectively asked, "How can you blame someone for wanting to leave a country like that and become a refugee?" Followed by, "Japan needs to help."

Questions, questions, questions. But others seemed more interested in asking me some questions.

*

You know I talked to Mark. You have the recording.

But do you know of the conversation before the recording?

"Jason, glad to see you've recovered," Mark said sitting in a folding chair with green cushions, in a plain room with four white walls, his grin one of satisfaction. I didn't see any two-way window or none of that other shit you see in the movies. But I did see a camera sitting on a tripod looking in my direction along with Mark's grin as he motioned for me to sit.

I sat down.

"You've seen the news?"

"A little…" I sat for a moment "Am I—are Mandy and I—"

"No," Mark leaned over and hit record. "Actually, let's get that out of the way. As you might have seen on CNN or wherever PureLight has links to Adina's death."

"But…"

"I know. You were in the compound. You were kidnapped, right?"

I didn't say anything as I tried to remember the events.

He leaned back over to stop the camera, then looked at me. "RIGHT?"

I remembered my blacking out.

"I…I guess."

"Don't worry then. You're covered. You're not going to be framed or even implicated. It's not that type of story."

"Not that type of story…"

"Right…everything is being wrapped up."

"What about that bombing?"

"Tragic, isn't it?"

"Of course."

He paused. Just stared at me...

"What..."

"PureLight will probably be no more—or at least reduced to non-entity, with their links to _____ and the refugees and all. Hopefully we'll get your friends Matt and Min—god you guys here in Hiroshima, Japan are causing a shit ton of problems."

He reached for the camera.

"They're dead."

He pulled his hand back abruptly, focused on me, leaned forward, both arms sitting in the table as he rubbed his hands. He made one glance to the recording device then settled on me.

"They are? They're dead?"

"I saw them...they were kidnapped and brought to the compound..."

"They were?"

"Yes, and I—there were images of Robert Kaplan? The scientist kidnapped in China who did psychic research, I think I saw him too, like he was monitoring shit. I knew there was tie to _____. I should have known."

Mark wrote this down on a pad of paper, then looked at the camera, almost dismissing it with his glance.

"So you're saying that you saw these two, who are now on television in _____ prison, good chance they're dead, were at the PureLight compound in the Akizuki region of Etajima, a small island in the Seto Inland Sea. Is that what you're saying?"

"Yes...I...I used to have dinner with Matt sometimes and even went out with Min a couple of times..."

"I know."

"You know?"

"Jason..."

"Yeah?"

"Before...don't put too much faith in your memories. Just like the heart, they can be deceitful."

"*Jeremiah*...the reference..."

346

"Thanks, I know." He then put his hands on the table. "But more importantly, when we found you, my god, you—I mean you had a good time cocktail of propofol, opium, and even sodium amytal. They create all types—shit can fuck you up."

"You're sure? I was on drugs?"

"I know you were."

"But before that, I think saw Yu—or was it Hanako at the port. Koyo Port? Remember we took a taxi from there and I think I saw her near my apartment—but at the compound she was in a wheelchair…"

"Jason. Stop." Mark waved his hand, then wrote something on his notepad. "Sounds to me like you have some Fregoli Syndrome too…"

"What's that?"

"Google it."

"I can't right now…"

"I know."

"I mean it felt real…"

"We'll have to get you talking to a psychologist, because that's really not my alley…"

"But…"

"It all seemed so real? I know."

"But, no, it can't—"

"Are you really going to dispute me? How much do you know about narcotics? We can't find or know any record of usage from you save caffeine—which fuck, you're single handedly keeping the bean economy of Columbia afloat."

"Well, I kind of prefer—"?

"A Salvordoran medium roast, particularly from Platform in Henderson, Nevada. I know. I've been to El Salvador. Can't tell you why, but I can tell you they have good brew. And I can also tell you aside from being a dick with women and associating with Nazi's—let's just say you're not the best at controlling your worst impulses online—you're pretty much a straight arrow. Maybe too much of a straight arrow. Oh Millennials…"

"Well, um, we all have our vices," I said. I tried to grin. Looked up then looked back down immediately upon seeing his stare. "How's um, how is Mandy?"

"Aside from the MDMA we found on her?"

"I don't…"

"Right. Straight arrow. That's Ecstasy by the way. And it's a mixture of probably recreational plus what PureLight gave her. Real good Thai shit."

"Oh…"

"And she's fine. And I mean, she is fine, right? At least when she heals up. Like that time we met on Christmas."

"Yeah, she's…I don't know. We've had our disagreements."

"I know."

"You know?"

Mark looked at me square in the eyes. "What do you know about her?"

"I don't…I just always kind of thought her to be some…some brainwashed liberal, you know? Even in the compound, she just seemed to take shit in, hook, line and sinker, you know?"

"I do know."

"What do you know about her?"

"Me? I mean, she's not really my type."

"Right." I giggled. "I'm kind of in to Japanese women."

"I know."

"Sto—you just, um, just know everything huh?"

"About you? I can make a pretty good assessment."

"What? What asses—"

"We'll get to that, don't worry. How you're not so much in to Japanese women but just exotic beauties and I'd include blondes in that—at least given your search history—but really your tastes run the gamut from blondes to big chested Jews, to housewives both American and Japanese…right?"

He didn't give me time to answer.

"But with Mandy, also a good looking blonde, I'd say she's just like most women."

"Most women? You mean their hypergamy demands a high value male to take care of them while they wax poetic and give lip service to liberal causes and the myth of equality and feminism?"

"Who is controlled now?"

"What?"

"You just repeated a bunch of lines from some manosphere website dude. I know you liked Justin Bangs and all those other guys and all they're so-called redpill lit explaining the truth behind the world encapsulated in opening a pair of female thighs—oh, did you know that photo of Bangs or rather Dimitri in front of the jet? Did you know the plane and the models were just rented?"

348

"You know…you've said you know like…"

"That's because I do know, Jason. We have everything. We knew about you before any of this started. The Japanese knew about you too—fuck it, I'll tell you. They were worried about PureLight's presence on the island, Etajima. They didn't want another *Aum* incident. They knew about your online activity, they knew you liked martial arts from all your YouTube searches…and that you'd settle for any girl really that even accidentally might wink at you. Yu and Kenji were perfect case agents for you. I advised that making contact with you might be a mistake. 'That's a mistake,' I said—"

"I'm a mistake?"

"Didn't say that. Using you as unwilling asset was a mistake, though."

"Mistake…using me…like you know…"

"Doesn't matter what I do or don't know or thought because they, the Japanese did their thing, like they always do. But it's over now. That I do know. We're out of that mess and in to this mess."

"They were observing…"

"Yeah, once again, I shouldn't tell you this but Japanese Directorate of Signals Intelligence—kind of like our NSA—was monitoring your traffic from well, since a little after you came here. Not so much you but who was following you…"

"My work didn't get much engagement…"

"Yeah, well…the little you did have was, well some, was from accounts ran by PureLight. They were taking an interest in all your work and they were viewing similar posts as you. Even your ANON comments. "'Hitler did nothing wrong'? Wew, that thread got a lot of traffic from them…so, they, I mean Japanese intelligence, wanted to investigate on the ground any possible connections you might have to them while surveying the influence and activities of the cult on the island."

I didn't say anything. I thought of all my security, my VPN and using a sock account. "But my security…"

He laughed. "Think we can't break that? We knew who you were from the beginning. I could bring up your first tweets and Reddit posts as General_TOHO if you like?"

"No…that's…"

"Why did—how did you get caught up in all…"

"I just didn't like the way things were going…I felt helpless, so I started thinking of ways…I just remember thinking—or did I read it? 'In the information age, we're all wielders of po—"

"In the information age, we're all wielders of power."

He said it same time as me. In stereo.

He then laughed. "You think a guy on a laptop in his apartment in Japan thinks he has power? What about the government with all the resources up to a nuclear arsenal? Look…" he pulls up an iPad then goes to Kai10 and starts typing in a post. "I can troll with the best of them. Let's write a story that I'm a government insider and I know the truth about the relationship between the Japanese government, CIA, the PureLight cult and Jason Reudelhueber-Katz. I'll even add some screenshots from my phone to make it authentic. Wait, I'll even throw in a photoshopped picture of you near the bank before the explosion—I mean you have been to Tokyo, right? You live in Japan. You booked a hotel near Yasukuni Shrine. You've posted about it on Instagram— fuck, I'll just add an archived link from your now banned IG account and…think of the mental leaps people will make." He then posts it. "Wow, quick replies." He looked at a few. "Wow, look at that 'Jason RK is typical Jew. An agent of subversion', 'these are Jew lies'—that was quick, huh? Oh, I found my favorite 'PureLight dindu nuffin'."

He then slides the tablet towards me.

I look at the post then refresh. I then see Mark's handle and what he posted under: Ultima_Thule.

I took a deep breath.

"Click the next tab."

"What? Look, I know about how images can be faked. Think I don't understand post-mod—"

"Click the next fucking tab."

He leaned over then selected the next tab to Kai10. "Here—". He then sat back and grinned. "You want to see the wielding of power…" And there was video of special forces, were they Navy SEALs or were they Delta Force or SOG? I couldn't tell…but the drone footage over the PureLight compound…the way they moved with such precision…looked almost perfect…their blasts were what shook the building that night…Mark then leaned in for another tab…article with headline: "Japanese Police Raid PureLight Facilities Across The Country" with photos of different arrests, specifically Ando-san, in hand cuffs being led away from a compound in

350

Karuizawa looking humbled and pathetic along with profiles of the girls kidnapped to work there…including Yuri. He then looked at me with that Han Solo grin. Perfect performance from pro spook. "You helped us. So, thank you."

"How did I…"

"Look at your posts…"

I look through my accounts across Social Media: Twitter, Instagram, YouTube, Reddit, Facebook and the like.

"I've been banned…"

"No, no, no. LOOK."

All my Alt-accounts were gone. Including the archived versions. "We had the article at *NewsGrind* removed. By using our own ANON account's we put out how they had the wrong guy with screenshots and the like. They printed a retraction. On both stories. You've been erased. We made it all go away. The Stephanie woman? Her phone was wiped. She tried to conspiracy post about it but was convinced to be quiet." My old IG profile, the one under my name and my blog *Katsura's Lair* sat present in the invisible chair of cyberspace, the last post being one of that shelf of discarded game cartridges. "Oh we also had an agent visit your mom to tell her what a hero you were and used a connection to pay off her house and other bills. And your Uncle Murray is enjoying the new interest he's received from casting agents."

I took a deep breath.

"Want to still talk about power?"

I said nothing.

He grinned. "Don't worry. That post about you and PureLight is…" he tapped on the tablet then slid it back to me, "Gone, baby, gone. Speaking of which did you like that movie? I know you like David Fincher."

"Fincher didn't direct it…" I looked at Kai10, my existence as Agent Provacateur…gone…

"Right. That was *Gone Girl*. Got the titles confused. I don't have time to be a cinephile."

I slid the tablet back.

"I recommend you…actually, you don't have much choice right now."

"What do you want from me?"

"We need to know that your journey down the rabbit hole is over. That you won't leave here and shoot up a place like that guy in Tahoe because he thought it was a Reptilian stronghold. You made some comments that could be construed as violent…"

"Like…"

"Well, the rape comments or…" he fingered through the screen on his tablet. "You posting as General underscore TOHO in reply to Ultima underscore Thule in a thread about so-called 'white genocide': 'Fuck these people.' Thule responds: 'We know how to take care of them when the time comes,' to which you reply 'Damn straight.'" He then threw the tablet on the table. "That could be perceived as violent intent…"

"I…I don't think…"

"I'm pretty sure you won't…but I have to prove that to—it doesn't matter. You just have to prove it to me." He hit the tablet screen again then slid it back towards me.

As I looked at the screen, I thought about it all: Yu, our meeting, Min, Matt…as I see some escort website showing different high class Japanese models and there she is…Yu—or is it Hanami?—no matter her name is listed as "Kaoru", with a note she speaks English as some form of selling point.

I looked at Mark then he pulled the tablet back across the desk. And I thought that could just be a website, some professional designer could have made a mock up…a means of persuasion to corrupt my memory…"But how did…"

"If you need an explanation, then you don't understand. You're not as smart as you think or even I thought…"

"Yu was an agent. Or was it Hanami?"

"Go on."

"She didn't love me…"

"Obviously."

"But the psychic stuff…I know what I saw…I saw Doctor Kaplan, I swear. And my monitors, any time I was around Yu—Hanami—or whatever—I'm just going to call her Yu, whenever I was around YU I just remember there being digital, like you know, flare ups, break-ups like she was communicating something or channeling it's energy, I saw that Kai10 post that…that…you, um, recommended…and it reminded me of the movie *Akira* about the psychics you know? You know that old movie? It's like from 1988…"

"I've seen it."

"I have too."

"I know."

"STOP!—shit of course you know. You know all this. You know the real story."

"I know what you know. Actually, maybe I don't because we're talking, or maybe I'm just trying to see where your head is at."

"I know what I saw. I saw Kaplan, I saw Yu, those disturbances, maybe that post was right in a way."

"Or maybe you're associating things, like electronic disruptions, with a story made up by trolls."

"Or maybe it's true. Like—like—how did you know I was there? How did you know the layout of the building?"

"Maybe Japanese SigInt hacked the architect's PC or maybe the architect gave them the layouts?"

"Or maybe Yu—I mean Hanami—was communicating with me—she was programmed by them—she was able to see the inside of the building due to our, um, connection you know?"

"Do you know how ridiculous you sound? But whatever helps you sleep at night, entertains you—meh!" he waves his hand.

"I don't...really sleep."

"Then whatever distracts you or helps you move through the world. You talk about psychic programming but who has been programmed? You've been thinking about psychics since you at least wrote that script of yours..."

"Did you read it?"

"*Distort?* That it?"

"*Distortion.* I lost it when my hard drive crash—fuck was that..."

"Well, one of your conspiracy theories is right. Ops don't always work out perfectly. And yeah, someone read...*Distortion*—that's the title, right?"

"Yeah, but..."

"Not me, they, someone, scanned through it and gave it a half-assed write up."

"Yeah, nobody reads my shit."

"Don't be so down on yourself. We love people like you. People with the knowledge and imagination enough to be dissatisfied with everything, wanting to upend order—well everything. We use people like that. And then you deny yourself. Even better."

"But I didn't deny myself."

"You did. You risked your life to save another. Because you wanted to be the white knight. And no plan goes perfectly."

"Like that night Yu—she's Yu to me…that night Yu and Kenji came to the Ryokan. What was that about?"

"I could tell you what Japanese intel told us but that's classified and what they told us is probably not really true either."

"But…"

"Don't worry about it."

"But there was an explosion—an electric explosion and…"

He raised his hand.

"Just be happy you're alive. We were worried that you might be found dead. And Mandy too. You surprised us in many ways with your courage. PureLight was going to use her as a hostage for leverage due to her brother's position. They had a child trafficking ring they thought they could continue if they made enough threats and got enough leverage and dupes in the West."

"Like me?"

"Like you. But in the big picture you, guys like you, always help."

"I do, huh?"

"Sure. You know what the best marketing or propaganda is?"

"What?"

"The type we do to ourselves. The stories we tell our heart. We find things, clues, confirmations, that confirm them on the inside, something we can actively participate in or that just helps us sleep. It's our job, well, guys like me, it's our job to just help confirm it all."

"But I don't—"

"You may not believe what everyone else believes—if you even believe what you claim to believe online or to your friends and family. Your behavior probably says otherwise. But that's common with everyone. Regardless, we can use that too. We're the storytellers but it's useless if no one is listening or buying. People like you help make the sell."

"I do?"

"You do. You, they, them, create an opening through chaos—call it a void. We fill it. Sometimes people need to be reminded or persuaded that left to their own devices, all sorts of hell could break loose. But they also need to know someone can keep it reigned in. You helped the good guys win, Jason. Be proud."

"Helped with what? I might've died. You didn't stop me. You didn't stop Mandy—you even suggested—is that moral?"

"Don't lecture me about morality."

"What, because I'm not moral?"

"Do I need to read your own, deleted posts to you?—you're welcome by the way."

"I don't kill people—at least I don't think I killed any…"

"Fuck posts…need I bring up the photos of Adina Iscovitz? What about your texts with her the night of her murder? We know you didn't kill her but will you continue to lecture me about ethics or morality? What did you guys talk about that night by the way?"

"Before the texts?"

"Naturally…"

"Well, Israel and Palestine…I kind of trolled her and made her upset…I mean, that's what I think we talked…"

"Yeah?"

"I didn't kill Adina. Maybe what we did—sure it was not traditional. But it was consensual. Maybe my attitude towards her was a little…I mean, since when was difference of political opinion a cause for—"

"It isn't. You're missing the bigger point. Whatever happened between you two is one thing. In the eyes of authorities' it's another."

"Meaning?"

"Morality is what we say it is."

"Who? You?"

"No, the government. Us."

"Doubt you'd hire me."

"Well…if someone Against American interests? Removed. Someone anti-Israel in the State Department? They're removed. Racist? Removed."

"What if someone is anti-Israel yet pro-US? Like the Saudis at least were…"

"Or you? You don't love America or Israel—even though you're Jewish—or aren't. I know, you prefer to think you're German or whatever. It isn't for me to decide. If you suit our purposes, then we use you. We can look the other way on other things."

"So, the overwhelming morality is just maintaining power?"

"Whatever keeps us in the game but what also maintains order."

"The game…being able to control. Being a bully."

"It isn't about being a bully. The state exists to stay in existence. We can spend as much blood and treasure we can muster but it means nothing if you no one is buying what we're selling. The state stays in existence by providing

355

security and freedom and making sure everyone knows who is providing it. Does it work? Countries like Japan and Israel want us around."

"Are you trying to convince—"

"You're not the one who needs convincing. You're inconsequential."

"The masses need convincing?"

"No. They need confirmation. I mean…the reason Japan, you like Japan, right?"

"You know I do."

"Good. You're catching on. But the reason Japan, South Korea, Western Europe—all of them—the reason they tolerate our military umbrella, is because they enjoy the comforts of it, not having to pay for and man a full military and all that. They enjoy the comforts of a stable currency. Just like you enjoy the comforts of a stable and crime free Japan. Any threat to those comforts and you blanch, right? People only tolerate a power as long as it brings them good, as long as it protects them. The minute that changes, the apple cart gets upturned. Power is about protection. Power is about pleasure. The key in keeping things stable providing a justifiable fear of the alternatives."

"I'm the alternative?"

"Didn't say that."

"So, you are trying to convince me…"

"Stop thinking about yourself and think about others. Think about your mom, your dad, your uncle. Do you want chaos in the streets? Do you want your family fighting for their lives? Do you want a might is right, survival of the fittest barbarian class ruling?"

"No…"

"But you hate the way things are?"

"Yeah…I do…"

"You think anarchy would fix it?"

"Is that how you sleep at night? Is that what you tell yourself?"

"Me? No. It's easier and more enjoyable for me if viewed as a game, not a religion or a belief system, just a game. The quicker you make peace with that, the more enjoyable and bearable life becomes."

"I wish I could be like that."

"Maybe you can, maybe you can't. That's for you to decide. After you're released, you can read or watch or return to whatever, whatever reality tunnel you decide to hide in as long as you don't hurt your country."

"Hmph…my country."

"I haven't see you turning in your passport…"

"Yeah, you know."

"You want to say 'Hitler did nothing wrong'? You think the world would be better with Hitler and the Nazis in charge—okay, I'll give you this: That may or may not be the case. Maybe we'd all be doing Roman salutes right now if they won and we'd be happy playing in fields with our blonde headed kids—oh wait, doubtful you would have been alive, though a version of you I suppose, I don't know, you're being half-Jewish and all, but let's go back to that Hitler did nothing wrong quote. He did do something wrong, something very, very wrong…"

"Oh god, the Holocaust?"

"No, actually…"

"Then what? What did he do wrong then?"

"He lost. That's what he did wrong."

"Yeah but…"

"You can make all the excuses and pleasant explanations you want but bottom line is, the Nazis lost, Hitler lost. A religious cult that looked as political work as a divine service, where Nietzsche's own sister said Hitler was more like a religious leader than a political one. Do you want PureLight running a country?"

"No, of course not…"

"That's what the Nazis were like. A cult. A cult that served our purposes."

"Ever heard of 'The Focus'? It was a Jewish led…"

"Ever heard of The Thule Society?"

"Ultima Thule…"

"Right…"

"You're handle, I saw…"

"Ever heard that one could be manipulating the other? A group like 'The Focus' pushing the Nazis to war, pushing them to attack the Soviet Union. Creating chaos and a vacuum in Europe, one that a power like the Allies could fill?"

"That's anyone's guess. It's just tea leaf reading. We weren't there. We weren't in the upper corridors…"

"You say that now."

"Have you seen the world? The white race, Europe as we know it could be facing extinction and you sit here."

"I sit here, doing what I can. Doing what I'm paid to do."

357

"Keeping us in the game?"

"Right."

"But it's all unraveling. Did you know the US funded the Bolsheviks? Mainly Jewish Wall Street financi—"

He put his hand up. "You talk about bankers, but you ever think the Allies post-WWI fucked with the German financial system to weaken the Germans to make room for a Hitler? You ever think that?"

"I, uh, don't know much about Weimar aside from the degenerac—"

"Did you know we funded the Nazis too? Prescott Bush—yes, those Bushes—his bank gave them funding. Captains of US industry gave them patents by the boatload. THINK General Motors, THINK Standard Oil, THINK Ford, THINK ITT…How'd those Stukas get such good engines? You know all this? Ever think we might have allowed Nazis to take power, knowing they'd help us and the British subdue Europe?"

"First I heard, I'd have to research…"

"Wait, have you even been to Europe?"

"No."

"You claim to love 'The West' or Europe but don't know how so-called Western culture was formed in the Mediterranean by Semitic peoples like the Greeks, how they colonized, spread their culture in places like Aeolia, Ionia, Doria and all of Asia Minor up to Rome itself which conquered but also absorbed cultures—it was an exchange—like the Japanese absorbing Chinese writing, Ramen from Manchuria and well, modern capitalism from us, while you sit at home playing Nintendo, watching Pikachu or whatever it's called and doing Karate. Ideas and cultures that are great are infectious and spread…people are convinced they're better, that it will improve their lives if adopted. It isn't abstract."

"Whatever."

"You love Western Culture or Europa, but you're only saying what you know by the images you see on a phone screen, curated for you and your tastes and biases?

"Yeah, um…yeah…"

"So you don't know that the British were the Reich's main trading partner?"

"No."

"And the Nazis had bought their raw materials for weapons manufacturing from the Soviets? Did you know that?"

"No."

"Think they weren't smart to Hitler? He all wrote it down in a fucking book. Hell, the Nazis even made deals with Jews like the Haavara agreement."

"They wanted Jews out. They were communists…"

"Yeah, some were. And the Soviets did support Israel at their founding but…after the post-war Jewish persecution in Russia, they're leaning towards Arab states and noticing the relative health and prosperity of Jews in the US, they came around to being our ally. And did you know Israel supported Apartheid South Africa and Rhodesia? Remember—you're probably too young—but Israel was considered a pariah state by the left, the left you hate, along with Taiwan and South Africa. Anti-Communist states all."

"Did you read the Clean Break memo? Fuckers got us in Iraq—"

"Israel—Netanyahu—didn't act on Clean Break memo. Many Jews didn't support the war in Iraq, but the Israeli government did, sure. They've made mistakes like thinking us invading Iraq would make them more secure and their overreaction to terrorist attacks and their invasions of Lebanon…they're not the genius conspirators you think they are—they aren't even the biggest lobbying power in Washington."

"Who is? The oil companies?"

"AARP."

"Boomers"

"Why don't you wage a crusade against them then? Israel has their own internal issues including demographic problems not to mention trouble neighbors like Iraq and Iran…they just want to exist."

"My cousin died in Iraq…"

"Yes, I know."

"Of course, you do. You know about Tyler, don't you?"

"I know. I know about Tyler. But how do you remember him? How do you memorialize him? By fucking around in Japan, blogging and shitposting online? How does that do his memory honor, aside from being a crutch for you to be perpetually angry? Those who killed him are dead by the way."

"The terrorists, you mean?"

"Yeah. The ones who pulled the trigger."

"But that doesn't bring him back…"

"I—we both know that. But there's more constructive ways to honor his memory. Like getting involved in government or trying to influence us to stay out of places like the Middle East. But that's work."

"Yeah…"

"The world—isn't as simple as you want it to be."

"I guess I don't know anything…"

"Didn't say that. You're a smart kid stuck in a cave. But do you want people to paint you with a broad brush as a cisgendered white male Nazi? That explain you well?"

"No."

"Think the world with all of its diverse unknown fractals and complex figures like yourself roaming it is any more simplistic? It's only that simple on a screen my man. There's a hell of a lot of chaos out there. Some are trying to keep order, while some are trying to keep power…usually a mixture of the two…""

I looked down and stirred in my chair as I thought.

"What?" Mark asked.

"But the demographic imbalance, refugees, the open borders…"

"I'm not disagreeing with you. But let me ask you a question: You win, then what?"

"What do you mean?"

"I mean, you win. You and your ideological crew take over the government, reactionary forces take over all of Europe too, hell, even here in Japan…then…what?"

"I—that's not…"

"You think it will all return to plowing lands, blonde haired virgins walking in the fields, pulling stalks, heroes wearing steel helmets, lighting fires on snow peaks, while everyone labors in the fields happily and singing? Is that your ideal? Sounds about as possible as bringing back knights, fair maidens, jousting and chivalry."

"I just care about my people…"

"Then why are you in Japan then? I'm your people. Think they assigned me to you by happenstance? Mandy is your people."

"It's different…"

"No, your 'people' is just a catchall for an invisible mob or crew that you can't even see. Meanwhile your uncle has some acting gigs lined up, your mom's house is paid off, your cousin Tyler is getting a new gravestone, and you saved a beautiful girl's life but you're still being pouty. You claim to hate globalism yet you live globally, watch anime, play Japanese video games and by your torrent history love Italian horror flicks…"

"They're more like slashers."

360

"Let's not forget the Nazi stuff. German. Not American. Like you or me."

"They had good aesthetics."

"That's about it. All that other shit, the anime and whatnot—is trashy. Termite art."

"It's what I like…"

"For someone who claims to be worried about high Western culture, your impulses are fucking low. Real low."

I shrugged my shoulders.

"I know you feel a hatred towards those on the left or the Jews or blacks or whoever, don't you?"

"'Hate' is a harsh word."

"Why didn't you ever do something about it?"

"I did. I tried to create awareness online…"

"Yeah but look does that change anything?"

"What else could I have done?"

"I don't know. Learn to box. Knock some brothers out, like *Rocky*. You seen *Rocky*?"

"I've seen it."

"Or find some banker, or leftie—that Avi guy is a real sanctimonious prick, huh? God, that Queens accent…why not him? Maim, attack, destroy even murder…"

"That's…"

"That's the solution though, right? There's an impediment to your plan , your people, so they need to be removed."

I sat staring blankly. I mumbled out, "I don't want to go to jail."

"Find someone else to do it."

"But…"

"They're ruining everything! And you just fret and shitpoast?"

"I…"

"Did you fret and worry in the compound?"

"No…"

"Why?"

"I didn't want…well Mandy looked…"

"You wanted to survive?"

"Yes."

"You didn't need to think about it?"

"I…I guess not."

"Don't worry, you can come up with the heroic version of events later. But you wanted to survive, and Mandy too because she was there, looked vulnerable, a damsel in distress…"

"I…"

"You were thinking about immediate survival. But what about cultural survival or civilizational survival, the things you posted and worried about so much online? Why didn't you do anything? Why didn't you even try to remove the threats? A country is just its people, and you're sitting in a *zaisu* chair across the pacific complaining about it!"

"I don't…" I felt my body tremble with tears.

"We see your history of watching movies, shows, fucking around, jaunting all over the city—pretty nice fucking life. I don't blame you for wanting to mess that up. Don't blame you at all."

"I don't care what you think," I said wiping a tear from my face.

"You do."

"No I…"

A long pause.

Silence in the room.

He leans forwards, muscles bulging from his forearms. "You do. You want a reaction. You want people to think you're important. So you care."

Another pause. I feel my skin tremble. My mind races. I realize. "I do?"

"You do."

I care what you think.

I feel my eyes getting moist, I'm about to hold my hands up in defeat.

"Political action is fun until blood is spilled. But I know your anxiety. I feel it. For all your faults, I can tell you ain't a bad guy."

"Tell that to Mandy…or the others…"

"I think Mandy is just looking for a good man. Man being the operative word."

"Like you?"

"Remember? She's not my type? But maybe she's yours. I don't know. Are you a man?"

"I…try to…"

"But are you?"

"I don't know what I am anymore."

"I've seen what you've been reading. What you want to be. But reading isn't enough. It never is."

"Yeah..."

"I said I would stop. But I can't help but say that, 'I know', again."

"Know what?"

"That reality irks you more than its image. The image you want to project but it won't conform to your screen."

"It might. It did."

"Reconciling your construction with reality can be a bitch, huh?"

I shrugged. :shrug:

"Happens to many. Especially now."

"I just...Min and Matt what will happen...god I couldn't stand Min the way she nagged..."

"You know what happened."

"I do."

"And you know, ever think that maybe Min dated a guy like Matt to send a message to you? Think she might've been a little insecure that you were dating or fucking Adina or whatever?"

"You know my answer..."

"Never thought of it, right. Good. You're sharp. Catch on real quick. You weren't a mistake. Glad I was proven wrong. It's always good to shake our thinking a bit. Get some different perspective, huh? Thinking about this shit is the realm of schizos and philosophers my man. We aren't either."

For whatever reason, that comment saddened me most. All I could do is shrug my shoulders again.

"Doesn't matter. 'The theorist has always been worsted by the man of action.'"

"Is that, um, a quote?"

"Google it—oh, I forgot. You don't have access to any of that. Sucks for you."

He smiled again. I had nothing to say. I was jealous of him, the way he sat there and seemed to revel in the chaos that is the modern world, a man flying in to and enjoying the eye of the storm. A man who accepted the Devil's bargain and is maximizing it to greatest potential. I attempted same but failed.

Reality is a bitch.

"Well, um, what now?" I asked.

"We talk..."

"What have we been—"

"We've been chatting. Off-the-record. Now it's time..." he leaned over to the camera.

"Wait—what then?"

His finger hovered over the red record button. "You go home."

"Home?"

"Yes. America. Our country."

"Home...my country..."

He hit record. Then looked at his notes.

Timecode 00:00:01: Now, Jason. What did you and Matt talk about?

But you know that, don't you? You've seen the recording, time-stamped, fuzzy picture, camera in locked position, looking down on me in the chair, arms crossed, painted with the look of defeated from top to bottom.

Broken.jpg

BTW, fuck you Mark.

*

While some Marines, mostly black, played basketball on the court, I sat in the adjacent courtyard leafing through an old PureLight brochure discarded around the base. The fonts were awkward, even a little dated, the pictures could have been framed better, the English writing downright embarrassing, making me embarrassed for ever being taken in by them. But also, my mind raced and I couldn't give it full concentration.

"Hey," Mandy said. She sat herself down while glancing back at the court.

"Hey." I continued to look at the brochure while I mentally travelled across the universe, from the Jupiter of how to the Andromeda of why and everywhere in between.

Mandy's facial bruises were more pronounced in closer view. She glanced over again at the game then back at me.

"Like what you see?"

"What?"

"I mean, you know—I guess, you're, um, um, you're not a basketball person? But you were looking so..."

"I was just looking over there because you were."

"Right...I mean I thought for some reason..." I stopped. Returned to the brochure.

"Yeah? Jason?"

I felt my thoughts return to Earth. "Wait." Mandy locked her gaze on me. "Did anyone hear from Adina's boyfriend, Maxwell? He lives in New York or something?"

Mandy grinned. Shook her head.

I took a deep breath. "Maxwell, um, he doesn't exist."

"No."

"Huh."

I opened and folded the brochure in my hands, thoughts back in Japan, in the central region to be exact, *Chugoku*, where all this occurred. Adina...

"Have you talked to your family?" Mandy asked.

"Yeah. You?"

"Sure. My mom. She's glad I'm okay."

I thought for a moment. "Um, they live in San Francisco?"

"No. That's where I lived before coming here. My family lives in Houston."

"Houston...'H-Town'...that's what Matt called it."

"And you're from Vegas or was it LA?"

"Originally? Like where I was born? I was born in Seattle...does that make me from Seattle? That's how Japanese would measure it—but I lived mostly in San Diego and Vegas. More Vegas actually..."

"Oh in that case, I guess, I'm from Dallas but I grew up mainly in Houston, well, I lived a few years in Switzerland, but I went to Berkeley for college. I guess—I mean, I considered San Francisco my home."

"You feel San Francisco is your home?"

"I don't know—my heart feels like it's there—that's—I'm liberal—well, I just felt like its home."

"Kind of like me and Japan."

"But..." she leaned forward held her hands out open.

"I know. I'm not Japanese. By any measure."

"No, no, I mean if it matters in your heart—"

"I just speak their language...kind of..."

"It's all in our mind a construct, if you want to be—"

"No, I'm—I'm an American. I'm American. There's nothing more American than thinking you can be something else, right?"

She shrugged her shoulders. "If—speaking of...did you see..." she leaned in to me and whispered, "Did you see Matt and Min on the news? Captured for helping refugees? If I remember—actually I don't trust my memory

365

because of drugs, but I could have sworn they were there, at the compound. Everything is a blur at the moment, you know?"

"Yeah…a blur…"

She looked around—not at the basketball game but at the surroundings in general. "It's so weird…I mean, you talk about Japan and feeling comfortable here. But I really never got to know the place. I just floated through it in a way." She paused. "Not very tolerant or open of me, I guess."

"Hmph…"

She looked at me. "Are you okay—stupid question."

"Why?"

"Of course, we're not okay."

"I don't know. I'm just thinking…"

"What about?"

"What's next I guess."

"They said we could go home soon."

"Right. But where to go?"

"I don't know it's just…"

"You said San Francisco is your home, right?"

"My home? I—there are times when I visit Houston and I'm happy to be there, to hear the accents, eat the kolaches and Tex Mex but it just feels like another city."

"Another city…"

"You don't want to leave?"

I shrugged my shoulders. "I feel…I feel…like I'm a guest here. But actually, I've felt like I'm a guest everywhere I go."

"You do?"

"Wherever I go I feel like an alien. Explains my attraction to Area 51 and aliens…reptilians…I was in to conspiracies" I let out a nervous laugh. I stopped when I saw her neutral face. "Never mind." I started looking at the brochure again.

I embraced the long silence thinking about Mark, PureLight, politics, God, Satan, my dad, my mom, Uncle Murray, Americans practicing Buddhism like Christians, Japanese practicing Christianity like Buddhists, what became of my anime alter—

"Jason…Jason?"

"Yeah?"

"You might be on to something. I feel that way too sometimes…"

366

"Really?"

"Maybe more than I thought. Especially here…but I felt that way before here…coming here…you know?"

"Huh. At first, I thought it was because I was Jewish, well, half-Jewish or the child of divorce or…"

"Your parents are divorced?"

"Yeah. When I was a kid. My mom, um, she had an affair. After the divorce, she got custody, and, um, we moved to Vegas to be near my grandparents and family, like my Uncle, funny he always said he was a Buddhist—but off topic, she, um, she just kept trying to justify her behavior when I brought it up."

"What do you mean?"

"Like you know, always talked about being pressured to meet 'his needs'— I don't even want to think what that meant…"

Mandy laughed. "OMG, I know. I hate it when old people talk sex."

"Boomer feature not boomer bug."

She laughed again.

"But, you know, she'd talk about his needs and say 'what about my needs?' Or how she fell in love with someone who more reflected her values better than him…my, uh, my dad."

"What were those values?"

"I don't know. They broke up about the same time before the divorce was even official."

"Oh…but your dad?"

"My dad was—or became a Christian youth minister. He ministered to all the youth…hmph…all except me, I guess. He stayed in Southern California then the Northwest. He 'forgave' my mom. Even went on a trip to Israel and sent her pictures. But he got remarried and I was kind of an inconvenient memory. I saw him less and less."

"But you saw him?"

"I did."

"Make you go to church and stuff?"

"Sure."

"Oh…"

"I mean, I didn't mind it. I did the Christian thing. I liked it. I studied the Bible, went to services my dad took me too, he even recommended one in Vegas, big mega-church type place with rock music and a light show, you know?"

"Not really."

"Well, that's what it was like. But outside of it, I did my research, dug in to the history and archaeology of it all and when I had the rare opportunity to talk to him, I'd bring up what I learned and he'd say 'that's interesting' or 'I see'…just…dis—well, not interested…"

"Your mom didn't mind?"

"Not really. She encouraged me to go on 'my journey' but also not to ignore the Judaic aspects of scripture. When I once said at dinner that Jesus talked about money more than any subject, my uncle, his name was Murray, said 'Well, Jesus was a Jew after all,' my mom busted his—well, she got angry. Secretly, I thought it was funny."

She smiled. "But you stopped going?"

"Well, I got to talking to the youth pastor and tried to have dialogue because I had some questions but they didn't really have answers nor care to—I don't know."

"They wouldn't answer?"

"No. They just replied with platitudes. But I suppose that's all they needed because that's what helped them so they thought it could help me. Like, I mentioned how I didn't see a, um, a scriptural or Biblical reason for supporting Israel, not like that's a position they championed but it was in the air, and I just pointed out how the New Covenant really made it a moot point and they were like dumbfounded, you know? Or uncomfortable I'd go there but…never mind…"

"So you do or don't support Israel? I know at the conference you defended Adina…"

"Yeah…that was…"

"So I'm confused…"

"It doesn't matter what I think. They exist. And they assert their right to exist. My opinion? Means nothing."

"Oh…"

"But it was important to Adina…"

"Yeah…"

There was a silence. One I wanted to fill…

"It's not their fault I guess—you know the church? It's wasn't their job to answer all my nerd questions. My whole life I've been a try hard…to make up for something."

"Like what?"

"I don't know. Insecurity? Whatever. I learned how to be friendly. How to be a fake. Technology was a reliable friend as was anxiety. I think I went to UCLA because like subconsciously, I remembered the Pacific Ocean as a boy, I think. I thought about the movies, working in them but I was always too scared to pull trigger I guess…never mind. Enough about me, what, um, what about you?"

"My parents were divorced too. They said it was mutual but my dad remarried quickly. So, I don't think it was mutual. I kind of saw him. Kind of. I remember one day, just before the divorce…I remember he came to my school for parent day, where the parents could be with their kids for a couple of periods? I was so happy he was there. I looked up at him and smiled and he looked down and smiled but then he disappeared and my mom remarried. She was adaptable like that. But her next husband was distant and she didn't want any other children. He complied. He bought us stuff. He saw no need to make more effort. So, it was just me and my brother hanging out. He always—my step dad—he always talked about overpopulation and stuff."

"The birth of a liberal?"

"No. I think that's when I was a teenager and became a vegetarian."

"Right you're a vegetarian."

"Kind of. Depending on my mood."

I smiled. "Moods…I, um, I know about those."

"My brother was in college in Arizona. I visited him one summer and he took me to some Navajo reservation near Sonoma. You been to Sonoma?"

"No."

"Well, I saw the difference between the two places. One was fake, a rich people playground and then…the reservation. You could sense the, like, the poverty?"

"Reminds me of when I saw Itsukushima Jin—I mean, Itsukushima Shrine--at Disneyworld as a kid…last vacation with my parents."

"It's at Disneyworld?"

"Yeah. A parody but it's there. No poverty aside from the spiritual sort."

"Right, well there was this ritual where they sacrificed a goat. Cut its neck and everything, then the blood poured in to a bowl. Then they cooked and ate the meat. There was true joy among like the people but I saw the animal suffer. I thought of how easy was to eat meat but not recognize the death associated with it." She paused. "I don't—you wouldn't be bothered by that?"

"An animal blood ritual? I don't know. I like primitive stuff."

369

"Well, it was just a jumping off point for me."

"I mean, I could see..."

"It's just—I don't know. As I heard people talk about politics, I also thought about those poor people on the reservation and heard how they got there. The world seemed so...cruel, I guess? Why couldn't others understand or be kind? Why didn't they care? What was wrong with them? Everyone just wanted to be selfish, get what was theirs. I don't know, I don't know. It seemed white men—I mean, I hated you and everything you represented. At least I thought I did. I mean, you could be useful for what I needed..."

"Like translation?"

"I shouldn't have said—I'm...I'm..."

"No, no..."

"God it sounds..."

"It's okay..."

"I'm such..."

"It's fine."

"But..."

"Mandy."

I grab her hand.

She calms down.

"I understand. It's okay."

"Really?"

"Yeah..."

Silence.

"I was the same way. I thought all the same things about you."

"Wow. Right..."

More silence. My thumb caresses the top of her hand.

"I mean—huh, I'm trying not to think about it but I just can't stop—GOD. I'm going to need so much therapy. I'm so...so...naïve...and I should know better. I don't know any minorities, you know? Did those Navajo ask for my help? I've never been to the ghetto—is that even the word?"

"Some say 'hood' but yeah 'ghetto' can be um, a catchall, yeah..."

"I don't even know much about Japan or have tried to learn. At vacation time, I was looking to go to Thailand but more to be on the beach or visit temples but I stayed for my brother. I couldn't wait for my contract to end. I spent a lot of time on my phone..."

Mandy told me about her past online history, her relationships, the falling out with her brother and the allure of PureLight. No need to go in to details. You know them already.

"So how did you…"

"How did I what?"

She shrugged her shoulders.

"Become a Nazi?"

"I didn't say that…"

"But you were implying…look I don't want to talk about politics…"

"I don't either. But…"

I began to stand up. Felt the wind. She then put her hand on my forearm. I sat down again.

"I'll listen." She shrugged her shoulders again and smiled. "We have nothing else to do." She rubbed my arm. "I won't judge. Really. I won't."

"You sure. Because I when, um, when I get talking…I tend to ramble on…" I laughed.

"I have nowhere else to go."

"I don't know…I've been wondering how I got here myself, you know? There's no easy answers."

"There aren't."

"But radicalization, I've been thinking about what causes it."

"What type of radicalization?"

"Any type. Any type of extremist from the Hezbollah to the Weather Underground to the Ku Klux Klan or even Greenpeace."

"You'd call Greenpeace radical?"

"I'm just saying um, the need to dedicate one's self to a cause no matter the cost, even death—whether it be to them or others, you know? Not like there's some, um, one common blanket factor…"

"Okay, okay. Don't worry. I'm just asking. Go on."

"Well, I'm thinking and it doesn't necessarily come from disenchanted youth or a need to rebel or whatever. It comes from one who is a good person, one who tries to do what's right, what they're told, but gets upset when he sees errant lawlessness all around him or those have a blasé attitude."

"What type of attitudes?"

"Like greed or selfishness or I don't know. Just no ideals?"

"Like I said earlier? People only caring about themselves?"

371

"Sure and maybe don't care about the bigger world or even their country save some lip service."

"You felt that way about America?"

"Well, maybe. People love America for the ideas it represents, what it used to be, not for what it really is, or you know, what it's become."

"What's it become?"

"A bus stop on a never-ending journey of chasing the carrot...well, in my opinion..." I thought for a moment. "Funny..."

"What?"

"I um, I sound like Ando-san. He said something similar...I guess there's appeal because there's some truth..."

"I see." Mandy looked down at the table.

"I said something similar to Matt too..."

"By the way, what did you guys talk about. Min said something about you guys having a talk..."

"Funny how everyone wants to know..."

"Never mind. What were we talking about?"

"Chasing the carrot?"

"Right..."

"So, um, someone, he—they—they're upset others don't care or see the looming disaster that they see awaiting if people don't wake up. Or they're just upset they haven't gotten their piece of the pie. So, he—they—want to take action against those responsible."

"But who's to blame for all that?"

"Some say whites, the, um, the, the, white male culture. I'm sure you and your friends would say that, right? Some say Jews."

"I'm sure you'd say Jews."

"I'll meet you in the middle and say boomers."

She laughed.

"You know thinking about it, we blame left, right, capitalism or socialism but really it's all of us. We're corrupted at some level. We're like the seed planted on the thorns or rocky ground—you know Jesus' parable?"

"I don't."

"Well, like that's—there's something in our core hollowed out and rotting. And we try to make up for it by chasing the carrot or causes...like religion or politics or you know, social justice..."

I stopped. I waited for her to contradict me, or to shift blame or anger on to me (even though I extended to olive branch) like a spoiled child slaps away food they hate from a smiling parent.

But she just asked: "You felt this as a child or teenager?"

"No, not necessarily. Only thing I remember from childhood—that I could, um, link to that, is going to the library and renting a book on Renaissance painting that my dad recommended. Not that he's the artistic type but he recommended it. So I looked at it and admired the beauty of it all, Sistine Chapel and all that…"

"I've been there."

"Oh…I've always wanted to go."

"It was cool."

"Right on. Well, my dad, he, um, he then took me to a museum, I forget which one after I said I wanted to see more of the paintings. There was an exhibit of Japanese *satsuei*. You ever seen those?"

"No."

"Well there was those and some choice paintings from European history, like Impressionism, Post-impressionism and all that, you know what I'm talking about. It made me think of art. Guess it gave me an appreciation of beauty, female beauty, god I sound like fa—I can't believe I'm talking like this…"

She tapped my arm, "No, go on, go on…"

"I was just happy that art honored that spark of love that beauty inspires. But no one at high school or wherever, no one cared. I felt embarrassed to talk about it. I guess I do care what people think. Hmph…"

I paused.

"Jason?"

"Yeah, um, it put the seed in my mind that…many in the West, the modern world, are begging for extinction. Call it God, call it nature, but it has a way of eliminating those who want to harm or just take from others or those who don't look out for their own well-being. And that's what I saw in us, in America. I stopped caring."

"But…"

"Yeah, I guess when I stopped caring, I was angry I stopped and even angrier no one cared I stopped."

"Seriously? You thought that?"

"Maybe sub-consciously. This is all—I forgot the word, it's just looking back…"

"'Retrospect'? 'Reminisce'?

"Something like that. And my cousin getting killed in Iraq kind of—I guess it clarified it…"

"What was his name?"

"Tyler."

"You two were close?"

"Well, the closest I guess of my cousins but we didn't see each other much. He lived in Washington, around Seattle and I lived in Vegas but…"

I feel her grip my hand. "I'm sorry for your—"

"It's okay."

Another silence as I think about Tyler and what Mark said.

"And it made you political?"

"I don't know. I figured out quickly that American political discourse is, um, controlled by progressive liberal framing. Everyone tries to uphold its ideals. Neo-reactionaries revel in being its antagonist. I guess I, um, decided to join them—at least online—but that's just feeding the monster of activist politics, giving the so-called Social Justice Warriors a target. I—we? We're just materialists dissatisfied in material existence trying to bring change, even if it's through chaos. Capitalism, National Socialism—you know Nazis?—and Communism are all just materialist ideologies but emphasizing different aspects of material life whether they be, um, individual capital, race or class. But the ideologies, the ideas, are themselves aren't as important as the power holder anyway—usually it's just an ideological means to an end for power, you know? And really, they're—ideologies or political systems that is—are most destructive when reduced to their bare essence, their logical conclusion, stripped of human forces that keep them in check—like religion or the arts or the family—or worse corrupting those same forces to reach their respective endgames. I mean, I wasn't looking for dialogue. Were you?"

"Well, I thought I—we—I thought I was on the right side. The side of good."

"So why debate, huh?"

"I guess."

"I can't, um, I can't speak for you but I didn't want to be understood. I wanted to be confirmed…and maybe conformed to. Attention and power, I

374

guess…and the accolades it brings. Ego is a sponge looking to things to soak up and expand…"

"This might be the most we've ever talked…I never bothered to talk or ask…"

"Sure, I mean look at ourselves. Everyone used to just grow up, get married, have babies, then they would grow up have babies and on and on you know? In between that, life would happen, some would die in battle, some of the plague and child birth, but it was all just considered a part of life with grandparents, in-laws and cousins there to support and ultimately the support or maybe, um, comfort of God himself."

"You think God is a man?"

"I know, I know, I know I used the masculine pronoun but still."

"I'm sorry. I'll stop."

"It's okay…programming. God knows I have my own biases."

"Please, please go on…"

"Most people's worlds did not extend beyond their hamlet but it was more than enough world for them. We now have the world at our finger tips and nothing is enough, nothing is satisfying. Our discomfort is immeasurable. The first sign of struggle or suffering paralyzes or at least traumatizes us. We're privileged yet crippled."

"But I don't want to live with my family. I don't really have a family."

"You don't want to get married?"

"No, I mean…" she thought for a moment. "I mentioned my brother but I barely saw or spent time with anyone else. My mom just follows my step dads lead to keep everything in order…me and my brother haven't seen eye to eye for a while…and your family like you mentioned…"

"Right." I took a deep breath. "I mean, a basic organisms life cycle is birth, toil and pro-creation, so it can keep the cycle going. Like a beehive. But we can't even get that right."

"So you just want to go to my room and maybe pop out a kid or two?"

"What? No, no, I'm saying…"

"It's…"

"I'm not saying we're bees…"

"I'm joking. I'm joking."

"It's obviously more complicated…"

"I'm joking. Sorry. Sorry."

375

I giggled. "It's okay…" I thought for a moment. Shifted my legs to adjust to the slight erection I felt. "Maybe we're locked in our histories both family and culture, even as we, um…try to escape them."

She rested her chin on her palm. "How so?"

"I remember…was it in high school? My mom was getting all self-righteous about the Holocaust or wanted to force me to attend some memorial or something. And I cracked a joke about wearing a SS outfit and her and my grandma got pissed."

"Were they Holocaust survivors?"

"No but I felt they just liked having something to mourn."

"Do you feel that now?"

"I don't know…I've never really talked to my mom about it. I just thought it was interesting that outrage is the only thing people bothered to do or get passionate about. So, I started surfing online and began noticing others noticed what I noticed. It felt good. They would post articles, I would read, lose my shit…it's funny, you know looking around out here with the weather, the cool air, the guys playing basketball…really it was only my inner world getting angry you know?"

"Yeah, it's not so cold today."

"It's interesting being without the phone or computer or most electronics…at least for me…"

"No, me too. I read articles all the time and just get upset."

"Right? Right! That's what always pissed me off about the left. They were just an outrage machine with their protests and SJWs, making emotion based decisions which was really just a need for personal significance. But that itself can lead to chaos by its very nature with regret or shame being the only form of reflection. But I'm the same way. A lot of what we do, I do, our world view, is shaped by a faith in many things that we have little to no understanding nor material grasp of, things pertaining to experiences we've never experienced or places we've never been. We haven't been to or seen refugee caravans, or the Middle East or Africa—"

"I've been to Dubai…"

"Oh and?"

"The hotels were nice but…" :shrug: "And I was interested in PureLight because they were helping refugees."

"Okay but do you think Matt and Min went?"

"I don't know."

"We only have that image of them on the screen. Our memories say different."

"Right…"

"So, so, um, so…we just trust what we're told and manipulated by many, including mainstream establishment outlets with ulterior or impure motives or maybe they just misunderstand things or they're manipulated themselves by misunderstanding and they're also in competition with other outlets and other ideologies. Does that make sense?"

"I kind of see…"

"It's survival of the fittest. I get angry at the likes of you but it's really like looking in to a mirror. I look down at the pit of all my anger and raw experience, the chaos inside me, a void and project it out. We both, I think, I mean, our doctrines and ideologies or just us period, have a death instinct. Instinct, emotionalism and reasoning don't mix too well. But neither does chaos and compassion. Maybe they do mix but we're trying to separate them. I don't know. There is no there there on both sides. It's all just reactionary false morality, emotional nihilism and a false traditionalism built on nothing, trying to get outside a hold of something we can't grasp inside. The end result is nothing.

"By replacing religion and community and family with ideology and radical individualism and liberal capitalism, we've destroyed the value of everything by putting a price on it. But, you know, um, systems and countries are just the product of its people.

"I've internalized this. I'll admit. We all have, I think. I was willfully and sub-consciously programmed. The object of my ire was also the object of my desire and pleasure. And In a way, that's why maybe I'm jealous of the Jews or the Japanese, or even those guys playing ball, the way they've preserved…they have something in this modern world. But even if I did have it, I'd probably fuck it up. I'm condemned to being a loner. My heart and soul are divided and distributed in many parts, completely separated or at odds with physical existence and when brought in to that world it only brings chaos."

"Wait—Jason…you jumped off…I'm lost first you're talking about modern capitalism then some form of programming…"

"Yeah, yeah my mind tends to wander. It's like I have many floating notecards that aren't really connected and I'm trying to connect them all. Really…that's what I've always tried to do. Make the connections. Sometimes failing miserably."

"It isn't a Master's thesis...actually maybe I'll just go back and get my Master's but that all seems so boring..."

"Like my talking..."

"No, no..." she said putting her hand on my arm. "Last thing I want to do is be looking at a wall. Keep talking."

"Where was I? I don't know actually. I guess I just wanted to pour gasoline over everything and watch it all burn."

"Why?"

"Because it all seemed so fake. Fake morality, fake outrage, fake moralism as the mask for greed and power lust. Burn it all down is what I thought."

"But then what?"

"Hmph. Funny. Mark, um asked me the same thing?"

"You guys had a conversation?"

"You didn't?"

"No. He just asked if I was okay. And told me my brother was safe."

"Good. I'm glad, um, I'm glad to hear that."

"Thanks." I watched the guys leave the basketball court. Mandy looked their way then back at me. "So back to...then what?"

"Well, what was all this fake morality referencing? Was there a true version that wasn't a parody? A true source? I came here and began to wonder. I think I hated everything from my past, so I just ran away. Ran away to college then here. Ran away online."

"Yeah. I ran to San Francisco. Then here. It's not Houston."

"Right..." I looked down. I looked at the court. The sun was out in full noontime force. "Everything I thought I hated...the suicidal, destructive tendencies of modernity...I guess actually I embody them. I'm just a—a mirror reflecting the same image it hates seeing. I too am the embodiment of the destructive duality between spirit and flesh..."

Mandy leaned forward and put dropped her arms between her legs, dripping her shoulders then leaned forward.

"I wonder...do I even exist?"

"Of course you do Jason...you're here..."

"No, no, I mean am I just a sum of my parts? Online I'm one person, in the flesh another. To my mom, I'm a son, to my 'friends' those I associate—" I thought of Yu, she'll always be Yu to me. I thought of Adina. I gulped. "But when I'm alone, I feel one way one day, even one moment and completely different the next. Don't mean to get all religious I'm not really that type of—

well, there might be something to the Trinity. How God is still one, a unity, but out of that flows a multifaceted persona—you know? And if, you know, my dad always said we're made in His image, so…I dunno…I guess there's a unity of multiplicity. If that makes sense…"

"Sure, yeah…"

"But even worse there's corrupt parts of our nature that ruin it. We try to flatten out or organize the unity, but that brings destruction, forcing things to fit where they don't. And our need for significance and acceptance. To be God's ourselves, you know? This need to make the world in our image but really don't know how and what the ideal truly is. And really, there's nothing beneath my skin. Nothing. Nothing of any depth. Just shallow wants and ideals. So the world in my image is no image. Nothingness."

"I think you're being too hard on yourself…"

"Maybe we haven't been hard enough."

"Do you really—?"

"We just go marching in to—or at least I did, in to that fervent conflict between utter nihilism of forced collectivism and detached individualism—I don't know. Yet my upbringing won't let either have carte blanche—or at least I feel guilty doing it. There's the quietest of voices maybe the most powerful yet drowned out by others. Everything is drowned out though. Everything is a pendulum of emotions and attitudes. Erratic behavior, confusion and chaos. Maybe I just think too much."

Mandy giggled. "You might be on to something. Maybe. That sounds like a world—god, I wonder, it is a struggle to navigate when you have everything."

"And, um, I think… we were both attracted to PureLight for the same reason: We feel unmoored from the world, exiles, and um, you know, we um…we want some escape from it, the world, or at least some order…even if it means destruction of the rest of it—or at least we're committed to a path regardless of guilt, you know?"

"I don't know if I wanted that…"

"Okay, okay, you say that but…um…look…I mean, I mean…" I rubbed my temples. I sighed. I looked at Mandy. She smiled. I collected my thoughts. "Think how—you mentioned getting upset reading articles online…"

"Right…"

"Think of all those things and think of um, the anger—you know and you get mad! Don't you get mad when you see something contrary and and and you say when will the fucking world wake up? When will things be fixed? You know…like…don't you feel that? You don't? You just said it…"

"I don't know…I've never really…hmph…"

"You don't or haven't but okay…"

"But what does PureLight have to do with it?"

"I don't—well, I guess…it's like you're sick of it all, you feel like no one cares and here comes a group or person with answers you know? But not just answers. But with a chance to escape the or fix world, right? A world that's alienating. And better yet, they say we care—not just about the problems but about you." I pointed at Mandy.

"But isn't that just all, you know, organized religion?"

"That's what they—I don't know who they are—but I guess that's what we think or have been led to think. But religion is more…what is it? It's, um, I guess, it's more a way to interpret the world and live in it, but, um, I'd hate to just, um…be so—to reduce it to that. But it's one facet. You take it away, religion I mean, take it away and it creates an empty space that needs to be filled and, um, and possibly mutated and perverted. But I hate all this psychological construct bullshit."

"It's not bullshit, I think. What you're saying I mean."

"Well, I just mean, we only call it 'organized religion' because we see it as an institution distanced from us, bigger than us, because it you know, it operates, um, regardless of us, it seems to only care about its existence rather than caring about us as individuals…and it's running in competition with other power structures and institutions for influence. It only loses relevance, organized or not, um, because we lose personal connection to it. Many of these things, work in kind of a circular exchange of meetings of people then the um, the people giving their resources in to it to sustain it…until it becomes corrupted or targeted by other forces. It's a vicious circle."

"You don't think things have progressed?"

"In certain ways, sure, but all this materialism…we call ourselves privileged, I suppose we are but really it's a material prison in ways with those seeking our loyalty in all sorts of manners. Yet here we are. And I don't want to give up anything I have."

"Same…"

"Yeah…"

Silence…

"And someone like me…I could be the superman and join in the rivalries of the world or be the sovereign individual, happy to watch the shit show as it happens. But both ways don't help I think. They either make it worse or, um, allow evil to happen."

"So you're saying—which one are you?"

"I don't know. I tried both. I tried to be an individual. My own ruler. The island, a place like Japan is the perfect model for building character. But islands can be invaded. If we're islands unto ourselves then we're connected islands, like the Florida Keys, sharing real estate…god a business reference…well, I am Jewish. Part Jewish."

She laughed and tried to cover her mouth.

"The other? The Overman, a god? A master of his domain? I don't know what the fuck I'm doing. I just now know the demons inside of me. The ones in need of exorcism or at least a need to be tamed. My desire for amoral pleasure. My nihilistic streak of just letting it all burn and providing matches. The pleasure in getting power from controlling others…well, the only thing I know how to do is to destroy. But maybe there's value in that too? Maybe fear of commitment is the problem. Or maybe God just has other plans. I have no idea how to build. I guess one needs to be humble. I guess it's time to maybe seek out God and bow to his universe knowing we are in control of very little. I don't want to be a devil. But they—I feel that powers that be don't want us to truly feel. To think. Or have children or just…live what used to be normal lives."

"Who is they—oh! The boomers."

I smiled. "Right the boomers. But assigning one group too much power, like Jews or Boomers or white males, just ascribes them power in your mind. Like with cults or religion we always seek to find an evil ruler behind all the suffering. Maybe it's the elites or maybe it's the just the hive mind or the general spirit of the age that flows through us all, who just want to externalize all problems in the name of progress."

"Progress…"

"Right. We always must progress. To what though? The future will take care of itself, I guess. I know I can't run away anymore. But I don't know what I'm running from…I guess I need to find out and at some point—I'll take a stand for something. Hopefully the stand I take, will have some effect. Maybe…"

She grabbed my hand. Squeezed it. Tears slowly rolled down her face. "Jason...you did have an effect. Already. You, um, you saved me. It may not mean much to you but...I—I treated you so...I was such a bitch to you. I'll admit it. I hated you for you wrote—and Adina she was my friend, but I never bothered to, I know you didn't kill her or ever mean to hurt...I'm sorry. You risked...you almost died...for..." she put her face in to her arms and cried loudly. I walked over and put my hand on her shoulder, but she stood up and embraced me in a tight grip, like she didn't want to let me go, her rapid tears moistened my sweatshirt on my shoulder, a touch of saliva creeping from her mouth on to my chest. This wasn't an abstraction or a body on a screen or a construction of my mind that I could tear down at my will. No, no, no, it was physical lamentation of a wounded soul, bruised, battered and fragile.

Actually, words can't express...

I embraced her.

I hugged tighter.

I did what I did. I don't know why.

Over-analysis is a mistake.

Action really trumps everything. It's easy to come to the wrong conclusions—

"Jason."

"Yes?"

"You think way too much."

"Yeah, I know. A lot of time by myself will do that."

"I hate being alone. So..." she tried to wipe the tears from her face. "So...maybe we can help each other out."

"Sure."

I pulled her towards me and held her longer. The sound of jets filled the sky above.

You don't know that, do you?

*

Feelings, feelings. Feelings that betray and destroy but feelings that also give enjoyment and excitement to the dull life...

As Mandy and I walk around the grounds, after our own pick-up game of one-on-one, I grab her hand as we walk back to the barracks. She doesn't fight my grip. I feel the welling up inside me—*let's never separate Mandy. We're bonded through violence; our pact in blood. No one else can understand. Maybe even we can't understand it.* I feel so when she asks "So what did happen?"

How do I tell her about Yu and Kenji, about how they were probably sent on some mission to find Hanako, and that I resembled vaguely some scientist or psychologist who was nice to them as children before they went under the knife, and that I was targeted by Japanese intel because PureLight liked my tweets even though US intel didn't quite approve of making contact—though Mark eventually signed off—and I was the mark to attract, with Yu (or Hanami) willing to use her body, Kenji as her handler, to somehow find her sister who had been taken in by the cult, and I in my inclinations, only made it worse, leading to the murder of Adina, and then somehow they came looking for me or due to my inner state I went looking for them—or maybe I was programmed to go there, a little nudge from Mr. Mark Ultima_Thule himself with his smug grin and statement "Your actions surprised us but still…they helped," meaning they might have just left us for dead, just like PureLight thought they could flip me and find Hanami (or Yu) for them, but either way I participated in this mess. And yeah, it doesn't add up and sounds far-fetched in parts but when has life ever given one a perfect equation with everything perfectly answered and everything seeming perfectly reasonable?

To say I feel a sense of guilt for what this all caused, the Neo-liberal global outrage that has come down on Japan since the explosion in Tokyo—though they insist Mandy and I had nothing to do with it—if it hurts Japan slightly then I'll feel some regret, even though I'll soon be leaving, which honestly is for the better. I feel living here that I'm just polluting the country and the culture I love.

But that's giving myself too much credit.

Being loathsome about the misfortune one causes is just the inverse of bragging about it. In both ways, you're acknowledging your power and superiority. I'm neither powerful nor superior, though I'd like to think myself so.

*

I saw on NHK News Akiko Fujiwara being interviewed, her head now shaved out of deference or just low nutrients given her gaunt physique due to hunger strike. "I don't care what people say about The Master. I don't care about the accusations. He was a great man and his teachings blessed."

It's tough to undo the programming.

But you know that, don't you?

You know about appealing to one's sense of freedom and individual identity thus making it as generic as the faceless mass. Just as you know true

383

freedom is a lonely and isolating experience. An experience I'm actually suited for…

*

But it's tough…especially when you're alone with your thoughts. Mandy and I can't be together all the time. There's the Bible in my room. One of my only things to read, when I have nothing else to do…and I talked to the Protestant Base Chaplain, a down-to-earth guy from Arkansas. He was amicable enough, comforting, but at the same time didn't have all the answers. However, he gave me a book with collections of Alexander Solzhenitsyn's writings. And I realized the same thing Solzhenitsyn realized: There is no great guru, prophet or elder, an Obi-Wan Kenobi or mystical negro, to expound it all, to give us a moment of *satori*. No, no, no, one has to learn and figure out things on their own, take the journey themselves though markers and guides may appear to point the way forward. The wise sage's in stories are usually just fictional creations of the artist in dialogue with himself.

But I also learned from Solzhenitsyn that our course is not fixed. We're not just computers discarded upon upgrades presenting themselves. And that's a relief. But it also means we will encounter hardships and evils directly affecting us—and then and only then must we take a stand.

But I try to focus on my sense of excitement and rest, the true new world dawning on my horizon. Mandy has noticed it too as we talked. But I felt the same way at PureLight too before it all fell apart.

But in a way, I understand the feeling of relief Abraham felt once he realized his son Issac wasn't to be sacrificed. He felt determined—locked in—to put his son on the altar, thinking it God's will. Yet…he stopped when the angel ordered him. How must he have felt, dedicated to one course of action, a certain fate, even one he dreaded but performed with duty, how must he have felt when he listened to the angel and realized a new world of possibility open to him?

I suppose Christianity continued what started with Abraham: There isn't heroic death but rather redemption after death.

Don't worry it's not that type of story.

But after certain events, past events take on different meanings. For the Apostles, the Crucifixion had one meaning on Friday and a very different one on Sunday. First, they were hiding in fear then they were preaching to 3000. In a way, I feel a sense of resurrection. The same Jason…but different…renewed.

But this may all be me trying to explain and rationalize my actions.

I care what you think, after all.

*

No more conversations with forced political musings. No John Galt-like monologues.

Just me.

My thoughts.

It's not a confession.

Maybe it is.

Who gives a shit?

I'm not like the writers of old who took the full journey, fought battles of every sort, then wrote something as afterword to a fully lived life. But no one has an ideal situation...

I'll just write.

Analyze me through this all you want. Write your papers no one will read. You're midgets looking up towards a giant, trying to bring him down with all your combined yet puny might.

But really that's the heart of it, a heart of a lot of struggle these days: I'm significant yet no one realizes it. Why won't anyone recognize my genius? A question that is a constant source of my frustration and maybe the source of my nihilistic urge to see it all burn.

Maybe I just have to do the hard work to prove myself.

Maybe I'm just lazy.

Maybe I'm just too different.

Maybe I'm more like everyone else than I realize.

I thought my intellectual spelunking was over. I thought that I found the light that was manipulating the shadows on the cave walls. I thought wrong.

I just found myself in another cave, where the sinister Director of Photography tells the gaffer where to adjust the lights accordingly so it's just enough to spurn us in to unending conflict with one another. And who benefits from this chaos?

My notes say I need to emphasize how there's an elite that rules and will do everything to maintain that rule. Call them white males, call them Jews, call them globalists, call them the US Empire, call them bankers, call them tech moguls, call them reptilians. The techno power structure will promote its doctrines, selectively emphasize a set of moralities and narratives to maintain power, just like all historical powers. There's always going to be elites. Numbers never distribute with equality. Neither does wrath, and the elites are just much at risk of destructive termination as I—maybe even more so (which is why they do everything to keep a grip on power, sometimes with an iron fist of tyranny or with prosperity—or both!—but as the grip tightens, the power leaks like sand from a fist). One must learn to navigate and live within the structures, trying to minimize and avoid the evils but utilize the good it provides (THINK Christians in the Roman period who utilized the roads, commerce and common tongue to their advantage while also suffering persecution and avoiding pagan sacrifices).

In our global Neo-liberal Democratic age, where getting enough votes is the key to power, politics becomes the religion, ideology its dogma and marketing its means, the modern commercial world working hand in hand with the political. But rather than trying to give life, it demands passionate dedication but returns no heavenly nirvana, coarsening and hardening the soul, destroying any need or desire for nuance, dialogue or recognizing degrees of disagreement. No, no, no, just dichotomies. And it overtakes the individual like a demon, hijacking our identity, holding it hostage for its own ends, only helped by the modern tech oligarchy.

And the establishment classes of politicians, money and hierophants could care less.

And the modern order of consumerism and politics, creating consumerist politics, is probably the biggest cult of all.

It tries to hold our inner life hostage but in the most sophisticated ways, appealing to our deepest vanity, thinking all decisions are our own as we build a temple to freedom in our minds rarely considering it may be a mirage.

But it's better not to dwell on the invisible armies you've been led to think are seeking your destruction and give all your attention to them. THINK Jesus warning his fellow Jews about the disastrous consequences of picking a fight with Rome and his mission to defeat the "ruler of this world", which wasn't Caesar but the accusing demonic undertow that pulls all men in to the pit.

Men like me.

Yet they killed Jesus for such talk (amongst other things). And Jerusalem burned, the Abomination That Causes Desolation realized.

But the Gospels were written after the Jewish-Roman war, so it served as a bias confirming contextual framing device. The Jews found a way to survive in the diaspora and the Christians also dispersed throughout the empire, the Gentiles slowly embracing their announcement, the message morphing in to new meanings from its Jewish roots, taking on the character of its host ("Rome" now means the Vatican after all) and Jesus' own warnings becoming a general apocalyptic pronouncement, the historical and particular becoming ahistorical and universal, thus causing its own conflicts and misunderstandings giving rise to the likes of Marcionites, Docetists, Arians and Gnostics in general.

But I know these things because they survived in some form of record. Societies and civilizations may fall or burn but their ashes always provide a soil for the next one to grow in its place.

And historical disputes are inconsequential to the never-ending mental and spiritual battles to which I must confront every day. Yet, here I am without phone or PC, alone with my own thoughts, semi-incarcerated, and I've never felt as free in my life. It feels like grace. Meaning there is truth in the texts of my spiritual and racial ancestors, meaning they all survived the fires of history for a reason. The words of Jesus still cut like a life-giving sword.

But it's not that type of story. Really, it isn't.

But why have we become so corrupted as to sneer and recoil upon encountering such stories?

*

I remember those words, *Kenji is coming* (sorry I lied; had to write them one more time) but more for reference as I reflected on everything that happened after it. And when my TV breaks up in the room, CNN disappearing, I think of the psychic distortion fields.

But reflection alone can't move reality, only passion or love that creates will to act. We externalize our hopes just like we externalize our demons.

But I'm too reflective to let myself revel in passion. I know I told Mandy I would stop trying to think but it's hard to break conditioning (as stated above). But I think I have a capacity to love, but to love properly one must be sufficient in themselves.

Not that is matters at the moment.

*

Some might say "Jason isn't like that" or "that isn't the Jason I know" but they really don't know. They haven't dived in to my soul and explored its depths just as I haven't theirs. They've only seen its surface and seek to understand and reconcile its varied reflections.

Some might understand why I rescued Mandy instead of going with the plan of PureLight (who I seemed to be in complete agreement with). Maybe I was weak. Maybe I was a cuck. Maybe it was my nature. The void in people that kill, because they have no other option, or rather no inner mechanism to

387

halt their actions isn't present in me. Or rather there is something present. Maybe there's a failsafe within my genetic code that returns to default factory settings, my operant conditioning being white knight. I suppose I should be happy. But we all do things we don't understand. Decisions are not based on logic alone or pure information. We're not flesh machines like futurists would have us believe. We behave on emotion (which can be manipulated), on memories that are constantly be re-arranged and re-framed by feelings from fear to love to excitement to malaise triggered by outside and inside events that engage with them. We are anything but automatons with a pre-programmed course.

*

There is no virtue in being weak. Even St. Paul himself said in weakness he finds strength, a stoic paradox. The course of society today is a weakening of will, especially aggression and moral fortitude (of which I barely have any) because it either sells more stuff making one a prisoner to comfort but also makes one more passive, easy to control. In the modern world, courage is cancelled out by conformity. Mark is right (as much as I hate to say it): Power comes from giving pleasure.

How is one to navigate this modern world then?

The scariest thought (to me) is the world is fine the way it is, that it's where it needs to be. But no time or era was or is perfect in an imperfect world. No, no, no—the scarier thought is I was meant for this epoch, made for it, and I must confront it. There is no escape to Middle Earth, Feudal Japan, Merry Old England or Ancient Rome though all sorts of media (content) try to take us there, to that mind space of ideal worlds without our modern complications, but a hollow experience nonetheless. But maybe there's an even more frightening idea that undergirds our malaise and FOMO—a world that is moving, changing and unyielding regardless of us, regardless of me.

But trying to do my own thing...being the supreme sovereign fenced-in individual is just as destructive and deadly as rabid forced communalism. Both seek to put to death identities that are important to many (group identity for one, individual identity for the other). Both need homogenized nothingness to thrive (for the radical individualist, the open borders open commerce world state, for the corporatist, the group think masses).

However, in the West, we're not in gulags yet save the ones of our mind. Perhaps that's the deadliest prison of all...

Maybe focusing on the individual, results in its negation. If we (I) turn inward, only seeking our (my) own pleasure and leisure and my will, then I in turn am needing of things from others, like a woman's embrace or someone to make some content (oh, content, content, content) so compromises are made to attain these things. We (I) give away our principles for a kiss or a LIKE. Our never-ending desire for pleasure and approval leads to others having power over us.

But do we find individuality by turning outward? Is this what John the Baptist meant by saying "I must become less"? By seeking God's pleasure (or approval or purpose), rather than that of men—this is what helps build and give someone "character", the true mark of a true individual? And from this outflow comes selfless love and sacrifice…is that individuality's ultimate expression?

Could the most rebellious act in this age be to suppress the egotistic drive in all its tech guises of social media and the like, to shrink back from themselves from the mirror or camera lens, deferring to God's will of whether they step on history's stage or not?

I'm getting ahead of myself.

It's not that type of story.

I've no desire to be an inward ascetic.

And maybe in its perverted way, narcissism brings positive outcomes to both individual and societal levels. The bodybuilder putting selfies on Instagram inspires someone to lose weight, a (cam)whore provides desperate men a form of pleasure while providing herself an income, the artist whose terrible egotistical paintings provide at least (derisive) laughter, a developer constructs a tower to his ego that provides construction jobs and office space and lastly a man tyrannizes his staff with his warped sense of reality that leads to the birth of a life-altering technology. History is full of such outward looking genius. But said genius collapses under the weight of the hubris that made it great. A feature not a bug. In a way, we admire and look to the men of industry, whether they be Howard Hughes, Donald Trump, Tommy Wiseau, Walt Disney or Steve Jobs because they provide a face to grand vision, even if its failure, as opposed to faceless corporate boards.

But enough second-rate Kierkegaard.

And a conversion like Paul on the Damascus Road is usually a re-framing of what one desires around a different perspective, a new way forward. But I don't know what I want and Paul noted the dividing wall of hostility had been "broken down", and in a way, as both half Gentile and Jew I'm a representation of it, but I am nothing but hostility…and fear. But true love casts out fear…have I found this true love, I wonder?

*

But one can't sit stewing. One must do something every morning. Thinking alone is meaningless.

Gnosis, having knowledge, a secret knowledge, you hold to yourself, to make yourself feel above others is quite an amoral spirit. It feels good to possess or acquire parts of. We get an arousal. But one must be fully dedicated to this spirit. Not flesh or matter. It doesn't necessarily have to be fleshed out. Knowledge—information—and spirit become more important than life. The phone more important than the passenger next to you on the train…

We talk about post-modernism, how all traditional structures are in an ideational, even spiritual realm, and how they define reality and need to be deconstructed…yet the experiences are very real. They are not abstract or intellectual. It's backwards. Intellectualizing experiences or events or even stories are a form of paralyzing observation and produces only stultifying action.

This can also give rise to self-importance. "As long as my spirit and mind is pure, I don't care what happens."

Cyberspace in a way is a very pure Gnosticism. Spirit and mind detached from reality, reveling in the physical chaos it brings whether it be through a disastrous Tinder hook-up or a troll campaign or a doxx or an election. We live in an age of social platforms created by asocial people. Technology is a nerd medium; an engineering attempt to flatten three-dimensional experience in order to understand, codify and streamline it by an industry largely founded by utopian hippies. But not everything can be coded and still I'm hesitant to give up the comforts it brings. No, no, no, they smartly appealed to our spirit. Our spirit of needing comfort and our spirit of vanity and just turning us inward on pure spirit in general, a form of technical meditation, thinking we have a community though we're alone.

But the divine spirit itself is useful. It can help you cross physical restrictions of time, place and self, and find common spirits in others for better or worse. But it needs to be grounded in the physical.

Too much time in the esoteric will just lead to the complete disregard of flesh and form and the world it inhabits. In short, physical destruction from neglect. But completely indulging the flesh, total nihilism, a complete focus on

390

materiality whether it be race or the latest color TV, will also lead to destruction as it has no regard for others. But in a way the polarized worlds of exclusive spirit and exclusive flesh are repellent partners united in pushing civilization towards ruination, both with a disregard to the essence of life (balance). One wants to completely transcend physical space, therefore making flesh ready for all varieties of mutilation, the other wants to suborn physical space with total indifference for its inhabitants. Transhumanism and sub-humanism are feuding brothers in a race towards annihilation. Our organizational hive brain has become too left side dominant, self-contained in its own creations, abstractions built upon abstractions, layer upon layer, conclusion upon conclusion, all a house of sand without proper right side support and connection, making the world flat and lacking depth, a societal autism, all fueled by that good mind cocaine that is dopamine that the left side is dependent on, being pushed by the narco traffickers of social media and tech. It becomes easier to drop bombs, build gulags, concentration camps and commit executions in the killing fields when it is all seen through a monitor, 20,000 feet away from the destruction, or just 5 feet away of physical distance but a million feet away in emotional distance, try as we might to ignore or disregard that nagging, unsettling feeling we can't name.

But pure reductionism is also a left-brain habit. A better illustration would be like that fall day, I remember it was raining and I won't even ask if you know about this incident because I know you don't know, right? Adina and I were at the Edion on the north end of Hondori near the Peace Park, she in immediate need of a laptop and I agreeing to help translate for her. Why did I agree to help her? I found her annoying, yes, but I didn't hate her, I really didn't hate anyone, but I was in the city with nothing else to do…in the middle of a Kai10 board discussion waiting for a reply…when she texted me, "Where's the best place to buy a laptop?"

And I replied "An electronics store."

And she immediately replied, "Haha, very funny. But where in the city?"

"Just order from Amazon."

"I need a new one. Like literally RN. I can't wait. I have a project."

"Try an Edion."

"Where's an Edion?"

"There's 1 in Hondori near Peace Park."

"R U in the city?"

"Affirmative."

"Can you affirm that you can meet me there? I need translator?"

"I'm busy."

"PLS."

":thinking_face:"

"I'll buy coffee :coffee_cup: My treat."

":thinking_face: :thinking_face:"

"Ur going to make me beg…"

"Might help."

":pray:"

":tired_face: fine."

Well, you know the text conversation.

But you don't know when she met me in her black The North Face windbreaker and tight red t-shirt that was low-cut enough to expose her cleavage, her thick hair slightly unkempt, frazzled by the rain amplified by her freckle face sans make-up and skinny jeans that didn't make her look all that skinny but it all gave her a sort of charm and for reasons I can't understand, maybe being amid the delicate Japanese women who carried umbrellas and walked in tiny steps as they tried to negotiate puddles in their heels, her relaxed look relaxed my guard.

And you don't know outside the Edion, the first thing I said to her was: "You need me for translating right? Not haggling?"

"Translation. Why I would need you for haggling?"

"You're more Jewish than me."

"Correct."

"But Japanese don't haggle."

"They don't?"

"So no Jewish to Japanese haggling, m'kay?"

After her smile and headshake we walked in to Edion. We were all business, as we looked and Adina deciding on a Toshiba Portege. But after I notified the salesman and he went to get it, I started to look at my phone…screen away from Adina…saw the Kai10 post with some libertarian harping about Nazis…I heard Adina say something…she asked "Jason? What did he say? Do they have it in stock?"

I put my phone up…

"Um, yeah, they have it in stock but…"

I let it hang.

She put her hand on my forearm. "What?"

"They don't sale to Jews. Strict policy."

"Stop."

"Don't worry, I convinced them I was German. Said I was a descendent of Goebbels."

"You…" She slapped my shoulder.

"They've agreed to sell. You can thank my Aryan persuasive skills later."

She rolled her eyes again but with a smile…again.

At the cashier, she pulled out her Fluffy Fluffy Cinnamoroll wallet and I said, "You bust my balls about a Pokemon pencil but look at that!"

The way she looked like she'd been caught then looked away and mumbled, "It was cute…and cheaper that the Gucci wallet I was thinking of getting…"

"And you say the Jew is strong with me?"

"I didn't say that. Avi did."

As we walked out, she held up the paper shopping bag with the blue and yellow Edion colors holding her Toshiba and said, "Here, you can hold this."

I stared at it without motioning. "And here I thought you just wanted me to translate."

"Well…you're good for more than that."

"Too bad Max isn't here for that."

"But you are here." She held out the bag. "Come on. Please." The tilt of her head and her cleavage rising and lowering…

I took the bag.

"What a gentleman."

We started walking towards the Peace Park for no particular reason and just outside the Lawson's *konbini* Adina asked "Where's a good cafe?" but before I could answer a big man in black suit and no neck bumped in to me. I nearly fell back but stayed on my feet, but he dropped a plastic bag with a couple of drinks. "*Shitsuree Shimasu!*" he said bowing. I noticed a petit woman in glasses and black business suit and skirt that emphasized some of her rolls, stood next him also bowing and loudly declaring "*Sumimasen*". Adina immediately picked up the bottles and bent over…I glanced at her cleavage. I said "*Iie*" more than once as they bowed and apologized and kept on walking towards the alleyway across from the convenience store.

"They said they're sorry," I said.

"I figured," she said looking at her bag.

"*So ka…*"

"Great you saved my laptop…" Adina noticed my looking towards the briskly walking couple that looked all business.

"What?" Adina said.

I pointed in the direction of the Love Hotel nestled at the end of the alley. "What?"

"I think I know where they're headed."

"Huh?"

"Look."

"What is…"

"A Love Hotel."

"No."

"They're going to make sex."

"Stop. What?"

"It's business time."

"No."

"Look. Can't you read…"

"Japanese? No I can't read. It's why you're here?"

"*So desu ne*," I said then looked at her cleavage. "Maybe you should take some lessons."

"Lessons in what? The sex world of Japan?"

"Best way to learn about a culture."

The couple was near the door.

"So…are they going…" they walked in. "OH! They so went in!" Her chest heaved with excitement as she covered her mouth.

"And have the drinks for pillow talk."

"O. M. G."

"Who do you think is on top in that arrangement. I mean, he's kind of big, she's kind of tiny…"

"Missionary is totally out of the question."

"Right. Totally."

"That's all oddly exciting." She grasped her hands then looked up to me, chest still heaving.

I felt my dick groan. Crude but true.

And it just came out. The words: "I can think of something more exciting." :smirk:

But Adina smirked too.

"You're probably just lying to me. Like you did in the store."

"Aryan subversion? First I heard it called that."

"Call it whatever you want."

"So I need to prove it too you?"

"How will you prove it?"

I started walking towards the Love Hotel, breathing heavy at the excitement I might get laid, a random hook-up, but also the audacity of my action, like reading those posts by Justin Bangs. But then I realized I still had her laptop and hadn't said a word. Second guessing. I stopped in the seat of fast traffic, but felt soft flesh bump in to my arm. Adina. "Why'd you stop?"

"I have, um, your, your laptop."

"I know. You forgot you're carrying it for me?"

"No, um, just…" I kept on walking.

Outside the door, we stood there looking at each other. She tried looking in through the tinted glass door. "Can't see much?" I asked.

"Not really."

"I guess we need to go in so you'll believe me."

She smiled and shrugged her shoulders.

I opened the door. She looked at me then looked inside and slowly stepped across the threshold. Inside the gaudy interior, I said, "I suppose you need to see a room now, just for confirmation." And she blushed.

Afterwards, we walked aimlessly in the early evening of the Peace Park, damp from the ceased rains and a luminous quiet as the street lamps reflected off the wet paths and river. We said little, I still carried her bag, looking around grunting as couples took selfies in front of the A-Bomb Dome.

"What?" Adina asked. First time she said anything since she put her clothes back on.

"Huh?"

"What's wrong?"

"Just thinking…"

"About us?"

"No, uh…" maybe I was but I said, "No, um, you know this is like, um memorial to mass destruction yet people are taking selfies smiling probably going to post on Inst—"

"Jason…"

"I mean…it's kind of…"

"Jason."

"What?"

"You think too much."

"Huh?"

"I said you…"

"I heard you."

"Can you hear me out on this?"

"What's 'this'?"

"This is…look, let's just keep this our secret, okay?"

"You mean sex?"

"Yeah, sex," she cracked an apologetic smile then looked down. "I mean, it's just sex…but…"

I looked down for a moment too.

She then started shaking her head, "Actually, forget it—I'm sorry…maybe we should talk about—I owe you a coffee right?"

"No, no, no…it's okay. Our secret. I promise."

"Our secret. Right. Thanks."

"If anyone ever says anything…just…" I shrugged my shoulders.

"Yeah?"

"Just tell them I'm a Nazi. You'd never sleep with a Nazi, right?"

"I don't know. That might make you sexier."

"Like sleeping with your oppressor's type of sexy?"

"Yeah, kind of like that movie, was it German? Have you heard of *Black Book*? Is that what's it called?"

"I have. Hold on." I pulled out my phone and went to Wikipedia.

"OMG you nerd."

"*Black Book*. 2006. Directed by Paul Verhoeven. DUTCH not German…"

"Stop…"

"Written by Gerard Soeteman and Verhoeven with cinematography by Karl Walter Lindenlaub."

"God you're such a nerd but that makes you cute."

"Reminds me about that movie *Masculin-Feminin* where Jean-Pierre Leaud walks in to the projectionist's room to give him the aspect ratio specs…"

"I don't know what you're talking about."

I pull out my phone again. "You don't know *Masculin-Feminin*? 1966. Written and Directed by Jean-Luc Godard…"

"ENOUGH," she said smiling. "Take me to the bus station and tell me all about it."

As her bus arrived at the SOGO bus station, I handed her laptop bag but she said, "Wait," and ran to the vending machines against the wall. She then ran back and held out a can of coffee. "Trade ya."

I handed her the bag and took the can. Boss Coffee with cream. "You didn't need to buy me coffee, I think…"

"I'm not a ho. I didn't trade sex for translation."

"I didn't say."

"A promise is a promise. I promised you coffee."

"Right."

"Friends keep promises. And we are friends, right?"

"Right…"

She smiled, put her hand on my forearm and walked on the bus trying not to look back at me.

I'm sure she lamented that fantasy of a hook-up with the enemy didn't match the reality. But I don't know. Maybe she didn't regret anything.

But I do know that I regret I couldn't keep my promise.

But that's only in retrospect.

At that moment, immediately after the bus left, I turned to my phone and returned to thread on Kai10 that led to me replying "Hitler did nothing wrong."

But you know that, don't you?

*

But isn't there nothing more human than to be flawed, contradictory—in short, a mess in need of some grace? Trying to ultimately transcend and detach from flesh, from matter, the human, results in the end of grace, the end of humanity. Maybe I'm being overdramatic. But maybe the ruins of Hiroshima Bank at *Heiwa-koen* says I'm not being dramatic enough: The A-bomb, the very symbol of destruction, splitting the very building block of nature, the atom (don't @ me about protons and neutrons), ends up destroying everything. I can't help but feel our social bonding shield, the strong force that helps bound together the social atom, is permanently damaged. What dark energy will be released by the societal mass lost as it moves at immeasurable speeds? Will we see the mushroom cloud or will we be too busy blinded by the light, pathetically trying to shield ourselves or just looking at our phones? One question I pondered living in Hiroshima.

*

I don't know why I was chosen for survival. Why I saw the face of Jesus. Maybe it was just my past revisiting me or calling me, light from my dim cultural memory attempting to provide assistance. I'm influenced by Protestant views of Christianity as well as modern, secular pop-psychology, focused heavily on words, rather than the mystery of The Host. I carry it like luggage or an albatross. But we must take our cross and bear it.

If I were a Japanese in a reverse situation, caught up in a Christian cult stateside, would I seek the Buddhism and Shintoism of my heritage in the aftermath? I can't even begin to consider it since the religious cultural dynamic of the Japanese is different than my own (much like when Americans start practicing Eastern religions, it's through a paradigm of Western style devotion). I'm not here to understand then explain everything. It's not that type of story. Just as there's cultural limits to understanding Japanese past the technical aspects of its language, so it is with life itself. We hear a dog's bark differently; Fuji film had a more subdued color palette than the brighter Kodak. We see life in a different hue and hear it at a different pitch. But you know that, don't you?

But do you know, that it requires faith to move forward knowing that the future is a shadow even when some things seem arranged in your favor?

This is not cheap Jungian synchronicity—no, no, no, I know I'm not the center of the universe, I know the sun doesn't revolve around me with everything aligning *pour moi*.

I'm the one rotating around God's light choosing to participate in events, my virtues and my vices helping or hurting the proceedings.

I'm merely a player on the stage, not knowing when the play will end.

*

I decided to make Yu my world. Put her on the pedestal, everyone else be damned. Even with all the knowledge about male/female relations, all that reading—really reading all that stuff only makes you fool yourself. You're the mark.

I loved an image but I'm neither the first nor the last to fall for a mutually projected illusion nor love myself in the nearness of beauty.

*

Yu…her beauty still haunts me. The dream I just had…I'm in a post-apocalyptic Walmart, the fluorescents flicking about a drab queue of people in uniform grays looking for goods, the Ridley Scott directed Apple *1984* Mac launch spot but in an end times consumerist setting. And then I see her. Her clothes are black, almost shimmering, not gold but she stands with Kenji next to her. I immediately walk up to her but we say nothing, no exchange, but she's

398

aware of my presence and not protesting—in fact she leads me, in to another room, a room that is refrigerated but the same drab grays and fluorescents dominate now, Ridley Scott directed *1984* Mac launch meat locker edition in full color. But she quickly leads me to another room and—BAM! Full of life, noise, blacks and golds, a Korean Vegas as shot by Paul Verhoeven circa 1995 and how do I know it's Korean? Because K-Pop blasts over the speakers as girls with gold tight pants and black tops with a gold streak across simulate doing a backstroke on the floor while others are held up by topless Korean beefcakes painted gold.

And then I woke up.

And nothing flickered. Not even my television.

But I still remember it.

It lingers.

It was gaudy but beautiful. Kind of like her.

*

Another dream: I was on a tour bus, a girl driving. Thin, brunette, with wide gentle smile. She asked me which route I wanted to take as we drove through narrow passages, up impossibly steep hills that progressively inclined. But I didn't care. She was happy to be with me.

*

There's something to be said for beauty. Even if the moment is fleeting. Maybe we tend to overrate the power of art, the elite transmitting its values to the masses for conformity and the artists themselves overplaying their importance. But there's worse things in the world. It's not a religious experience though it can assist in providing one.

Like the old churches—well, the older buildings in general, stand as a reminder, as do the Shinto Shrines standing in nature. The *torii* of Itsukushima planted in the *Seto Naikai* dedicated to an entire island, venerating the creation knowing the humans passing through them are only temporary—it all calls out to us to honor the eternal, knowing we're just drops in the waterfall of history and continue the tradition going, rather than only thinking of now. The vulgar now.

But maybe vulgarity serves a purpose. The old world had a violence and ugliness that needed beauty in the realm of religion and architecture. It needed a call to something higher…or rather in the midst of sorrow, it created a need to find and give hope.

Then life improved. The dirt disappeared, and art took it upon itself to remind everyone of vulgarity, the grotesque, the violent and the dangers of self-seriousness. I live in the latter period but I desire the former. But it's no use wanting for an age past.

Beauty in itself, as an idol to be worshipped, or its offspring, style, lack depth in and of themselves. Like drugs, they'll eventually stop giving their buzz. But put it as a puzzle piece in the greater picture of the heavenly grand design, not the lynchpin or capstone, but to be enjoyed and revered as you look at the greater picture the puzzle displays.

We try to attain the image of truth through science, religion, the arts and philosophy. People see and read then interpret their complex reality through these mediums and then try to form reality from these interpretations, a cycle of creation inspiring us, then us inspiring creation. It works beautifully when it is in harmony. A series of engagements and inspirations, flowing, bouncing and reflecting off in to and off one another.

It's never perfect but whatever is?

Nothing is an end to itself (at least for eternity).

*

Feelings ungirded is destruction, a spoiled entitled need to be recognized, world be damned. Intellect ungirded is de(con)struction too. To the have the harmonious whole is love. As Augustine said love sees the "whole at once" because no man should imagine God with just the lust of his eyes (no, I haven't read Augustine, just a passage I found in a philosophy article).

I saw a love, felt a love, not a lustful love but a love I can't explain…when I reached for Mandy. Dear Mandy, will you ever understand? Will I?

*

And yes, they gave me some temporary internet access to help research and provide clarity. On a lark, I visited the Facebook and Instagram pages of Adina. Aside from the posts about hate and political platitudes and messages to the deceased, I see her with a selfie holding the Fluffy Fluffy Cinnamoroll doll I bought for her.

*

"Kenji is coming" (I know, I wrote those words again) is just a fixed point for me. I wasn't the root cause but I decided to play along and fight against the invisible armies that I thought were taking civilization in a path towards certain doom.

400

It's human error and arrogance to lock events in to a chain they weren't looking for and reduce the profundity of events to a flattened deformed metal, our universe diminished to human line of sight.

Fatalism is a mistake.

But tying in beauty, God and Jesus himself…I think of the drummer Yoshiki who would almost die after a concert performance…or the artist or writer who toils without little reward. Why? Its presumptuous to compare the two, but Jesus was a model since the beginning of the world (according to John). He's supposed to represent its nature. If he didn't sacrifice and die, there wouldn't be a resurrection. If the artist doesn't create then what? Some might suffer, like the immediate families and friends of a frustrated creator who just uses his time to drink coffee while surfing Kai10 thinking it all pointless, being an emotional burden to everyone surrounding him.

We can sacrifice ourselves or sacrifice others.

But sacrifice requires faith.

But if we have this faith we can move forward in sacrifice knowing there are no fixed points in the future, only potentialities. I THINK of Yamamoto-sensei being able to learn and teach English while his father was forced to hide his light under a bushel. One generation the door closed, the next generation the door wide open. There may be moments of doom awaiting us but there may be moments of grace too.

Art points us toward potentialities too. We make it for one reason, hoping for it to be perceived or received one way but it may result in something different and unexpected (THINK Vincent Van Gogh). At that moment, we may feel forsaken but that's when the work bursts forth with a new and unexpected life. A life of its own, that gives life to others.

*

Kind of like the new relationship that developed around Mandy and I.

They allowed us to watch some movies, under supervision. I watched *Eyes Wide Shut*, *Demons*, *Tenebrae*, *Phenomen*a and much pestering the canon of David Fincher. Mandy joined me (she'd never seen his movies before).

MOMNDF: What was her favorite?

JRK: Se7en. Yu's favorite too…at least that's what she said.

MOMNDF: Happens like that sometimes.

JRK: Why are you here again? I thought you left…

MOMNDF: I never leave. You can quiet me down but I'll eventually speak up again.

But after a while all the blood and guts in the films left me numb. So, we watched Godard, Antonioni, Tarkovsky, and *Jeff Who Lives at Home* which made us both cry (not proud to admit, just trying to be truthful).

One evening we watch the jets lift off from the runway, and I look at the mountains of Iwakuni, the castle sitting atop as a speck in the distance, one ancient warrior tradition looking upon another, and I'm thinking and thankful of life in the whole. The beauty of the view adds to it. The jets lift off with a loud roar. Mandy puts her head on my shoulder. The sun sets. I feel at rest.

"I really don't know much about Japan. But after talking to you, I got curious but now…I'm leaving…I'm jealous you get to stay."

I'm not jealous.

After she left I even received a letter from her. You know that, I'm sure you've read it as I shared it with the shrink from Tokyo who I'm forced to talk to almost daily. I'll just note the passage I think of import: "It's also weird saying (meant writing oops) in fact, I'm shocked myself but I miss you. After our shared experience and all we talked about, everything and everyone seems so plain LOL (do you write even "LOL" in long hand?). My conversations now, here at 'home', are boring and predictable (I think you'd use a word like "banal"). I feel like we have a secret we can't tell anyone else and even if we did, no one would believe it or at least understand it…" ending with "I hope we can talk again sometime. Love, Mandy." I got the letter just a day before I started writing about our time at the compound. Left me feeling high. Kind of changed my perspective on things earlier. We've always been holding hands, I realized; the grip tighter the further we're apart.

Bad metaphors aside, I wonder—no, I worry—If getting closer would loosen the embrace.

*

The black nurse, the first person I saw when I woke up on the base, her name is Crystal, from Wilmington, North Carolina. Do you know Crystal? Her hair was short and always pulled back. I noticed black spots on her arms as she took my vitals weekly. But after Mandy left I was happy to see her smiling when she walked in my room. "We should probably stop meeting like this," I said.

"Maybe we will one day."

"At least I know I'm alive every time I see you…"

And on and on. She asked me about Japan and good places to visit on the weekend as well as how to say certain phrases. It was pleasant conversation. No, we didn't fall in love and fight the racial protestations of our respective families as we stood strong. It's not that type of story. We just enjoyed each other's company for the five minutes we saw each other.

*

They gave me back some of the personal effects that I had from my apartment. I realized then that I would never see my apartment again and maybe even Japan at large. One item being of particular note was the letter Yamamoto-sensei wrote me. I know you have read it.

But one passage had particular effect on me. "I felt emotion flow through me as I thought about you Jason. The way you would walk with me and talk, like no other English teacher. I feel you understand *Aun no Kokyu*. I cannot even explain or translate. I have reached limits of my English! But that brings me joy. You can feel something that can't be taught or explained, and it is only something I can understand in my heart. You have so much potential waiting to explode like a beautiful firework that brings makes everyone smile with awe just like I smile thinking about our talk."

I'm not afraid to admit I cried upon reading. A letter I received so coldly now deeply affected me in different situation and state of mind. It felt like grace.

It's not that type of story, I know.

*

As I surfed the internet for research for all this, whatever this is, I logged on to Kai10. There was no Ultima_Thule save for one post about his doxx with a link to the *NewsGrind* story: "Meet the Single Nazi Provocateur Hotel Clerk from Branson, Missouri,"—and no, it wasn't Mark. But you know that, don't you?

I also noticed all the guys like OingoBoinGoy were gone. Disappeared in to the cybervoid. Justin Bangs deleted all his tweets and went to India to meditate while Scott Nash announced he was studying Kabbalah after his co-host Jimena did an interview with *NewsGrind* claiming he was "a sexist and a racist" getting him banned from YouTube, Facebook, Twitter and his sub-Reddit shut down, and then the revelation she used to be a webcam girl under the *nom de plume* "LatinaHeartCock" with tweets in the variation of "I would love to get smashed by some black cock today" and "Who is going to cum on my big titties?" while new e-personalities appeared, both anonymous and

403

namefag. One of them, a blonde Iowan called Jenny Hawkeye stated she had "researched" PureLight and did a 100-part tweet thread about (TL;DR) how they were the target of a Globalist cabal because they were trying to open the eyes of the Japanese and world at large. OFC there were bald and tank topped boomer men replying "Thanks for the hard work and keeping us informed." And these posts spilled on to Kai10 with their own threads. All half-truths and speculations, some short like "PureLight dindu nuffin'" or longer ones speculating "Even if PureLight is nefarious, there is good that could come of this. The arrest of their leader and crackdown on operations helps expose to the world the true (((rulers))) and shows how frightened they are." I logged in anonymously to post a reply but Mark quickly got smart to it.

"STOP THAT SHIT! YOU'RE DONE!"

"But what about the truth?"

"No one cares about the truth."

And I lost my internet privileges.

And they forced me to talk to the shrink more and he made me fill out a long description he wanted in free form and free association to describe my experiences. I'm unsure if it was for intel purposes or just for him. But I tried to cover all my bases.

*

INT. WALLED ROOM—NIGHT

JASON sits at a desk as MARK sits across from him and slides him a notebook.

JASON

What's this?

MARK

You need to write

JASON

Write what?

MARK

Everything.

Jason sits in SILENCE.

MARK (CONT'D)

Everything that happened. They
want to know.

JASON

Want to know what?

MARK

They want to know what
happened. Who, what, when,
where, why and how.

JASON

I've told you everything. I've
already written, done
interviews…

MARK

I know. We need more. I'll be
honest. Japanese intel isn't
being forthright about their
activity. We need your
perspective.

JASON

Can't you just use what I wrote
for the shrink?

405

MARK

That was unintelligible and
confusing. He concluded you
were an isolated self-hating
Jew who fucked over women to
get revenge on his mother while
at the same time putting the
exotic other on a pedestal.

JASON

That's a little Freudian.

MARK

Is he wrong?

JASON

No. I...writing...I fucking hate
writing...

MARK

I thought you were an artiste.
I figured you know how to do
basic writing. Maybe all those
arty flicks you watched with
Mandy warped your creative
simplicity.

JASON

How'd you—never mind.

MARK

Good you're learning. Maybe
you'll learn you're not going

406

anywhere until you give us what
we want.

                    JASON

But I...

                    MARK

FUCK THIS! WRITE!

                    JASON

But—

                    MARK

It's not negotiable. You've
learned the score. I mean, I
could get you a book on how to
write.

                    JASON

Fuck you Mark.

                    MARK

Now that we've established you
care what I think, I would
really care if you gave us—me
in particular—the most
straightforward A-to-B story of
your journey.

                    JASON

Something comprehensive?

MARK

As comprehensive as you want
but keep the bullshit to a
minimum.

JASON

You care about no bullshit?

MARK

I do care.

JASON

I know.

MARK

Funny. Write. It's simple. It
just needs a beginning, hook,
middle build and ending.

JASON

I know how to write—

MARK

Don't forget the inciting
incident.

JASON

It's not that simp—

MARK

Quiet.

JASON

What?

MARK

Be fucking quiet. Kenji is coming.

JASON

Hub?

MARK

Kenji, remember him?

JASON

Of course I—

MARK

Shhh. I said quiet. I don't want him to see you.

MARK looks at JASON and points at the PAPER while opening the DOOR to leave.

MARK (QUIETLY)

Write. And keep it inoffensive.

Door closes. Jason sits there alone with a pen and notebook. He notices KENJI walking by the door as Mark obstructs his view near the WINDOW.

JASON (MUTTERING)

Kenji is coming...keep it inoffensive...fuck you Mark.

You wanted the story, I gave it to you. Maybe on the second draft I'll have a more polished prose worthy of Thackeray (maybe I'll read him next) with enough clear stated contrition you can sit in it like a comfortable La-Z-Boy serene in your self-satisfaction the wrongs have been realized and the right (as you know it) has triumphed.

And yet…protest as I may and given it might have been a pointless exercise to write it all out, share my thoughts and experience, I still felt a need every day to put pen to paper. A need to propagate, extend something beyond myself. Even if its ideas and passages few will read. Because it may be the only offspring I produce.

And maybe it will get me out of here. LOL.

>Being hopeful.

>Has no choice.

>Faithhope&love.txt

>unironically writing that

But certainly, it'll all just get filed away, maybe appear lost in the e-stacks of another hacked document dump, maybe due to a disgruntled bureaucrat like Mark himself, but who will read? One or two people—five tops? A casual glance or tweet thread summation for something I've put my heart and soul in to? Doesn't matter. No use wasting energy on what-ifs. And…

I don't care what you think.

It had to be this way.

To me, it's me, my life. To you, to them, to everyone else, it's just…content.

Made in the USA
Monee, IL
11 October 2020